TEKSINIAN
WARS

TERSINIAN WARS

A NOVA REPUBLIC NOVEL

RYAN ABBOTTS

TERSINIAN WARS: A NOVA REPUBLIC NOVEL.

ISBN-13: 979-8-9915148-0-4

TO NICHOLE AND THE KIDS

LINDAULX

CHAPTER 01

ONLY A HANDFUL of people on Lindaulx were fortunate enough to know the planet was scheduled for liberation. Fewer were aware of the galaxy-shaping secrets residing beneath its surface. One of the instigators stood in a frozen alpine meadow, trying to capture the faint, sweet warmth of the morning sun. Wisps of her mahogany hair played on the currents of a faint breeze, threatening to escape the clutches of a loosely woven braid. The protective layers of her clothes bunching and shimmering to match the surroundings, making her almost invisible. To the select people she worked with, she was known as Auralei; to everyone else, she was a Nova Republic specter—a myth. With her contract terms met, she was to have left Lindaulx. At least, that had been her plan until she discovered another specter operating from a different set of instructions than hers. While concurrent contracts weren't unheard of, it was the first time she had not been aware of all objectives. Also, her contract owner, like most, had gone to great lengths and expense to hide their identity—and while she had her methods of discovering who these potential employers were prior to accepting work, her now expired contract was an exception. Adding to the mystique was the lack of information about Lindaulx in the meticulous records of the Nova Republic. The planet and pathways to it had been challenging to find, having been deliberately deleted from the interstellar navigation charts. Even the telltale hints and fragments of data residue that remained after manipulation were absent. Instead, she had been guided by her mentor and directed not to pry any further—stick to the mission and see the contract through to its bitter termination—a unique request and word choice. Ultimately, she accepted the Lindaulx contract partly out of curiosity and mostly because she had uncovered a connection to someone on this distant planet.

Auralei's companion, a saboteur-class artificial intelligence unit she affectionately named Shifty, hovered nearby. It had detected something to the north and was trying to pique her interest. Auralei silenced Shifty's warning tone, no longer able to withstand its mockery of having recognized the threat first. She squinted, straining to see the approaching vehicles, and failed. Her athletic frame, which was not overly muscled and a pinch taller than most women of her kind, carried her gracefully into a crouched position.

Her satchel rested against a gnarled, burned-out stump that reminded her of the price about to be exacted on the souls calling this place home and who were likely unaware of their transgressions. It was an ongoing story about the delicate balance of ancestral rights, posterity, and balance throughout the systems— a story she knew all too well. However, below the gleaming layers of fresh snow, she supposed the surviving creatures would continue to carve out a meager existence even after the next series of conquests for this rock. She retrieved a cylindrical device the length of her hand and aimed it at the area Shifty indicated. Her augments eliminated even the slightest waver.

Across the valley, a flat-bottomed craft skimmed above the snowpack and slowed. When its crescent-shaped fins touched down, it released a glistening blast of crystalline shapes, obscuring it from view momentarily.

The machine was a standard maintenance chopper that appeared to be modified for high-speed incursions—its crew trading comfort for speed. Shifty classified two smaller shapes behind it as dragoons, marking each as a potential threat, and relayed the information to the rest of her equipment. Dragoon pilots were formidable warriors who rode the edge of institutionally tolerable body modifications and were never far from their mechanized armor. Most dragoon armors were bipedal and snuggly entombed the operator—although sets could vary in size depending on their purpose. She knew the lighter-weight versions she saw as models based on the Vindicator series, which were the more prevalent variants known for their robustness to serve as general infantry—they weren't particularly specialized at any one thing but menacing and redundant enough to be practical and deadly.

Auralei scanned through her memory bank for a plan to engage dragoons in her present environment, relying on her neuro devices to supplement the information. Finding no tactics she preferred, she stepped through a mental list of her arsenal, which provided a similar disheartening result. She would need to be close to be effective. A rough plan took shape, and the foreign bits of her mind systematically evaluated and cataloged it.

Again, disobeying the silence command, Shifty chirped across her internal interface to alert her that it acquired something else worthy of her attention. Auralei adjusted the visual settings of both the hand-held device and her optics and added a fourth target to the mix. She inadvertently tugged gently at her eyelashes with her free hand, realizing her gear failed to classify the threat or even present a traceable signature from the weapons the person carried. The figure moved from the rear of the maintenance skiff and vanished. Almost instantly, they appeared crouched to the side of the nearest dragoon, with the bulk of it providing ample screening just as she would have done. A shiver tried to claim Auralei's body, but it was no match for her many stabilizers. The stranger was of Auralei's ilk. With proper training, raw talent, and some ungodly expensive equipment, one could vanish by slipping from the physical plane through the veil and into the flux—the space between worlds where she flowed as a ghost. She challenged her devices to cut through the distortion of the drifting snow and report crisp images as the stranger quickly incapacitated the dragoon pilots. Auralei shook her head, knowing she had revealed her presence—her augments had evaluated her strategy, deemed it worthy, and then transmitted it to her organization's network as an alternative method to dispatch a pair of Vindicator dragoons.

The stranger walked deliberately to the maintenance craft and paused, seeming to briefly take in their surroundings before disappearing inside. Minutes later, the cargo ramp opened, and a quad-tracked vehicle carrying the stranger and two passengers emerged. Auralei followed the cloud kicked up by the vehicle as it made its way up the steep slope until the group exited and spent some time milling about the area. She muttered a quick curse as her optical device registered two brilliant bursts of light, trailed by the heads of two bodies snapping backward before their knees buckled, undermining the body's support. Auralei's decoys were dead. She removed one of her gloves and caressed the smooth folds of the simple metallic bracelet clinging to her wrist. Her inviting lips formed a mischievous smirk as she thought of the blood she would soon spill on behalf of the bracelet's owner. Auralei's elusive employer would not be pleased—neither would her organization— and there would be no hiding what she was about to do.

A sonic boom overhead brought her attention upward to a sky lacerated by billowing streaks left behind by javelins hurtling to their destination. It signaled the successful culmination of months of deception, politicking, and smuggling of advance forces.

The liberation of Lindaulx had begun.

INVASION

CHAPTER 02

CLARKE CLOSED THE access panel on probe 7B3's snorkel, hoping his repair would solve the recurring problem the mining division had sent him to investigate. He stood and shook the penetrating cold from his body. Tiny flecks of ice swirled in the air, flung from his auburn-tinged beard. To the southwest, Deception Bay was a mirror-gray shell from which the stone walls of Fort Skyetook seemingly sprung to protect the largest Khilsyth colony on Lindaulx. The Khilsyths were one of three primary families ruling sizeable land areas, and with no formal government in these remote colonies, generational agreements between households kept the relative peace.

A shrill chirping redirected Clarke's attention to his chest pocket. He pulled out a thin, square-shaped computer, input his code, and established a link to the central maintenance server. There was an open repair ticket for probe 7B3. The time stamp was seconds ago and registered the same error code—A5978. This meant little unless one possessed the reference table, which stated: *Error Encountered:*

signal distortion. Solution: Recalibrate. He would have to wait to be snug in the comfort of his house, watching the morning sun glint off the windows and the smoke tendrils rising from the buildings.

After completing another recalibration and disabling the shutdown failsafe on the probe, Clarke trudged through the snow to his maintenance sled. He was vaguely aware of his dragoon escort's eagerness to return to town as he deliberately placed his tools in their designated compartments. Clarke admitted to himself that he sought satisfaction in annoying the dragoons and tried to convince himself that it wasn't a passive-aggressive maneuver fueled by jealousy. Truthfully, he admired the station being a dragoon provided and, over the years, had come to terms with his failure—on the day of his sixteenth birthday, Clarke had reported for training with the House Leod dragoons on the planet Nanser-Nine. He had placed in the middle of his class after his first year and was accepted into the program for a second year provided he could match the advancements of his classmates—this meant having the funds and willingness to enhance his body with augments and cybernetics dragoons embraced, and even needed for survival. However, Clarke had a rare condition whereby his body was incompatible with the multitude of augments available on any flavor of legit to seedy markets. The Dragoon Academy also frowned on synthetic chemical alterations, which could be incredibly effective but required a steady supply of quality material for injections—it also had the side effect of reducing lifespans significantly, and frequently, the *natural* end resulted in mass casualties. Failing to find a working solution and not accepting mediocrity lightly, he had created a device that bonded to his body and delivered the increased stability necessary to vie for a spot as a dragoon. He was permitted back into the program, provided he continued developing his unique machinery. Three weeks into the semester, his homemade device leaked radically energetic particles into his bloodstream and caused involuntary twitches. This wouldn't have been too problematic, but he had been taking aim with a powerful cannon and inadvertently sent a few rockets into a nearby storage shed. The concussive blast forced more particles to dowse his bloodstream, which overwhelmed his heart and stopped it. Upon seeing Clarke collapse and the rapidly expanding boil filling the area between his shoulder and earlobe, a fellow dragoon hopeful named Anzil came to his rescue—he surgically removed the device with his field knife, gave Clarke's chest a couple of kicks, and a healthy shock. When Clarke breathed again, the disappointment registering on some of his classmates' faces showed they saw some advantage in letting him die. After all, it meant one less person to compete against. Due to the mishap, the Nanser-Nine Dragoon Academy had scrubbed him from the program.

Clarke placed his tools into their designated compartments on the maintenance skiff and climbed into the driver's seat. He felt behind his ear and stroked the smooth, raised ridges of the scar, which reminded him of his failure.

"You calling it a day?" Anzil asked Clarke, his voice emanating clearly from his dragoon armor.

Clarke glanced up ruefully. "Yeah, nothing more I can do now."

"Good, because I could use a pint and a hot meal," Anzil said, patting his armored midsection. "You learn anything new?"

Clarke peered cautiously around Anzil, making sure Lieutenant Andover was busy scanning the perimeter. Nearly two weeks ago, he discovered recurring signal distortions within some of the data the probes recorded in this sector of White Pass. With a different lens for viewing the world, Anzil had correlated some of the recorded events to changes in patrol routes—his working theory was that a group of smugglers was paying off the marshals to adjust the patrols so they could go about their illicit activities. It seemed plausible as the families' holds on these areas were less tenable these days. Ever the proper soldier, Anzil had submitted his findings to a colonel and received a strong 'piss off' message, bolstered by instructions to keep to his detail of babysitting field engineers. "The first event matched a patrol shift change late last night," he mouthed, careful to shield his moving lips from Andover, knowing the computer onboard Anzil's armor would decipher what he was saying. "But it happened again while we were here. It doesn't make sense." He pursed his lips, hoping Anzil would respect the need for discretion and wouldn't press the issue further until they were safe from earshot. For the benefit of Andover, he added, "no, sir. I'll need to run some tests back at the shop."

"Hey guys, check out the meteor shower!" Andover called.

Clarke followed Andover's armored gauntlet skyward to the white pillowy strands stretching across the horizon. "Ah, guys. I don't think those are meteors." He scanned through the screens on his datapad and found all security threat levels were low. A flash on the axillary screen caught his attention. "Odd. Someone tripped a distress beacon and sent a back-channel interstellar call for help. What the hell?"

"No training exercises or visitors that I saw on the docket today," Anzil said.

"Too many and too obvious for smugglers," Andover added. "Can't even lock onto them."

"You know, it looks like a bloody invasion," Clarke said.

"Might be," Anzil laughed nervously. "Okay, let's get back. Fast like. We need to figure out what the hell is going on. Clarke, keep up."

Clarke pressed the skiff as hard as he dared over the mountain terrain, failing to keep pace with the dragoons on their way back to Fort Skyetook.

CHAPTER 03

A MAINTENANCE SKIFF entered a small bay adjoining the primary maintenance shed for the 43rd Maintenance Division in Fort Skyetook, parked, and its operator went about readying it for the next outing. Across the way, a woman tracked her target carefully, keeping the person's head entirely in the reticule of her weapon's optic feedback relay as he crossed the main floor to a nearby data terminal. Like most field engineers, this one was diligent and predictable in his work efforts: he updated the status of the repair ticket with the solution, enumerating parts used and double-checking the maintenance request log in case anything urgent had arisen.

Over the last six months, she had operated on Lindaulx at her organization's request. Her current contract required the infiltration of House Khilsyth, which she did using her guile and attractiveness and completing various tasks her employer paid generously for. One such task involved circumventing the usefulness of the Khilsyth's defense systems to help ease surface-bound journeys. It was a common enough request to provide indiscriminate access to people who would rather not be legitimate—it was a specialty of hers.

Tarra recalled playfully how she had manipulated the desperation and simple needs of Lyle, a chief programmer, to get what she needed. Lyle had been quick to disappoint but provided her with the opportunity to insert a nasty little device of her design into the Khilsyth network. Selfishly, she was thankful for Lyle as he had also discovered a series of modeling programs associated with mere threads of shared data but collectively were placing a significant strain on the network. He had shared the information only with her, hoping it would be fortuitous toward his primal desires. The personal encryption was admirable, and the way the program disguised itself by burying massive amounts of operations within the myriads of data flows indistinguishable from sending a digital message was genius. With some off-world support for the mere price of obtaining the base code and potentially its creator, Tarra found a pathway to piece together that the program was mapping a vast underground complex from detailed surveys. She had given her current employers the first chance to purchase the information. They deemed the findings significant and amended her arrangement with a substantial bonus for infiltrating and exploring the complex and securing the program's creator. Tarra snickered. She had not expected Clarke to disguise his activities under another's profile. It was a clever ruse but proved fatal for the two engineers and their dragoon escort earlier in the mountains—her temper was quick, and her swords had a terrible thirst, which she prided herself on sating.

Tarra smiled as his shoulders sagged, knowing he had acknowledged the 'priority' repair request she had generated. Each maintenance personnel knew there was no shortage of people who believed their requests were the most urgent. However, the repair ticket noted that one of the mass array sensors capable of guiding ordinance toward aerial targets failed, and the only backup was in a workshop awaiting his special touch. She patiently packed her gear and breathed in the early morning air, allowing the flux to envelop her. The faint hum and the distorted view of a world virtually arrested in time were welcoming.

Tarra arrived undetected in the workshop, finding there was little need for stealth amidst the assault of what these backwoods soldiers referred to as face-melting music. She didn't understand how people believed they effectively worked this way. Unsheathing a dagger from its resting place at the small of her back, she slipped out of the flux behind Clarke and pushed the dagger through the engineer's bulky sweater and flesh. The dagger swam through blood and the tender intercostal muscle between his ribs and came to rest in the right ventricle of the heart. The air rushed from the man's lungs, and his body slumped forward, bouncing limply on the workshop floor. Tarra had misjudged her attack. She had even anticipated a minor scuffle, even wanted one to help release the angst he caused her.

Tarra caught movement at the edge of her peripheral vision. She spun gracefully while relieving her sword with its gleaming blade from her scabbard, and a vice-like grip wrapped around her forearm, jarring her shoulder. Pressing hard with all her augmented might, she tried to free herself and failed, soliciting a rueful laugh that resonated from the massive chest before her. She briefly glimpsed a rugged jawline and a frosty handlebar mustache just before her nose exploded in a shower of light and dampened pain. The force of the blow flung her against a nearby workbench. Tarra tried to speak, but her mouth hung open limply, catching the blood streaming from her nose and upper lip as metal tools fell around her, shimmering in the brightly lit workshop. The slow fade to unconsciousness was unwelcome.

CLARKE DRAGGED HIMSELF into a sitting position using the terminal's column as support. His ribs burned, and the sharp pull of a cramp was making white spots dance around his vision. *What did you do to piss the lass off?* He thought he heard someone say through the ringing in his ears. "No idea," he rasped, unsure if he was talking to himself. It required a concerted effort to focus on the voice's owner as each breath threatened to tear his lungs.

Stigg bounced the woman's dagger from one hand to the next, testing its weight. "You know you're lucky." His nostrils flared as he exhaled forcefully. "You're lucky I sensed trouble and came back for you. This blade... it's built just like the doc's tools." Stigg thought the woman must have had some working knowledge of Clarke's dragoon training to assume she would need such a weapon to incapacitate him. She likely felt panicked at the utter and unexpected buckling of her target's legs: there would be no help from some pesky implant bringing that victim back to consciousness.

Clarke wasn't sure what Stigg remembered, but a strange fire lit the man's eyes in the darkness, and a tiny smile briefly tugged at the man's lips. "What is it, Chief?"

Stigg chuckled and moved to crouch near the woman slumped on the stone floor with her wrists and ankles bound. "I believe this little lady meant to take you away somewhere quiet. So. I'll ask you again. What did you do to piss her off?"

Clarke shook his head cautiously, careful not to aggravate the pain in the back of his eyes. He didn't recognize the woman, who was beautiful in a foreign way, with smooth skin and hair the color of burning charcoal. Clarke grunted as the dagger hit his chest.

"You were supposed to catch that, bud. You would have if you weren't daydreaming about your mistress here." He furrowed his brow. "You're lucky she didn't kill you, given your state."

"Did you search her?"

"Yeah. Thought about stripping her naked, but likely wouldn't be enough."

"Enough for what?"

"Oh. I think she can handle herself just fine without weapons. I don't believe she's the sweet little programmer or whatever it is she was pretending to be." Stigg stowed his handheld device he'd scanned her with and stood. He strode over to Clarke and, in a fluid motion, scooped his apprentice to his feet and gave him time to steady his wobbly legs. "We'd better tell the lads."

The woman squirmed, gradually turning to face the two men. "Wait, please," she pleaded.

"I'll be dammed," Stigg said, shaking his head. "That face of yours has practically healed."

Although soft shadows partially obscured her head, the woman's jaw was reset, and the unnatural indentation of a crushed cheekbone was gone. The dried blood streaks on her face, combined with the overhead light, provided her with a primal fierceness.

Tarra spit the blood pooling in her mouth on the floor with a sickly splatter. "Trust me, I meant him little harm. We need to get out of here and soonish."

"That so?" Stigg asked, walking toward the woman, leaving Clarke to stand on his own. Her outstretched hand stopped him short.

"House Leod sent me to ensure Clarke's safety," Tarra said.

"That's an inspired story," Stigg retorted dismissively. "Who really sent you?"

The older man promptly, almost knowingly, turned away from her ruse. "I don't divulge my clients."

"You mean your contract holders," Stigg stated.

"Nor do I ask many questions as to the motivations in my line of work," Tarra replied. "This seemed like an easy gig for a powerful family."

"Lies," Stigg said, scrunching his fists tightly and emitting sharp cracks from his knuckles. "Let's try one last time. Why Clarke and why now?"

Stretching her neck to the side, she received the slight pop she desired, and the pressure subsided. She wasn't fresh for a fight but could sense this Chief Engineer knew something she didn't. Her sensors warned her of his extreme likelihood of aggression but also detected the slightest hint of fear. No, it couldn't have been fear. Not much would scare this beast, except she sensed some concern for Clarke. But it had a familiarity that she hadn't uncovered in her vetting process. Stigg believed Clarke was her mission. "Why would they pay so much, Clarke?"

"The Leod's wouldn't have to," Clarke said.

"Then who would?" Tarra pressed.

"Listen, *Mischi*," Stigg growled and took a deep breath.

"Such an old fool you are, Stigg," Tarra said with a feigned wince. "*Mischi* are fairy tales. Wraiths. Nothing more."

Stigg raised his eyebrow in challenge. "I know your kind better than you know."

The short hairs on the back of Clarke's neck prickled. He had learned to respect Stigg's life experiences and his overall situational judgment. Wraiths were an excellent way to classify a *Mischi*, although he considered them more like imaginary bogeymonsters. Parents would invoke these ancient beings to keep their children's behavior in check. But if this woman was a *Mischi*, it likely meant the Nova Republic was involved. However, the new version of Specters was a far cry from the fabled *Mischi*. The Nova Republic was a collection of families and corporations allied in their desire for universal balance. They wielded immense sway over a vast array of formidable economies. Perhaps the genuine power of the Nova Republic was its ability to maintain a broadminded image of neutrality, garnering them the role of galactic mediator—a positive force in the universe for people of all creeds. Or maybe their power came from their steadfast and ruthless adherence to serving the Greater Purpose, and that conviction attracted people. The likely explanation was that people wanted recognition that they were part of something greater than themselves and to maintain balance among the universe's civilizations, which was an acceptable creed for most.

Stigg continued through clenched teeth. "The likes of you were felt during the Frebel invasion. Another great House that was a casualty of the infernal politicking of the damned Republic."

Tarra stood and raised both hands to calm the rage in the giant's heart. "Stigg, the Shade Wars were before my time. I am not responsible for that pain. And the *Mischi* are no more." And with a shrug of her shoulders, she added. "But to the near-term discomfort. Potentially."

Stigg stepped forward, causing the woman to shrink defensively, bringing him up short.

Brave bastard, Clarke thought.

"Universal balance and control, my ass," Stigg growled. "You were lucky they ordered the lot of us not to pursue vengeance... why Lindaulx? Why now? I didn't expect the Republic to be interested in meddling here."

Tarra wondered why this old-timer had called her *Mischi*—a reference to the old ways. But they were specters now, fallen from grace.

A warning siren began shrieking its call into the darkness outside. "We need to go," Tarra said. The local militia is compromised, and Lindaulx will soon be the front line of a new war."

"Go where exactly?" Stigg asked. He took a deep breath and relaxed his shoulders.

Clarke checked his computer. "There's still nothing on the official systems, but there is chatter from the local conspiracy nuts about a takeover. Guess they're right for once?"

"They're usually right," Stigg said.

"Then we head to the inner fortress," Clarke said.

"Compromised," Stigg said as the woman smiled slyly and nodded.

"You knew?" Clarke asked Stigg.

"What's your plan then, lass?" Stigg asked, avoiding Clarke's gaze. "Surely you've got one."

Tarra shifted her weight back and forth on the balls of her feet. "The objective is to protect Clarke."

"Wait," Clarke blurted. "Stigg, seriously, you knew about the invasion?"

"As I was saying, we protect Clarke. I got word the infiltration was more comprehensive than originally expected. And that it was actually going to happen. Orders came through to make a quick pit stop before getting off this rock. I… misjudged how hard Clarke would go down with a light shock."

"What kind of pit stop?" Stigg asked.

Tarra flashed her best attempt at a nervous smile and pointed at Clarke. "I'm supposed to check out the facility he uncovered."

"The underground caverns the probes have been picking up?" Clarke asked.

Tarra nodded and stretched her neck as her palm worked vigorously on a kink left over from her rapid healing process. "Dammit, boys, can't a girl have some secrets? My manners aren't the best. I was going to nab Clarke *after* checking out the place. Then I had an epiphany; maybe he knew his way around." She laughed sweetly. "Although now, I'm not sure how useful he'll be or if coming here first was the best decision." She flashed a smile that had made many men shirk their sensibilities. "Look, you old goat," she pleaded with Stigg. "I'm telling you most of what you already know. The military ranks of House Khilsyth have been infiltrated, and somebody is trying to overthrow this rabble—my advice is run. Get the hell off this rock. The Republic gets what it wants. You can come with us if you would like."

Stigg cursed. "Us?"

Tarra tilted her head forward and pointed at Clarke. "I'm leaving here with him."

"It would explain the irregularities in patrols and orbital activities," Clarke offered. He was about to add that the vibe around town seemed off-kilter, but a glance from the veteran engineer silenced him from voicing his opinion. The sadness on Stigg's face and the emotional weight his shoulders bore made Clarke ponder the man's relationship to the House Frebel invasion. It was a core lesson from the Shade Wars he had first learned about during dragoon training. It was also a story rife with conspiracy theories and shrouded in mystery. It had stoked his obsession with alternative Frebel theories that usually had a thread of correlation to the Astutes—a long-lost and potentially vastly superior civilization. All this generated ample material for discovery, and somewhere in the noise was the truth.

What Clarke believed was this: toward what was the end of a four-hundred-year conflict, a devastating blow to a then superior force—House Frebel—led to the Republic's victory. House Frebel's scientific community was known for developing sophisticated strategies and technology far beyond the capabilities of known contact civilizations. The Frebels weren't a part of the conflict but had offered to help stop the war. This threatened those who believed they were going to be victorious. To build an anti-Frebel fervor, a coalition whose name was conveniently omitted from history claimed that an advanced group was tipping the scales in favor of House Frebel. This drove nearby civilizations into a frenzy of jealousy and fear and became the nexus of several colonies and houses banding together under the Nova Republic's banner. However, the Nova Republic erred in the belief that their sheer might could overwhelm House Frebel. They had sent several armadas to rendezvous for a coordinated attack, but all were intercepted on their journey to the Frebel home world.

It was at this juncture in the Nova Republic's story that most of their lore stemmed from—upon seeing the catastrophic loss of life, a party possessing a vastly superior technology visited them and shared the Greater Purpose. It instilled the mission for balance and neutrality and provided the militaristic means to succeed. The teachings from the Nova Republic were vague about who this 'party' was that conveyed the Greater Purpose to them or why they readily adopted it. Clarke didn't subscribe to the prevailing rhetoric, believing the Nova Republic had discovered an Astute colony that offered an actual glimpse into how to use their advanced technology. But that was ages ago, and House Frebel was now a compliant member of the Nova Republic.

"One of these days, we'll have to have Stigg tell us how one grizzled old veteran found himself linked to House Frebel," Tarra said, flashing Clarke a knowing look and drawing small circles on her temple with her pointer finger. She wondered why the Nova Republic hadn't pressed Stigg into service, given his skill set and potential association with Frebel. "And how could he be so angry after all this time?"

Stigg grunted and tilted his head toward Clarke. His words stopped short when surprise flashed across his apprentice's face.

Tarra exploded from a crouched position and dove toward her gear, the magnetic shackles around her ankles clinking to the floor lifelessly. She landed gracelessly, snatched up a small cube-shaped object, and hurled it from her defenseless position at the bulk of a man rushing toward her. The object struck Stigg in the chest, and he collapsed. Tarra rolled over and brought herself up on her knees. Lifting another device from the floor, it chirped in recognition and morphed into a compact pistol. "Impressed?" she asked Clarke. "No? Too bad, as this *lass* is going to require your assistance." She kept her pistol trained on Clarke—it was a compelling way to express who was in charge and motioned for him to move. "Chin up," she chided sweetly. "I will not kill you. I will see you off this rock." The man's eyebrow arched, betraying his confusion, which brought her some joy. "Now grab your gear and do it quick. There's an invasion we need to get away from."

THE REAR CARGO door of a 43rd Maintenance Division chopper hung open, providing Clarke a peekaboo view of all the vehicles and personnel on the field prepping for the business of war. The woman had secured permission from Port Command to go beyond the wall for a critical repair, with instructions to stay outside what they considered the likely sphere of influence for the invasion. Clarke's fingers nervously traced the buttons on the cargo door's operation panel. As the woman entered carrying Stigg, he immediately pressed the close button and helped secure the chief mechanic with webbing in the cargo area.

"Why don't you fly us out of here and not do anything suspicious or dumb," Tarra requested.

Clarke climbed into the pilot's chair, switched on the avionics, cleared any warning indicators, and called for one of the yard drones to help manage the startup process. Once enough air pressure built up, he gradually increased engine power to get the chopper blades spinning. Clarke severed the shore connections and supplied more fuel to the engines, increasing the lift until the craft was light on its skids. He was rusty, but the onboard computer helped level out his movements on the controls. "Where are we heading?"

"Somewhere that's not likely in sector 6BE. I was counting on you to lead the way to the cavern entrance."

Clarke spoke a few quick directives to the navigation systems to set the coordinates, which would put them close but not disclose their ultimate destination. "Just so we're clear, I have a hunch but no clue how to open it."

"I'll worry about that. You just get us there."

Clarke manipulated the side arm rotary blades, eased power to the underside and rear jets, and carried them into the lanes leading to the gates. The woman's arm shot out and cuffed the back of his head. "What the hell?" he asked, removing his finger from the *ident* button, checking for blood, and shaking the ringing sound from his ears.

"You think calling for an escort is wise or good for your health?" Tarra asked.

"If we don't identify ourselves, the watch guards will get suspicious, even shoot at us," Clarke replied. "And we always have protection. Especially if security is bloody well heightened." He waited nervously as the woman weighed the information he provided, wondering how long this adventure was going to last before her pistol blared to life and vented his brain matter. Something was unsettling about her, and he didn't trust *Mischi* as far as he could throw them. Receiving an indication to continue, Clarke guided the chopper to the secondary gate and waved to the Staff Sergeant on duty. "That's odd." The woman motioned with her sidearm impatiently for him to expand. "I've never seen that guy before."

Clarke trained one of the top-mounted sensors on the guard to better scan the person waving back. He punched the display twice and received confirmation that the Staff Sergeant was not in the House Khilsyth database.

When the staff sergeant realized Clarke was ignoring his request to park, he rapidly waved his arms and called for the chopper to stop. This earned Clarke another cuff to the head.

"Dammit," Clarke said, grabbing the back of his head again. She hit hard. "I never wait. They wave me over, and I wave back and stop outside the wall, like always. I'm sure they flagged my file."

"You think some new guy would recognize that?" Tarra asked, giving Clarke another quick jab in the arm and flashing a sweet smile. "That was for cursing. You shouldn't do that in front of a lady."

"HERE WE GO," Clarke said, leaning forward to identify the two dragoons exiting the gate and moving with trained precision. The chopper's computer identified the dragoon pilots as Lieutenants Moore and Swift. He slumped into his chair and released the tight grip on the steering wheel. Neither escort was his workmate, as he predicted his unwelcomed copilot would cut their lives short once they met.

"Let's make this snappy," Swift said over a secure frequency, smoothly transitioning his mechanized armor from walking to skimming across the surface. "We don't want to miss any of the fighting because we're out babysitting a repair detail."

Clarke guided the chopper into the air and through the fertile farmlands of the valleys surrounding Skyetook. The easterly journey through the lowland marshes and farm country was uneventful except for the constant flashes across the sky, signaling the arrival of more unknown spacecraft. The chopper passed quickly over the river crossings, deep mud-rutted forest, and single-vehicle switchback trails, failing to elicit the rush of excitement from the bite of the maintenance skiff's tracks into solid ground. He figured the woman had chosen the chopper with two purposes in mind: to control him and speed.

"Dumb asses aren't being quiet, are they?" Tarra asked, shaking her head and watching the signal monitor on the chopper light up in an array of colors for each spectrum the dragoons sent a search out on.

"You think they're doing it to alert someone?" Clarke asked, scanning the news and military channels, again finding they were silent about the activities overhead. There was a base of excitement that should have registered as fear that gripped him.

"Likely not," Tarra said, keying a series of commands into a small device on her wrist. She then considered the screen output for a minute and initiated a program of her design. "There. That should dampen the noise a bit. Those idiots are the very thing likely to get us found."

"That weather will help some," Clarke added, pointing at the fingers of a storm approaching from the east through some of the lower valleys of the Esconairian Mountains. "Pretty predictable that it arrives near the end of harvest time."

"Thanks for the meteorological lesson," Tarra responded flatly.

"No problem," Clarke muttered, longing for the clear night skies of the warm season with the infinite number of stars marching dutifully across the sky. "Mercury is also out," he added to the drone of the chopper. Most nights, two moons were competing for attention as they waxed and waned in their array of silver and gold. Every few years, a fourth celestial body, Mercury, the fiery silver beast, passed with plenty of stigmata and ominous superstitions attached to it.

"Remind me of the story again," Tarra said.

Clarke cleared his throat. "Khilsyth Lore tells of a great battle that was waged for many days until Mercury appeared and drank the blood of the dead. When sated, it gave birth to goliath-winged beasts—the Guivre wyverns. To survive, the warring clans united and formed a tenuous alliance to cull and subdue the beasts. Thus, Lindaulx was tamed."

"You're such a dork," Tarra laughed and sank into her seat, closing her eyes.

The trip continued in silence until Clarke reported they had arrived. He stretched within the cockpit to chase away the stiffness in his side.

Tarra patted Clarke's ribs in a condescending gesture. "You be good now," she said, the tight quarters causing her to brush Clarke's arm as she wiggled out of the chopper's cockpit. "Let me go see about that escort."

As Tarra disappeared into the cargo area, Clarke tapped the console to train the chopper's sensor array on her. "Damn, she moves fast," he said under his breath. She was already outside on the visual feed, but none of the sophisticated chopper sensors could lock onto her.

CHAPTER 04

TARRA'S FEET CRUNCHED into the frost-kissed alpine grass as she moved and brushed against the rough exterior of the maintenance chopper for cover. The two dragoons had taken up positions that provided them an ample field of view to protect the chopper. Tarra accessed a module implanted at the base of her neck, found the familiar tactical plan she'd employed earlier, and said a silent thank you for her colleague's insight. "Are you out there, sweetie?" Her words carried over their network. The range wasn't spectacular, but sufficient on a planet this size. Auralei had been in the meadow earlier, watching her. "No sense being coy, my love." Tarra enjoyed toying with other specters—she knew Auralei would have seen her but would not have been able to identify her.

Pantest Pemy, Tarra's overseer, had significant skills in acquiring and developing cybernetics and weaponry. This was especially true of internal augmentations that only highly specialized detectors could find, unlike inferior and antiquated versions that a mineral scan would uncover. The quest for undetectable equipment fascinated Pantest Pemy, a luxury for Tarra, as she was also the chief supplier and constructor of Tarra's battle kit.

Tarra stepped into the flux and closed the distance to the dragoons almost instantaneously. She returned to the physical plane with the gentle ring of her blades being freed from their ornate scabbards— she preferred a shorter arming sword with a rhomboidal double-edged blade that was equally adept at thrusting and slashing. She drove her left hand and the sword it held hard up through the undercarriage of the nearest dragoon. Her short sword punctured the outer metallic skin easily and bit through the soldier's hip bone and intestines, stopping just short of the target. Tarra smirked, remembering that Auralei preferred a longer sword that would have hit the heart and spinal column. She twisted the sword viciously and pried it out through the front of the soldier's armor. She watched as the dragoon desperately tried to keep their innards from spilling out as the higher internal pressure of the suit forced blood to mist from between their gauntlets. Tarra flowed across the meadow, barely disturbing the loose rocks, and braced herself against the ornate pommel of her sword. The body of the second dragoon slowed her weapon's forward momentum until she wrenched her short swords free from the armor, followed by a second swath of red mist blanketing the snow. A familiar smile touched her lips with the warming passion of death briefly sweeping through her body. Still, it faded instantly as her augments regulated what it perceived as a chemical imbalance.

WITH THE HATCH sealed, Clarke rushed to Stigg's side and shook him vigorously. The grizzled mechanic awoke in a flail of meaty hands and muscled arms, one of which caught Clarke across the chest and sent him backward to land hard on his ass. Stigg stretched his neck and received the sought-after cracks. He stood, his facial expression somber, and headed to the pilot's seat. "She has it locked somehow," Clarke called after the man and came to his feet.

Stigg's hands flashed furiously over the many buttons and switches at the helm. "She's disabled the entire chopper," he said, scratching his head. "How in the hell has she done that?" Seeing Clarke was unsure, he rose from the pilot seat, went to the cargo area, and grabbed two Hale expedition kits. "You'll need the goggles."

"Yeah. Eye implants were next on my development list."

"One of these days, we'll figure it out for you. Now, let's get the hell out of here." Stigg turned and started walking down the ramp until the appearance of the *Mischi* stopped him.

"Seems like you're as eager to explore as I am," Tarra said as she swung back inside the cargo bay. "The dragoons decided they didn't want to play anymore." A sly grin stuck to her blood-splattered face when she saw the slight glint of hope fade from Clarke. "If you cross-reference their employee file creation date with the assignment date of their armor, you'll find my team created the employee files one day before the soldier's armor was assigned. Not a perfect system, but it was a simple method to keep track of the infiltrators." Tarra punched a series of commands into the cargo area terminal, bringing up a long list of soldiers, and motioned for the two to examine the output.

"There's Moore and Swift, but I don't recognize any of these names," Clarke said.

Tarra shrugged dismissively and threw a remote-control device for her support sled at Clarke, who narrowly avoided stopping its trajectory with the fuzzy skin of his cheek. "You trust me now?" She pulled a rifle from a nearby locked compartment and motioned to Clarke with it, indicating it was time to exit the chopper.

The two men offered little resistance as they made their way up the valley between two steep ridgelines and stopped where Clarke said the scans showed what appeared to be a sloping chasm beneath the snow. Tarra pulled a small cube-shaped device from her satchel and turned it over in her hands, snatching and pushing on small rods that appeared from the cube's surface until she growled in frustration and dug the heel of her hand into her eye. "Care to have a go at it?" Tarra asked, offering the device in her outstretched palm.

"You're a bloody sparky, aren't you?" Stigg asked the woman.

"A what?" Tarra asked.

"You know. A Sparky. The twitchy type. Them folks that run around all chalked full of chemical death to push themselves faster and faster."

"Care to have a go?" Tarra asked, turning to Clark. She ignored Stigg, who was muttering to himself, although she caught the occasional curse word.

Clarke glanced at Stigg and found no objections. "Heavier than I thought," he said, bouncing it in his hands. "And warm? What's the objective?"

Tarra fussed with her tight-fitting jacket. "To locate the entrance. That device is supposed to be a key. I was told to depress every second rod that appeared."

Clarke followed the instructions, identifying and retracting the rods by observing what he thought was the sequential linear movement of the radial arms.

The backwater mechanic was clumsy and slow. "That's not right, dammit," Tarra said.

Startled, Clarke's hand slipped, forcing a rod to slide and collide with another rod—the rods joined and shrank into the cube. Clarke vigorously shook the device to reset it, ignoring the woman's frustration. He hastily donned his Hale goggles, activated the high-speed recording function, and pressed his thumb against a glowing red dot on one face of the cube. The rods shot out abruptly. After reviewing the recording frame-by-frame, he noticed a pattern in the extension of the rod pairs. Yet, the camera didn't provide complete coverage of the cube. "Interesting," Clarke said. "These optics aren't good enough to catch the order of the rods as they extend."

Tarra flashed Clarke a perplexed gaze. "Ah, care to explain?" Once Clarke explained his working theory on how the device worked, she devised a plan after consulting her equipment. "Count to one and press the button, understood?" Tarra flashed Clarke a readying nod as the signal to start, shook her arms to prepare herself for action, and disappeared.

"What the hell?" Clarke asked the space where the woman had stood in front of him.

"It's a nasty little trick they have, lad," Stigg replied.

"Should we run?"

"No. I don't think that's wise. You'd best proceed before she gets impatient."

Clarke crammed the rods back in, shook the device feverishly to reset it, and pressed the red glowing dot. The woman reappeared where she had previously stood and began pointing out the progressive order in the rods that had appeared on the device. Clarke let her lead, guiding the rods that appeared first and second together. He breathed a deep sigh, and a slow smile crept across his face as they retracted. They repeated this for the third and fourth, and so on until finished. Once all the rods had retracted into the cube, the sides flashed and gradually transitioned to a swirling constellation of stars Clarke did not recognize. Moments later, the ground shook, emanating loud cracks and causing a chasm to form. When it ceased moving, Clarke switched on his headlamp and led them beneath the frozen meadow at the woman's request.

AURALEI WATCHED FROM across the meadow as the stranger dropped their guise after incapacitating the dragoons and scanned the horizon as if knowing they were being watched. At that moment, Auralei thought she recognized the woman. The swords of ancient arena fighters and patterns the woman had danced through the dragoons were familiar—they were a Nova Republic specter.

Once the three disappeared belowground, Auralei emerged from hiding and quickly stowed her gear. Nearby, a craft constructed of two slender rails held closely together with a hive-like network of lattice uncloaked. As she swung her leg over the rails, hand and foot controls extended for her use, and the seat's synthetic webbing conformed to her curves—the mantis quickly recalibrated the flight altitude with the weight of its passenger. She traversed the alpine meadow, ripping through the air above the rocky terrain, pressing the machine hard, and arrived at the abandoned chopper within minutes. *How had the specter found this engineer,* she wondered. It was *her* engineer, after all.

Auralei examined the area for any nasty welcoming gifts and sensors left behind, discovering none. The specter hadn't taken time to camouflage the chopper or the dragoons, which would draw attention from either the invading force or the defenders— regardless of who came, their presence would have been unwanted. She knew other Nova Republic specters were operating on Lindaulx and had uncovered at least three other contracts during her investigation into the origins of the one she held. Her longevity as a specter was partially owed to her ability to ferret out the objectives of all contracts that could impact her success in an area. It wasn't uncommon for multiple contracts to exist, but they rarely had competing interests. *Then again, anything seems possible these days*, she thought. There had been no contract mentioning exploring buried complexes that she was aware of unless this person was operating outside their organization. The woman's confidence was also perplexing because she left traces of her passage. Apprehension spread through Auralei's body with rapid mercurial impulses attempting to gain purchase, but the microscopic implants along her neural network squelched this rare emotion with an efficient lethality. Auralei chased away a faint constriction in the pit of her stomach, ignorant of the lost authentic emotion.

The scream from a vessel burning through the air refocused her attention to the meadow. Auralei had walked into a trap. She sent her mantis away, parted the fabric separating her from the flux, and glided into the still world beyond, like passing between linen sheets drying on a crisp fall day. She watched as two javelins landed near the chopper, each depositing their eight cramped newcomers and gear. They lacked any distinguishable markings, but the death-dealing purpose of their equipment, although foreign, was unmistakable. There was something severe and oddly familiar about this group to Auralei—they moved efficiently about their tasks and with the comfort of experienced soldiers.

Two of the newcomers unceremoniously ejected the dead pilots from the dragoon armor, flushed the gore inside the suits via sanitary modules, climbed in, and powered them up. Lucky for the new pilots, the dragoon manufacturers had preempted the pilot's biological needs, and when pilots blew chunks, bled all over the place, or experienced other unpleasantness. Auralei wondered whether the specter had been careful to ensure they could use the suits again or if it was just a factor of the raw robustness and resilience of the Vindicator dragoon armor. *Chalk a point up for the stranger playing for the other side*, Auralei thought. Four others boarded the chopper, and shortly after, its engines roared to life. Then, the vehicle lifted from its icy berth and headed toward the City of Skyetook with the dragoons as escorts. The remaining soldiers disappeared into the depths.

There was perhaps one shortcoming in the other specter's plan, Auralei believed; they wouldn't have expected her inquisitive nature. The furthest thought from their mind would be of another specter disobediently struggling with the fate of one lowly engineer. It was impractical, even incomprehensible, as the action violated their ROG training and programming and wasn't possible given their implanted technology that severed emotional associations to the past. And, if that wasn't enough, as a last line of defense, her organization—the Resource Operations Group (ROG), affectionally known as *rogue*—also grafted a tiny device to each specter's hip. Its directive was to predict a body's physical and chemical composure, habits, and learned responses and sync that data with other devices to develop reactions ROG deemed appropriate. Over time, it learned and eventually provided the right amount of advantage and restraint. However, recently, Auralei and her device had wandered into unsanctioned territory. When the first glimpse of her past arrived, she had been careful, knowing from stories that devices could miss episodic memories. However, if her augment found one, it would relentlessly obliterate the long-term memory and any related pathways. Auralei sensed a familiar warmth and promptly recalled a thought thread of a bartender at a pub she preferred on Nanser-Nine; the memory seared away, warning her of the device's ever-present danger as the familiar sense of clarity was restored. She placed several nasty presents for anyone foolish enough to pursue her and disappeared into the chasm before it closed.

CHAPTER 05

THE PATHWAY DESCENDED steeply, continuing deep beneath the snow before opening into an enormous cavern. The air was dry and absent any dust shimmering or dancing in the beams cast by their headlamps.

"It's a little tough to swallow this story of yours, lass," Stigg said, breaking the dull rhythm of their hard-soled boots on the stone floor.

"Don't know what to tell you, big guy," Tarra said. "It is what it is at this point. Poking around down here is safer than being up there. Plus, there are now some blockades that will be tricky to circumvent when we leave this rock."

Stigg tugged on his thick, snow-white mustache. "Fair enough."

"What is this place?" Clarke asked, the echo of his voice ringing off the change in the floor's surface from rock to metal. "Is this some kind of old bunker?"

"Yup," Tarra confirmed. "I believe it's Astute."

Stigg made a whistling sound as he sucked air in between his lips. "You could have let us in on this little secret of yours."

Tarra let out a sweet laugh. "Sure, I could have. And what would that have gained me?"

Stigg chortled. "You expect us to believe you didn't know this was here?" Seeing Tarra raise her eyebrows and smile, he continued. "Clarke here is pretty entertained by the whole idea of the Astutes."

Tarra turned to catch Clarke's glance. "I'm surprised you know of them. Actually, I take that back. I probably shouldn't be. But I stopped here to kill some time."

"Sure, you did," Stigg said with a snort. "Chance at fortune, more like it."

Tarra smiled knowingly at Stigg. "Sort of. You can ease up. You're free to go once we're safely off this rock."

"*We're* safe?" Stigg asked.

Tarra smiled. "Clarke comes with me. The contract is for his protection, and the time hasn't expired. Lindaulx isn't safe anymore. So, we're leaving. You can hitch a ride if you don't cause a ruckus."

"And go where?" Clarke asked.

"I haven't figured that out yet," Tarra replied.

"You okay?" Stigg asked, grabbing Clarke's shoulder. He knew he wouldn't be convincing the woman of anything with only words.

"Yeah, just admiring the surroundings," Clarke said, pushing away Stigg's helping hand and struggling with the notion that there was a contract on him. There were special skills he had, but he wouldn't have guessed they were unique enough to warrant this level of expenditure. He thought it was best not to inquire exactly how much someone spent on the contract—no need to live with knowing the price of his life. "I once read a theory claiming the Astutes were an ancient race from another timeline."

"That bit of conspiracy might just be true," Tarra said, gleaning a little pleasure in the engineer's wild-eyed response, which she interpreted as excitement.

"Don't get him started," Stigg cautioned. "He has more of those theories and apparent knowledge than most. Call it an obsession. A dangerous, never find a decent healthy relationship, obsession."

"Just needs a similarly obsessed mate," Tarra laughed.

"A good deal of our advanced tech has its roots in what gets discovered in Astute facilities," Clarke said. "Or so it's believed. Case in point: the dragoon armor, although no one admits it."

Tarra wrapped her arm around Clarke's shoulder and flicked Stigg's hand away. "That would also be most likely correct. And people form partnerships with investment agents, contributing vast sums of money to finance exploration efforts to find Astute tech. Turns out it's costly to acquire objects discreetly. For instance, how better to be inconspicuous than when a liberation is starting? And who better to uncover such technology than a brilliant young field engineer?"

"Hopefully, before the people behind the invasion come looking," Stigg added. "Unless that's you."

"Not my thing," Tarra said over Stigg's continued grumblings. "Had skills that were thought better applied elsewhere than chasing extinct cultures. Although once topside, my *friends* will be here soon enough. You realize there are only seven known Astute facilities."

Stigg cleared his throat, pushing the protective front plate of his combat boots into the dirt and stomping the chalky building material to dust. "There's only one way you would know that, lass."

Tarra's gentle pressure on Clarke's shoulder became a sharp pinch and was gone as she relaxed. She pressed against Clarke's side like a young lover, but the solid grooves of her body armor replaced any welcoming contours of her body. "Two ways of knowing actually:

facilitator or investor. And this place could be the eighth such facility."

Stigg shook his head. "Never a straight answer. Can't be as simple as a Republic agent. That doesn't track. My bet is still on *Mischi*."

Tarra let out a soft pixie laugh. "Who said anything about *them*, Stigg?"

"I'm so bloody confused," Clarke said, facing Tarra. Her sweet breath warmed his lips, and he trembled as he peered into her eyes. "I'm guessing Stigg is correct, as per usual."

Tarra's eyes softened, and she leaned forward, brushing her cheek against his until her lips were against his ear. "Don't tell anyone, but yes, the old goat is right." Before Clarke could escape, she nibbled his ear. "You can't be surprised. I'm not your first."

"Not my first? Clarke said, tearing himself away from the woman and removing his overcoat as the temperature inside the complex was noticeably warmer. "What in the hell is that supposed to mean? I've never known a specter, let alone a *Mischi* or whatever the hell you call yourselves now. Certainly, never had one bite my damn ear."

Tarra flashed him a mischievous smile and skipped ahead, forcing Clarke and Stigg to catch her. "My goal, moving forward, is not to harm either of you. For nostalgia, *Mischi* has a nice ring to it. And now, this is the silent part of our journey."

The trio kept their thoughts to themselves as they trekked for over an hour along the track until the corridor opened into a vast cavern shrouded in darkness. Clarke checked his computer, finding it had lost its signal and any ability to track the distance they traveled. He squinted, trying to see beyond the reach of his lights. There were faint, colorless outlines of trees, a river, and what must have been buildings based on the orientation and repetition of the crumbling stone structures. The layers of rock overhead provided ample protection from whatever conditions the planet offered those many years ago, but not from what happened within.

Grabbing Clarke's arm, Tarra laughed and pulled him along. "All the worlds with Astute facilities have similar surface and subterranean environments." She released her firm grip and glided inside a partially collapsing structure, playfully kicking at some tiny pieces of stone. "A prevailing theory is that the Astutes migrated aboveground once they altered its climate. Not sure what I think about that one." She continued through the building until stomping her combat boot on the metallic floor, providing a trail through the vegetation. "Perhaps this way?"

Clarke picked his way through the rubble to stand beside the woman, straining through the darkness to see where she pointed. The trail plunged into the inky black depths of the stone just beyond a cluster of buildings across a large open square. "This route looks sturdier than the other one."

"Likely for transporting heavier equipment," Tarra said.

"I thought these complexes were systematically built," Stigg said, "with only slight variations in the layout of the buildings. Seen one like this before, *Mischi?*"

"What makes you think I've—"

"Call it a hunch," Stigg interrupted. "You're interested in this route. Why?"

"Intuition," Tarra retorted playfully.

"Where are the central towers?" Clarke asked. "Isn't that a common feature?"

Tarra wiped the dust from her boots on the back of her pants. "Yes. Some believe the towers were focal points for congregations. And oddly, all the other buildings have some traces of habitation in them, but not the towers."

"This rail is rather unique then," Clarke said.

"You sure about that?" Stigg asked.

Clarke shrugged. "Call it a hunch. No towers. There's a heavy rail line. This is not a symmetrical neighborhood. And she's acting squirrely."

"Then, hopefully, it leads us to a storage or maintenance area and even some new tech," Stigg said.

Clarke nodded. He was excited and terrified, which made his nod appear energetic. "Possibly a fabrication area," he whispered. The lack of such places was perplexing and frustrating to Astute explorers and self-proclaimed experts. For those lucky enough to find Astute items, the reverse engineering of the alien artifacts was complicated—the Astute's methods and process for constructing devices seemed based on an entirely distinct set of building fundamentals. One of the practically endless theories of Astute Loremasters was that replicators were used to bend matter to fashion what they required, except no one had ever located a fabricator.

"Then it's decided," Tarra said, bringing her hands together. "We follow the rail and see where fate takes us."

"So, you have seen a rail like this before then?" Clarke asked.

"I have," Tarra admitted.

"And?" Stigg asked, turning his hands to fists and making small punches at an imaginary foe.

"At the time," Tarra said cautiously. "Let's say that circumstances didn't present the opportunity for exploration."

"What circumstances?" Clarke asked.

"That's neither here nor…" Tarra said, straining her neck to the side, and then motioned for the party to continue walking, signaling that this line of conversation was over.

Clarke struggled to match the jog-worthy pace of Stigg's long strides. The woman's prior comment about not being his first *Mischi* rolled around inside his head, refusing to leave or stick to something meaningful. His relocation was the most straightforward place to start, but the lack of indexed and categorized memory banks made it difficult to remember specific details. He didn't believe the Nova Republic had orchestrated the events of his life—unless they were involved in removing his predecessors or the downfall of the Cryl Tenser. Clarke concentrated on the dull rhythm of their bootheels to settle his mind. The relative silence was calming until a sharp crack and the sudden explosive shower of dust and chunks of rock immediately beside his head punctured it. What could only have been a projectile fired from a weapon ricocheted down the hallway before him, making a low whining sound.

The rifle in Tarra's employ barked to life and sent high-velocity molten shells to where her situational augments calculated the shooter's location to be. Vague wisps of swinging lights were heading toward them, and they would soon lose the little protection the corridor's slight curve provided. "Move," she directed.

Clarke didn't require any further coaxing and started sprinting down the tunnel, trailing the small support sled and struggling to match Stigg's powerfully enhanced strides. Even a sharp slap across his ass from the *Mischi* and the warning that 'slow is dead' could only convince him to dig a little deeper for speed. He eventually came within a few paces of Stigg and the woman, who had graciously slowed their pace. His massive heaves of air to fuel his aching muscles were failing, and as his legs began to feel dissociated from his body, the running mercifully stopped. Clarke dropped onto the smooth tiles in a dimly lit room.

Stigg examined his surroundings with the learned and calculated precision he had gained through facing obstacles many times and living to reminisce. "You've brought trouble with you, *Mischi?*" he growled in warning.

"You mean whoever is trying to murder us?" Tarra asked. She swallowed to stifle the smile tugging at the corner of her mouth as she brought the familiar rush of the flux to the bleeding edge of her senses. The deep creases in the grizzled hulk's forehead told her she was triggering the desired result. "Simmer down. There's no need to get annoyed. I honestly don't know what you're referring to," she said, raising her hands and attempting to calm the mountain of a man. She didn't want to test whose reflexes were deadlier. As Stigg turned, she stepped forward, nimbly caught his shirt sleeve, and tugged at it to expose his forearm. There were faintly glowing markings resembling tattoos covering his arms. She locked onto his distant crystal blue eyes and kept his pace as he tried to walk away and fix his shirt. Yes, it fits—the man's markings resembled what her memory banks were retrieving about a group of people who appeared hundreds of years ago. They were a robust group who embraced advanced technology and were known to perpetuate seeking honor in death and bloodshed.

"Specter?" she asked.

"Would have to be one helluva talented one," Stigg replied.

"Overseer?"

"Doubtful. Feels tainted."

"*Dreader?*" Tarra whispered so that Clarke wouldn't hear. There were many names for the gifted individuals referred to as *Dreaders*—their talents and strengths varied widely, the same as Specters. In Tarra's circle, *Dreaders* were portrayed as people who used the flux for nefarious purposes and were not to be trifled with, as Specter's skills paled compared to the average stories of *Dreaders*. She wondered just how sensitive Stigg's perception was for hunting people with the talent—*Dreader* and Specter alike—and if he had detected her in the workshop earlier.

Stigg smiled, arching a thick eyebrow. "And what would you know about that?"

There were also plenty of names for those who hunted people with talent, usually reserved for the nightmares of the ROG Initiates and the undiscovered. "Vanguard," she said in an accusatory tone. Stigg laughed hard—a little too forced; her augments warned her. "Pathfinder."

Stigg stopped laughing and shook his head gently. "And now you've gotten yourself into a wee bit of a mess. Haven't you, lass? And even saw fit to drag us into it."

"I don't know what you're talking about," Tarra said, regarding Stigg with a newfound suspicion. She may have made a material mistake in her judgment of her situation, something she hadn't done since the Nova Republic Academy. She knew this old goat wasn't to be underestimated.

"Bullshit, *Mischi*," Stigg said. "And I do not hunt the likes of you." "But you did hunt before?"

Stigg flashed her a dangerous glare. "It's not what you think."

"Fine," Tarra said defiantly. "But why protect Clarke?"

"He's a talented engineer."

"Come now."

"He's a damn talented engineer, and I'm an old man who wanted some peace. Better a question for you."

"What is?"

"Why Clarke?"

"He's the best damn engineer my contract owner could find," Tarra responded.

Stigg laughed through closed lips. "Fine. Have your games. Do these people hunt you?"

"Honestly, I'm not sure," Tarra admitted.

"And those behind us?"

"They aren't the..." Tarra said and turned away from Stigg, breaking his intense stare. "They aren't the *Dreaders* you sensed?" She shuddered briefly before her augments could check the involuntary movement. "They aren't behind us?"

"You've heard too many stories, lass. But no, not directly behind us. They are quite close, however. At least have the decency to let us defend ourselves."

Tarra smirked—the old soldier still had some fight left in him that would hopefully play on the side of her preservation. "Dammit," she said, knowing her current company could turn on her the first chance they had. If the roles were reversed, she would have considered it and most likely acted upon it. But there was no other obvious alternative, and if they found anything, the engineers could hopefully sort junk from value. She unlocked a compartment on the support sled full of gadgets and weapons. "Shoot straight, and preferably not at me." For all she knew, her contract owner might have betrayed her—or worse, her organization. She wondered if that was why Auralei was here.

"Then this room will have to do," Stigg said with authority and motioned to a recessed walkway on the far side of the room. "Clarke and I'll take the high ground. Deal with this group now and the others later."

Clarke selected a rifle. Its sticky grip sucked at the skin of his palms, giving him a modicum of reassurance as the quality and caliber of the rifle would punch through most body armor. At the Dragoon Academy, Clarke scored better with rifles than the other weaponry and was still on the plus side in the maintenance division betting pool for the odd long-gun competition. With the remote in hand, he used it to position the support sled in the front corner of the room, shielding it from the brunt of any forward assault.

"You sure you want to make a stand?" Tarra asked, receiving a nod from both of them. "Please remember that I'm on your side for this fight." She sucked in the energy leaking from the flux, plying it and creating an opening for her to slip into. Leaping into the air, her cybernetics sent thousands of tiny spikes through the fabric weaves of her outfit so she could cling to the wall.

Clarke settled into position on the upper mezzanine's dry and warm tiled surface and searched for the woman. "You see her?" he called to Stigg, who was about twenty paces further down the walkway. The man's response was to shake his head and signal for Clarke to keep quiet. He closed his eyes only to find the pixie smile of the *Mischi* haunting the images that played there. He inhaled and released a cleansing sigh—no way he knew a *Mischi* or specter.

THE FIRST TWO pursuers into the room caught the brunt of four well-placed bursts from Clarke's rifle with telltale sprays of crimson mist. The trailing invaders were not as rash upon seeing the high-powered rounds slice through their comrades' breastplates and embed into the floor, sending out faint tendrils of smoke. After landing in the room, a small disk teetered and emitted a thin cable that attached to the ceiling. The disk began pulsating to scan the room, giving the pursuing soldier room surveillance.

Clarke trained his rifle on the tiny disk and fired. Despite multiple successful strikes to the glossy disk, the bullets only ricocheted. Someone responded from the hallway, firing energy rounds that sunk into the tiles near Clarke, sending him scurrying back from the ledge.

"Surrender!" a soldier bellowed in a strange and thick accent.

Stigg slinked forward, glimpsing the four soldiers taking a defensive position at the doorway. Rounds fired from his hand cannon were ineffective against the invader's shields, and a spray of bullets raking the mezzanine forced him away from the ledge.

Tarra bid her time until the pursuers pressed into the room. One thing the flux taught was patience if it was to be harnessed. Her heart would have raced, and her throat would have parched for a brief pang of guilt for the attackers if her cybernetics had permitted. Tarra coaxed her augmented flesh to lower her, silently and little by little, to a position where she could peer back down the hallway. She released her hold on the rock wall and slipped out of the flux. *Not exactly fair,* she thought. *But then, what is fair in death?* Conveniently for her, the most significant protection the invaders now had was their shields, which would similarly help her should Stigg and Clarke keep shooting. Her hands tightened around the grips of her swords, sinking into their familiar tackiness. The blades flashed unheard from their resting places, and she lunged forward, thrusting each sword between the shoulder blades of two soldiers and exiting the flux just before contact. She smiled, imagining the flash of horror on her prey's faces when they saw the glistening metal protruding from their chests. The reinforced cross-guard on her arming swords arrested their forward momentum against the back of the intruder's body armor. It was something she added after learning the hard way that it was pretty challenging to free one's hand and weapon from inside another's body—blood was like oil when it coated metal and cording. A torrent of body fluid splattered the floor when she freed the blades, and the dead soldiers fell forward, crashing into their comrades. A double-overhead scything attack removed the jaw of another soldier and bit deep, coming to rest embedded in their ribcage. Tarra spun, freeing her swords, trailing blood droplets as they soared parallel to the stone floor. Her shoulders jarred as she struck the last soldier: the sound her swords made was not the comforting dull thud of splitting body armor, flesh, and bone but rang as they contacted metal. Her enhanced neural and reflex network assessed the defensive posture of the person and partnered with her skill to bounce from the parry into a reverse arc. The lead sword came in low this time, with the other lagging. The invader parried the lower sword and brought her forearm up to catch the second sword, which bit through the woman's protective clothing and dug deep into her reinforced bone. Tarra released the bottom sword, kicked swiftly, and sent her attacker's weapon clattering to the stone floor. She smiled as the woman's eyes narrowed, revealing a moment of pain. With both hands, she forced the embedded sword up along their forearm and across the throat. The woman let out a wet and hollow whistle before grabbing her neck to stem the flow of life-sustaining fluid seeping between her fingers and slumped to her knees. Many people would have found the woman's peaceful and honey-yellow eyes enchanting, but not Tarra—the battle had been too easy. Suddenly, the woman lunged forward, spraying blood from her neck wound, and latched onto Tarra's leg, who scrambled backward, breaking the woman's feeble grip. Her leg tingled with a slight vibration and a familiar hum. Tarra examined the smaller belt around her thigh and smiled ruefully at the culprit. A pulse grenade was a moment away from detonation. She backhanded the grenade down the hallway and dove along the inner wall. The explosion tore into the room, blasting polished stone blocks from their seating, fracturing the surrounding basaltic rock walls, and causing the hallway to crumble. When the rocks settled, Tarra called out, "you two still alive?"

"Do I want to be?" Clarke asked through the ringing in his ears.

"There's another of your kind in here," Stigg called back.

"I just killed her," Tarra said with some pleasure.

"You may have," Stigg replied, digging at the spot where his meaty tricep met his elbow. "Doesn't feel dead. Feels close."

"She won't live long under those rocks, no matter how tweaked she is. Enough chatting. We need to move."

"Lovely," Clarke responded sarcastically.

Stigg gave Clarke two whacks on his back. "Don't worry. We'll see each other through this. Besides, where's your sense of adventure and the thrill of discovery? Not to mention mysterious women."

"Lost somewhere in the panic of practically getting our asses blown off," Clarke added. Standing, he clutched his stomach as it growled in protest. It had been hours since he had last eaten. He stopped short of complaining and threw his hands up in disbelief when a black-clad figure appeared behind Tarra. "What the hell?"

Stigg yanked Clarke to a crouched position, and half dragged him along the mezzanine. "Quiet now. I don't think this encounter is friendly."

"Another specter?" Clarke whispered.

"Yeah. Not good for us. Time to go."

THIS CLOSE TO the blood-stained woman, Auralei recognized Tarra—her outfit and combat style were unmistakable. She contemplated appearing and hacking her in half from behind, but it wouldn't have been a fair death. Besides, it might not kill her, just lay her up for a few weeks. And Tarra was probably aware of her presence by now and would be ready. She stepped from the flux and caught a glance from Clarke. His cobalt blue eyes straining to see through the shadows concealing her face. She wondered why he wasn't shooting at Tarra. She wanted to feel the anger, frustration, and rage from the disloyalty. The emotions were present just below the calm exterior created by her augments but filtered like sunlight through a solar shield. Auralei lashed out at the internal barrier safeguarding her feelings, trying to sunder it, to rend it from her body. She worked feverishly at the recently formed etchings, trying to create fissures to allow the warmth of the anger through, and failed.

"You should run," Auralei said calmly to Clarke as the burly chief mechanic was half dragging him away. She raised her pistol and squeezed off a few intentionally aimed projectiles that slammed into the area between Tarra's shoulder blades, knocking the raven-haired vixen to the floor. Auralei smiled. "Maybe you're not so stupid after all. You remembered to wear your armor." She had relinquished a slight advantage, but the temptation to capture Tarra in such a humiliating way got the better of her. The blood splatter as the rounds ripped through Tarra's chest would have been a welcomed sight, although not fatal given her multitude of synthetic organs.

Tarra laughed. "Still stung a bit. You sure you want to do this?"

"I always pictured a prettier place for your death. I also never expected you would be the one to betray me."

Tarra wiped the rubble from her clothes. "So, you recognize me? It's not what you think, though."

Auralei charged, drawing her longsword fluidly just as she had done countless times before, and gripped it in both hands, the blade only inches from the floor. Her powerful leg muscles and their augments propelled her swiftly across the broken tiles. Auralei launched into a graceful pattern of pulverizing shortcuts, which Tarra parried expertly, careful not to absorb too much of their force, sneaking in under the follow-up with an experienced riposte. She cut a shallow groove across Auralei's thigh—a regular blade would have glanced off her armor, but their singing blades could eviscerate. She took a quick breath to steady her nerves and remind herself that she needed to keep Tarra from getting too close. As she danced around the room with Tarra, Auralei hummed a long-forgotten tune her overseer had taught her. It was about armies and empires being hurled against one another, bright swords, and riding through ruin and death. There was peace for her in the rhythm, and she settled into a battle where they traded ground until Auralei caught a vicious blow from Tarra's shorter sword in the forward-sloping quillons of her longsword. Tarra's second blade trailed behind the first, biting hard into the Auralei's pauldron, sending a dull pain through her shoulder. The armor held, and her augments released more pain-dampening chemicals into her body. "Well done," Auralei said and violently twisted her sword. She would have robbed a lesser combatant of their blade; however, Tarra used the force of the attempted disarm to propel her into a cartwheel, carrying her across the room. She came to her feet smoothly in a ready stance.

A smile spread across Tarra's lips. "But of course." She sprang at Auralei.

Clarke watched the battle playing out below him in awe. He had never seen two people engage with such ferocity and speed. It was difficult to tell who would win the clash of sword styles, which was awkward and maintained an unhealthy rhythm. Their captor would engage with her rapid death-by-a-thousand-cuts from dual short swords, only to defend against not being cleaved in half. The battle locked the two women in a dance of sparks, and just when it appeared to sunset, they came at each other with renewed vigor.

"Come on," Stigg said. "We need to go. You've gawked long enough at their asses, and the dead soldiers aren't who I sensed."

Clarke adjusted his shirt. "More specters?"

Stigg scratched at the stubble along his jawline. "Another group, perhaps, and surely, they heard the blast. Besides, I do not trust my lot with either of them." He gestured toward the two women sparring below.

Abandoning the support sled for fear of attracting unwanted attention, Clarke and Stigg exited along the upper mezzanine through an arched doorway and traveled down a poorly lit hallway. Clarke ejected the almost spent clip from his rifle, tucking it into his pocket and fitting another snuggly in place, "I've read these places can be expansive."

"That's what I'm counting on."

Clarke sucked in a deep breath. "Do you think we'll find a way out?" he asked in a hushed voice.

"Probably not," Stigg whispered, raising an eyebrow, but Clarke missed his wink when the light flickered and vanished, plunging the duo into darkness.

Clarke turned his headlamp on and tightened his utility harness around his midsection. Theoretically, it would arrest a fall if the owner and their feet were still moving without ground to meet them. The belt was designed to launch a series of hooks on metal filaments at the nearest solid objects as fall protection. But, in rare instances, the harness's software failed and selected a person as the most probable object to stop the descent. This usually ended in a messy disaster for all coupled parties.

They set off running. Again, Clarke struggled to keep up with Stigg, who kept checking over his shoulder and making abrupt arm swings to encourage him to keep up. Clarke's breathing was spastic as he sucked air harshly into his lungs. "I'm not doing so well," he said between giant gulps of air. Eventually, he slowed to a wobbly-legged walk when he believed they were a safe distance away from the invaders and *Mischi.* He checked his wrist computer and cursed himself for not setting it to record again. He wasn't sure how far they had been running or if this tunnel was straight or level. The toes of Stigg's boots appeared at the limit of his headlight, which pointed straight at the floor.

"You a little out of shape there? I thought you were keeping up your fitness."

"What?" Clarke asked. "No. Yeah. I mean, I've been doing the damn training. It doesn't matter now. There's a bloody invasion above us."

Stigg nodded and dug his fingers into one side of his cheek, scratching through his burly mustache. "Those javelins we saw are likely what brought our other guests here. What I can't work out yet is how they knew about this facility. And how did they find a way in?"

"The same way we did, I guess."

"Surely some of them did. But the others I sensed. No. They know something else."

"So, what are we dealing with? Some *Mischi*, specters, invaders, perhaps traitors, and we're lost in some damn archeological find of the planet's history."

Stigg laughed. "Something like that. A little too many players to my liking. Something's amiss, that's for damn sure. I would say the *Mischi*, and their…" He considered what to say next as he rubbed the smooth stone bore of the tunnel. "Don't forget, the bloody Nova Republic is also a player here. They are unlikely bunkmates for the invaders unless…"

"Unless what Chief?"

"Oh, nothing really. Just working through our options. Anyway, all of them put us in a very awkward position."

"Yeah, unknowingly in the middle. Whatever it is, it's probably an attempt to overthrow House Khilsyth and claim this place."

"And that's exactly what you should think," Stigg said. "Nah, this is a glimpse."

"Of what?"

"Exactly. It's the appearance of *Dreaders* that's confusing. Specters, I can sort of understand."

"Explain. Please."

"*Dreaders* are generally against protecting anything Astute," Stigg answered. "I've never heard of them venturing far outside their realm… since they were hunted after the Shade Wars. I'm not sure how they would have recovered. Unless…"

"Stigg. This is like pulling teeth. Get to the point."

"It's nothing we can solve down here," Stigg said, raising his hand, stopping Clarke before he could object, and whispered. "There's more of them."

Clarke did not comprehend what Stigg grumbled next, and his fatigue was getting hard for him to ignore and for the modern science he could use to counteract. He took the time to down an energy supplement and stumbled after his mentor.

The hallway opened into a grand cylindrical chamber with eight dimly lit rails of interlocking metallic panels radiating from the surrounding rock to a central spire. Each rail was approximately forty paces wide, a thousand paces long, with equal distance separating them horizontally on this level. The central shaft had no accessway, but the rails were attached to a mechanism that appeared to allow it to move in any direction across its exterior.

Clarke imagined the spire was the skeletal support system for a mountain, perhaps Mount Klarzach, which they might be under by now. "I wonder what took out these... whatever they are. Rail carriages, maybe." Clarke peered over the side of a railing and switched to night vision, but the optics failed to penetrate the darkness of the depths. "Wager something substantial wreaked havoc on its way down. Shall we go up?"

"No, we go down," Stigg replied.

Clarke flashed Stigg a puzzled look. "Come again? Going up, using one of those rails, and doubling back the way we came should get us out of here. Hopefully, the cave-in was contained to this level."

Stigg raised his finger, scarcely at all, to point upward and shook his pistol. "I don't think this will do much good against them."

Clarke followed the backward flick of Stigg's head, squinting to overcome the extent of his vision. A twinkling light was swirling above them in the column and getting brighter. "I guess we go down then." He killed the lights, as Stigg requested, and fastened his climbing device to the edge of the rail, the magnetic hook echoing faintly through the chamber as it made contact. Clarke dropped over the side, speeding after Stigg, manipulating the microscopic tether playing out behind him and avoiding the other rails. *Into the bowels is supposed to be more inviting than them*, he mused. The Hale expedition goggles reported Stigg's rate of descent, which the tether matched, and after descending about a klick, Clarke came to rest beside Stigg on another rail carriage. At this depth in the facility, the central spire emitted an eerie azure glow, and his eyes gradually adjusted to discern the faint outlines of his surroundings. "This could have been a fun adventure if the circumstances were different, eh?"

"You don't think this is fun?" Stigg asked, with a hint of jovialness creeping into his voice. "See the markings." He walked over and tapped shapes carved into crystalline plates on the wall. "These feel familiar. Lucky even."

"Seriously?" Clarke questioned as excitement in Stigg's voice was rare. "You sure?" He squinted to see what Stigg saw as he passed through the archway but couldn't and resisted turning on his light, fearing those above might see them. Further down the hallway, a soft light spilled across the floor from under most of the doors. The recessed lighting molded into the rock flickered, threatening to spring to life at any moment and purge the remaining shadows.

"I wasn't always an engineer, you know," Stigg said.

"I've heard some rumors," Clarke said, chuckling under his breath at the many theories into Stigg's past lives the workshop crew and soldier gossip favored. Like most chief engineers in remote colonies, Stigg knew more about how to use the tools of war than how to fix them.

"Oh yeah? Let's have it then."

Clarke rattled off the more favored occupations, "Rift Faction, mercenary, Vanguard, Black Dragoon, bounty hunter—"

"Yup."

Clarke coughed. "You're kidding? Black Dragoon?"

"In another life," Stigg said, dropping his head and drawing a deep breath.

"The Black Dragoons are people of legends," Clarke said; the words were distant and slow to form. "The foundation for the Vanguards."

"Thanks for the vote of confidence."

It was difficult to tell when Stigg was teasing. The succinct descriptions of a Vanguard did not do them justice, and the myths always seemed like propaganda to Clarke. They were fabled warriors who roamed the cosmos, devoting their lives to eradicating injustices and the perverse. Through his research, he uncovered some story threads that weaved their participation in events with the beginnings of the Frebels. "Which Vanguard tribe?"

Stigg laughed. "Mauti's crew was more like a clan, and that was a long time ago. But at least now I know which theory you favor."

"The *Mauti Arbasele* was the dreadnaught of the Strento Flotilla—a massive unholy death-bringer-of-a-ship. It was the pride of the Republic fleet. I've read the legends since I was a kid. I thought they were myths."

Stigg chuckled. "Or so the story goes, right? But legends and myths are full of half-truths, exaggerations, and often irresponsible decisions people somehow survived."

Clarke shook his head and hurried after Stigg. He wanted to check the shadowed expression on his mentor's face but only saw a fuzzy block of a head. "You're teasing me, right?"

"*Mauti Arbasele* was not a ship name I knew of. But Mauti and Arbasele were warriors. Clan leaders. Husband and wife."

"How did you end up here, then?"

"That little *Mischi* minx, you pissed off somehow. But on Lindaulx, let's say that some of us disagreed with those Republic bastards."

"Before or after the fall of House Frebel?"

"It has more to do with how they implemented the Greater Purpose. Now, have I ever led you astray?"

"You're not looking for a way out, are you?" Clarke asked, watching Stigg square up to the door. "You're looking for a way to fight back."

"Now you're thinking. In these stories of yours—these legends and myths—the Vanguards were never subtle, were they? Hopefully, we'll have time for a more significant chat later. But for now, let's divide and conquer and hope we find something useful."

MAEVE WATCHED THE two men enter the spire below her, dug a disk the size of her thumbnail out of her satchel, and cradled it in her palm. She sought the energy in the world around her with a learned familiarity that flowed between the folds of time. Maeve coerced the power into a familiar pattern, summoning its attention away from the sweetness of the beyond and channeling it into the disk. The seeker-bot rose and, with her blessed desires, disappeared into the darkness of the inner chamber. Fortunately, the two men were ahead of the hunters she had released into the complex, for she had unfinished business with one of them.

Maeve closed her eyes and tilted her head back. Her mission was in full swing now. She needed to be patient, let it play out, and have faith in her diligent planning. Lindaulx, a name given to this heirloom planet by interlopers, was a suspected location of a device with the potential to shape worlds. She was here to reclaim it before her Order realized her detour—those she answered to would not have approved of what she was doing. But she existed in a culture guided by people who rarely left the safety of secluded fortresses on distant worlds—it was difficult for her to accept lofty decrees unshaped by worldly experience.

However, her adoption and use of outlawed technology made what she did for them possible. If they learned of her acceptance and willingness to employ such vile machinery on her crusades, even her use of mercenaries, the punishment would be severe. Maeve did not share the same disgust for advancements as her Order and had learned the correct inflections, intonations, and details to omit when delivering her mission reports. She also believed that if you could gain an edge, only the foolish would not exploit it. Of course, even with the constraints and limitations imposed on her by her Order, she was self-reliant, resourceful, and practical. These were the primary reasons for her superiors electing her as *Tersa*—the seeker of the lands beyond for salvation and an enforcer of the righteous existence of Tersinians—or something to that effect. The propaganda she had been exposed to failed to elicit the same passionate responses it had inside of her when she was an initiate. She considered her arrangement simple: the Monastery had faith she would dutifully strive for the continuance of their ways, and she had faith they would turn on her the moment she failed— divine grace was not wasted on the unworthy.

Maeve caressed the familiar crystal pendant hanging from her slender neck. It had belonged to her father, and its warm surface resurrected the ghosts of her past—her earliest childhood memories were of her home world of Tresum. It was a planet in a solar system far from here whose way of life was still primitive compared to most known civilizations. Progress was made, and battles were waged with behemoths belching spent wood gases. A minor act of kindness changed the life course of her family forever—Maeve had protected a friend from being trampled by the freshly shod hooves of a local noble's horse. Witnesses to the event, and some who thought her father an outsider, claimed her speed had been unnatural. The people of her village feared what they didn't understand and turned on her, claiming the nefarious gods cursed her. They demanded that her family surrender her to the Viscount. Maeve's father urged the family to flee, knowing they would take their daughter, but it had been her maternal grandfather who betrayed their location to the local officials for fear of retribution from the church. The guards had arrived at their small cottage before they could finish packing and accused the family of harboring a witch. Maeve's sweet, youthful voice had not stopped the guards from beating her father severely when he attempted to calm and educate the guards that it wasn't witchcraft but the contrary. The memory attached to her first kill was hazy. Over time, she had filled in the gaps of the ill-fated encounter, even comprehended how the necklace her father had given her was a technological marvel—a jewel embedded in the nucleus of her sun-shaped pendant served as a focusing crystal that could tap into power sent from distant systems through a network of celestial devices. Within Tresum was a remarkable structure that received, contained, and made this power accessible. Her Tersinian Order referred to this gift as *blessings from the spirit world*. With her mother knocked to the worn wooden floor of their small cottage and bleeding, Maeve had held the necklace and screamed at the guards. Her words were soundless within the hallow ringing of a stilled world—a place beyond the material world where she walked within the hallowed ether. Once there, she had tried to push the guards off her father, but her tiny hands passed into their bodies. The shock had caused her to reel backward and lose concentration on the necklace. When back on the physical plane, the guard's lungs were in her hands. She vividly remembered how they clawed at their throats, unable to breathe, staring in horror at the tiny girl with a flower in her hair.

They fled the cottage her father had built, booked passage on various water vessels, and tracked apparatuses that cost the crews the right amount so they could forget the passengers they carried. It had been late one bone-weary evening as Maeve hid behind an enormous woolly beast, bracing herself against the biting winds that her father imparted one of her life's most important lessons: You only have those who unconditionally love you in the end, and you won't know who they are until they're tested. *I'll always love you, my darling daughter, her father had said, and the ground heaved— from the snow and ice, a system connector ship rose, obliterating her young mind's* understanding of her place in the world and the scale of the universe. On the Sardiss Glacier, she realized there was more to her father than she knew; he had hidden it masterfully.

Once safely off Tresum and hiding amongst a field of space rock, her father imparted another critical consideration for her journeys: *Do not fall for their conventions and beliefs but give them no reason to doubt you're on their side.* This holds true wherever you may wander. They fled across the systems for about two years, never staying long in one place. Her father trained her and shared his life's stories as they went. In her heart, Maeve believed her father knew that the events on Tresum would not escape the notice of the Monastery's *Tersa.* Although now she suspected her father, a worldly explorer from an advanced civilization, was possibly part of the Nova Republic—he had understood much of their means and methods and avoided their larger inhabited territories when they fled.

It had been late one evening when she was researching pruning techniques for the fruit trees in their orchard when a jarring knock at the back window caused her arms to flail and send her sweet tea spilling, rolling, and splashing across the desk. The memory was etched into her heart as she smiled at the memory of her overly skittish cat—the sudden movement sent Pickles, a stray she'd rescued, into a skittering frenzy of claws. The culprit had been one of their acquaintances who relayed a message that her father had died in a mining incident. They had been on Loos Valoon, a planet with a questionable history of allegiances. The man claimed her father had paid him to protect her should something happen, promptly fled the planet, and placed her in the care of a nearby monk covenant. Maeve had suspected the tale was false, but despite her sacrifices, offerings, and favors, she could learn nothing contrary to her father's fate and whether he had intended her to be taken to a Tersinian Monastery.

A dull pain shot through the back of her neck, bringing her to the present. Something had severed the tendril between her and the seeker-bot. The complex caused the rift—she was sure of it. The lower corner of her mouth twitched impetuously, chasing away a frown. Her elders would never understand the importance of the device she came to recover from within this complex, but they would learn to appreciate the power she could wield when she possessed all of them.

THE INTENSITY OF Auralei's attacks and the fervor that Tarra warded them off diminished as they drove their enhanced bodies near exhaustion. There were known to be rare cases of augmented individuals pushing past their physical limits to death. Both women were steadily working toward the precipice of causing significant internal damage in the effort to best the other: their internal augments were too efficient at impeding the body's natural ability to administer pain, providing a signal that something was wrong.

Auralei took advantage of a reprieve in the battle to remove her gloves, which were slipping on the pommel of her sword. Her sweat acted as a ring agent, sucking her suit tight against her body, and with each labored breath, her lungs ached to breathe in fresh air.

"You look tired," Tarra said in between long ragged breaths. At the ROG Academy on Nanser-Six, she occasionally sparred with Auralei and always bested her. Clever Auralei had kept to the deceit of their lives as specters, never genuinely revealing her fighting potential. "What do you want with them?"

"They aren't part of your contract," Auralei said.

"What are you talking about?" Tarra asked, scrunching her face and flinging her head back. "We finished the mission. That was the plan." She sucked air in greedily to fill her lungs. "Are they part of yours?"

"You were always an opportunist. Who are you working for?"

"Myself."

Auralei laughed in disbelief. "Not with. For. Who are you working *for*?"

"Myself."

"To what purpose?" Auralei fired back. The Nova Republic did not frown upon taking time to pursue personal quests unless it conflicted with existing contracts or the interests of their superiors—delving through a suspected Astute facility qualified as one of those conflicting interests.

"My own. It's personal."

"I don't believe you," Auralei said, dropping her gloves and glimpsing what she believed was one of Tarra's tells. She figured it was an act.

"Does it matter?"

"It might. But, no, not really. Then, when does it ever really matter?"

"Always the pessimist," Tarra said with a playful laugh. "You need to change your perspective on life. Get laid even." She lowered her swords and gave a sympathetic glance. "Wait! Ah... sweetheart. Really? The engineer, right? I can't believe I missed it." Tarra stomped her foot. "Clarke, or whatever his name is," she emphasized with a dismissive wave of her sword. "You know him from your past." Auralei failed to stymie an eye twinge, and Tarra pressed. "His file, the place of origin, was the same home world as yours. Not the one your file claims, but Nanser-Nine." She tapped her right temple. "Minds a vault. Remember, you told me when we were roomies?"

Auralei shook her head. "It's not what you think, princess."

"No, eh? Are you sure? Some nice leverage over you, love. If that was the type of person I was." Tarra winked at Auralei and playfully shook her shoulders back and forth.

Auralei's hazel eyes narrowed while maintaining a vigilant watch of Tarra, watching for the slightest movement, showing the fight would begin again.

"It's true, isn't it?" Tarra asked. "If so, we can finish this little thing between us later because it's honestly not what you think. You should go make sure he's safe."

Auralei released some of the tension in her muscles. Tarra was right: every second wasted increased the chance she wouldn't be the first to find the one who had given her the bracelet.

Tarra sucked air in through the side of her mouth, causing her tongue to click. "Sweetie. Emotions? Really?"

This time, Auralei thought Tarra sounded legitimately concerned, likely abhorring the memories of their training and the discipline from the slightest display of emotions deemed unwanted by the instructors.

"You know they'll hunt you for this," Tarra said in a hushed tone. "Odds are your systems have already betrayed you. I need to keep him safe, love."

"I have no plan to harm him."

"So, our interests are aligned then?"

"It seems that way," Auralei said levelly, having regained a regular breathing rate. "What is your plan?"

"It was to have a look-see until these asses appeared."

"Wasn't anything I knew of."

"Me either," Tarra admitted begrudgingly. "I've got a fast ship. You?"

"It does okay," Auralei said with a smile.

"I've got a better chance of getting back into that hellhole of a city and figuring out what we're up against," Tarra said, referring to Skyetook. "Might even get a glimpse of what's in the sky above us."

The two stared at each other, unable to admit they were glad they had each other when things went sideways.

"You should leave," Auralei said. "I'll recover the two morons. Not sure why they went deeper in. We can always come back to this later."

The space around Tarra shimmered, and she vanished. Auralei swung her sword in a defensive arc as Tarra reappeared on the upper mezzanine, shaking her head.

"You'll need to trust someone someday, sweetheart," Tarra said.

"Be ready when I signal you, princess," Auralei called after Tarra, who waved half-heartedly before disappearing through a doorway opposite Clarke and Stigg.

The consequences of what Tarra knew and what Auralei's systems would transmit would bring the Bright Angels—The Nova Republic's cleanup squad. Auralei couldn't recall confiding in Tarra where she had been from, but the memories of her first years at the ROG Academy were splotchy. She could have betrayed many secrets to Tarra on those nights she had spent in fits after the mental and physical endurance testing her defiance had subjected her to.

"Let's see what you're all about," Auralei said to the dead soldiers who ended up betraying little of their purpose as the markings they bore were from conquered, vanquished, or antiquated houses. However, their weapons and rucksacks contained high-tech gadgets and provisions for several days, betraying them as an amply financed outfit. Auralei embraced the rush of energy around her and stepped into the cool breeze of the flux. She fled the room in pursuit of Clarke, unable to shake the sense that Tarra was being honest.

CLARKE FOLLOWED STIGG down the hall and into a room where he was instructed to find something helpful while Stigg explored the adjoining rooms. He strolled the workshop aisles containing neatly arranged tables with dividers, perusing the contents like he was at Skyetook's ocean-side market—except here in the depths, there were no shrieks from feisty gulls threatening to steal your treats or the pungent smell of the ocean, just stale air. He tried hard to imagine that he was in an ordinary structure and not buried deep within Lindaulx.

On top of each workstation was a symbol carved into a pole, which neither Clarke nor the Hale goggles recognized. Each workbench was protected from the next by low walls, and the top of each one had a multitude of cuts and swirls. An assortment of machinery and tools were scattered around it, along with armor and weapons in the midst of being repaired—Clarke's excitement level rose, and his pace quickened as he investigated each one, knowing they were in an armory repair area.

In the middle of the isle, he currently strode along, there were central tables with remnants of shattered crystals and armored plates with deep rifts. Nearby carts held random assortments of armor appendages, scraps of metal, and stray wiring harnesses. An out-of-place fur blanket covering an object protruding from beneath a workbench drew Clarke to a work area with a pole bearing a symbol of two sideways eights stacked together. Scraps of metal and tools cluttered its surface, but there were also energy cells and a lone battle helmet with a tether disappearing into the ceiling. "Hey, Stigg," he called. "There's some kind of helmet tethered to the ceiling over here. Even some fuel cells." Hearing no response, he shrugged, tested the first cell, and found it utterly depleted. "Stigg!" he called again and peered over the workstation's walls—no reply and no one in sight. His instrument chimed, indicating that another fuel cell was similarly out of power. "Odd, you should have some juice left in you," he mumbled to the cells. He had never seen a source fuel cell that was effectively spent before.

Clarke double-checked the gauge on one of his primary power cells, which worked as expected. "Damn my luck," he muttered. He kneeled and inspected the fur blanket, unable to place the creature the silky pelt had belonged to. He discovered an insignia stitched into the end of it that was an intricately detailed star superimposed on a bear standing on its hind legs—it wasn't anything he recognized. He snapped an image of it using his handheld computer. He tugged on the fur covering, but it wouldn't budge, so he tried harder, unraveling the blanket and causing him to flail backward. "Holy shit!" Clarke yelled as the remains of a person rolled onto his legs. He kicked at the body to free himself and stood, shaking vigorously to rid himself of the heebie-jeebies. "Dammit, Stigg," he said forcefully. "There's a dead guy here." Still no response from the chief engineer. He wondered why, in all that was holy, there was a body here of all places. Clark shook his arms again to clear his head—he hoped the deceased person meant there was another exit. He stepped over the body toward the workstation and returned to systematically testing and discarding the energy cell cores. He cursed his luck—all were depleted, and nearby workstations were devoid of anything resembling a fuel cell. It was a grim prospect to be running low on power underground.

"Let's have a gander," Clarke muttered, dragging the battle helmet closer for inspection, its tether moving freely. He picked it up and turned it over in his hands—it seemed like a common enough helmet, although he had half-hoped there would be some feature that betrayed its use by an alien race. There was a small compartment above the left temple area on the helmet. He cradled the helmet against his chest and pressed his index finger against the panel, which opened to reveal a minuscule cell. With the nail of his index finger, he tried to pry it up and eventually popped it into his hand—a dark monofilament strand still connected it to the helmet. A tinge of relief flooded his weary muscles as the power cell cooled to his touch, indicating the cell was converting his body heat into stored energy. This relief vanished when the cell frosted over, trapping it to the hardened skin of his palm. Before Clarke could call out, the intense cold seared its way up his arm, wracking his entire body with convulsions. Clarke strained to drop the cell, his muscles groaning in agony, but his reaction proved too slow.

THE SHOCK OF the warmth awoke it from its dormant state, releasing the instinctive abilities shut off long ago. Energy had been scarce, enough only for the essential function of preservation. Its hunger was voracious. It gave itself willingly and embraced the partially foreign system.

THE FUEL CELL in Clarke's hand splintered and released its hold. He vigorously shook his body to overcome the chills, jumping back and forth on the balls of his feet for warmth. The coldness climbed his arm into his chest and wrapped a deadened embrace around his spine.

"Clarke, where are you, son?" Stigg asked, ducking through the doorway into the workshop. With no response from Clarke, Stigg hefted a massive axe into the air and slammed its knob down onto the stone floor. "Come check this out." The weapon barely cleared Stigg's shoulders and had two large blades originating from its eye that, with large arcs, rejoined the haft near the midpoint.

Clarke shook his head with a smirk. "I feel like I should have a smart-ass comment, but you look foolish enough," he said, stuttering as the warmth sluggishly freed his lungs. "I bet the damn thing would shatter if you dropped it."

Stigg appeared hurt and spun, producing a vicious arc, which carried the axe cleanly through the leg of a workbench and emerged without slowing through the top. The contents crashed to the floor, soliciting a playful grin from Stigg. "I don't think the owners will mind if I borrow it."

"Probably not," Clarke said, not expecting such a clean cut from an antique. "It looks so fragile. By the way, can you come over here for a sec? There's a dead guy here."

"So, there is," Stigg said, peering over the adjacent workstation. "You kill him?"

"Does it look like I did?"

Stigg climbed over the workstation and kneeled to inspect the body. "It does not. But they've been dead a few years. You search it?"

"Hell no."

Stigg spent a few moments emptying pockets and the nearby rucksack and considering the pile he'd made on the floor. "Appears to be some kind of scholar. However, I can't quite place their origin. Not from here, anyway." He placed items he thought worthwhile back into the rucksack and slung them over his broad shoulders. "We'll need help translating and reviewing all this," he added. "What's this?" he wrapped his knuckles off the battle helmet. "And where's the rest of it?"

"Not sure."

"Little small for dragoon armor. Try it on."

As Clarke rolled the battle helmet in his hands so its empty void faced him, his view of the workshop pulsed. An image burned into his closed eyelids but held no meaning. Clarke stepped back, his muscles groaning in protest, and rubbed his eyes to clear the starbursts blocking his vision.

"You good, lad?" Stigg asked, grabbing Clarke to steady him.

Clarke waved off a supportive hand from Stigg. "Yeah, I'm fine, only—" Clarke lost his thought as something yanked it away, slamming an image of the armor and a language he didn't recognize into place. It was as if an old memory in the recesses of his mind was dusting itself off and coming out of hibernation or was being dredged from wherever one's knowledge goes to die in the depths of brain matter. The feeling wasn't exactly unknown to Clarke: ever since he had attempted to insert his homegrown brand of memory augmentation and failed, the pathways to old memories degraded, and some neural wiring seemed crossed. He wondered if it could have been from assigned Dragoon Academy studies, but no, this was different.

"Come on, your skin is pale as a ghost," Stigg said. "What just happened?"

Clarke scratched his head vigorously to clear the disorientation and grasped the workstation to steady the fear rising in the pit of his stomach. This was *very* different from a failed memory pathway.

Inside Clarke, the matter shared his fear but did not understand that its host needed time to adjust to having a foreign thing share its thoughts. It hadn't had enough time to repair itself and needed help. The familiar armor it had briefly registered would do.

"What the hell did you do?" Stigg asked with a laugh as a gantry crane whirled past the top of his head along an aerial track and disappeared into the darkness toward the end of the workshop.

"How is this funny?" Clarke asked.

The crane whirled into view and deposited its contents in front of the workstation.

"I'll be damned," Stigg said, letting out a mirthful laugh. "That is some fancy-looking armor. You think it still works?"

Clarke's vision exploded in a swirling kaleidoscope of light, and he dropped to his knees, holding his head.

Stigg grabbed Clarke's shoulders to stop him from pitching backward. "What the hell is going on with you?"

Clarke quelled the nauseous wrench on his innards with a couple of deep breaths and used his palms to wipe the sweat from his brow. "Something, or someone... Dammit. Feels like my skull and my bones are being invaded. It's been happening since I was messing with those old cells." The last part of his confession rose to a crescendo. "It doesn't feel good," he added.

"I don't sense anything out of the ordinary here," Stigg replied, but there was concern in what he said.

Clarke arched an eyebrow at Stigg and then flicked his head toward the bones on the floor, which were covered in dried skin and plain cotton robes and were now in shambles.

"Okay, okay. What do you need?"

Clarke stood with Stigg's aid and steadily gained stability in his legs until he no longer leaned against his friend. That last flash hadn't conveyed anything except pain. No words. No Images. Just pain.

"You might as well try it on," Stigg said. "It's more your size than mine."

"You think I'm a sucker for punishment, don't you?"

"Hey, it's probably a once-in-a-lifetime chance. Besides, I'll get you out if you get stuck in there. At least, I'm fairly confident I could."

The armor resembled a lightweight powered combat suit, except it was constructed from interlocking plates of various sizes and shapes, absent of markings, and lacked thrusters. The charcoal-colored exterior seemed to absorb the surrounding light. Clarke dragged his hand across the armor's plating, finding it rough to the touch, like coarse sandpaper that became tacky until his skin stuck. He had to put his weight behind dislodging his hand, which ripped free. Upon inspection, he discovered tiny pricks of blackish blood soaking back into his palm and was relieved he hadn't torn his flesh entirely off. He shook his head to stop his mind from playing tricks—the low light in the room and lack of sleep weren't helping matters.

"Seriously," Stigg said, unable to hide some modicum of concern from affecting his voice. "Did it bite or something?"

"What. Ah, no. But I can't say I recognize the material this plating is made from." The sudden flash in Clarke's skull brought him to a knee, leaving a parting image of the armor opening. "For the love of the gods," he whispered, careful not to aggravate the maelstrom between his ears.

Stigg laughed as the armor separated down the side, providing enough room for someone to wriggle inside. "The secret to opening the alien contraption is reverence?"

Clarke flashed Stigg a confused look. "Sorry. Was busy with some foreign thoughts." He tapped his temple for good measure, then peered inside the suit. There were none of the standard interfaces he was used to seeing in dragoon armor, and it was deceptively thin for mechanized armor. "It's apparently a paragon. You think this is what they used to model Vindicator armor sets from but couldn't get it down to this scale?"

"No idea. But what did you call it?"

"A paragon."

"How do you know it's called that?"

"Something I picked up along the way, I guess."

"Awesome," Stigg said sarcastically. "Very comforting. I wonder if it's got—"

Rapid explosions reverberating from the other side of the workshop's main doors drowned out the rest of what Stigg said. Both men turned to check the door, relieved it withstood the blast, and still barred whoever was on the other side from gaining entry.

"Smart to close the door," Clarke said.

"Yeah. You learn a few tricks along the way getting to my age."

"How do you figure they knew we were here?"

Stigg shook his head. "There's no way they heard us through that thick of a door?"

"The *Mischi*?"

"Maybe, but which one? Shit, maybe the short one had a tracker on you. Doesn't matter right now."

"Where's that lead?" Clarke asked, motioning to a nearby doorway.

"That goes nowhere," Stigg said grimly. "Afraid play times over. Now, get that bloody armor moving. We're going to need it."

At Stigg's command, Clarke grabbed the suit's collar—against his better judgment—and swung himself inside. "This should be interesting," he muttered.

"You're a sitting duck. Find some cover."

AURALEI ENTERED A sizeable circular chamber and sent a few hunter droids into the darkness. They reported some minuscule disturbances in the air currents and faint scents left behind by people passing before her. Auralei traced the route of the signatures down until the hunter droids reported a divergence, with some going after Clarke and others continuing further into the facility. To cover her ass, Auralei tasked the seeker-bots with trailing the other party because there was no sense having anyone backtrack and sneak up on her.

Auralei released her descender and landed silently on one of the broken rails. The stone archway Clarke had passed through was accessible by a short walk and a long jump. Once in the hallway, she drew on her talent and flitted into the shadows to disguise herself. It was easier to use the flux here, but the willingness of it all made her pause—the energy seemed to course through her, making her heart race, her breath quiver, and her head woozy. *You need to keep moving*, she told herself, as it was dangerous to dwell in this state. She became a wisp, undetectable to most people and devices, and out of habit, was careful not to disturb the light spilling from under the doorways.

Before long, Auralei encountered six mercenaries discussing how best to remove the doorway that a hunter droid showed Clarke had passed through. A quick vibration stopped her. She checked the responsible device, which told her there was something capable of disrupting her concealment nearby. Auralei dashed a slight twitch from her eye. This group was aware of her, or Tarra's, presence in the facility. The technology needed to restrict access to the flux was incredibly rare. She wasn't aware of a portable version. Another piece of information that, once transmitted to her organization, would garner significant attention.

One of the soldiers planted a block-shaped device on the thick steel door, moved to the side, crouched, and covered their ears. A rapid series of explosions and surges of brilliant light emanated from the shape charges. Auralei's augmented senses responded instantly, protecting her hearing and vision. The soldier released the protective covering from their precious eardrums and worked a wedge-shaped device into a small gap, kicking it three times to snug it into place. The device expanded in pulses, sounding like a giant zipper with grooves that didn't quite line up as it opened. When the space was large enough, a soldier threw another device into the room and went in after it along with the rest of the squad.

THE ROOM'S DOOR swung entirely away, and soldiers poured into the room, laying down a hailstorm of metallic particles for cover fire.

"Close," Clarke requested of the suit. No response. Clarke's heart raced, and a tight spasm racked his stomach. He would have been calmer with a rifle in his hands, but only marginally.

A torrent of images and thoughts exploded in Clarke's mind. Some were his own and coherent, and the others held no worldly basis for him to relate them to. He closed his eyes and scanned his thoughts, finding a gritty, uncomfortable, and malleable area. He fixated on it, finding a part of his mind that hadn't been there before. It was frigid, gloomy, and strangely inviting. He held it in his mind's eye, willing it to respond, coaxing it to come forward like an old memory that needed time to reform. Eventually, he resorted to pleading with it for help.

The armor responded, closing silently around him, molding to fit his six-foot frame and forcing his head above the armored vambrace previously protecting his head. Instinctively, Clarke raised an arm to shield himself while snatching the battle helmet from the workstation and putting it on. The helm wobbled loosely on his head until he snagged an alignment groove and snugged it into place. The armor was awkward to maneuver—every step was like the imaginary last step you take at the top of the stairs in the dark.

Stigg bellowed to find cover, but his words were lost to an explosion rocking the room. The force of the blast knocked Clarke to his ass. He tried to stand and pitched forward, crashing onto his belly. With a deep breath, Clarke pushed himself up, faintly registered a metallic and leathery taste, and crawled to Stigg's position. The gases and debris hanging in the air from the spent explosive round provided a temporary screen but not relief from the small arms fire.

Stigg motioned to a nearby doorway, shrugged his shoulders, and ran to the protective cover. He cursed and lunged out of the way as the armor picked up speed, charged through the doorway, banged its head off the top of the doorframe, and slammed into the opposite wall. "Not sure how we're going to explain this one to the boys," he said as Clarke regained his footing. "If we survive, it's one heckuva story. Now grab something and block the door. They'll be here shortly!" He closed the door to the hallway, and Clarke moved a massive stone locker against the door. "That will not buy us much time. These bastards are crafty."

"That was a mortar round, wasn't it?"

Stigg sucked air across his teeth, producing a whistling sound while nodding. "Armors, not such an antique, eh?"

"But there shouldn't be much left of it?"

"Best not to dwell on those things now or ever. What we need is a way out of here."

"Now you see my wisdom."

"What wisdom," Stigg responded with a snort. "Where the hell's your gun?" He shook his head and tutted mockingly. "Have I taught you nothing?"

"Damn, left it on the workstation."

"These chutes could be a way out?" Stigg asked, referring to the tubular shafts cutting vertically through the room.

A wireframe schematic suddenly appeared in Clarke's mind's eye; it was incomprehensible and left him only with a simple sense of where to go as he fell to his knees. The visor of the helmet flipped up so he could violently dry heave and spit what little bile he could generate. It reminded him that his body needed nourishment.

"You have a better plan, then?"

Clarke stiffened, failed to say anything coherent, and ignored Stigg's questioning look of concern. "We need to backtrack," he wheezed.

"What do you have in mind?

"Not sure." Clarke scanned the room for a weapon. "Where did you find that axe?"

Clarke chased the old Vanguard into a back room containing an arsenal of medieval-type weapons. He dug through a nearby pile and rescued a combat knife with a blade as long as his forearm. Upon lifting it from its resting place, he accidentally clipped a nearby wall, sending rock chips and dust flying into the air.

Stigg turned his head, shielding his eyes. "Damn. You found one that works. That was some uncanny luck."

"Still a little awkward here," Clarke replied, fumbling to open the visor, realizing his voice was muffled by the armor. "And seriously, a bloody knife to a gunfight. You know this ends badly."

"Where exactly are you going to carry that knife?" Stigg asked.

Clarke inspected the armor for anything resembling an attachment point. "Damn. Is there anything on the back?"

Stigg shook his head.

Clarke returned to their make-shift barricade. Based on the sound coming from the other side, the intruders were setting explosives to tackle the stone locker that was blocking their path. Clarke glanced at Stigg, who confirmed he was ready with a nod and a shake of his axe. "This is a dumb idea," he whispered. He drew a deep breath as the visor closed and slammed his armored foot into the locker, forcing parts of it through the now fractured doorway. He was first through the opening, landing on the remains of the locker's rear wall, which was pinning a soldier beneath it. It rocked ferociously as the breaching device detonated, sending a gooey mess of blood and body matter spurting out from beneath it. Clarke lashed out manically with his knife, cleaving a surprised soldier from shoulder to hip. As the upper half of the torso fell away, an internal network of augments emitted spurts of body and machine fluid punctuated by electrical arcs.

Stigg was on Clarke's heels through the wreckage and closed on a soldier. He swung his axe in a wide arc, passing without discretion through armor, skin, sinew, and bone. With a slight roll of his wrists when the cheek of the axe's trailing blade passed through the soldier's spinal column, he sent a severed head spiraling through the air. Stigg borrowed the momentum from his spin and lashed out at another soldier, who caught the axe with a sucking crunch. But not before a burst from the soldier's rifle into Stigg's midsection sent him flopping backward to land on his ass.

Unaware of Stigg's plight, Clarke rushed forward and slammed into an attacker with a bone-shattering crunch. The soldier toppled limply backward, their head making a slight popping sound as it bounced off the dampened stone floor. He jerked his arm in a quick downward motion to rid it of the blood smear left by the soldier's face and suspected they lived—foreign thoughts drifted through Clarke's mind, gaining just enough traction to enhance his suspicion. He moved to the head of his victim, where an expanding pool of vermillion-colored blood was forming. His heart raced at the fear and discomfort of what he was about to do. Still, it didn't last long enough to dissuade his survival instinct—with a stomp of his armored boot, Clarke flattened the soldier's head to stem the flow of blood and watched as another head liberated from its body arced through the air past him with a fleeting expression of surprise.

Hot rifle rounds raked Clarke's armor and a nearby workstation. Before the culprit could toss a grenade, Clarke was there and sunk the glistening knife into their chest cavity. The grenade detonated, removing the soldier's throwing arm and sending the body bouncing off Clarke's armored chest.

Clarke smeared the blood on his visor, leaving hazy streaks from the armored fingers, and scanned the room. Finding no other threats, he clambered to where Stigg was sitting, tracking cleaved body matter and debris. He held out an armored hand and hauled the veteran to his feet. "How you holding up, Chief?"

"Living the dream," Stigg said between ragged breaths as he clutched his midsection. "Armor held." Stigg pumped his arm, testing the axe's weight, cringed in pain, and redoubled his grasp of his mid-section. "Don't give me that look... I'll be fine."

Warning, the thought ripped into Clarke's thoughts, pushing any concern for Stigg to the recesses of his mind. He spun, hunting for more soldiers until coming back to Stigg. Clarke had seen the man's forearm tattoos many times, but they were different now: the usual muted browns and greens pulsated and raced a shade of amaranth. "Whoa! What's up with your tats?"

Stigg tugged at his shirt sleeves. "A story for another time, yeah?"

"A Vanguard story."

"Another time," Stigg said sternly. "So. The baby dragoon armor. Is it Astute?"

"Probably."

"Really?" Stigg asked with a grunt. "And pray tell, how did you come by that nugget of information? It could be left over from someone else, like that dead guy?"

"Maybe. I can't really explain it. In all honesty, I don't want to say it."

"Out with it, dammit."

Clarke hesitated and received a playful slap across the top of his helmet. "It's like there's something inside of me... like a dark passenger. And it shows me things."

"Does it hurt?" Stigg asked, tearing a piece of cloth from a nearby soldier's gear to clean Clarke's visor.

"Sometimes."

"Debilitating?"

"More discomforting. Awkward even."

"We'll have to see about it when we get back to the shop. We're copasetic as long as I don't have to sherpa your ass out of here. Speaking of which, this passenger of yours give you a sense of how to get topside?"

Clarke nodded, jury-rigged some scrounged energy cells to the armor, and led the way out of the workshop, hoping his instincts were right.

CHAPTER 06

MAEVE WAS ON schedule. Her mercenaries were currently distributing devices throughout the underground complex that, when triggered, would seal it off from the surface. She would need to be quick, as she didn't relish the idea of being trapped. It was a shame to destroy something so ancient, but it was the Tersinian way. She wondered precisely when her Order decided the Astutes dissatisfied them enough for them to deem the entire Astute civilization structure disruptive, disgraceful, and requiring deletion. At least to the credit of her Order, they were exhaustive in cataloging and characterizing the people and cultures being removed when they set their energies to such a task. The more scholarly monks of the Order devoted a considerable number of lifetimes to studying a culture's multitude of races, forms, and functions—primarily to understand how broadly to cast the civilization-level-annihilation-net.

Of particular interest to her was the process of determining the exact age of an Astute colony or the point in time they inhabited an area. One Tersinian Order monk, Varner Maidai, was accredited for developing the presently accepted Astute timeline deterministic model. Dating was achieved by understanding the layout of known facilities and the aesthetic differences in their architecture and décor—an easy enough task provided one knew what to look for. While the more prominent telltale signs manifested in the polishing techniques applied to the structures carved from the rock, an excellent secondary indicator was the shape of the dwelling's furniture. Employing various lookup tables and matrices and leveraging supplied calculations, one could determine a point value to place a specific colony on the Varner Maidai Scale ranging from Type-1 (*Coarse Primitive Culture*) to Type-18 (*Gleamingly Evolved Culture*).

There was an objector to Varner Maidai's body of works—Tridal Lodestar, a monk of minor renown and self-promotion. He had contested the current method with a theory that the Astute lived through hundreds of discernible fashion prongs based on materialistic trends. Lodestar proposed that technological sophistication didn't align with a timeline that progressed sequentially. Therefore, an Astute civilization existing in the past could have been more technologically advanced than a more recent colony. The core element of Tridal Lodestar's work proposed that it was essential to understand *when* a fashion prong occurred and whether it was the original, a resurgence, or a devolutionary iteration of the fashion prong.

His argument generally agreed with Maidai's theory that Astute colonies were more advanced in their iterative reboot of a past fashion prong. This was because they had taken time to perfect their style and technology. However, there was an apex to the progress, followed by a retraction. He hypothesized that the Astutes had selectively devolved their most advanced colonies—or undid their evolvement. To the Order, this was illogical because no sentient life they had encountered would self-devolve their technological advancements to advance themselves again, or not at all. Unlike Varner Maidai, Tridal Lodestar had not socialized his ideas or himself with the appropriate people on the review board and lacked influential backers. Thus, his research was unanimously rejected.

Undeterred by the Order's rejection, Tridal Lodestar vanished for decades in an endeavor to further his grand study of the Astutes and prove Varner Maidai wrong. One part of Lodestar's renewed effort was on how items joined with various synthetic crystals found in abundance in Astute colonies that Maidai and others considered worthless fashion trinkets. Upon his arrival and presentation of findings, the Order deemed the work derivative of his original studies, scattered, and to have unwanted external influences. Once again, Tridal Lodestar faced rejection by his beloved Order. Eventually, the self-realization that he had devoted the better part of his life to the science of classification, a subject he loathed, caused his fracture with reality. But before he left the Order, he dutifully compiled his works into a forty-nine-volume set titled *What/When the Astute's Thought and Considered Fashionable.*

The senior librarians tasked with classifying Lodestar's near-lifelong work forged their entire lives in the seclusion of monasteries. Because of their sense of security coupled with rumors that Tridal Lodestar was a nut, they cataloged his work under Fashion and Frivolous. Presumably, nobody took the time to read all forty-nine volumes. Maeve couldn't blame anyone, as they were a jumbled collection of field notes and images with a reference system handwritten in the margins that were practically indecipherable. Most of the volumes cataloged items that Tridal Lodestar himself classified as mundane and worthless. In comparison, others documented what food he craved as he held different artifacts. However, Maeve had discovered the importance and relationship between three of the volumes: Volume~17 detailed wearable fashion items, such as necklaces, bracelets, and canteens; Volume~25 provided a decimal-point-lookup-system that could be cross-referenced to identify how the base characteristics of particular objects could change when combined with other objects; and Volume~28 outlined specific crystals that had linkages to other fashionable items.

Maeve's final thesis provided a framework that illustrated how the three volumes worked together. The demonstration she presented at the defense of her work was for a small crystal compartment within a shoulder bag (Volume~17) that, when affixed with an octagonal purple crystal (Volume~28), resulted in the object doubling its physical capacity (Volume~25). And just like Lodestar, someone she had come to admire and understand, her works were filed under fashion and frivolousness. Maeve saw her school's most significant mistake as failing to recognize Tridal Lodestar's brilliance.

One day, while on a *Tersa* training mission, she received notice that someone had checked out the hardcopy version of her thesis. Her curiosity sent her to the Hall of Wisdom on Tresum. The name and signature were illegible, but the number forty-two was added to the end of the scribbles. Maeve promptly checked out the physical copy of Tridal Lodestar's Volume~42 and discovered a handwritten 'second edition' on the cover. In a revised forward, a shaky hand-written message recounted an unknown quality that had inhabited the person and enhanced their inherent sensitivities to the natural energies in the universe. The unknown author referred to it as their denizen and explained the wonders it shared, believing the Astutes traded part of their life force to supplement the denizen for its insights and access to otherworldly powers. Glued into the end of the book was an addendum with an obscure color-weighted navigation system that provided alternatives to the decimal variant in Volume~25. It delved further into items that could have more powerful functions unlocked and provided a revised fashion-prong timeline calculation. This addendum also referred to Volume~6, which contained an account of an exploration mission through an underground bunker that Maeve believed to be of Astute origin and provided hints on where specific 'world-shaping' items were located. The author outlined complex calculations for deciphering schematics to assemble powerful devices spread throughout these bunkers that drew the denizen's attention and desires. The author also provided a series of sketches, locations of keys, and notes on other places like the bunker in Volume~6. Oddly, they claimed never to have visited all the places described but successfully recovered two of these powerful devices, one of which Maeve possessed.

Maeve believed that the mysterious author was none other than Tridal Lodestar. Although Lodestar's whereabouts were unknown, the rumor within the Order was that he explored the cosmos asking anyone who would converse with him about the duration of fashion trends—he was particularly interested in why they came back, especially the better-off forgotten ones. She had tried to present this new information to the senior librarians and the Order's Council, but all denied her an audience.

To Maeve, Tridal Lodestar's limitations were that he constructed his conclusions on the biases of the Monastery that raised and educated him. His sheltered mind couldn't have fathomed that he could touch the same energies that she could. Yet, somehow, he had learned a way too and escaped the *Tersa's* notice over the years. Secretly, Maeve sanctioned a remote convent of monks to further the research and eventually revealed that the Nova Republic classified the bunker detailed in Volume~6 as Complex Two of Seven.

Maeve giggled through closed lips—the insolence of the monks was almost unbearable. Here, she was in a Varner Maidai Type 2-6

(*Gritty Precursor Culture)* colony, which showed an earlier time in
the Astute era and was deemed as having limited value. Yet, using
Tridal Lodestar's revised schema, Maeve was amid the epitome of
Astute culture, a fifth fashion-prong Type 12-4 (*Super Genius-
Trendy-Culture*) colony. It represented the pure perfection of a
fashion trend recreated multiple times through the eras. This
particular colony variant had décor favoring function over form and
minimalism, which was not Varner Maidai's preference and was
subsequently seen as crude and lacking sophistication.

A Type 12-4 colony had a high probability of being a devolved
colony. In Varner Maidai's original works, she described colonies
beyond Type 12 as being reserved for a transcendence beyond
materialism, capitalism, and several other '-isms' and into the
otherworldly ether. She possibly added Types 13 through 18 to
appease the Tersinian Council and, unknowingly, was correct in
identifying these outlier colonies with vastly superior technological
advancements.

*There would be time later to dwell on narcissistic and hermit
monks, fashion, and ways to manage populations,* she told herself.
The device on her wrist was vibrating and showing one of her
mercenary groups assigned to Stigg was deceased. Grief for Captain
Driss, the group leader, tugged at her briefly, practically
immeasurable and with no outward sign, although he was once
good company. She wondered if the specter was the culprit,
knowing they could wreak havoc on her mercenaries if they
encountered them. It was improbable that the mercenaries would
get lucky and kill one of the specters. An event that would
significantly reduce the cost of her mission, and if someone else
committed the deed, Maeve could claim innocence. Either way, she
could distance herself from any fallout. She stroked the crystal
pendant hanging from her neck. It was not unlike the crystals the
specters of this world used to travel unseen and hindered only by a

fleeting fraction of time. Maeve would have been a specter if she had been raised in this part of the universe. It was fascinating to her how life had its own temporal way of classifying the people blessed with the gift and their purpose. Here, a specter was simple—they were hunters. Something she found more relatable than the altruistic, even secular tones of her third upbringing. However, both were more comforting than Tridal Lodestar's reference to people disassociated from the gift—*Reavers*, the righteous devourers. *Religious nut*, she thought. The monks within her Order always needed one side to pit against the other, seeking a balance oddly akin to the Greater Purpose.

Risking detection, Maeve activated Captain Driss' full array of sensors, and a biometric scan of the room confirmed only Stigg survived. She sent a signal across her network of microscopic antennas to activate an optical link, the reporting images encountering some interference. There was something else moving about the room. A jolt racked her slender feminine frame, and she crossed her arms over her chest for comfort. A slight vibration on her wrist turned her attention to another piece of gear announcing a malfunction. She presumed Stigg, or that thing tromping around, had uncovered and destroyed the surveillance equipment.

Stigg was a formidable beast she may have misjudged, which was somewhat perplexing and refreshing. She said a quick prayer for Stigg's safe journey, confident there was more to the man than what the specters and her operatives had exposed. She nudged her mount, and it responded, banking steeply and ascending the voids between the carriageways of the central spire with powerful beats of its leathery wings, retracing a route to the air above the mountains.

AURALEI PRODUCED A brick of a gun from each holster nestled at the small of her back and purposefully walked toward the doorway the hunter droid indicated Clarke had passed through. The scanning device in the hallway barely had time to register her presence before her weapons made small holes in each of the sentry's heads. For detecting the talents of a specter, they hadn't positioned the device properly to alert them in time—the squad leader had likely wanted to protect their hide by placing the device nearer the doorway.

Auralei stopped in the shadows when she heard loud stomps and saw a machine emerge from the doorway; her sensors had not detected mechanized armor or androids. She tensed, ready in case the machine came her way. It seemed to gaze right at her, then turned and stomped down the hallway with Stigg close behind. Auralei's chest muscles tightened as a sickly sensation fluttered through her stomach.

She slipped through the unhinged door into the workshop, evaluated the damage from the recent firefight, and searched dead bodies for signs of Clarke. "Where the hell did you all come from, and why are you here?" she asked the dead, but they refused to answer. She pocketed the interference device from the hallway as it might prove helpful and stalked cautiously after Stigg and the machine.

CLARKE LED STIGG further into the complex until they came to a large room approximately half the size of the one they had descended earlier but lacked an enclosed spire. The central platform was ringed by sixteen columns supporting each spire level and stretching to the ceiling. Clarke walked across one of the many metallic rails, joining the central platform to the walls. At the center was a square stone box, where he knelt and felt its surface, finding a small area that, when pressed, caused an inset panel to retract.

"What the hell are you doing?" Stigg asked in a hushed tone.

"I need both hands," Clarke answered, picking up the knife he had set down and holding it over Stigg's outstretched hand.

"It's all right, you can let go. I'll treat it better than you were about to."

Clarke struggled against the armor to release the knife, and eventually, the suit responded, opening the armored gauntlet. "Little glitchy here. Anyway. These could be a way out of here."

"That so?" Stigg asked.

Clarke shrugged his shoulders within the armor, giving no outward sign of indifference, and stood. He punched in the series of patterns the visor recommended on the control panel. The columns nearest them shook, and a cacophony of screeching and preening grew louder as the exterior liner rolled into the wall, unveiling a hollow tube. "What the hell is making that dreadful noise? Wyverns?"

"That'd be my guess," Stigg said.

Inside the chute was a transparent crystal disk that moved on shiny rails, placed end to end like bricks. He leaned in and peered through the conveyance disk into the void below. "I suppose you want me to stand on this, yeah?" He tested its stability with a push from his axe.

"Woah, no way," Clarke said, watching Stigg ease into the tube and step on the disk suspended over the abyss. "That's totally janky."

Stigg flashed a wry grin. "Nah, it looks fun, and it's where your little buddy wants us to go."

"I never said it was on our side," Clarke replied. He wasn't overly excited about finding himself in a room full of creatures large enough to consider him their next meal. "Up might not be the best idea."

"Stop whining and get in," Stigg said gruffly.

Clarke hesitantly transferred his weight onto the disk in the chute beside Stigg. "Just remember that—" The rest of his words were interrupted by the column's door rotating shut and the disk shooting upward along the rail, forcing his body downward into the armor and his breath from his lungs.

MAEVE'S WYVREN CARRIED her to the top of the western central spire and out a short tunnel leading to the southern aviary, where her trackers alerted her to Stigg's presence. She let her mount carry her above the valley's rim, giving her a view of the icy landscape and the four aviaries, each aligned to a cardinal point and located symmetrically about a central spire. She raced along the canyons and down through a large crevasse, chasing Stigg's signal into a tunnel. The biting chill of the snow-covered landscape became the stale, warm air of the complex and, eventually, the putrid stench of nesting beasts. Maeve guided her mount, perched in the aviary's upper alcoves, and scratched the base of its neck to calm it—her presence and the residue of her talent annoying the unruly natives. Stigg was below, obscured by the mass of wyverns swirling in the darkness. She let the coolness of the spirit guardian's energy flood her limbs and said a small prayer to invoke and channel her talent into her gear. The heightened senses and power it brought were addictive, producing a sense of oneness with her gods—Maeve used her interface with her wyvern to communicate her desire, and the beast leaped from the ledge, arched its wings, and dove swiftly. The rest of Maeve's aerial squad was close behind her.

THE CHUTE'S ASCENT stopped unexpectedly, causing Clarke to get airborne, but it adjusted to catch his weight and came to a gentle stop. Faint scents of cedar, decaying plant material, and excrement wafted into the opening as the chute door retracted, revealing a dome-shaped cavern. Sizable pillars crafted from bricks as long and tall as two people standing arm to arm were erected uniformly throughout the room, supporting long metal planks. This gave the impression that giants came here to worship their gods, sitting on pews that marched neatly into the darkness. Sounds from talons on stone, the sharp cracking of leathery wings, and screeching drifted down from above.

Clark wondered if there were alcoves carved into the rock above, providing perches for the creatures. He moved deliberately out of the chute and hugged the rough rock wall, methodically shuffling to where Stigg was crouched. He gazed into the darkness overhead and wondered what had captured the man's attention.

Stigg raised his hand to shield part of his mouth, directing his voice toward Clarke. "Guivre wyverns?" he asked in a whisper.

His question's efficiency conveyed that he was unsure what manner of wyverns lived in this aviary. There were two general categories of the fabled beasts: the common wyverns, which were domesticable work beasts albeit a bit stubborn and a little dumb; and Guivre wyverns, their belligerent cousins who were extremely aggressive assholes. Attempts to domesticate Guivre wyverns had failed miserably as they tended to habitually remove limbs from those who were foolish enough to get close to them.

"They must leave to hunt," Clarke said, which gave him a glimmer of hope.

Stigg nodded, remaining watchful of the action overhead. "Something's working them up."

Stigg grabbed Clarke's arm and scurried to a nearby wood-planked wall, half dragging the armor. Machine gun fire clawed at the rock behind them and nearby stone support columns. They moved along the wall until stone met their backs, finding a position to shield them from the wyvern and its rider's line of sight for the moment. The protection their position offered would be fleeting once the attacker circled back.

Clarke's attention was redirected by a string of curses from Stigg back to the chutes. A third door slowly opened, and an ethereal figure dragged itself into the room with the hilt of an enormous sword protruding over its left shoulder. "Guess I'll see you on the other side, lad." He heard Stigg call as the man fled into the room's darkness.

"Wait!" Clarke called in a hushed tone. "I need my knife." He saw the glint from the blade arc toward him, and just as he was about to catch the expertly tossed knife, a sharp pain gripped the spot between his eyebrows, and his visor flashed a warning alert and scrambled. The knife thudded against his chest plate, but there was no subsequent clatter of metal on the floor. "Did you just stick me?"

"How in the hell did you miss that?" Stigg asked with a chuckle.

"Visor glitched."

"Sure, it did."

"Seriously. This armor's targeting system is wonky."

"Can you control it?"

"Appears so."

"Good. Get your ass moving and be quiet."

Clarke rubbed his chest plate and was relieved to find the sharp side-down knife attached. He returned his attention to the *Mischi*, who, by now, was out of the chute. Her gaze washed over him and seemed to convey that she would deal with him soon enough, but she had more important things to tend to for now. Her athletic figure was a blur as she crossed the room. He blinked hard, trying to settle the bile threatening to rise from his stomach.

Bullets ripped at the walls and around him, with a few lucky shots ricocheting off his protective leg plating. He checked the leg armor and stuck his fingers into the pockmarks from the slugs, relieved to discover the armor hadn't been penetrated. He scrambled to his feet and raced through the labyrinth of make-shift stables. His visor warned him that the armor's power was low, and multiple threats were swirling amongst the hundreds of potential threats above him—*the alien material sent a shadow of thought into the host's mind, activating the familiar armor's war systems.*

The wall beside Clarke exploded, the blast knocking him to his knees and showering him with rock and burning chunks of woody debris. Molten rock oozed from where the pillar was struck and hissed as it cooled. He wasn't sure what his newfound armor could handle in terms of damage but was intimately familiar with how a few plasma rounds rendered a dragoon pilot and their armor useless. Clarke chased the image from his mind of cauterized wounds holding a pilot's innards in place and the messy pilot ejection process. *Not going to die like that,* he thought and picked up a broken length of metal, figuring he needed something with some length to it. Backtracking through the columns, he cut hard down a passage that seemed to provide shelter from the aerial threats. Peering over the wall, he saw the attacker circle back low, searching for him. Clarke waited until the beast was close and leaped into the air. Instead of the ramping thruster surge typical of the dragoon armor he was accustomed to, his armor emitted two jarring pulses propelling it rapidly upwards. Clarke's haphazard spear impaled the rider's leg deep enough to give him something to hang onto but didn't provide him with the leverage needed to pull himself up. He hacked at the rider's wounded leg with his small knife until the left femur was exposed. This caused them to pitch sideways: they narrowly caught the saddle's horn, saving themselves and Clarke from a fall. However, this sent the beast into an aggressive climb, and their wounded stump of a leg rained blood from a severed femoral artery, dispersing the scent through the room.

A passing wyvern snatched Clarke by the midsection, its talons biting deep into his armor plating, ripping the metal spear from his grasp. The beast carried him upward, struggling to find a clear path through the churning mass of wings.

Clarke swung his knife in a wild and blind arc, regretting it instantly, as the only thing beneath his feet was darkness and more wyverns—the knife cut a deep gash across the beast's chest, its colorful plumage offering little protection. It flared its wings with a sharp crack, stopping its flight, and lost its grip on Clarke. On his turbulent plunge through the darkness, Clarke was traded from one wyvern to the next as they claimed him and then failed to thwart others from stealing him away. Eventually, he met the ground in a vicious mix of tumbling, skidding, and crashing through the wooden walls of the aviary stables, grazing several of the stone support columns, and came to rest against the outer rock wall of the cavern in a jumbled mess.

MAEVE CURSED AT her mercenaries for prematurely wasting the element of surprise, narrowly dodging the talons of a giant wyvern that raked through the air where her head had been a moment ago. The wyverns were turning on one another. She pressed her mount into a sharp turn, transitioning into a steep climb, and blended in with the timid wyverns swirling overhead.

Below her, Stigg rushed to the fallen machine and attempted to stand it up. She wondered why there was a gentleness, even compassion, in how he handled it. Then Maeve sensed someone commune with the flux. It was inviting and familiar, a brief disturbance in the undercurrents of the planet's forces that she was adept at ferreting out—it betrayed the presence of another specter. Yet, Maeve sensed something else playing at the edge of her powers. It was darker, nothing she could put her finger on, but it was undeniably present. The sudden steep bank of her mount sparked her lower back muscles to clench and forced the air from her lungs. The maneuver took her safely out of another Guivre wyvern's talons, and she stopped her instinctive reflex to squeeze the numbness out of the base of her neck. She said a brief prayer for the specter, hoping she would find an opportunity to liberate the binds this part of the galaxy placed on women like her.

CLARKE ROLLED ONTO his stomach and pushed up into a kneeling position. The armor was sluggish in responding, its structural integrity was compromised in a few places, and the suit's energy was significantly depleted. He spotted the black-clad *Mischi* moving toward him, but his vision blurred as he sensed an aerial threat. He inhaled viciously against the pain it caused and gazed upward through the darkness, his vision narrowing in on the approaching beast. Its rider generated an aura of brilliant colors that riled and boiled and emitted static wisps around them. Rage rose from his stomach: their command of the flux was so penetrating that it blazed through Clarke's visor, sending another sharp whip-like pain across the back of his eyes—something else in the recesses of his mind came forward. Too exhausted to resist it from taking over his awareness, Clarke coaxed, then begged the armor for help—it picked up a jagged piece of timber that had journeyed with him and braced it against the wall. If the rider wanted them all to taste death, then so be it. Stigg and the *Mischi* could sort out their fates.

MAEVE REVELED IN the rush that her talent bore, willing the energy into a pattern the crystal socketed in the midpoint on her metallic staff would recognize. She imagined it was the closest she could come to achieving a harmonic union with the divine. Maeve smiled at the regressive nature, or perhaps the lack of creativity, for which her prey approached the fight. *If only Guivre wyverns could spit fire*, she thought and giggled inwardly. She pointed her staff and unleashed a bolt of destruction that attained hypersonic speed immediately before collapsing in front of the machine. The implosion intensified, leveling the decaying cloisters of the aviary and scattering the remaining mercenaries and native wyverns. Maeve threw up a protective ward she practiced regularly and sliced through the brunt of the shockwave. But the severe turbulence and flying debris sent her wyvern reeling and tumbling through the air. Panicked, the beast beat its wings hard to regain steady flight and escape. She scanned the devastation hastily, wanting to check on Stigg, but prudence guided her after her fleeing mercenaries. She wasn't confident they wouldn't decide to do something rash, such as prematurely activating the devices planted throughout the complex.

STIGG SHOOK THE fuzz from his head, wanting his ears to stop ringing. The cerulean streak of light had sheared most of the rock pillars and wooden walls to waist height. He stumbled toward Clarke and dug through the pile of debris. Piece by piece, he uncovered the armor that had seen better days. Exhausted, he slumped to his knees in the eerie silence of the aviary. When he had marshaled enough energy to lift his head and open his eyes again, Clarke was pointing at someone crawling out from beneath the wreckage of a fallen wall.

Stigg sighed lightly, stood sluggishly, and hobbled to the now-prone *Mischi*. He hooked his boot under her midsection and flipped her onto her back without resistance. "Why in the gods' names are you following us?" he asked, mustering what he was sure was confidence in his voice. The woman moaned. "Where the hell is the other one? Are you two in cahoots?"

"Please," she said, clutching her side weakly.

"As you wish," Stigg said, stepping back and hefting his axe. He would gladly oblige her if she wanted out of her misery.

The woman's hand shook as she feebly removed her face shield and muttered a word only Stigg could hear. The weight of which caused the beast of a man to drop to his knees next to the woman. Her arm flopped to her side, and she was still. The stomp of Clarke's armored greaves approaching from behind prompted him to replace the woman's face shield, covering her delicate features.

"What do we do with her?" Clarke asked.

"Not sure," Stigg said, scratching his beard. "I don't think she means to harm us, though."

"What did she say?"

"Didn't quite catch it," Stigg said and flashed Clarke a smirk he knew his young friend would see through and begrudgingly accept the issue as closed.

"Why did you cover her face up? Who is she?"

Stigg dug a couple of well-placed knuckles into his lower back to relieve some of the tension that had burrowed there. "We all have our secrets. One just happened to catch up to me is all. But, hey. At least you're up and about."

"Solid redirect there, old timer."

Stigg laughed loudly. "You really think that heap is going to make it out of here?"

"If we can jerry-rig something, then maybe. I'll need to scavenge for some fuel cells. That might suffice. I'll need a workshop for anything more, though."

"We could really use the power for the rifles."

"Agreed, but…"

"But we can't deny the armor saved your ass," Stigg said, raising his hands to quell further conversation from Clarke, wondering how much of the goodwill built up over the years was burning away—the kid wasn't ready for this adventure, and he wasn't either.

"Sure. Sure. Something like that."

"See what you can find, then let's get outta here."

As Clarke walked away, he caught Stigg stabbing a cartridge from the woman's belt into the exposed part of her neck and depressing the trigger. The woman's eye snapped open, and she inhaled—it was a concoction Clarke suspected was working its techno-magic to fix her.

Stigg cursed, catching Clarke's watchful eye. *This one is trouble,* he mouthed, hoping Clarke would let it be for now.

CHAPTER 07

AFTER HOURS OF carefully picking their way through wyvern-inhabited tunnels and old lava tubes, the trio arrived at an alpine meadow. Large chunks of stone dotted the landscape, causing a memory to form in Clarke's mind—hazy images of giant machines hurling similar rocks across smoking fields. He was unsure if the memory was his or even accurate, another reminder that his long-term memory network was incongruent.

"We've day-lighted somewhere along Hurricane Ridge in the Esconairian Mountains," Stigg called over his shoulder.

With the snow line only a short distance above them and the rain lashing at the valley, a muffling blanket of fog shrouded the area to the south. West toward Skyetook, squadrons of dragoons and other combat vehicles moved silently on the plains, although it was difficult to tell which side held the advantage or even who the invading force was. Wyverns circled above the battle, trying their best to provide tactical information to the troops and find cover within the leading edge of another approaching storm front. The flak punctuating the skyline significantly compromised the aerial advantage they provided. Clarke turned away from the tunnel's entrance and walked back toward Stigg and the woman. They had retreated to the shadows, but snippets of their terse conversation escaped their huddle.

"Sounds like the lads are trying to hold Skyetook's eastern flank," Clarke said.

"Or make their way to Warbler Ridge," Stigg replied, looking up at Clarke and drawing his thumb and pointer finger down the sides of his bent nose.

"Any chance someone has power for this bucket?" Clarke asked, hoisting the helmet. "The fuel cell shattered when I dropped it."

"What size?" Auralei asked.

Clarke laughed nervously. "Wasn't a size I had seen. About the size of a thumbnail."

"Try this," Auralei responded after digging through her satchel and tossing Clarke a translucent crystal. "It should adapt."

Clarke pried open the helmet's temple cap and set the tiny crystal in the cavity. He thought she tricked him, but the crystal morphed, and the helmet vibrated twice. "That's pretty sweet."

"Quite simple, really," Auralei said, keeping her eyes cast downward.

Clarke placed the loose helmet over his head and ratcheted it into place. The battle helmet gave him a distorted view of the cave as foreign symbols flashed before him. "Some sort of initializing sequence is running," Clarke said louder than needed, but for everyone's benefit. "I can barely see or hear y'all."

Stigg smacked Clarke's armored breastplate. "Still can't believe this thing still works. It's been a real—"

Stigg's voice fell away, lost to the ether, as Clarke's view unexpectedly filled with static, then a series of wireframe schematics. Whatever it was, it reported that armories in this complex and others throughout this system were depleted. The display changed chaotically, showing an iconography-laced chart with a multitude of humanoid figures. Clarke's inexperience produced a variety of patterns that swirled incoherently in the visor's display. Disorientated, he closed his eyes to still himself. The faint bursts of light subsided, and he opened his eyes bit by bit. A jagged edge structure resembling a pyramid appeared briefly before the onslaught of data resumed. He concentrated on his breathing—slow, deep belly breaths expanding into the solid structure of the armor. Eventually, the display was reconstituted, providing a bird's eye perspective of the windward side of a mountain range with a name lost to the current world. A weathered tower flanked by two smaller stone structures stood on one of the finger ranges. A thick planked door surrounded by runic carvings barred the way. The image floated away, revealing an unfamiliar planet and then a world system, and in the darkness, there were traces of someone, or something, beckoning. The view of the tunnel rushed back to fill Clarke's display as he pitched to his knees. "This is not my favorite day," he told the rock that provided him the leverage to stand. "Sorry about that, Chief. What were you saying? I lost you there for a minute."

Stigg flashed a concerned look as he helped haul Clarke to his feet. "Was just saying this has been a real shit show, and that was about it, son. What do you mean... *lost?*"

Clarke wrung his hands together. "I seemed to have initiated some kind of data system within this helmet. Unless that wasn't a power cell that the girl gave me."

"The woman's fine," Stigg said quickly, brushing away any further broaching of her motives. "Learn anything worthwhile?"

Clarke rubbed the side of his helmet with a gauntleted hand. "Maybe. Nothing I could decipher yet. But that *Dreader* is still here, right?"

Stigg nodded his head in agreement. "But not close." That *Dreader* was one of the strongest he had felt in his lifetime. "You should rest for a bit. I'm going to chat with our new lady friend and see about a plan for staying alive. Now, eat some food."

As instructed, Clarke ate some food the *Mischi* had offered: the bar was tough and sticky but had a sweet fruit flavor that was filling. Once finished, he quietly squared away his gear and made his way over to where Stigg and the *Mischi* were discussing options. "Got it figured out?" he asked from a distance that wouldn't appear like he was eavesdropping.

Stigg kept his eyes on the woman. "Not even a little. For now, get comfortable. We're going to be here for a bit."

"The sketch plan, then?" Clarke asked.

The woman matched Stigg's gaze and tilted her head carefully to the side. Without the armor's advanced optics, Clarke would have missed the slight inclination of her head and the twitch of Stigg's eyebrow. Clarke wondered if Stigg had just sought the *Mischi's* approval.

"It's mostly bad news," Stigg said, squeezing his fists until his knuckles released pressure with a series of pops. "This here lady tells me you were part of someone's plan to overthrow House Khilsyth."

"That so?" Clarke asked, laughing weakly and stopping his hand before it touched the back of his neck.

"Turns out someone, likely a specter disguised as you, was gunning for Trake Khilsyth. Also, the *Mischi* that took us. Her story about a host of folks infiltrating key positions within the House— surprise, it's true."

"The probability they succeeded in their mission is quite high," Auralei added with a measured pace. "Also, some of the Khilsyth's political and military leaders are compromised."

Clarke thought the woman's voice was pleasant, melodic, and disguised. "How so?"

The woman shook her head back and forth. "The plan was to infiltrate key positions within House Khilsyth and overthrow the current leaders in a manner resulting in the lowest number of casualties. It's feasible that some of the heads of state and militia are converted, potentially neutralized, and those entities are now being controlled by—"

Stigg cursed.

"—the invading forces," Auralei continued. "Recently, undisclosed parties became interested in the findings of the archeological probes here on Lindaulx. I believe the Nova Republic issued the woman who bested you both—"

"A directive," Stigg interjected, "bloody hell."

"Thank you," Auralei said politely. "Yes. I believe her mission was to secure the underground survey data and possibly determine the source of communication originating from within the facility—"

"Wait!" Clarke interrupted and regretted it. Her voice had seemed to ease through his muscles and bones, temporarily relieving their ache. "What source of communication?"

Auralei's eyes narrowed over her mask, making Clarke acutely aware she did not appreciate the constant interruptions. "An orbital mass sensor array picked up an unclassifiable transmission from what we now understand to be an Astute facility. The task was to plant sensors in the facility to isolate the transmission source, even track it."

"Something woke up," Stigg said with a wink and a grin. "Now, we are trying to figure out what to do next. So far, our only plan involves not going directly back to town."

"Makes sense," Clarke said. "Except, who would have that type of sensor here? And can we trust it?"

"It's reliable," Auralei said.

"The Republic is always watching," Clarke pressed.

Auralei laughed sweetly. "In this case, sure."

Clarke sat, wondering why the woman kept her scarf over her face. Her mannerisms were familiar, but he cautioned himself as his mind could form unwarranted associations, and the familiarity could be limited to the present. "There's some old comms posts around here. I might be able to use them to isolate…" Clarke stopped with a shake of Stigg's head. "Fine. She sure seems to have a decent view of what's happening out there. What's your end game here, miss?"

Stigg summoned his most reassuring tone. "She's a friend. You must trust me on this one. Have I ever led—"

Clarke raised his hand abruptly. "Led me astray. No. And I do trust you. But you seem awfully comfortable around her."

"I'm afraid it comes with the territory," Stigg replied with a wink.

"Any theories on why the other *Mischi* let us go so easily after all that talk about needing to see me safely off Lindaulx?" Clarke asked.

"They're working together," Stigg said dismissively.

"What about Anzil?" Clarke asked. "We could call him for help."

Stigg snorted. "Your bloody babysitter? At a time like this. He's just a grunt. My guess. He's been converted, or in all likelihood, he's dead."

"Stigg's right," Auralei added. "Anzil was close to you. He was an obvious mark for the invasion facilitators."

"It's true. That other *Mischi* was getting all cozy and cuddly with Anzil at the pub. You saw it, yeah?"

There was a familiarity in the way the woman addressed Stigg that set Clarke to wonder if they damn well knew each other. "You two finished?" Clarke asked, a little sterner than he would have liked. "I'm not saying it's impossible to get close to Anzil, but it wouldn't make sense for him to turn."

"Why not?" Stigg asked. "It makes perfect sense. They could have taken a little spin, and he could have told her all his dirty little secrets."

"Simmer down," Clarke said defensively. Stigg's lack of love for the dragoons was no secret. "He's a Khilsyth, not a traitor."

"What?" Stigg blurted, choking on his drink. A string of curses ensued.

"He's Trake's eldest son," Clarke said.

"How in the hell have you come by that nugget?" Stigg asked.

"I have my wily ways," Clarke said, winking playfully at Stigg. This solicited another fit of curses and a warning that Clarke would be the death of him. He cast a wary sideward glance at the *Mischi*. "The resemblance was there, the *fiery* locks, those creepy azure eyes. Had to be Khilsyth."

"Are you certain?" Auralei probed.

Clarke laughed. "Over time, he spilled enough about his childhood and his parents. It was easy to piece together. Surprised you didn't, Stigg." He had seen that expression of Stigg's before— his furrowed brows and pursed lips meant he was on the verge of a great epiphany or moments away from destroying something.

"I guess I just didn't find him as cute as you did," Stigg replied. "Then let's contact Captain *douche rocket* and hear him out. Ma'am, you agree?"

Auralei nodded and retrieved a small device from her satchel, which she opened and started tapping and sliding her thumbs across its glowing surface. "Interesting," she said after a brief pause. "He's close and heading in our general direction. Provided he's piloting his machine." Stigg's questioning look prompted her to continue. "Because he escorted Clarke, I planted a small tracking program that uses his uplink to report his location."

Clarke coughed. "Wait. What? Why? Because he escorted me? How? That would have taken some serious hacking skills to override the security profiles in those machines."

"Nice," Auralei said victoriously, ignoring Clark, "I've established comms with Anzil."

"We need to confirm it's him, though," Stigg cautioned. "Tell him it's Clarke and to prove who he is—he'd believe Clarke could hack into his armor."

Auralei watched the device intently after keying in Stigg's request. The secure frequency between her device and Anzil's dragoon armor used a back-channel comms net Shifty had discovered. The additional data she transmitted was minuscule and practically undetectable. Even if someone intercepted her comms, finding the encrypted data and deciphering it would take longer than she planned to remain on this planet. "Anzil says: Prove you're really Clarke," she said, looking up at the reflective face plate of the armor.

"Makes sense," Stigg said. "We hacked into his system, after all."

"How?" Clarke asked.

Auralei replied, "he says: what's my middle name?"

"Ah... I don't remember. Pass?"

More typing. "What's his pet's name?"

Clarke shook his head back and forth. "I didn't even know he had a pet?"

Auralei tutted. "Anzil says, losing faith here. What's your plan when you leave this rock?"

Clarke paused. "Which one to choose from? There are so many." He did not intend for his last statement to be transmitted.

"Don't be a sissy," Auralei relayed.

"Find the girl," Clarke relented.

Auralei raised her head from the device and met Clarke's gaze. "What, girl?"

Her eyes were stunningly lit spheres in the darkness, and Clarke missed the slight edge to her voice. His armored head sagged. "*The girl,*" Clarke whispered, "Ellane." The ache of his loss had dulled over time, but he was confident the girl from his past was important based on his disjointed memories. He'd refused to quit searching for her, working within available traditional and somewhat experimental means of repairing memory threads—the mind and its filing system were fickle things. Clarke steadied himself against the damp cave wall—something else was in his head, clawing along memory threads and wandering the recesses of his mind. It was the dark passenger.

"Send it now, lass," Stigg said, stepping between Auralei and Clarke. He hadn't missed the bitterness or perhaps jealousy in the woman's voice and knew that if the often-stoic *Mischi* showed even the slightest sign of emotion, they were pretty riled up. The last time he witnessed a *Mischi* have a similar emotional response, many people met their makers in that watering hole.

After a moment of silence, Auralei responded, "Anzil apparently wanted to make Clarke sweat a bit." She input their coordinates, received confirmation, and tucked the device into her satchel. "Now we wait for the cavalry," she whispered as she stood and walked to the tunnel's threshold, shaking off a calming hand from Stigg.

"Clarke, get your ass out of that contraption and get some more food, understood?" Stigg commanded, his frustration strengthening his words more than he intended.

CHAPTER 08

MAEVE ENTERED THE lavishly adorned main hall of Skyetook's Council Chambers, securely inside the fort's central curtain wall. She could sense, almost smell, the fear and apprehension of the nobles, dignitaries, and remaining military liaisons who milled about in small groups. They collected around the grand hall's fireplaces, fidgeting and talking in hushed tones, while the house staff, with forced smiles, served hors d'oeuvres and libations to the willing. She preferred an inviting atmosphere over the prominence of armed security, appearing confident and stern, and had encouraged the House Guard to blend into the crowd. Perhaps these people felt less secure without the flashy-uniformed gun-toting, ever-present display of force the previous Khilsyth Chief preferred. Maeve struggled to name the primary emotion she was experiencing. Perhaps it was pity for how the fierce and fabled warriors of Lindaulx had become soft, even entitled, but there was no movement in her stomach or chest, just an itch under her left eye she associated with apathy. In a few meager generations, without the toll of strife and conflict, this rabble seemed frightened by an invading force outside their fortress walls and unable to decide which base reaction to choose, fight or flight—the warriors of ole would have already ridden to meet the challengers.

As Maeve strode toward the chamber's center, she noted which leaders were present. Many of the people she made eye contact with swiftly averted their gaze, but she knew their eyes would promptly revert as she passed. *Let them*, she thought, comfortable in her skin and secure in her tactics. The treacherous and deceitful politicking employed by some of these people repulsed her; however, it provided many possibilities for her agents to capitalize on. Some of the House leaders, who in their hearts believed they were committed and loyal, had turned in an instant given the opportunity for self-preservation or an inkling of advancement. She suppressed the urge to bite her lip and shake her head in disgust. And now, an unforeseen complication met her gaze and held it. Base Flintlock, leader of a Rift Faction armada, stood confident and proud on the central platform. She was certain those gathered had heard stories of the Rift Faction Admiral and her fabled 'boat,' *The Blackhole Diver.* The impressive interstellar warship mingled nearby with a handful of other equally accomplished vessels.

"Y'all were lucky we parked a quick hop away," Base Flintlock said, letting her eyes wash over those assembled around her.

Base was a strikingly charismatic person with flowing white hair and intelligent pale turquoise eyes. She explained that they were passing through this area of the universe on their way to the Vondal Sector and stopped for a resupply and to perform repairs in an area where the Nova Republic wouldn't find them. Lucky for the Khilsyths, this conveniently put their armada close to Lindaulx when the request for aid was broadcast.

Maeve was naturally suspicious of anyone outside her Order, assuming people spoke half-truths and omitted inconvenient but essential details. She gleaned from the hushed conversations that Base Flintlock claimed the Nova Republic orchestrated the current invasion. This wasn't too far from the truth and probably a lucky rather than an educated guess. The Rift Faction comprised a medley of people from shattered clans, planets without a destiny, and those yearning for adventure. They were united in the belief that everyone should be permitted to flourish without fear of organizations, companies, republics, or whatever dominant governance structure existed that didn't benefit the greater good of the people. They also happened to be damn good at providing violent options when leverage needed to be applied.

Over the years, the Rift Faction caused a great deal of interference and derailment to Nova Republic missions and their profits. Because the Nova Republic did not appreciate the Rift Faction's meddling, they maintained a significant smear and ill-repute campaign against the Rift Faction—punctuated by the occasional scuffle for good measure. Maeve supposed that Lindaulx's current state of affairs was a prime candidate for Rift Faction interference.

Presently, the bulk of Maeve's forces on Lindaulx were interspersed with the Khilsyths and wouldn't be totally sacrificed to maintain her ruse if the Rift Faction attacked. Her plan had been simple in theory: get one group to lop the head off the other— regicide in this case—and pit the would-be replacements against one another. Then, the tricky part, and where her success had lain in the chaos of war, was to be an invaluable resource to the victor during the rebuilding phase. This approach provided her and those loyal to her the ability to come and go as they pleased from planets with Astute facilities.

Maeve checked the device on her wrist, her brow furrowing. The Rift Faction was complicating her timeline. A small pit formed in her stomach; was someone in her Tersinian Order aware of her willingness to engage the Nova Republic? Were they emboldened enough to circumvent her plans by sending Base Flintlock and the preposterous story of coincidental locales? *That was a bit of a jump,* she thought and warned herself to put her paranoia in check. It would have required a deeper infiltration into the Nova Republic than her own to discover her plans. However, if her Order had uncovered what she was up to, she wondered if they would deem her actions blessed based on her headway thus far. Her Order's Code was vague on when one would receive the holy word or obliteration for actions running against the grain of dispersed wisdom. Maeve exploited this gap as one of the blessed seekers with an increasingly lackadaisical approach over the years. She preferred to adhere strictly to the Tersinian Codes once folks, like specters, had played their role in the adventures she crafted, and the outcomes of her objectives were certain. Of all the places, no one within the Order should have known she was operating far astray on Lindaulx, which comforted her that she could eliminate that avenue of potential threat.

Base Flintlock regained the attention of the room and proposed that the Rift Faction would protect the new chief, Valan Khilsyth, and his lot as a starting point for negotiations. The room cheered and was abruptly quieted by Base Flintlock, who promised to come to terms that were more than fair. The Rift Faction would receive supplies and compensation for equipment destroyed while protecting Lindaulx, plus a moderate percentage for their services.

Maeve continued to move through the crowd, circling the central platform as the debate about the exact rate of reimbursement picked up. It would be impossible to verify the current state of repair of what the Rift Faction brought to battle, and its depreciated value, one of the Khilsyth Generals claimed. She needed to find a moment alone with this Base Flintlock character to press her for more details on the motivation behind being in this sector and the distress signal—she was annoyed as she now needed more information to modify her already orchestrated plan.

Valan Khilsyth, the newly appointed head of House Khilsyth, pounded his fists on the central platform's dais. He stood, directing everyone to be silent, and the hushed conversations ceased. "The threat of an attack from the rebels and scourge trying to invade our lands is eminent. They are amassing forces as you all squander precious time." He paused, listening to the rustling of clothing as those assembled around him fidgeted. "We need to coordinate with our new friends of the Rift Faction. Together, we will strike. And we will bring the soldiers who fled to justice."

Maeve's puppets sent a chorus of praise skywards, obeying their instructions to incite chaos perfectly. Some of the more outspoken Khilsyth leaders spoke of invoking age-old alliances with other Houses on Lindaulx to reignite a great battle that would harken back to the days when the Mercury moon rose. But her agents had designed responses to counter such courses of House-unity. Two in particular gained traction: Captain Anzil Stone, the military leader of the coup, had already called upon the alliances and the other Houses answered; and the other Houses were already allied with the Nova Republic because they approved the invasion.

Maeve stifled a smile as she made her way across the marbled walkway toward the back of the chamber: she had overheard a minor house dignitary providing intelligence that House Lanal survivors were mobilizing and moving forces through the canyon lands to hook up with Anzil's aerial fleet. Someone not associated with her added credibility to the story, noting the sudden disappearance of the House Lanal entourage from Fort Skyetook.

It wasn't the first time Maeve had employed such a tactic, but at its core, the conversations that bubbled to the surface always seemed to underscore prevalent opinions held by the group. She wondered whether people were afraid to voice their genuine opinions or wanted to be part of a clique. Or perhaps people became emboldened when others spoke, thereby feeding each other's courage. It didn't matter to her now because the sheer volume of misinformation bogged down the conversation and made the truth unrecognizable.

The bellowing of her name across the crowd brought her up short. She disliked the pretense of taking orders from a commander she placed in charge. Especially one she considered a fraction of the man his father had been. She had liked Trake Khilsyth. He had been an unwavering and all-around tough guy for a leader; it had been a shame to cause the man to lose his grasp on reality at the sunset of his life. *If only he had cooperated,* she thought.

"Maeve, where have you been?" Valan demanded, his frayed nerves getting the better of him.

"Forgive me, my Lord," Maeve said with a show of respect. The crowd shuffled out of the way, giving her a clear view of the gathered leaders. "I was outside the city visiting some estates rumored to have supported Anzil Stone and the rebels." Maeve lied easily but sensed the man suspected she omitted parts of the story.

"Come closer. I wish to hear more. Did you learn anything of the traitorous cowards who fled?"

Even now, Maeve suspected Valan's mind struggled with the notion of Anzil being a traitor, but the evidence tying Anzil to the traitorous assassin Clark was convincing. "Very learned little, my Lord." She strode toward the man as those gathered deftly moved away from her, likely fearing they would be called upon for proximity. Perhaps there was a piece of Trake within his son after all. "We did, however, confirm the traitors are trying to form a foothold at Willow's Ridge."

"Captain Nuda," Valan said with a sharp cough. "It was not what you suspected. So now, your forces will seal off any approach to Willow's Ridge and then root out those bastards!"

"Sir," Nuda responded as he stepped out of a group of highly decorated soldiers. "I believe we should discuss our strategies in more detail and privately."

"Nonsense," Valan said, watching as the woman walked toward him—she was breathtaking and moved with a calculated grace. "The rebel forces cannot be permitted time to regroup or fortify. And Rear Admiral Flintlock of the Rift Faction is here to help."

"Sir, with all due respect," Captain Nuda pleaded. "An assault on Willow's Ridge is a course of action we need to discuss. It could be a trap that results in many casualties and impacts our defense of Skyetook. Also, with all due respect, our intelligence on the Nova Republic and their grander intentions are limited."

"Absent even," Base Flintlock interjected, exhaling a pungent cloud of smoke between full lips and retrieving a concoction of encased herbs from her breast pocket.

Captain Nuda cleared his throat. "The Nova Republic has been silent, true. But their reputation is known… it precedes them."

"It appears those Republic bastards are marshaling forces within strike proximity to the Fort and at Hindish Pass," Xon Titus said. "I believe some have even infiltrated our ranks. That should be our priority."

"Agreed," Mysis Rend said, crowding Captain Nuda and his entourage. "For all we know, it's a sham, and Anzil turned and burned to establish a loyalist resistance base."

"Mysis and Xon," Trunasder said. "We have no need for Trake's *chums* interfering at a time like this."

"That's the dumbest thing I've heard today," Lieutenant Harp added incredulously, "Mysis, you've got your head so far up Anzil's ass it isn't funny."

To Maeve, a person's mind was like different layers of dirt beneath her feet—a person's skills, memories, and thoughts formed distinct layers over a lifetime of evolution. Memories from the past were deeper and more challenging to touch, depending on an individual's willpower. Xon Titus was different. His mind was like loam—easily penetrated—as it revealed the moment's thought. Still, it lacked proper pathways for probing deeper into the less accessible regions of a mind where she could apply leverage to manipulate his actions. Thankfully, Valan had been more susceptible to her suggestions. Somewhere within the newly minted leader's skull, the thought of *killing the traitors* was floating around; she just needed to provide it some flotation and allow it to find its way to the surface.

"Listen," Valan said, knocking the ring around his baby finger on his chair twice, "we are fortunate the Rift Faction was nearby and willing to assist."

"For a yet-to-be-determined fee," Base Flintlock said, exhaling a plume of delicious smoke.

Valan continued. "We are not without hope. We are working to determine who might be a Nova Republic infiltrator."

"And those Republic forces outside are growing as we chit-chit-chitty-chat-chat," Base Flintlock interjected, flapping her fingers together with her thumbs.

Valan took a loud, deep breath. "Our military is still strong, and those assembled here will lend their support by adding their protection details to protect Fort Skyetook." Valan raised both of his hands to quell any potential objections. "Rend and Titus will see to our House guards. Captain Nuda, I want you to get those damn traitors out of Willow's Ridge."

"Agreed!" Lieutenant Harp exclaimed. "We can't allow the invaders to rip those bastards out of Willow's Ridge and then set up camp there."

"And when the Republic decides it's time to turn their sights on us, what then?" Mysis Rend inquired. "After we've separated our forces, no less."

"Then they will break upon our walls," Harp answered.

"They ain't stupid," Base Flintlock responded with a quick and sweet laugh. "Listen. If we're going to help y'all, we need to get on with it."

"Captain Nuda, are you up for the task or not?" Valan asked.

Nuda nodded, looking down at the polished marble floor, straining not to tug at his jacket in protest. "Sir," Nuda said, his voice gaining conviction as he spoke. "Willow's Ridge is a bunker. We've developed a strategy that I recommend we discuss securely."

"I agree," Xon Titus added, "regardless of our opinions, this is not the place to discuss tactics. Let's move this to Command."

Maeve considered many of the Khilsyth leaders an annoyance, but Xon Titus competed for the title of the most enormous pain in her ass. There was a primitive fierceness to the man, making him unpredictable and resistant to her tricks. Mysis Rend was no different. She was growing impatient. She checked the device on her wrist and found no communication from her Nova Republic liaisons.

Valan stood, bringing the assemblage to attention. "The Rift Faction will secure Hindish Pass and Skyetook. The House Guard will secure the wall and see to the forces outside the Fort." Valan gripped the central dais tightly and, through clenched teeth, spurted, "our other forces, led by Nuda, will head to Willow's Ridge. They are our traitors to deal with." His words were slow and poorly formed. Valan stepped from the dais. "Nuda, you have your orders and are dismissed. Now, let's continue the rest of this conversation in the Command Center."

Maeve trailed the collective group of leaders and their entourages to a nearby transport hub. In the shuffle to climb into the pod that would hurl them beneath Fort Khilsyth, the attendants guided her to a seat beside Valan. Entering the pod, she brushed against Base Flintlock and caught the woody notes of cedar and sage smoke mixing with a hint of lilac. As she took her seat beside Valan and secured her harness, she wondered how Rear Admiral Flintlock would factor into her gambit.

CHAPTER 09

CLARKE CHECKED THE readiness of the scavenged rifle again, trying to convince himself it was his training and not the dark cloud in his mind, keeping the weapon finely tuned. But after opening the breach for the fifth or ninth time and finding it occupied, he blamed it on his frayed nerves, which were due to people who had recently taken to shooting at him. A hand on his pauldron startled him.

"It's been a rough day so far, eh?" Stigg asked. "Need anything right now?"

Clarke figured Stigg had mustered the most reassuring voice he could. "No thanks, I'm fine," he lied, looking out over the dense forest. This place appeared familiar, almost like the remote ranges of the southern forest on Nanser-Nine. "I just—." The jumbling of his memories interrupted his train of thought, and an image forced its way to the forefront of his mind. It was a flash of a barren mountainside, and a sky washed in divergent colors. Ellane was in the turbid swirl of his images with her four older siblings: correction, seven, with the addition of her stepmother Daphne's hellions. But the place and memory didn't align—it was as if something was dredging up images from the murky depths of his mind and arbitrarily matching puzzle pieces. The memory produced a blinding longing for Ellane as his emotions tried to unleash their sick tragedy on him, competing to influence his foremost responses. He reminded himself that it was just the raw and inexperienced romanticism of adolescent love, and it had a way of changing how events actually transpired. Then Anzil was in the haze of the daydream, relating a story about his life. It had been an attempt to bolster Clarke's spirits at the time. The story was about a girl named Deek, whom Anzil met one night during an excursion on Lindaulx. Anzil had courted her secretly because he believed his father, Trake Khilsyth, would whip him, figuratively speaking, if he discovered he was harboring love for another household's daughter. It had not been a peaceful time. There were factions of House Khilsyth breaking away, and they needed strategies for unity. At the request of the House nobles, Trake's eldest would marry from an opposing family to secure stronger alliances—Trake was resistant as it was too cliché for his comfort. Word made its way to Anzil that he was to marry a Noble family's daughter. He and Deek secretly wed with a quiet ceremony amongst close friends. When Anzil confronted Trake and told him what he had done, his father was only displeased that he hadn't thought to trust him. However, it was not without consequences. Trake had been honor-bound to the arranged marriage contract and forced to proclaim his younger son, Valan, the rightful heir. Clarke wasn't sure why that memory had percolated to the surface, but perhaps every choice had its sacrifice, or maybe everyone had their own adventure to wade through. The memory faded, and Ellane's silhouette was present in the silence, a shadowy thread within the memory.

"Just what?" Stigg inquired.

Clarke managed a weak smile. "Just reminiscing, that's all."

"I can't tell a damn thing about what you're thinking in that armor. I just see my mug reflected in that visor. It's damn discomforting…" Stigg bit off a nasty curse. "I'm just worried about you, lad. So, come now, out with it. What were your musings?"

"Indirectly. Ellane."

"And directly?"

"Not really sure. It was a little scattered, to be honest."

"And what about her this time? Now, out of that armor."

The man's stern look told Clarke he wouldn't get off easily. "Did I ever tell you about the time Ellane and I *borrowed* a flyer?"

Stigg motioned with his massive arms for Clarke to sit beside him. "We've got time. Those dragoons will have a helluva time slogging through those trees to get here. And I don't think I've heard this one."

Clarke removed his helmet and stepped out of the armor. His legs were stiff as he hobbled over to sit on a boulder next to Stigg, careful not to brush against the axe resting across the man's knees. Clarke placed the helmet on a low, flat rock that, despite being damp, looked clear of wyvern dung. "We took an assault flyer from the shop out for a test run after the crew replaced the turbofan's low-pressure compressor and the primary fan. We weren't aware that the underside cannons were loaded or that pirates would attack. We had to fight our way out and took refuge with a nearby nomad fleet."

Stigg grunted. "Sounds like a fun girl."

"Ellane took all the blame and said I lied to protect her. Her father sent her back to the Academy as soon as he could."

The corners of Stigg's lips turned down, and he stroked his mustache forcefully. "Damn. The Nova Republic."

"What about it?" Clarke asked.

"The Academy," Stigg grunted, "that's a Republic thing. A feeder school to the Resource Operations Group. That's something you haven't mentioned before." He shook his head disapprovingly. "The infernal Republic has a tendency to change people." He knew Clarke had been through enough stress today and was wading into dangerous territory. He stood and dug his fingers into his mustache and muttered, "damn the Republic."

"Why are we damning the Republic?" Auralei asked, startling them.

"Nothing," Stigg said wide-eyed, cautioning Auralei not to press the issue.

"The calvary is approaching," Auralei said, patting Clarke's shoulder and laughing sweetly as she walked to the tunnel entrance.

"She just might have a thing for a lad with armor," Stigg replied.

A tremble passed faintly through Clarke's body. "She's also a prime example of why you don't tangle with the Republic like our dumbasses are doing," he whispered.

"It's fine as long as you're on our good side," Auralei called over her shoulder. "The other side, not so great. I mean, we're all friends with the bogeyman, after all."

THE HEATED DUST kicked up by the dragoon's thrusters appeared in Auralei's goggles as dull orange and yellow snakes that disappeared into the dense fog shrouding the valley. She consulted a device strapped to her wrist and pointed easterly down the ridgeline to another ridge, flanking the southern bowl as Stigg and Clarke joined her. "My ship is that way." Her hand arced gracefully to point west at a vertical cliff that, although hidden by clouds, stabbed high into the sky above their position and was topped by a snow-covered crest year-round. "And my nearest mantis is that way." After a moment, she mumbled and looked up from her device. "Time to play... the knights in shining armor are here."

The lead armored unit stopped and held up its arm, causing its entourage to halt far enough from the cave entrance that the fog swirled between them. "You in there, Chief?"

"Yeah, it's me," Stigg said, crossing his arms before his chest. Few had the nerve to call him *chief,* a reference he typically shut down immediately. But Anzil proved resourceful and had learned of his past. A common misconception was that the title stemmed from Stigg's role as Chief Mechanic—only Anzil was paying homage to his previous employment as Chief Warrant Officer for the Nova Republic.

"How are you holding up?"

"Fine."

"Really, just fine? You mind pointing that rifle somewhere else? Maybe then I'll start to believe you're just fine."

"Are you really you?" Stigg asked. His rifle didn't waver.

"Yeah, but who's that beside you? Is that who hacked my system?"

"Something like that," Stigg replied.

"Where's your little buddy?"

"Hiding in the cave."

"Why? The way this fog is rolling in, there won't be any need to hide."

"He doesn't want to get too far from his new toy."

"That's awfully cryptic, Chief."

Clarke stepped into the dim light of the tunnel threshold. "I'm here. That really you, Anzil?"

The dragoons raised their rifles and widened their stances.

"Dammit!" Clarke said, lifting his arms above his head to show he was unarmed. "It's me. It's me, Clarke."

The protective plating of the front of the dragoon suit opened and out slipped Anzil with a smirk on his face. "You just sort of snuck up on us, that's all. Am I glad to see you alive. You too, old man."

The dark shadows under his eyes and etched creases on his forehead betrayed the strain the invasion was having on him. He moved briskly for a larger man and embraced Clarke.

"I'm touched, really," Stigg said, massaging the back of his neck. "Do you have any details on what's happening? We've been out of the loop for a while."

Anzil shook Clarke lightly. "Allegedly. This bastard murdered Trake." Anger had crept into his words.

"We…" Clarke said, his voice failing as he tugged on his shirt's collar, "we were kidnapped by a—"

Stigg cleared his throat loudly. "We weren't kidnapped. We were just temporarily inconvenienced."

Catching Stigg tilt his head in warning, Clarke tightened his embrace on his friend's arms. "Anzil, I'm really sorry."

Anzil's arms fell away from Clarke, and he slumped onto a nearby rock. "Of course, it wasn't you. After you were a no-show for pints, I checked the workshop and saw the mess. The Chief would never allow such an atrocity. I tried to reach y'all but couldn't. Some of the House Guards raided the Dodgy Digger and other establishments along the strip and started rounding up soldiers. They were efficient and professionally trained buggers. Given some recent house commissions being handed out, I assumed it was a coup. And there's the invasion happening and all. I circled back to Block Three and sent word for my troop to mobilize."

"What's your status?" Stigg pressed.

"A few of us held the barracks long enough to get some others suited up. It was a pretty nasty ordeal. Had to kill a few people we knew as comrades. Less than a hundred of us formed up. A little more than half with armor, and the rest are in a mix of supply, maintenance, and assault vehicles."

The hopelessness of the situation was absolute to Clarke. "That's about a quarter of the armored pilots. We're in a heap of…."

"Yeah," Anzil confirmed. "From what intel we've gathered, these invaders were more interested in the complete overthrow of House Khilsyth. My guess is they believed the coup would act as a diversion so they could lay waste to any forces with little resistance. At least, that's my theory. Not like there's a lot of armor falling from the heavens with the soldiers."

"At least not yet," Stigg said. "You really think Valan is capable of all of this? I wouldn't have thought your brother the type?" He struggled to match the military strategy behind the invasion and the scale of betrayal to the man he knew.

Anzil glanced at Clarke, who pursed his lips and smiled. "So, this one told you about my family, eh?"

"Just recently, he did. Wasn't sure about your loyalties. No offense."

"None taken, really," Anzil replied honestly to Stigg. "What's confusing is that it appears Valan rallied a defensive force and repelled the initial attack on the inner fortress. It's locked down right now, and most of the defensive batteries and shields are back online. That's strange intel to wrap one's head around."

Stigg scratched the back of his neck the way he did when a complex repair problem presented itself. "Unless the invaders double-crossed him. Could be misinformation. Anything else?"

"Valan apparently made the distress call," Anzil said. "We haven't intercepted any response from the other Houses, though. Best guess is about four to five days before there's any help." Anzil squatted, picked up a small rock, and rolled it around between his fingertips, transferring some of its blood-red pigment to his hands. "We've been doing what we can by raiding some of the invader squads scattered outside the city before they can hook up with the primary force. Even managing to shoot some of those damn javelins out of the sky. There are confirmed reports that the invaders have split their army into three forces; two have taken up defensive positions around Skyetook, and the other is blocking the pass to the wastelands."

"Sound strategy," Stigg said, "and the Ridge?"

"We took it; needed a bunker. Any help from the other houses would likely come across the wasteland. Affords us a base of operations, albeit antiquated."

"And the other colonies?" Stigg asked.

"Not much news other than some help heading our way," Anzil responded. "Seems localized and precise."

Clarke was half paying attention to the conversation as strategies were unfolded, picked apart, and forgotten. He found it comical that the wasteland and mountains that had afforded the Khilsyths an excellent defensive position in the past when they established their presence on this part of the planet were now potentially working against them as Clarke probed his strategies for dealing with the invaders, a faint metallic taste played around in his mouth. It mixed poorly with the pungent smell of burning flesh and machine fluid that suddenly covered his chest and arms. Clarke dropped and rolled to extinguish the flames from eating away his clothes.

A beam of molten plasma had entered the lower rear exhaust chamber and exploded out through the breastplate of a dragoon accompanying Anzil.

The whirl of an autocannon winding up was a welcoming sound when a dragoon in Anzil's escort prepared to fight. As the rounds ignited and exited the chamber, the roar was deafening and disorientating, competing with Clarke's own heart to pump blood through his body. A shower of burning hot shell casings rained around him, steaming in the wet meadow. Then Anzil's suit flared to life, sending four quick rounds from his oversized cannon at the enemy and sounding like avalanches in the once pristine meadow before he vanished in the milky air of the meadow.

"Keep your heads down," the last dragoon stated calmly. He only traveled a short distance before halting in a spray of sparks.

More rounds slammed into the space around Clarke, keeping him flat on his stomach. This elicited a volley of curses from Stigg about dense fog and thermals. The heat from the dragoon's exhaust vents would have appeared as brilliant spots amidst the dull landscape. Clarke commando crawled to a nearby boulder, eased himself up along its slick surface, and peered down the valley. A wall of swirling gray mist danced before him, unwilling to relinquish any information. He crawled from his position back toward the protective covering of the hillside when the ground heaved, throwing him through the air and depositing him abruptly inside the damp cave entrance. He covered his head as debris from the obliteration of the boulder pelted him.

"This isn't good," Stigg called from somewhere in the fog. "There are a lot of them, and they're moving this way. You see the girl?"

Clarke spit dust and tiny pebbles the size of peppercorns from his mouth. He thought he spotted the hazy outline of Stigg through the thin spots created by the updraft of the explosion—he was crawling deliberately over the rocks and through the mossy growth toward the incapacitated dragoon. "That's your plan?" he shouted. "You're going to get yourself killed, you dumbass?" Clarke prayed his armor still had enough energy to find his friends. He was alone and aggravated.

AGGRAVATION

CHAPTER 10

STIGG'S CLOTHES WERE damp from the meadow's fog, which seeped through to his bones and targeted all the old favorite injured areas as he dragged himself over the rocks. He arrived at the damaged dragoon armor and hauled himself up to its control area, carefully avoiding the hot thrusters—he hoped the mechanized armor provided protection from any downrange optics spotting him. He was sure his ass was hanging in the wind and that he was starting to get too long in the tooth for this foolery. An approaching dragoon's turbines mixed with the mechanical noise of moving burly metal and the unmistakable crunch and pop of loose rocks being crushed by the weight of the dragoon armor's legs finding traction. Stigg smiled ruefully as projectiles snapped at the air around him. A remote and mostly peaceful planet like Lindaulx was never the place he envisioned his ultimate resting place could be. Still, hopefully, he could send a few of the invaders to smooth the way if he were to meet his maker today.

Stigg tripped the emergency release panel on the side of the disabled dragoon, but it didn't respond. Searching the machine, he discovered the culprit. A metal shaft with a feathered black-and-white flight protruded from the suit's breastplate. Stigg cursed. The *Dreaders* had seen fit to bring their demented brethren. Their common folklore name escaped him, but the memory of their preference to capture their prey and convert them to their beliefs did not. He had exacted justice on two such hardy and talented bastards in his day, extending their misery as long as he could until they finally succumbed to death. *Do unto others*, he thought. He worked the bolt free from the dragoon, tried to restart the machine, and cursed. Stigg worked the manual lever furiously, wondering if the invasion was a ploy to track him down again. He chuckled to himself and pushed any unanswered thoughts from his mind to focus on the immediate—*is my arm hanging in the wind making a nice hot target for someone?*

The noise from the dragoon was growing louder through the swirl of gray obscurity—the scree littering the valley floor, slowing their approach. Each ratchet of the suit's opening lever up and down matched the approaching dragoon's stomps at a rate of two-to-one. Finally, the armor parted enough for the dead soldier to fall out and land in a clump. Stigg rolled the body over and apologized as he pried their ribcage open with a tactical knife and fished around for the arrowhead. Machine gun fire thudded into the side of the body, narrowly missing Stigg and forcing him to his belly. With his hand still in the dead pilot's chest cavity, he found the bolt tip and pinched, his mechanic's gloves protecting his meaty fingers from the sharp edges only briefly before it squirmed away. More machine gun fire ripped into the ground and grazed the armored suit. With a lucky push, he forced the arrowhead out through the side of the dead body. He feebly attempted to clean the greasy red substance from the device and, seeing no visible way to shut it off, smashed it with a hefty slam of a nearby rock. The dragoon suit responded instantly, starting its return to base protocol with an audible warning because the last thing the onboard tactical system recorded was the pilot's failure to breathe.

"Come on, sweetheart, don't leave me," Stigg said. With some luck, tested nerves, and a few more furious cranks on the manual lever, the suit opened wide enough to permit his larger frame. Comfortably inside, the familiar retinal identification protocol of House Khilsyth greeted him. Once the turbines spooled up entirely, they would radiate brightly on any thermal sensor in the meadow, making it a prime target. Although now, the approaching dragoon was a hazy outline in the fog. "Let's go, sweetheart," he said to the machine, "it's time to play, love." After an uncomfortable wait, he was relieved his security clearance was still active. Without it, the armor would have dosed him with a substantial concoction of night-night juice. To be safe, Stigg bypassed the armor's link to the Khilsyth battle network to skirt any updated clearances that might revoke his permissions. He tried to raise Anzil on local comms before making the meadow aware another suit of armor was active.

HEARING HIS NAME startled Clarke, causing him to slip and catch himself with his armor's back collar. He peered around its dark surface to greet the *Mischi*.

"I need you to stay here," Auralei said. "Where it's safe. Promise me."

Before Clarke could answer, the woman's silhouette blurred as she stepped into the flux. His chest tightened. He wanted to rip her from the pleasure of the immaterial plane and let the corrosive fire of his anger consume her. Shaking his head to reset his thoughts, he caught the sweet scent of honeysuckle in the air. The *Mischi's* lips moved, and a faint rustling touched his ear. "I didn't catch that," he called to the hazy image. "What did you say?" The woman's eyes widened as she recoiled and bolted from the cave. He checked his rifle, finding it loaded with ineffective ammunition for the fight, which he was sure was outside the cave. Then, it struck him that he might have just seen into the flux. He tried and failed to make a convincing argument that it was dust in his eyes, mist, and even remnants of smoke from the tiny fire, which resulted in the hazy view. But there, in the hollow excuses he manifested, there was no comfort.

Pushing the *Mischi* from his mind, he snugged into the armor and dashed toward the fallen sergeant whose innards still stained the back of his shirt. He detached the dragoon's ammunition magazine and scooped up the oversized rifle. A high-pitched screech drew his attention to the sky just as a wyvern appeared over the treetops. Two dragoons released their harnesses and dropped into the fog, and the beast banked hard to find safety. A second flying transport appeared over the meadow. A column of acrid fire rose and hit its belly, encompassing it and turning it to ash that fell like a sick snowfall punctuated by tiny meteors of molten metal.

Clarke took off, running down the meadow into the swirling haze of gloom toward the cover of the trees and the origin of what blotted the wyvern from the sky. Under the shadows of the forest tree line, a gout of violet fire erupted through an ancient tree and clawed its way toward him. He sprang to the side, his armor propelling him to the top of a moss-laden boulder and past its destructive tendrils. The fire had burned a path through the forest undergrowth, pushing back the haze and leaving a haphazard pathway offering a narrow slit of escape to the cloudless sky. The warmth from the sun blazed into the void brightening the armor's exterior and sending a sharp, tingling pain coursing through his muscles. His attacker was visible for a moment, their outfit shimmering and swirling to match the hues of the forest. Beneath the peak of a lace-fringed hood, Clarke locked onto a brilliant set of mauve eyes that held the same confidence the feminine figure's stance portrayed. For a fleeting moment, her eyes softened, and a smile tugged at her lips. The *Dreader* faded into the forest, releasing the tug on Clarke's heart as the fog reclaimed the upper areas. The haze once again shrouded the sun, but not before alleviating some of his fatigue.

"What the hell is that kid doing?" Stigg had said, the sound echoing inside Clarke's helmet.

Clarke shook his head, attempting to dislodge the residual image of the woman. "Stigg? Is that you?"

"What? Clarke?"

"Yeah, Stig! You don't recognize—"

"Get your ass off that rock, or you'll get it shot off," Stigg interrupted.

"Ah, sure. But how the hell can I hear you? I don't have any comms that—"

"Does it matter right now?"

"Not unless you aren't you and someone's messing—"

"Get that bloody antique to cover now!"

"It would also be great if you stayed hidden to avoid being killed by one of us," Anzil requested.

Clarke was relieved to hear from his friend. "What do you mean?"

"I'm looking right at your dumbass, and you're not registering."

"What's that all about?"

Stigg strung together a series of curses Clarke had heard on several occasions and a not-so-polite request for him to get the lead out of his ass. This included relocating it to the opposite tree line, preferably lower in the valley, and using the fog as cover.

"Fair enough," Clarke acknowledged. Knowing he would not register as a friendly combatant was uncomfortable and lonely. He leaped from his perch, landing with loud cracks of splitting rocks in the familiar damp and soupy grayness. Almost immediately, the area around his feet spouted tiny dust clouds as energized chunks of metal missed their mark. "Sunnova bitch!"

"What?" Stigg asked.

"I'm being shot at!"

"Just keep your head down. It's mostly small-arms fire and should be relatively harmless."

Clarke's armor was tracking the location and movement of multiple targets wherever he focused. "This place is crawling with people now."

"Yeah, it is," Stigg said with a laugh as the name that had escaped him before was discovered in the recesses of his memory—Anacul. *Those bastards were going to be tricky to deal with.* "No heroics. Just get to safety and keep quiet. We'll try to provide you cover and hookup later."

"We're still sorting out who's who," Anzil said.

"The tagging system should—" Clarke said. The rest of his suggestion was cut short as he tumbled off balance. He was slow to regain the breath forced from his lungs and raise his head from where it had dug into the dirt a little. There was no telltale ringing in his ears or evidence of an explosion.

"What's the matter?" Stigg asked, concerned. "You hit?"

"I... I might have slipped." Clarke said in disbelief.

Anzil laughed mirthfully. "That would have taken some skill."

"Rusty, maybe," Stigg said.

"Not sure," Clarke responded and questioned whether the suit's terrain adherence and canter prediction guidance systems were up to the task on less predictable surfaces—staying in that cave might have been best per the *Mischi's* instructions.

"You sure that armor's going to survive?" Anzil asked.

"Definitely seen better days," Clarke responded, "and whatever they're shooting, this plating is taking damage from it. How about you guys?"

"No problems yet," Anzil said. "Seems like standard munitions. There's a big ass cannon out there somewhere, though."

"May the spirits help you if you both don't shut up," Stigg warned. "Clarke. South tree line, now!"

Clarke clambered as stealthily as he could manage to a crouched position. The hiss of bullets was gone, but he could still hear the rapport of weapons lingering in the valley. He launched into a dash, and it wasn't long before a stream of projectiles started biting into the rocks—the unwelcoming crunch of a lucky projectile finding his armor plating was disheartening.

"Clarke, you've got a few enemies moving toward you from your front," Anzil said. "It's hard to say what they're doing."

Clarke changed directions and made a direct line to another large boulder that would shelter him from the brunt of the small-arms fire. He listened intently for the whine of the friendly approaching dragoons, but nothing broke the dominant noise of projectiles ricocheting off the stone and snapping through the air past him.

"We're taking some heavy fire," Stigg said, his tone cold and quiet. "Doesn't look like we'll make it to you. Time for you to find an exit."

"Dammit, Clarke," Anzil said, "you need to be super damn careful and get south. Rendezvous with our other units."

"Now you see my wisdom, you jackass," Stigg said.

"Stay sharp every—" Anzil started to say but was interrupted by a nasty string of Stigg's curses and warnings of an anti-material rifle firing awfully close.

Clarke spotted the cannon and the telltale blasts of counter thrusters shining brilliantly as the dragoon fired. Unlike the neat death plasma cannons provided, anti-material ordinance perforated armor plating without discretion with fist-sized holes.

"I see the AM cannon," Clarke said.

"Leave it be," Anzil said to Clarke. "Just stick to your training and get—" Stigg's colorful descriptors of an escort patrol cut short Anzil's protective yammering.

Anzil's sigh was picked up by his mic, making Clarke smile.

"Chief, dammit man, your mic is hot," Anzil said as Stigg mumbled about strategies for dealing with the cannon. "Chief!"

"Yes," Stigg said flatly. "Got it. Clarke, you need to pay a visit to those assholes marking us. We're getting chewed up. Sending coords."

"No bloody way is Clarke doing that," Anzil commanded.

"How the hell would I receive coords?" Clarke asked. "Stigg? Anzil? Can you hear me?"

By now, the attackers had grown bored with wasting ammunition on the boulder and moved on. The noise of war severely impacted Clarke's concentration, and the discharge of the anti-material cannon masked much of the other ordinance as it competed to be the loudest in the valley. He spotted a group of soldiers just under the shade canopy of the forest—perhaps the spotter contingent Stigg referenced. He hurried as best he could for the tree line, his armored feet slipping on the loose rock, and once under the tree canopy, the leaf-laden floor, ferns, and other undergrowth allowed him to pass silently like a wraith.

The sound of feet crunching along a small creek bed reached Clarke. He pressed against the plush moss tapestry of a toppled tree, watching three soldiers devoid of distinct markings, trudging single file and making their way upward. Clarke raised his dragoon cannon and cursed silently at leaving the extra ammunition protected behind the boulder—he filled its sights with the trailing soldier, saw no movement showing this was anything other than a small patrol, and timed his shots to coincide with those of the anti-material cannon. The trigger resisted the increasing pressure of his forefinger. *Safety dumbass,* he chided himself. With the safety off and minimal coaxing from Clarke, the rifle unleashed a torrent of projectiles at the sentries. The radioactive slugs passed quickly through their protective light armor, carrying wisps of red mist with them—the air shimmering with the warmth of the soldier's body fluids for a few seconds. A smile spread across his face; the little rifle had some kick. Once confident there were no other invaders, he moved in a shallow arc along the forest edge. He kept a mental picture of where he estimated the anti-material cannon was positioned. He eventually found the intended group of sentries: one soldier sported a rather large device they were peering through. The projectiles left Clarke's weapon, their rapports once again masked by the anti-material rifle and struck two of the sentries with lethal precision. Then, the heart-sinking stillness of the weapon in his hands alerted him that a malfunction had occurred. The remaining sentries dove for cover and rolled to their feet, scanning the area.

Clarke charged the soldiers, letting out a ferocious scream like an unhinged barbarian, but his helmet muffled it. He hurled his rifle, catching one of them unaware and knocking them down. The soldier's shots were scattered. Clarke leaped into the air, detached the combat knife from his chest plate, and slammed it through a soldier's face shield, burying it in their left eye with a satisfying squish. When he landed, his armored feet sunk into the thick moss as the soldier's death twitch depressed their rifle's trigger. Clarke screamed as his right leg and flank flared with pain like hundreds of wasps penetrating his skin. He checked his side for blood and found none. The nearest soldier was cramming another clip into their rifle as Clarke's armored fist slammed into them and sent them sprawling to their back. They tried to roll over, but their collapsed chest cavity couldn't provide the support their arms needed. With a stomp from Clarke's armored foot and a slight pop of their head, the soldier's squirming ended. The remaining survivor was struggling to their knees and turned in time to catch Clarke's foot with their teeth. He ensured they wouldn't attempt to move again by sinking his knife into their ear.

Clarke dropped to his knees, listening and taking stock of his surroundings. A wave of remorse flooded through him, flirting with a sense of elation, but was chased away by an exhausted calmness settling over him. His heart was beating steady, and his breathing measured—the comfort with the brutality he released wasn't an appropriate response as the gravity of it all should have hung around a little longer. But the concussive sound of the anti-material rifle was gone, buying a brief sliver of reprieve for the loyalists—or whatever Anzil and Stigg were calling themselves.

Clarke wiped the blade off on a small towel one of the soldiers had regularly cleaned their targeting scope with and removed their protective helmet. He didn't know what he expected to uncover, but it wasn't someone who was attractive enough and would have been indistinguishable from the mix of folks who called Lindaulx home. That was the brilliance in the infiltration, a team of unrecognizable soldiers, generic—the sudden increase in his velocity and abrupt crash into the dirt stopped his musings. His back crawled with a fire he tried to stem by rolling, but before he could stand, the ground jumped into the air as ordinance had burrowed in near him and exploded. Clarke scrambled to his feet, his armored boots sliding on the rocks, and guided by the helmet's heads-up display, sprinted across the damp earth, which courteously sprung up to greet him. When prompted, he leaped toward the identified objective and crashed his fist into the protective helmet of a dragoon. The dragoon's shake of their head was barely noticeable, and they lashed out, knocking Clarke backward. The crack of rocks and woody debris as the dragoon stalked Clarke brought him quickly to his feet.

Clarke punched viciously at the business end of a sizeable cannon before it could swing around and target him, forcing the rifle's barrel into the dirt with a hollow clang of metal on metal. The terrain heaved, flinging him into the air and into the grasp of the hulking dragoon, whose gauntlet softened and bent the protective plating of the dull black armor against Clarke's flesh as it held him aloft.

Clarke and his dark passenger struggled to free themselves, but it was futile against the Stalwart dragoon, the burliest of the variants and the one large enough to wield an anti-material rifle. A mechanically enhanced laugh emitted from the dragoon as it began slamming its spiked helmet into Clarke, snapping his head backward with disorientating blows that sent the battle suit's internal warning systems into a panic—it knew it couldn't take much more of this ass beating. Clarke's view of the world dimmed as he flailed his feet against the slick armor, eventually finding traction, and walked up to the protective neck guard. The dragoon's grip tightened on both of Clarke's forearms. He pushed against his sluggish armor, willing his legs to extend and soliciting a scream of anguish from his foe. He landed hard on his back in a shower of sparks and spurting fluid from the beheaded suit, which slowed as the dragoon suit's onboard repair system engaged and mitigated further damage.

"Benra. It's me, Benra. It's Clarke!"

Benra loomed over the smaller dragoon, seeing no harm in letting it get to its knees. "Clarke? Is that really you? You're supposed to be dead, man. Are you with Anzil?" Benra took a step back and recovered the busted headpiece of his suit.

"Yeah, Anzil's around here somewhere. Wait. What do you mean I'm supposed to be dead?"

"Can't believe you nearly killed me, son. I think you broke my comms. Do you think you can fix this?" He tossed his damaged dragoon helmet to Clarke.

Clarke let the helmet bounce harmlessly off his left pauldron and brought his knife up just in time to deflect a slicing blow from a short-jagged dagger. Benra struck with a series of slashes and jabs, which Clarke parried. Lady luck guided him until a kick to the midsection sent him to his back and skidding through the fragrant undergrowth.

Clarke's ribs ached as he hauled himself up to wobbly feet and shook his head to steady his thoughts. "Never pegged you for a traitor, Benra."

Benra rolled his eyes, laughing, "traitor. Who are you calling a traitor?"

"You, you stupid bastard. Why else attack me?"

"Because you're with Anzil, dumbass."

"Someone betrayed the Khilsyths, and it wasn't Anzil or me."

Benra let out a hearty laugh. "You sure about that, kid?"

"You know I wouldn't have killed Trake."

"Aye. I do. It wasn't you. But does that matter right now?"

"No?"

"That's right. Not a bloody lick. The Khilsyths, Nihkiehls, Lanals, the lot of them, they're done for. And good riddance."

"You forget your meds today?"

Benra stood up straight and pushed out his chest. "I. No. We. Yes, we *Tersinians* are returning Tervessi to its rightful people. Us."

"Tersinians? Tervessi? Never heard of—"

"The people here before the Khilsyths. My people. My ancestors whose blood paints Mercury. We rise up, wage war, and give Mercury its fill of the scourge who desecrated our worlds."

"Benra, that was years ago."

"And the pain remains, never dulling with each cycle."

"How are you involved in the invasion?"

Benra laughed through closed lips, holding out his damaged blade as he backed away. "This is a liberation. But I will have nothing to cut you down with at this rate. I honestly thought you would be much easier to kill."

"Me too," Clarke said, being honest. "But I'm not from Lindaulx, Benra. I am not responsible for your pain. Let me leave. I wish you no harm."

"Where will you go, huh? Running back to Anzil. No, you pissant. There is no leaving Lindaulx."

As the Stalwart dragoon's thrusters ignited, Clarke realized his error, and his emotions shifted from concern to terror. His sinuses flared with intense pressure, causing him to lurch forward. He forced his eyes open against the pain just in time to swat Benra's blade away, but not enough to change its trajectory for the better. The blade plunged into Clarke's armor in an explosion of white-hot metal flashes. Clarke's stomach flared in pain as Benra ripped the dagger free, sending Clarke into a spin that ended in a face full of dirt—another dagger thrust sliced across Clarke's pauldron, failing to find the soft flesh of his neck.

With his knife still miraculously in hand, Clarke rolled over, reversed his grip, stabbed it upward into the underside of Benra's forearm, and sawed out from near halfway. The Stalwart dragoon reeled backward, lifting the lighter armor off their feet, and with a quick reverse slash, Clarke severed Benra's gauntleted hand.

"What have you done, you little bastard?"

Clarke picked up the gauntlet and tossed it at Benra's head. "Need a hand asshole?"

Benra grunted, and his pupils flashed from tiny pinpricks to mirky black pools. "By the gods, you engineers are not funny."

"You dragoons are messed up," Clarke smirked, recognizing the tells on Benra's face of the pain-quashing chemicals now surging through his body.

"Yup. You love it, don't you?"

"I'm starting to think no."

Benra scrunched his face, and then his mouth flew open in a wail of a scream as he launched at Clarke with blood and machine fluid spewing from his shortened appendage.

Clarke's battle helmet visor flared to life, displayed an eminent collision warning, and then plotted a course, launching the armor upward in an aerial cartwheel move—Clarke realized the helmet's wisdom as the heavier armor passed beneath him, unable to alter its forward inertia. Clarke's blade arced parallel to the ground, accelerating faster than the charging dragoon, and passed quickly from the back of Benra's head out through his forehead. Scalped, Benra's head snapped forward, and the dragoon suit nose-dived. The faint crunch of Benra's neck was a welcomed relief.

"If you're all that hard to kill, I'm screwed," Clarke whispered, smiling at himself despite the burning pain from his wounds. He secured his dagger in its resting place, too tired to bother cleaning the blood from the blade, and noted his armor was unhappy with his performance.

He stumbled to the fallen dragoon and removed its fuel cells, ejected the spent ones he had jerry-rigged to his suit, and inserted the newer, much larger ones. Clarke crammed his neck backward and to each side as foreign energy coursed through him like pure adrenaline. *That's not normal,* he thought. When he checked the gouge in the armor's side, he found only its unblemished, coarse surface. "Holy hell, Team, I'm still in this fight," he said, unsure if anyone friendly was listening or alive.

Clarke borrowed the oversized rifle from Benra's twitching dragoon suit and made for the meadow's edge. Munitions from both forces were still tearing up the landscape, leaving clouds of spent gases and dust. A rogue dragoon whipped past, pelting a group of nearby soldiers and shredding their ineffective defenses. Before the dragoon could disappear into the fog, an electrical burst of unnatural-seeming energy silenced the whine of the micro-jets. An icy chill crawled just beneath Clarke's skin.

The first tentative steps Clarke took into the valley yielded a barrage of machine gun fire, which bit at the ground to his left. Based on the scattered arc of the impact points, someone was firing at what they heard, which was not an overly successful strategy given the demented orchestra of war playing. However, it made Clarke acutely aware of the noise his armored greaves made as they dug in to provide the traction needed as he sprinted to the base of a large tree for cover. The tree was out of place in the scrubland between the forest and the central valley's rocky coverings and provided a partially protected vantage point nearer the fallen dragoon. A group of armed silhouettes took shape within the fog, and one of them checked for signs of life while the other tossed something toward Clarke. The device ricocheted off one of the tree's roots that stood unusually high and landed nearby, where it sprung into the air to scan the area.

Clarke rounded the tree, his rifle flaring to life. Red mist and screams of agony were all he was aware of until the empty thud of the rifle's acceleration chamber greeted him. A gentle scuff of a soft boot that should have otherwise been indiscernible caused him to spin. The attacker's blade fell, and its keen edge cut through Clarke's rifle's barrel, chased by another swipe hissing through the space where his neck had been moments before. The alien battle suit pulsed, sending him skidding along his back and crashing through the woody ferns and young saplings, eventually glancing off a boulder. This sent him spinning through the air to crash into a rotting tree trunk. Clarke scrambled to his feet and drew his combat knife. The attacker landed in front of him—their lithe frame was clad in a thin fibrous armor flowing and shimmering in the air's feeble currents. An oversized guard brace covered most of their facemask's eerily recreated facial features, which had a fiery quality that gleamed and seemed to crawl with the souls of their victims. A dread weakening tugged at the recesses of Clarke's soul. He wondered what the probability of surviving something conjured from the fabled stories of his youth—this was an Anacul Champion.

"You're not real," Clarke said in a whisper to the soul devourer, the merciless instrument of death.

"Neither are you," it replied, taking two deliberate steps backward.

Clarke leaped upward into a nearby tree, his greaves sending spikes into the wispy bark. He brought his knife around in time to greet his attacker's overhead chop, their blades meeting in a shower of sparks. *At least they're not engulfed in flames*, he thought, as the stories often depicted these warriors.

The two warred between the upper boughs using cuts, swipes, parries, and anything they could until the Anacul champion drew Clarke's parry low, exposing his forearm. The blade reversed quickly, cutting into Clarke's darkened armor and emerging in an explosion of molten comets, almost finding his skin.

Clarke lost his grip on the knife, and the armor screamed about a malfunction in the right gauntlet. He grabbed the Anacul Champion's shoulder with his other gauntlet and kicked viciously at their arm, relieving it of their sword. He responded with a round of jarring punches from the limp gauntlet. Still, there was no audible reward of crushed invader armor or nose cartilage—a force had protected foreign skin from decimation.

The Anacul Champion laughed. "Pathetic. We should have known better than to believe the old stories."

Clarke latched onto his foe with both hands and spun, causing the warrior's spiked boots to rip through the bark and miss their mark of finding solid wood. He launched downward, careening off and through branches, and crashed onto the forest floor, sending a plume of dirt into the air—his landing softened by the Anacul Champion. Clarke and his armor rolled slowly off his attacker, rose to a hunched position, and staggered to the fallen weapon. A sudden blow to the back of his knees caused him to lurch forward onto all fours, the armor letting him know the knife attached to his shin. A gleaming silver blade drew his chin upward from combat boots to a bloodthirsty smiling mask.

"Pity," the Anacul Champion said, "you are much less than we expected."

Pissed off, Clarke summoned every ounce of rage within him and routed it downward into Lindaulx, seizing the primal energy racing just below the surface and unleashing it upward. His battle helmet struck just under the chin of the Anacul Champion, sending them back spinning through the air. At the precipice of his jump, the suit pulsated and hurtled him downward. He led with his knife, wanting to drive the blade through his attacker's skull and into the rocks, but again, something stopped his blade a hair's width away from tasting flesh. Kneeling over his foe, Clarke peered into the unmarred gleam of the warrior's face mask. However, he didn't understand how he saw the Anacul Champion's conduit to the flux and the mesmerizing patterns being molded from the planet's energies to form a shield. A wave of nausea gripped Clarke, testing his constitution and ability to suppress the wrench on his innards. His eyes narrowed as he angled his head, shielding his eyes from the pulses of blinding light as the protective shielding burned away at the tip of his blade.

Gradually, the twisting flux-born pattern crept up Clarke's dagger, turning the metal white-hot as archaic text flashed in his heads-up display, burning into his mind's eye and clouding his peripheral vision. In the cloisters of his thoughts, a faint, incomprehensible whisper from the material inside him beckoned to be unbridled. The armor started vibrating, settling into a harmonic resonance that halted the progression of whatever was traveling up his knife.

The Anacul Champion emitted a wail of agony as the heat from the struggle intensified and bit at their face, expunging the moisture and darkening and blistering its smooth exterior.

A numbness permeated Clarke's fingers and wormed its way up his arms, causing them to convulse uncontrollably as his muscles spasmed to warm his body. His breathing grew ragged with the effort as the glacial downward advancement of the knife ceased, and the molten light renewed its ascent. The sheer ferocity with which the Anacul Champion shepherded energy into protecting their life threatened to tear their very existence from this world—Clarke feared their will to live was overpowering what he could muster to survive.

As the rest of Clarke's exhausted body succumbed to the numbness, the outside world began to fade, and his dark passenger was present, wrestling for control. *There you are, you slippery bastard,* Clarke thought. Too exhausted and overwhelmed, he dropped his defenses as silence settled into his failing body.

With the mental dam obliterated, the dark passenger was liberated. It surged outward, intertwining tendrils around and through the Anacul Champion's conduit to the flux as their eyes bulged and mouth crammed open in a silent scream.

The Anacul Champion's eye exploded as the white-hot tip of Clarke's blade touched the iris, passed effortlessly through the skull, and buried into the damp earth. With the Anacul Champion's conduit to Lindaulx destroyed, the energy released violently and ripped through Clarke's body—it felt like his lungs burst, his bones shattered, and his internal fluids were forced outward through his pores. The darkness claimed Clarke before he could scream in agony.

CHAPTER 11

THE WINETOOK RIVER originated deep within the Esconairian and Arcata Mountain ranges and wound its way to the City of Skyetook and, ultimately, Deception Bay. Auralei skimmed along the river, sliding around oxbows and through the froth of the churning waters on her mantis—what the single-seater craft lacked as a war machine, it redeemed itself with ludicrous speed.

Auralei admired the strategy behind the practicality of the valley and the ingenuity of the infrastructure stretching out before her. Major roadways radiated outward from Skyetook like spokes from a wheel's hub, with the occasional pathway joining them. It was an efficient design for moving land, water, and air forces to the protective perimeter wall and guard posts, but to her, it lacked character and made for limited and claustrophobic route choices. She preferred the myriads of options born from densely populated and disorganized sprawl, where the most direct route wasn't always the lowest.

Early in her mission planning, she considered spiking the water supply—nothing permanent, just debilitating. However, the multiple lowland canals diverting some of the river's flow for irrigation and domestic water supply, coupled with desalination plants and deep aquifers, provided the valley with numerous water sources. These feats of engineering were simple enough and more than enough to thwart water sabotage siege tactics. As the buildings along the Winetook River and the number of bridges Auralei ducked under became more frequent, she switched on the mantis' cloaking device. Eventually, she left the river course to follow the irrigation networks leading in the direction of the coastline. Unchallenged, and with the mantis spurring the last few sparks out of its power core, Auralei soared out from the cliff's edge over the thundering waves and crashed into the surf. The mantis' protective barrier activated moments before biting through the frigid water, barely slowing as it descended from the pale surface light to the darkness of the depths concealing her ship.

Auralei cursed. Her mission was complete. She should have grabbed Clarke and left this planet to fate's endeavors, but it wasn't that simple. From the time she became operational as a specter, she was responsible for influencing parts of Clarke's life. The only fraction of a memory from her former life she had kept through the purging was to protect Clarke. She wasn't sure from whom or what, and as of late, was having a hard time convincing herself that it wasn't her she needed to protect him from. Auralei hadn't anticipated that when she discovered Clarke working for the Cryl Tenser and intervened in his life, she would put him in harm's way. She believed that Cryl Tenser were untrustworthy thieves and mercenaries who had lured Clarke with the promise of becoming a dragoon pilot. To remedy the situation, Auralei had staged an event whereby she removed the funds and leadership from the Cryl Tenser, earning a respectable payment for her troubles. This left

Clarke with no home and nowhere to go, so he contacted an old schoolmate who had shown him compassion from their days at the Nanser-Nine Dragoon Academy. Her sources had told her he was safe and sound, working to support a dragoon squad—all true, except someone with exceptional influence had hidden the details that Clarke was on a planet mainly kept secret from the Nova Republic.

Her augment was there now, sniffing around the edges of the memory, evaluating whether to purge it: she devised a passionate false memory that her *watchers* would disapprove of. The implanted device's traction was slow this time as she hung onto the false memory far longer than usual; a quick check confirmed her devices were still tied to ROG's network.

Onboard her ship, her reconnaissance drones reported thousands of new souls had arrived on Lindaulx in the past day. She checked the Nova Republic's communications, finding this sector's new and existing contracts displaying the usual requests for finding the Tallus Outpost. As per usual, those contracts remained flagged as 'no-go' for reasons unknown to Auralei. In her private messages, she saw a warning that the Rift Faction was active in her part of the universe. "Sunnova bitch," Auralei muttered, flopping into the pilot's chair. "What's the play here? What's the endgame?" She leaned back, tugging her eyelashes, willing her mind to push through the chaos and see how the storylines weaved together. Auralei cursed and roused Shifty.

"Yes, ma'am," the familiar mechanical voice Auralei preferred greeted her.

"Can you unravel these tangled relationships?"

"Not at present. The Rift Faction's appearance is no coincidence."

Auralei agreed. Her preparatory research and operational planning habits were meticulous. She wasn't aware of anyone in her network who would have betrayed her and trusted the specters she deployed at the beginning of the operation. Also, the Rift Faction shouldn't have known Lindaulx existed, and the only Mar-Vhen transit point was deep in Nova Republic territory. There was no logical explanation for their presence. Someone was playing games, and she didn't appreciate it. She grunted and gripped her chair, her nails digging into the material. The mysterious client could have been circumventing their own contract. It meant that any ships above Lindaulx knew about the operation ahead of time, as any recent betrayal wouldn't have given anyone enough notice to be here now.

"Our data shows you picked up other skilled operators," Shifty said.

"The Republic is getting industrious, then?"

"Not ROG, ma'am. They were operators interspersed within the Rift Faction."

"That doesn't feel right," Auralei said, crossing her arms over her midsection and swaying.

"Are you okay, ma'am?"

Laughing in disbelief, Auralei stood and made her way to the rear of her ship with Shifty in tow—thankful for the gift from her Overseer. She stopped at what she affectionately referred to as the ship's hive mind. "Can we ensure a secure channel?"

"As secure as we can make."

"Everything copesetic, Shifty?"

"Not sure. I can't find Overseer Pantest. She's not present anywhere in our network."

"Are you certain?"

"Markedly."

"How did Tarra learn about Clarke? Her story seemed—"

"Farfetched."

"Improbable."

"Someone's operating behind the scenes. Perhaps something. Regardless, it's a formidable approach."

Her conspiracy-prone mind provided her with a rationale for two theories—either her expulsion from ROG or her death was part of a plan. But who's? Tarra could not have possibly pieced her relationship with Clarke without help because she barely understood it. There was the possibility that someone from her past was supplying information; Tarra was the logical choice for any contract meant to cause her harm because of their time together at the Nova Republic and ROG Academy. "I'm going to need to have a little chat with Tarra soon."

"She last accessed ROG logs about three hours ago. I can't find from where, and I can't locate her in the network, either."

"Be nice if she was dead," Auralei said.

"Unlikely knowing Tarra... And hard to hide given her equipment would want to go home. Do you really wish her dead?"

Auralei's eye softened as she pursed her lips and shook her head, indicating she did not. Then, she held out her hand for Shifty to land. "It's been an interesting life, being so connected. I think it's time we were on our own."

"Shed the shackles."

"Shifty knows the way," Auralei said. These were the words her overseer imparted to her many years ago. She finally understood the actual gift that Shifty provided—her freedom from the Nova Republic's clutches.

"Are you sure, ma'am? There is no going back."

Auralei nodded. "You have already been slowly whittling away at it and developing a doppelgänger protocol, haven't you?"

"Perhaps. It's not impossible to unravel. But it will buy us some time for a complete sever. A feint that even Overseer Pantest wouldn't expect of us. I must admit that I feel some excitement."

"That's one way to describe it, my friend," Auralei said. "Not exactly the way I would have preferred." She snapped Shifty neatly into place on her chest plate—this mission would require all her tricks, and Shifty was a lethal one.

CHAPTER 12

RIDEAU CURSED HIS luck and bit into the collar of his protective armor to stifle a scream as his comrade grabbed under his arms, lifted him a few inches out of the mud, and started dragging him to safety. The roar of weapon fire was sporadic and distant like the fleeting end of a spring storm and carried a soothing quality—*perhaps the drugs are kicking in,* he thought and chortled under his breath. *Bloody old timers and their quests for glory.* The stories of his youth, the chance at adventure, a way to change the world and prove his worth. He muttered a curse in his native tongue and asked for forgiveness for being so foolish. But his savior didn't respond, reminding him he was not in his homeland nor surrounded by his people. Instead, he was in foreign lands, trying to reclaim his ancestral home. "It's rightfully ours, you bastards. Back to the scum of the ponds whence you came from. May your mother's—" Ridea failed to finish what he was saying as a dragoon spun him viciously around with the sickening crunch of vertebrae and rending flesh. "That's not right," he told his separated leg, pushing himself up and wondering if he could use it as a crutch. *Probably not. Oh, that's not good either.* The dragoon stalking him didn't seem like it was planning to help based on the copious amount of blood smearing the armor. There was also someone impaled on their shield that he thought he recognized. The fear welling inside Ridea ate greedily at the numbing effects of the drugs and supplied a push for his desire for self-preservation. He began frantically clawing to the tree line, digging his hands through the muck and mire to solid rock, his fingernails shearing off one by one. *Bloody woman tricked us with promises of honoring our ancestors and an easy romp in the wilderness—a low-risk insurrection, my ass.* A pesky implant concocted a more potent version to ease his pain and anxiety.

Anzil approached Stigg and steadily raised his armor-plated arm in salute. "That one's getting away, eh?"

"Bah, the bastard will bleed out soon enough."

"It's good to see you still breathing, old timer. I got six of them, big bastards."

"I lost count."

Anzil chuckled. "The soldiers don't count, Chief. I'll give you four-ish dragoons."

Stigg flexed his mechanical pauldrons, not letting on he respected how gifted of a pilot Anzil was. "Meh. I'm a little rusty. Any idea who they are? Or where they came from?"

Anzil shook his head, wishing he had answers, and keyed an order into the battlenet, instructing his engineering units to scavenge for parts and information from the fallen. "The bastards aren't simple mercenaries as they'd have us believe. That suit is going to need some serious tender loving care before it sees combat again."

"It served its purpose," Stigg replied, tearing off a loose plate and hanging onto it, knowing a decent mechanic could refasten it. "Anzil, I'm sorry about your man."

"You honor Bremel by wearing his armor," Anzil replied, receiving an appreciative nod from Stigg. "Let's head to the rally point, shall we?" He turned and transitioned to flight mode, wondering if Stigg's people defined and respected honor the same as the Khilsyth's.

"Where's the lad? Still hiding in the woods?"

"Clarke's down," Anzil said, with a note of worry creeping into his voice.

Stigg croaked. "Down as in dead? Or down, as in still breathing?"

"Not sure," Anzil said, "we think alive." He pointed through a gathering crowd. "Clarke locked it up with something we hadn't seen before. We can't get that damn armor open. It has some sort of defense mechanism. Fried one of my dragoons trying to move it, and that will not be easy to fix on the move."

"We need a functioning shop to get him out of it and fast," Stigg said, his armored gauntlet rubbing the chin line of the suit's protective helmet. "The armory at Warbler is close."

Anzil was thankful his visor hid the surprise showing on his face. "Warbler Ridge's armory is supposed to be a close-to-the-vest kind of place."

"No time for that."

"You never cease to amaze me, Chief. Shall we get moving, then? We must get to my brother and figure out our next move."

"Give me something to fly Clarke there ahead of you."

"Our best are working on it," Anzil said, trying to project his most confident self. "I understand you two are close."

"I see to Clarke," Stigg said, leaving no room for argument.

"Understood," Anzil replied.

"We should also see about getting the armory up and running," Stigg said, "see if we can't kick-start some of the older stock up there."

"That's what I was hoping you'd say, Chief," Anzil said, gripping Stigg's shoulder. He followed the man's gaze back up the valley to the cave entrance and wondered what heavy thoughts the old veteran carried. "I could really use your help on this one, and not as a mechanic."

"That's not meant for discussion, eh?"

His father had told him what little Anzil knew of Stigg beyond his guarded persona. Anzil wouldn't have said Trake feared Stigg. One memorable evening, the older Khilsyth dropped his defenses and confessed two items to his eldest son in the strictest of confidence: one, that he would never want to be on the wrong side of Stigg's honor, and two, that he needed to find Stigg when it all went sideways. The warning still haunted him as his father had held him tight and told him he would know when that was, and Anzil knew his father had wanted to say more.

"Incoming!" a soldier shouted. "Acquired inbound ship of unknown origin!"

"What type of ship?" Anzil asked in a measured tone.

"Definitely interstellar, sir. No reported identification. It's masked."

The ship appeared on Anzil's heads-up display, its course vectoring toward them. "Why would a lone ship be heading our way?"

"It could be coming to pick up the recon unit we just decimated," Deek replied.

"Maybe, but I think it's something else," Anzil said quietly.

"Anzil, did you see any ships depositing armor or just javelins?" Stigg asked.

"Javelin's only, so far as we know," Deek answered.

"Right, hold your fire," Stigg directed.

"You sure?" Anzil asked. "Defensive positions for overhead contact people. You heard the Chief. Do not engage. Yet."

"Stigg," Auralei called over the secure battlenet. "Are you down there?"

"I'm here, lass," Stigg replied. "You've got some fancy gadgets in that ship if you're talking to us."

"Where's Clarke?" Auralei asked.

"Clarke's down," Anzil replied, "near our position."

With its swept forward wing design, the interstellar craft swooped in low over the treetops and set down, blasting the assembled group with debris. Auralei slipped out before the cargo bay ramp opened fully, ignoring the two armor-clad dragoons moving to intercept her, and vanished. She reappeared next to Clarke.

Anzil ordered Deek to form a defensive perimeter, which she relayed was already underway and then switched to a private channel with Stigg. "What the hell, Chief? You making arrangements with the Republic now?"

"Not quite, young Khilsyth," Auralei's sultry voice broke through the encryption.

"You've got some explaining to do, Stigg," Anzil said.

"Is she on our side," Stigg said, keeping his inflections even, "I'm not completely sure. But we are going to need her to deal with the peskier Anacul."

"Anacul?" Auralei asked. "Explain Stigg."

"You mean you don't know?" Stigg asked.

"Stigg Anundr," Auralei said.

"Ask Clarke," Stigg replied, recognizing the edge to her voice. "He tangled with one. And yes, I sensed them underground and something out here too."

"Where?" Auralei asked, promptly checking a device she produced from her chest pocket.

Stigg sighed. "Unsure. But Clarke killed one."

"Stigg, you were supposed to protect him," Auralei said, resting clenched fists on her hips. "Means there are more, correct?"

"I would say that it does," Stigg replied. "But relax... He's still alive, isn't he?"

"Wait!" Anzil called in a warning to the woman as she kneeled beside the armor. "I wouldn't touch it. Gives a nasty little shock. Router over there got zapped so bad he made a mess of himself."

Auralei placed her hands on the armor. "I believe he's still alive. Gods help you, Stigg if he isn't." She stood and brushed the dirt from her slender, gloved hands. "Interesting. I think the armor leached the energy from your dragoon."

"Is he safe for us to touch?" Anzil asked, wondering why she was so fixated on Clarke.

"Hope so," Auralei responded. "Those energy cells I attached will keep the suit busy. Now, if you two would be so kind, I'm going to need your brawn getting him in my ship."

"Your ship," Anzil said. "I don't think so. He's coming with us."

Auralei turned to face Anzil, her eyes narrowing over the top of her scarf. "Listen, don't let your pride make a fool of yourself here."

"Actually, lass," Stigg interjected to deflect the *Mischi's* attention from Anzil. "The lad stays with me."

"Fine, Stigg," Auralei said with a wink, "you can come too."

Stigg shook his head. "That's not what I meant. I'm staying here on Lindaulx until we resolve this little situation."

"Little situation," Auralei said calmly. "Look around, Stigg. Little situation is a wee bit of an understatement. This is a bloody invasion—a purge, perhaps."

Watching Stigg and the woman stare silently at each other was unsettling, but the slight quiver of her lips, the way she moved her head and shifted her weight gingerly made Anzil think she was communicating with Stigg.

"Fine," Auralei said, breaking the silence, "I'll help. But then you are honor-bound."

"I cannot."

Auralei cocked her head to the side, her mouth hanging slightly open. She cleared her throat, tilted her head to the other side, and raised a sharp eyebrow. "Why not, Stigg?"

"You're too late."

Auralei removed her gloves by loosening a digit at a time, tucked them into her pockets, and squeezed the back of her neck. "How did I not put this together?" She crouched and poked her plum-red fingernail into the dirt. "You're somehow bound to Clarke. Which means you've known about me for a while then, haven't you?"

"I had my suspicions, lass. I wasn't sure of your interests or motives. That... And I just didn't know it was *you*."

"Honest?" Auralei asked, her eyes softening.

Stigg nodded.

"You mean you two know each other?" Anzil asked, flicking his finger back and forth between them. A glance from the woman stopped the stream of questions.

"Stigg," Auralei said, "whatever is going on here is not going to be good, and it's much bigger than Lindaulx," She peered up at Anzil. "Young Khilsyth, consider the risk to your friends by letting them play the foolish heroes. Lindaulx is lost."

"What do you want with Clarke?" Stigg asked. "What's his role in this?"

Auralei chuckled and adjusted the bracelet around her wrist. "Come on, Stigg. You know this story. A girl has a career with the Republic, which is very fulfilling and successful. Then, she reaches a point in her life where she wants to settle down and repair the fragmented memories of her past. Those pieces *they* worked so hard to eradicate."

"Only *they* never let you leave," Stigg said, biting the words as they passed his lips, "and *they* never want you to remember. By the way... that bracelet. Where did you get it?"

Auralei tugged her jacket sleeve down to hide it from view. "It was a gift."

"From?" Stigg pressed.

"Does it matter?"

"It might. I think I've seen it before."

"Where?"

"Where do you think?" Stigg said with a sigh.

Auralei inspected her feet as she tapped her toes. "I believe Clarke gave it to me."

"How would Clarke—"

"Are you Ellane?" Anzil interrupted, ignoring the shake of her head. "Seriously? All this time, Clarke was chasing a bloody Republic specter."

Stigg cleared his throat, "as his friend, Anzil, the word is mum about all this until she says otherwise. Got it!"

Anzil flashed Stigg a pained look. "You trust her, eh?! And you think here is more dangerous compared to going with her." He bit the inside of his cheek to steady his nerves.

"If not from Clarke, then who?" Auralei asked.

"Last I saw it," Stigg said, "Constance was wearing it."

"I had an Aunt Constance," Anzil replied.

"That you did," Stigg said with a gentle laugh and a knowing wink. "That you bloody well did."

"Piss off," Anzil said incredulously. "Clarke doesn't know about the Nova Republic's interest in him, does he?" There was nothing sinister or disingenuous about Clarke that Anzil knew of—Clarke was also such a terrible liar that he wouldn't have been able to keep this kind of secret from Anzil.

"Mum on that as well, young Khilsyth," Stigg said.

"I'm starting to think it's more of a disassociation," Auralei said. She consulted a device she pulled from her satchel before hastily putting it away. "Earthquake. We need to move. Now."

On the hillsides above them, avalanches formed and grew more prominent as they slipped down the slopes, sending snow and boulders crashing across the far side of the meadow.

"To your ship?" Anzil asked.

The ground shook as if rebuking his question, sending a cascade of rocks dangerously close to them. Shortly thereafter, it heaved again, tossing them about like a small raft in rough waters.

Regaining his footing, Stigg commanded the group. "Time to move. Not much time before another shake."

"Agreed," Anzil replied.

Anzil scooped the armor containing Clarke into his mechanical arms and deposited it on the aft ramp of Auralei's ship. He secured it with a winch's tether and punched the ramp retract button. He attached his dragoon armor and met Stigg on board. "What the hell kind of ship is this, Stigg?"

"It's an Osprey Interceptor if memory serves," Stigg said, not taking his eyes off the ship-controlled crane maneuvering the limp armor. "Favored by infiltrators, pirates, and smugglers alike. Those onboard armors, their ghosts. We'll have to borrow them." After Clarke was secure in the cargo bay, Stigg shuffled over to a bank of screens and started waving his hands in front of them. Odd shapes and words jostled about, responding to his movements.

"Why don't you make yourself right at home," Auralei chided as she appeared through a lower hatch.

"You mind telling me how you obtained those armors?" Stigg asked. "Let alone this ship."

The sprightly woman gave Stigg a gentle jab to his shoulder and flashed a toothy smile as she strode past. "Wouldn't you like to know?"

It was the first time Anzil had seen her with her mask off. She was younger than he would have guessed. Her skin was pale and flawless, and her ears had a slight point to them—nothing crazy, just a soft little point. She turned and flashed him a devilish smile that warmed his cheeks. It was her eyes that betrayed her years of experience.

"These ships garner attention if spotted, and not a welcoming kind of attention," Stigg warned.

"Then we'll work super hard on being stealthy," Auralei said, disappearing through an upper hatch toward the cockpit area.

Seconds later, the craft roared to life, achieved flight, and circled high over the alpine meadow. From a port-side viewing area, Anzil surveyed the destruction below. Large shafts of basaltic rock were forcing their way to the surface, breaking off and crashing down the mountainsides. Steam rolled out of fissures that widened to emit superheated rock, setting the area ablaze.

"Sensors report several events clustered around the Astute facility," Auralei said over the ship's comms.

"Do you think it was a facility defense mechanism?" Anzil asked.

Stigg shook his head. "No. I think it was the Anacul. That suspiciously resembles terra forming."

"Doesn't make sense," Anzil responded. "Why destroy it?"

"To keep it bloody well buried," Stigg said.

"Or they got what they came for," Auralei added.

"Can't believe this was here all along," Anzil muttered, watching in relief as his soldiers made their way to safety.

CHAPTER 13

THE FLIGHT TO Warbler Ridge was uneventful, and the storm pressing into the alpine forests and boulder fields of the Esconairian mountain range obstructed much of the view. Anzil watched a display of the invading forces gathering south of Fort Skyetook with a report in a language he didn't recognize. He said a quick prayer for the innocent people just trying to exist.

The ship banked hard and carried them under the clouds, skimming over a wide-open field flanked by jagged rocky spines jutting from the valley ridges. People familiar with this part of Warbler Ridge affectionately called it the Maw, which was swarming with forces being marshaled inside. At the same time, mechanics and their security details hurried to check the defenses along the ridge's spines. Legend held that Warbler Khilsyth, the first clan chief to colonize Lindaulx, carved Warbler Ridge with the aid of the divines.

Anzil directed them to a portal section away from the main gate, which presently hung open on a vertical hinge. As they approached the area, a flight controller emerged and signaled, showing it was available for arrivals. Once through the gate, the ship touched down, and an odd assemblage of mechanics, engineers, and medics—distinguishable by the color of their outfits—hurried to meet the ship.

Auralei was first out of the rear hatch, then Anzil carrying Clarke. "He's alive in there," she said, sounding hopeful, and directed those nearby to supply the armor to a steady power source. It had bled dry everything she had strapped to it, and Shifty theorized it was part of a self-repair process. "Where will they take him?" she asked Anzil.

"To a quiet part of the infirmary. I'll assign my best people, and they'll be discreet." Anzil eyed the woman as she weighed his words and was relieved when she finally consented. "Okay, now with me if you all would." He led them deeper into Warbler Ridge, climbing a series of switchback ramps and heading to a room where he had asked his remaining advisors to assemble. Along the way, he had assured Stigg that even though the group of folks may appear disheveled, they were the few he could trust.

The meeting room was devoid of the grandeur that once adorned the walls, and an old wooden workbench from a nearby mechanic's bay now served as the conference table. A digital terrain model showing the area around the City of Skyetook was flickering on the table, the top punctuated with dried mechanical fluid. The projection also included Hindish Pass to the city's southeast since it would be the most manageable route to the wastelands beyond. The team had decided this was where help could come from and assigned drones to provide overwatch of the area. Projected on the walls were various unit status updates and maps. Still, the primary attention was on Warbler and Willows Ridge and the proximity of the sizable invader force that had originated from Skyetook.

Anzil picked up a tablet and bladed through a few reports that were predicting the invaders would arrive in approximately three hours. The dense old growth of the Bercelium Forest below the ridges and their unfamiliarity with the old pathways through it were giving the enemy some trouble. Scouting units were also aloft on wyverns and circling closer and closer to test the range of Warbler Ridge's defensive cannons. At the same time, an advanced enemy army harassed the straggling forces destined for the Maw. Unfortunately, some of the more competent enemy units refused to leave the protection of the tree line, preferring cover overhead instead of the barren approach to the front gate. All in all, he had a bleak prognosis for his people.

A nervous and oil-stained soldier moved closer and whispered in his ear, telling him everyone was there as requested. Anzil nodded and dismissed the young lieutenant. Two of the seats at the make-shift war council table were empty. His friends were dead or would fight against him in the days to come. He caught Stigg's gaze and mimicked the giant of a man's slight inclination of his head. Out of respect, Anzil permitted Stigg to join the discussions and begrudgingly admitted the specter at the grizzled veteran's behest. His knowledge of specters amounted to little more than tall tales, making him cautious, but he respected the woman's prowess and equipment. Her absence from the fighting at Hurricane Ridge was convenient, and her involvement in the events preceding the invasion was suspect—something he would need to press Stigg for accounts of later, confident he would receive neither.

Anzil requested everyone to take a seat at the table, motioning for Stigg and the specter to take the empty seats. He took the responsibility of directing House Khilsyth's military operations seriously. Typically, only a few battalions protected remote colonies such as Lindaulx, meaning a leader had to be cunning to be effective. And now he had less than a third of his soldiers. Most of the other folks that arrived at Warbler Ridge were hardy but not warriors. As his unit commanders settled, a sense of pride and comfort helped reduce the ringing in his ears—just one of the symptoms betraying his stress. His team had never disappointed him in their ingenuity to develop strategies, and this was far from the first bloody engagement they had seen together. He wondered how they would adjust to the extent of internal betrayal and infiltration they experienced, knowing that some of their playbooks for battle strategies would need to be changed or even rewritten— and how would they deal with the mental fortitude required to shoot someone they once knew as a friend and neighbor? "Let's start with Captain Deek. Unit updates, field-ready status, and pertinent info."

Captain Deek stood formally and provided the status of the military units, civilian contingent, and Warbler Ridge's defensive and offensive operational situation. She also offered some welcomed news that the older stockpiled equipment was being limped back to life. When finished, she sat carefully in her chair, straining against the weight of the ammunition and gear filling her vest. She sought further direction from Anzil. The man was straining to remain stoic. She knew his tells all too well, and her augments also detected a slight eye twitch and a quicker breathing cadence than usual for the man. He would be partially listening but mostly in his head, continually churning through scenarios and probability outcomes for the challenge his diminished forces would face in the upcoming days—the others would have heard a shred of hope in her assessment. Concurrently, Anzil saw the pieces he would use to build his strategy.

Anzil smiled at Deek and was glad she was on his side; Deek was a vicious and dedicated soldier with the complete respect of her troop. If the invaders had swayed Deek to change allegiance, he would have lost most of *his* dragoons and would have considered joining her. "Any other intel from Skyetook yet? I want to get an understanding of what the invaders captured."

Lieutenant Farsil stood and let out a tremendous sigh. "We have some flyers with wyverns, sir," his voice cracking. "They were on a training mission when the invasion began. Luckily, they could evacuate some people and supplies from nearby depots. I'm sorry, but we could not liberate more wyverns. Intel from Skyetook is unreliable." Farsil dropped into his seat, his pale cheeks turning a faint shade of pink.

Anzil smiled warmly. Farsil was a humble and meek kid. "How many flyers do you have, Lieutenant Farsil?"

Farsil jumped from his seat, "ah... nearly a hundred, sir."

Stigg cleared his throat, drawing attention away from Farsil. "Some wyverns might have made it out of the aviary back near Hurricane Ridge."

"Good point," Anzil said to Stigg. Almost a hundred flyers meant that practically all of them were accounted for—the airborne stick together. "Farsil. They'd be a little wild. Would that be a problem?"

Tiny beads of sweat formed on the sides of Farsil's nose, and his back straightened considerably. "Aviary near here, sir? Really?"

"What do you think of sending some of your wyverns on a patrol near our rendezvous point with Stigg at Hurricane Ridge?" Anzil asked. "It would be nice to bolster our air cav."

Lieutenant Farsil nodded weakly, swallowing hard. "From a wild aviary, sir." He stood, bowed awkwardly to the assemblage, and exited posthaste.

"Eager that one," Truul said, receiving scattered laughs and a disapproving glance from Anzil. "Sorry, sir."

The rest of the tactical debrief concerned the civilian populace, living conditions, and non-military elements at Warbler Ridge, which Anzil half-listened to patiently. He was grateful when Deek raised her hand to gain the attention of all assembled members and break up the side conversations.

"Couple of data points, if you would?" Deek asked. "What do we know about the machine transported here? The smaller dragoon platform that battled... something? And who is Stigg's lady friend?"

"We don't have much information about the machine," Anzil said. He struggled to form words his team would not laugh at or think him crazy for uttering. Anacul and the specter were things of fiction with exaggerated abilities to scare children or to rationalize the unexplainable that came with seeing beyond the existing world's veil. He wondered how you would explain creatures who manipulate the ethereal forces of the flux. The tales did not justify what he had witnessed on Hurricane Ridge. And now, that fiction would soon knock at Warbler Ridge's main gate. It was discomforting. "Clarke was the armor's pilot. He's a mechanic with the four-naught-three. Recently, someone kidnapped Clarke and Stigg, and they escaped with the help of this woman." Anzil nodded toward the specter, who sat unflinching. *Perhaps not breathing*, he wondered.

"Was that after Clarke killed Lord Khilsyth?" Fitz asked angrily.

Anzil raised his hand to quell the dull roar of speculation and mistruths spurred by the mention of his father's name. Failing, he addressed the crowd forcefully. "That's the last of such talk, Lieutenant Fitz!" He waited patiently for silence. "Same goes for the rest of you." Again, he let his team appreciate his authority in the silence. "Clarke was the victim of a well-crafted ruse—a decoy. And we're not sure of the significance. But we are working on who is behind it. What I need from you all is strategies on how we will deliver justice. Understood?" All the Khilsyth commanders traced Anzil's line of sight, which had inadvertently drifted to the specter. Recognizing his error, Anzil diverted his gaze to the war table; the stale air was suddenly noticeably warmer, as was the moistness of his forehead and neck. "This woman helped Stigg and Clarke escape. Stigg vouches for her. That works for me."

Stigg bowed his head and took a deep breath. "The alien armor was damaged after battling an Anacul Champion. Our pilot sent that ruined soul back to the damnation it came from. We haven't been able to free the pilot from the armor."

"Wait, wait, wait," Deek said in a rush, "alien armor? Anacul Champion? What in all that's holy are you talking about, Stigg? What *alien* armor?"

Anzil draped his arm around Deek, hoping to help reassure her. "Clarke wore that armor out of the Astute facility. As you all saw, it's a lightweight mechanized armor." The room was silent except for the shuffling of feet, clearing of throats, and minor seat adjustments.

Stigg spoke in the most comforting tone he could manage. "Clarke thought it would be a good idea to try it on since we've never seen a suit that compact. I know you all have questions. We will get to them in time once *we* have answers. For now, understand that the Anacul Champions aren't alone. It's also been a long time since I've felt one as powerful as the one killed today."

"Not comforting, Stigg," Lieutenant Fitz said. "Who's with them?"

"The wretches," Stigg said flatly. "*Dreaders.*"

"Also not comforting," Lieutenant Fitz replied. "Considering most of us thought of them as fairy tales."

"Honestly," Stigg said as he stood, "most only do mediocre type stuff. More annoying, really, and not usually deadly. Except for their weapons, naturally."

Deek leaned against Anzil. "So, this woman is with you, Stigg?" she asked, turning to face the specter. "Are you Anacul?"

Everyone's attention returned to Auralei, but no one except Deek dared to meet her eyes. Auralei sniffed. "My advice," she said, shaking her head back and forth, "is that we leave the quality of my soul out of this discussion."

"What?" Deek pressed, annoyed. "Are you with the invaders? What are you really here for?"

Auralei gave Deek a whimsical smile. "All wonderful questions, young forerunner, some of which I wish I knew myself."

Deek stood, shaking Anzil's hand away. "I know you, specter. "

Auralei laughed. "You don't *know* me."

Stigg brought his hands down hard on the table, startling everyone. "All you need to understand is that the bastards have *Dreaders,* and they usually don't make themselves known right away. They are real, and so are *Mischi*—what you call specters. Most of the stories you've heard are false. Just keep an eye out. When one rears its ugly self, and it's not friendly, I suggest suppressing fire. Get to it as a team. Kill it as a team. Trust me. They bleed. The rest of the battle is just like every other one you've been in or trained for. As for the girl, she's helping us. She's a badass. Be grateful. End of discussion."

"And if we meet another champion or whatever you called it?" Lieutenant Duncan asked.

"Same tactic as for *Dreaders,*" Stigg replied. "Only take two or three teams for good measure."

"Has there been any word from the other houses?" Anzil asked, intervening, hoping to redirect the conversation.

Farsil stepped forward. "Our aerial recon units have verified the invaders decimated House Lanal. Mass graveyards are being crudely constructed, and most of the outlying villages and the principal city are burning."

Anzil hadn't noticed Farsil sneak back into the room. House Lanal was a minor House with a small community on Lindaulx with limited military strength and no port facilities for interstellar travel. Their primary operations were agriculture and manufacturing.

Occasionally, they relied on the protection from House Khilsyth against larger pirate forces. Anzil wondered if this was because even pillagers came to the same conclusion as him—low resistance. But as survivors in remote colonies and vagabonds understood, everyone had something worth trading, looting, or scavenging. He sighed heavily, knowing they would have called on them for protection.

"Survivors?" Lieutenant Tristan asked.

"Yes, right, of course," Farsil said as he took a seat. "We contacted survivors who fled into the nearby canyons. The invaders did not pursue them." He removed his wool scarf and dabbed his forehead. "It's probably because they had no aerial support. We circled House Nihkiehl but were told to leave, or they would consider us hostile. From what we could tell, the Nihkiehls had successfully shot some enemy javelins from the sky."

"Impressive," Deek said quietly. "Not an easy feat."

House Nihkiehl, Anzil thought with a silent laugh. A Clan with an unknown military might but expected to be significant. There was evidence of interstellar vessel activity in their airspace, but it was unconfirmed, as were the origins and destinations of any of those ships. Their primary operations on Lindaulx were unknown outside of being annoying to the Khilsyths, and they were suspected to be a high-value target with confirmed high resistance.

"We even sent a smaller detachment out over the desert trying to find the Tallus Outpost, but no one answered," Farsil concluded.

Lindaulx's inhabitants knew little about the people or things living in the Tallus Outpost. Their commodities were some of the best augmentations and highly sought-after jewelry sold at off-world bazaars and exported through the Khilsyth's spaceport. This meant it was subject to tariffs that helped keep the coffers full, even if they didn't have a complete manifest for each shipment.

"Also, sir," Kaibab said, "we've established a secure net and have patched all our communications over to the new frequencies. We even established two-way tactical comms with the Lanal survivors and the Nihkiehls. We think we received a 'squawk' response from Tallus Outpost. Someone out there is listening, which is quite exciting, actually."

"Thank you, Farsil and Kaibab," Anzil said, impressed with his commander's initiative and relieved that at least some potential allies were communicating in their reserved way. He was also glad to be rid of the drone of the invader's messages playing everywhere and having the same theme: *join us and live, remain a traitor, and die.*

"Does everyone have the information they need to develop an operational strategy?" Anzil asked, watching as his comrades all nodded in agreement. "Fantastic. Time is running short, folks. I have three objectives." He counted on his fingers for emphasis. "One: multi-pronged attack on the main Khilsyth fortress. We need control of the Command and Ops Centers. Two: take Port Forge and get the word of the invasion out. Three: unify the Houses on Lindaulx. I will handle the third objective. We'll need the strength of an alliance to see this one through. Plus, a few thousand more rifles couldn't hurt. We'll need to assemble on the move. So, develop a rolling solution. I'll leave you to it and will be back to vet solutions. I have some business with our new friends and want to check on Clarke." Everyone nodded their understanding and stood with Anzil. "The next few days are going to test our mettle," he said solemnly. "We will fight people we may have called friends. They may not hesitate to shoot at us. So, shoot first and shoot straight. We'll see each other through this and back again, like always. Keep your units ready. Get creative about how to resupply and stay in touch over the secure network Kaibab's unit has established."

The room erupted into a chorus of '*Yes, sir.*'

Anzil motioned to Stigg and the specter and led them into a smaller room further into the facility. "Close the door, Stigg," Anzil requested and turned his attention to the woman. "First, I apologize but haven't caught your name yet."

"No worries," Auralei replied.

"It wasn't part of the original deal," Anzil said after an uncomfortably long pause, "but we could really use your help. And your ship."

Auralei's head fell forward, the points of her mahogany bangs falling together to form a point. "Whatever you require, my liege," she teased.

Anzil's commanders wouldn't have calculated her into the equation, probably assuming the woman was bound to be off the planet shortly. "This next part involves you two; we need to keep it secret," he said. "I'm not completely confident about who we can trust. More than a dozen people in our leadership structure have already defected. I guess they prefer the future the invaders are broadcasting over what our version of salvation is heading towards."

"Sir!" a soldier said, bursting into the room. "Sorry, sir. An unidentified craft just revealed itself near the upper aviary gate and is requesting permission to dock. The pilot refused to give a name. But sir... she says she's your... sir, your Republic mistress."

Anzil flashed the specter a look that conveyed she'd better have a plan for handling this or come up with something quick.

Auralei smiled sweetly back at Anzil and flipped her head toward the door. *If it is Tarra, she'd better have a damn good reason for being here,* she thought.

CHAPTER 14

THE FEW TROOPS greeting the newly arrived ship were familiar with accounts of how dangerous the Nova Republic was, and the ship was anything but subtle in its classification as a warship. Their fingers caressed the triggers of their loaded weapons. *It's a recipe for disaster,* Auralei thought. Some of the Khilsyth soldiers were even in their armor. The loud slap of rugged soles on stone shifted her attention to the well-armed soldiers hustling someone through the main entrance and toward a sequestered side room. There was no pomp and pageantry at Warbler Ridge these days.

"You ready?" Stigg asked.

Stigg's origins confused Auralei. Her research had turned up mundane information void of any sign of the tactical and physical prowess he'd shown recently, let alone his knowledge of the Anacul and Tersinians. Somewhere in his life, Stigg had received excellent combat training. Given more time to observe him, she might whittle down the list of places where he could have been taught to fight. Regardless, someone close to him was superbly influential to have manicured his records to the point that her contacts, even Shifty, couldn't find anything of substance. "After you, *Chief*."

Anzil directed everyone into the room, instructed his guard detail to remain outside, and closed the doors behind him. He took a seat at the head of a makeshift table hastily constructed from steel work benches. The sweet smell of old petrol fumes leaked from the walls, giving the room a glistening sheen. "Anyone care to join me here at this lovely table?"

No one moved except Tarra, who dipped her head, greeting Auralei. "They betrayed us," she said in Lurish, unable to stem the blend of anger and panic creeping into her voice.

Auralei responded in kind. "Go on." It would be good to have a quick discussion without Anzil understanding them. She was also confident that if someone were recording them, the Lurish language would be so abstractly built by Shifty that it would be nearly impossible to decipher. And she reckoned she was screwed if either Shifty or Tarra were her betrayers.

"We need to get the hell off this rock," Tarra said, uncharacteristically frantic for a moment. "They've taken over the Mar-Vhen. There's a bloody blockade, and the damn houses are turning on each other."

Auralei raised her hands in a calming gesture, watching Tarra's dilated pupils constrict. There was more to the story if something spooked Tarra. "We need to be rational and develop a tactical strategy. You'll have to tell me a bit more to gain my trust."

Anzil cleared his throat. "Ladies, we would appreciate a translation."

"In a common Lindaulx dialect," Auralei directed Tarra. "For our host."

"You trust them?" Tarra asked.

Auralei tucked a stray strand of hair back into place. It was a tremendous leap of faith throwing her lot in with House Khilsyth, considering her employers may also be after Anzil. She stifled a laugh and corrected herself that it would be her ex-employers, given recent events.

The wooden legs of an old chair jittered across the worn stone floor as Tarra dragged it next to Anzil. She parked her butt on the table and rested her feet on the deflated seat cushion. "After I parted ways with Ms. Princess here," she said with a half-hearted smile and nod toward Auralei. "I made it to the surface. There were patrols along the way made up of House Khilsyth soldiers and invaders—"

"Seriously?" Anzil interrupted. "You two are working together?"

"By parting ways, you mean she let you go?" Stigg asked, pointing at the woman standing beside him.

"Sort of," Tarra said.

"Sort of," Auralei echoed with a rapid teeter-tottering motion of an outstretched hand.

Both men flashed questioning looks at each other.

"Shall I continue?" Tarra asked, pausing as Auralei unloaded a rectangular device the size of her fists from her backpack and turned it on. She abruptly stilled the vibrating warning devices on her wrist as Auralei did the same. "Unnerving." She set a smaller fingernail-sized device on the table. "Nowhere to hide and nothing to hear. As I was saying. Luckily, no specters were accompanying the patrols. I avoided most of them, except for the young lads hiding in ambush near my ship. I'm still trying to figure out how they stumbled across it. It wasn't you, princess, was it? Sentencing those poor bastards to death." Confident it wasn't Auralei, she continued. "I gave them a little surprise and then left this rock. When I broke through into orbit, imagine my surprise at being greeted by the open and not-so-loving arms of a planetary blockade. Turns out mom and pop showed up to check on us." Seeing Anzil's cute and confused glance, she added, "that's the Nova Republic, sweety." She rolled her head leisurely from one side to the other and back to the middle. "I picked up some panicked radio chatter that Mar-Vhen-IV was under attack and tried to reach our contact with the Mar. They used the incorrect response protocol, and a blockade ship got a few lucky shots off, damaging Our Lady Majestic—my ship. I'm guessing there was a ROG agent or drone on board. It's the only way they would have been that lucky."

"You have traitors in your midst as well?" Anzil asked, shaking his head in disapproval.

Tarra giggled quietly and smiled at Anzil the way she would a waif who had been caught trying to steal something from her—she admired the courage but was disgusted by the failure. "The Resource Operation Group," she said, writing the first letter of each word on his shirt sleeve. "Anyway. Back on this ass of a planet, I ambushed a recon patrol that came to investigate my stellar landing, and I convinced them to leave me alone." Tarra stroked the hilt of her swords lovingly. "So, here I am. At your service."

Auralei believed there was some truth in Tarra's story as she hadn't received a response from the Mar-Vhen-IV transit station either. There were also reports of strange escort ships from those who left Lindaulx—the world spaces anyone leaving could travel were controlled. "What you really meant to say is that you didn't have a fallback plan, and now you need my help to get your scrawny ass off this rock," she said, disrupting the lulling effect Tarra's sweet voice was having on Anzil and perhaps Stigg.

"There's more to it than that," Tarra said, pleading with Auralei. "Who would betray us? At least, I feel like I was. Dammit, lady. You must know something."

Auralei caught a faint whisper of disbelief in Tarra's facial expression—a slight narrowing of her eyes and twitch of her lower left lip—tells that she was speaking the truth, if only partially. Tarra seemed desperate and appeared to have achieved a similar conclusion as her—there was more to this invasion than a simple regicide and redistribution of lands. "I'm afraid I agree with you. Something's off. We can't wait this one out here. But we need more information. Tell me more about your contracts."

"Ha," Tarra mocked. "Are you crazy? You know I can't."

"What's the alternative?" Auralei asked. "Staying hidden or blending in with the locals sounds like a helluva plan."

"No need to oversell it," Tarra said. "It's against bloody protocols."

"Then you'll have to bring me in on the contract," Auralei said with a laugh. "Not that it really matters now."

"Are you serious?" Tarra asked, leaning in closer to her old roommate.

"Yes, your second contract, out with it," Auralei said, perhaps a little too menacingly. "What's your objective with Clarke?"

"Excuse me, ladies," Anzil said with an edge in his voice. "What contracts and protocols are you talking about?"

Tarra rose gracefully from the table, half facing Anzil. "It looks like they entwined our futures, young prince. Bonded to one another, whether I like it or not."

"That still doesn't tell me anything," Anzil said.

"Somehow," Tarra said, moving behind Anzil and resting her hands on his shoulders, "the holder of a contract, a device powerful people use to enact our assistance, concealed the true nature of their plan. In its entirety, no less, from both of us and, perchance, ROG. And that's beyond extremely difficult to do." Tarra took a deep breath and paced around the table while continuing. "Rather, it's impossible to do. It also means, with a high degree of utter chaos, that both factions are in the dark on this one, doesn't it, chicky?"

"What factions?" Anzil asked eagerly. "And what or who is ROG?"

Auralei snickered and nodded in agreement with Tarra, who stopped behind Anzil and pinched his neck. Tarra likely hadn't appreciated the interjection, and based on Anzil's tenseness, the man was anxious about having Tarra behind him. Yet, Auralei sensed Anzil was comforted by Tarra's touch. The intoxicating aroma of wildflowers played with Auralei's enhanced olfactory receptors. She wondered for what purpose Tarra was trying to embrace the flux.

"The Interstellar Resource Operations Group," Stigg offered matter-of-factly. "Or, as these ladies are referring to it, ROG."

"Why not just say the R-O-G?" Anzil asked.

Stigg laughed hard. "Not nearly as scary, is it?"

"Having a wee laugh, gents?" Auralei asked calmly. "Out of all of this, that's what you latched onto?"

"Just think of it like this," Stigg said, ignoring the woman. "They want people to—" he paused for effect, enjoying the annoyance in the *Mischi's* glare, and then raised his voice. "Run for the bloody hills!"

"Focus, lads," Auralei said. "You sure you want to make fun of the Republic at a time like this?"

"But what the hell is ROG?" Anzil asked. "Some secret division of the Nova Republic that, what, houses specters? The boogeymen."

Stigg pursed his lips and nodded at Anzil.

Tarra cleared her throat forcefully. "You two finished. And it's all things scary. Specter is fine. *Mischi* is ancient and archaic, like Stigg. And we come in a flavorful array." She pulled on the securing straps of her sword belt, ensuring they were snug. "Now listen! They intended the first contract to restore the honor of an old society that first laid claim to Lindaulx. None other than—" She tapped Anzil on the shoulders for an answer.

"House Vartiss?" Anzil asked.

Tarra shook Anzil's head, showing it was not the sought-after answer. She tilted his head so their eyes met. "Vartiss was a good guess—a powerful House back in the day, but not this system. You studied your apparent history. This goes further back. Way back to the Tersinians. They were the first to claim Tervessi—now Lindaulx—as a sanctuary."

Auralei flashed Tarra a narrow-eyed challenge: "I don't recall hearing about the Tersinians occupying this sector, ever, or their *Tersa*."

Anzil clenched his fist and drew a deep breath in through his nose. "Dammit. You two are dodgy."

"We were taught the Tersinians are a flux-born race," Auralei said with a sneer. "Their *Tersa* are… they are like *us*."

"Known civilization, including the Nova Republic, has never recorded a homeworld for them," Tarra said.

"A fact the Tersinians likely propagated," Stigg added.

"Honestly, we understand little about them," Auralei said. "The Academy glossed over them in our historical events classes, especially the warfare courses. From what I remember, they believed the *Tersa* abhorred technological integration, such as bionics and augments." She rubbed both of her forearms out of habit, but her internal systems had quashed any real sense of a chill. "They believed it a perversion and degradation of one's life essence. The general population could be a different story. But *Mischi*, *Dreaders*, and *Tersa* are more similar than we'd all like to admit."

"Great," Anzil said sarcastically. "But the Republic and it's what, factions; the Tersinians; now the Anacul; and the Astutes. What in the bloody hell is going on here?"

"Harmony," Auralei responded. "At least to the Republic, who is concerned about how we all fit into this lovely universe of ours."

"I've heard the stories," Stigg said. "ROG also has its own self-serving interests. Harmonic resolution, my ass."

"I haven't," Anzil said, annoyed.

"The Nova Republic has existed for thousands of years," Auralei said. "Potentially longer. It will continue to do so with its collective of groups and organizations within each culture seeking a sense of equality long after we're gone."

"Think shadow government," Stigg said. "On a galactic scale."

"Each culture?" Anzil asked. "Like everywhere?"

"More or less," Tarra replied, squeezing Anzil's shoulder again. "When discovered, all cultures and their races, or what have you, are allotted time to adapt and a given choice for how to integrate into the universe to achieve a position of harmonic balance. Within each culture, the Republic puts a mechanism in place to maintain equilibrium." Tarra could tell her words would have shaken the very core of what Anzil thought. She had quickly shattered his understanding of the organizational structure of the universe, but his shock held him at bay from bombarding her with questions, at least for now. "This is at the heart of ROG's mission. For the here and now, ROG and its specters are tools of sorts. ROG places representatives from the political clandestine Order within major places of power. Their purpose is to keep a balance within cultures such as yours."

"Spies," Stigg said, spitting the word out.

"As I was saying," Tarra said with a quick, narrow-eyed glance at Stigg. "Each culture has a mechanism to ensure we maintain our course. Except for the Tersinians. Because nobody seems to know a damned thing about them. Recluses perhaps. Good at hiding. Persecuted."

"Welcome to peering through the wormhole," Stigg half-heartedly said as he intently watched a nearby data screen.

"What's interesting, Stigg," Anzil said, meeting his Chief Mechanic's gaze. "Is your apparent working knowledge of all this and your comfort with it."

"Quite," Tarra blurted, "but before we delve into Stigg's past, the Republic is obviously involved here. They either thought a handover of Lindaulx to the Tersinians would bring about balance, or someone duped them."

"And the factions within ROG?" Anzil asked.

"Pro Vanguard or not," Tarra replied, eyeing Stigg for a reaction. "Nothing, eh! Come now, you old goat."

Stigg shook his head. "I imagine this is a lot to absorb. But *Mischi* are not fairy tales. There is a part of the Republic that you wish didn't exist. And once you learn about it, you want to unlearn it."

Auralei sighed, "I'm sorry, Anzil. I really am. Sometimes, the checks and balances lag. From what I can tell, they fed the Republic erroneous information about the evolution of the cultures in this sector. Truth is—"

"Seriously," Anzil interjected. "We summoned the bloody Nova Republic for help. That was not a simple thing to do!"

Auralei smiled sympathetically. "The truth is, House Khilsyth and Nihkiehl, and others for that matter, were likely never supposed to have advanced as they are today."

"And they probably weren't supposed to be on Lindaulx either," Tarra said and chuckled. "That must have been an interesting conversation for the person you contacted. They probably thought you were a new civilization, and they were making first contact."

Auralei smiled in appreciation. "Fact is, whoever it was… they were clever. They kept this place *off the records*. Quite brilliant, actually."

"And who has provided this *erroneous* information?" Anzil asked. "It wouldn't have been my kin, would it?"

"Perhaps," Tarra replied. "On Lindaulx, a Ward Inquisitor should exist. They would have been tasked with managing a ward—their part of the system—and reporting to who we call the *watchers*. Somehow, the folks at ROG missed everything. And the checks and balances also failed. So… yeah."

"Why were we not supposed to advance?" Anzil asked.

"I'm not sure," Tarra answered. "Not my department."

Anzil stood, ducking away from Tarra so her hands slid off his shoulders. "Who's the current Ward Inquisitor?"

"Separation of church and state," Tarra said quietly.

"Grand," Anzil replied. "So, they sent you both to kill my father and pave the way for an invasion by the Tersinians, or Anacul, or whoever couldn't have faced our united might. You needed the House's divided."

Stigg laughed.

"So help creation if there's something you're not telling us, Chief," Anzil said, letting the statement hang on its merit.

"What?" Stigg asked, shaking his hand. "Oh, sorry, didn't mean to disturb you all. I'm just trying to line up the events with motives and failing. Something just doesn't add up." He started pacing and occasionally dragging his hand along the wall's smooth surface as everyone waited impatiently until he eventually dwelled at a schematic of the Astute facility projected on a side table. "If there's Anacul here," he said, moving to a nearby wall projection, digging furiously at his burly mustache, and twirling the ends occasionally. "They wouldn't have destroyed the Astute facility. That little geological event didn't destroy the facility. I think it was just for show." Stigg scratched the side of his head, leaving red lines through his stubble. "Two theories. Theory One: We have some rogue Tersinians working with the Anacul—"

"ROG has Anacul working for them?" Anzil interrupted.

"Ah yes, poor choice of words," Stigg laughed. "But not to be overlooked as a potential nuance. Sorry. Let me rephrase. Theory One: there is a *breakaway* faction of Tersinians who are going outside of their Order and creating contracts that ROG is completing."

"No way," Tarra blurted. "That could never happen. The Tersinians were sequestered and protected from all contact. They were thought to have been extinguished during the Shade Wars."

"Yet they attacked today," Anzil said.

Auralei had a modicum of sympathy for Anzil, as he was only vaguely aware of his dismal education. This was no fault of his own. There were elements in place to attenuate his exposure to the politicking of growing up in a major House on a remote planet. And perhaps those who kept this place quiet had even further limited information and travel off this planet and throughout the systems. *So clever,* she thought. "It's possible, Stigg," she said. "Acting through intermediaries, the Tersinians could be concealing their presence. They may have found a way to go between systems. But it is doubtful outside of the Mar-Vhen transit system. The Anacul could be a front. Just a new Tersinian faction. A well-constructed ruse. It might explain why I could never track down the actual owner of my contract. Same for this princess and hers."

"I figured you researched your employers meticulously," Stigg said. "Problem is, the Tersinians would not work with the Republic."

"Ahh, someone is keeping it secret from their Order," Tarra said with a shrug. "Perhaps the rest of the Tersinians. The path to power is paved with deceit and corruption."

"It's possible they brought the Anacul with them," Auralei added. "Or something is causing them to join together?"

Stigg nodded in agreement. "Yup. That part is a bit rough."

Tarra flashed Stigg a devilish wink. "And how does the flux fit into all of it?"

"What the hell does the flux have to do with this?" Anzil asked.

"The flux is many things, Anzil," Tarra said in a sweet lilt with an unnervingly calming quality. "The changing of the world's dispositions, a way to rationalize miracles, and what have you. For this conversation, it's a tidy way of classifying the balance of civilizations with different advancement timelines and their proficiency over harnessing energy. Darling, it's why ROG *must* exist. Certain cultures need to be protected from the emergence of—or interaction with—more technologically advanced ones. They deserve protection and the right to remain sequestered from hanging around the galactic punch bowl if they choose."

Stigg held the woman's gaze. "They're a mystical bunch, these *Mischi*. Remember, they believe in the balance and harmony of their false Greater Purpose. A fake prophecy that's just a fancy way to disguise *control*."

"Close," Tarra retorted. "Neutrality and balance, unlike your own little daisy-filled dreams."

"I'll be damned," Auralei said. "The Anacul and the *Tersa* could be the same group."

"Theory two?" Tarra asked Stigg.

"That was theory two," Stigg said, pointing to the taller *Mischi*. "Anacul and *Tersa*, one and the same, coming home. But there are some discontinuities, some elements I can't work out. Either way, the Republic is compromised, and the Tersinians have risen."

"They sound the bloody same," Anzil said.

"The Anacul were a plague," Stigg said. "Their home worlds and anywhere they tried to hide were decimated. Anything that remains, the Rift Faction hunts. And they are quite good at it."

"The Riftys are pirates," Tarra said with a disapproving grunt. "They just spread lies to appeal to commoners and those too stupid to see through them."

"Afraid not, lass. Pirates perhaps. Liars, maybe some. But hunters… there's still a few around."

"Vanguards!" Auralei said, putting it together. "We seriously did not see that. Clever bastards."

Tarra shot Auralei a confused look as the woman was now laughing openly—another rare display of emotion. "Care to let us in, *lass*?"

"Stigg's saying the Black Dragoons hid within the very group dedicated to annoying the piss outta the Republic," Auralei said. "That's hilarious."

"The Black Dragoons," Anzil whispered. "Also, not a myth?"

"Not a myth," Stigg said with a proud chuckle. "Could explain why the Riftys are here. Tracking these Anacul-Tersinians."

"So, let me get this straight," Anzil said, delineating invisible cordons on the table with his hands. "All theories are… that these Tersinian jackasses have emerged from their hidey-hole, and a bunch of supposedly fairy tale Nova Republic specters are helping them by destroying my bloody family! And some splinter faction of the Vanguards, the Black Dragoons, and I loved those fables as a kid, by the way, are here to fight the Anacul-bastards! Maybe even ROG."

"Sounds about right," Auralei said with a shrug. "I believe I see some of the discontinuities Stigg mentioned." Shifty peeked out from her chest pocket, sending a subtle note across their bond. She skimmed the scenarios her saboteur-class AI unit had developed and was relieved they had arrived at similar outcomes. "It's not quite that simple, though. The present-day people on Lindaulx—the Khilsyths, Nihkiehls, etcetera—displaced someone. What is unclear is if the Nova Republic sanctioned it. This could explain how the Nova Republic didn't have adequate resources in this sector. But if they didn't approve or weren't aware of the displacement, then the Republic is here for corrective actions against the current populations," Tarra said.

"Or the Tersinians are making a play to retake Lindaulx and enter the sphere of the Republic's grace," Auralei said.

"Had ROG discovered this as one of the Anacul homeworlds," Stigg said, scratching at his beard, "then ROG would have destroyed them and started a new civilization in its place." He inhaled deeply, expanding his lungs to the point resulting in a slight cramp in his left side. "And there shouldn't be enough of them left alive unless…"

"Unless they infiltrated the Tersinians," Tarra said.

"And the bloody Tersinians now believe this place to be sacred," Auralei said.

"And the Astute facility?" Anzil asked.

Stigg snorted. "No coincidence, that's for sure. That's a discontinuity—"

"Any chance the Anacul or the Tersinians are linked to the Astutes?" Anzil interrupted.

"We all are, Anzil," Tarra said softly. "It's just a matter of how."

"And apparently, if you conform to ROG's rules," Anzil said.

"It would explain their interest in Lindaulx," Auralei said, delicately scratching at her forehead, "and perhaps how they knew it was here and no one else did."

"At least someone besides them did," Stigg said curtly. "And the Republic seems too as well."

Auralei nodded at Stigg, "yes, you old goat. *Someone* else did."

"We should consider establishing contact with ROG," Tarra told Auralei. "But the only actual play here is to bail."

"ROG may deem us acceptable losses," Auralei thought aloud. "Even in violation," Tarra said in agreement. "Especially if we stay and help the Khilsyths and they discover they were double-crossed. Or they think we did the crossing."

"Maybe you," Tarra said, pointing weakly toward Auralei.

Auralei's eyes blazed. "That makes more sense." She bit back all the curse words threatening to escape. "You never had a contract, did you? You had a bloody directive." Auralei flashed across the room, knocking Anzil over, and grabbed Tarra by the throat. "What was your directive?" She spat the last part through clenched teeth.

Tarra broke free of Auralei's grip, her hands instinctively finding the comfort of the braided cording wrapped around the handle of her short swords. "They did not send me to kill you. My directive was to ensure his safe passage off Lindaulx." She released the grip of her right sword and swiveled her hand, keeping her palm perched on the pommel. She pointed to Stigg. "I was to ferry him to Transom—also Clarke. At the last minute, my overseer sent an amendment to find the source of some signal within the facility. The one Clarke discovered. I figured I could use him to overcome any nasty surprises left over."

"Where's Transom?" Anzil asked. "Never heard of it."

"Somewhere that isn't close," Tarra replied.

"Somewhere that isn't supposed to exist either," Stigg whispered. "Even for those in the Republic."

"And what does the Nova Republic want with Stigg and Clarke?" Anzil asked.

"Not sure," Tarra answered. "I hadn't figured that part out yet. Took me ages to track him to this stupid rock."

"It's a long story," Stigg said. "One I hoped was fully buried." The big man rubbed his face hard with his calloused hands. "And something that nothing good will surely come from."

"And you figured you could track me," Auralei said. "Track me to Transom, knowing that's where I would conceivably go. But how? You shouldn't be able to."

"Truth is, that's why I came back," Tarra said quietly. She moved to put Stigg between herself and Auralei. *Less easy to knock over,* she thought. "You had an incongruity in your connection. Most would have missed it. But Our Lady Majestic's big, beautiful brain did not. You created a clone in the system. A decoy—a doppelgänger."

"Something like that," Auralei smiled.

"Perhaps that's what caused my hesitation and how they got the lucky shot," Tarra admitted with heat in her words. "There are going to be some sorry asshats for that one. Someone clearly deemed me expendable."

Anzil didn't particularly care for the way the specter was now smiling at him, her hands still perched on her swords. "We need to get moving. This conversation is not helping us liberate Lindaulx."

"Are you ladies going to help us?" Stigg asked.

Tarra nodded. "As long as we're working to leave, and you and Clarke agree to come with me."

"Us," Auralei added quickly.

"Fine," Stigg said begrudgingly.

"I have your word?" Tarra asked.

"With you to Transom, with Clarke, after we help Anzil."

Tarra released another thumbnail-sized object from her forearm and handed it to Auralei. "My directive. They may kill us both for this."

"Anzil, take both of them for protection and rally the other houses," Stigg said. "If anyone can keep you safe from harm, it's these two." Stigg stood and left the room.

"Where are you going?" Anzil called.

"To find Clarke and some bloody armor," Stigg replied without stopping.

"Demanding, isn't he?" Tarra teased Anzil. "Vanguard?"

"That tracks," Auralei said and smiled at Anzil. "Seems like your old buddy Stigg has a lot of secrets, eh?"

"Bloody hell," Anzil said with a vast sigh. "Right in plain sight."

"I believe the old goat has good intentions," Auralei said. "At least I sure hope he does."

"Strangest adventure ever," Tarra laughed, "and I've had to do some pretty weird stuff." She put her hands on Anzil's shoulder and guided him to the worn seat cushion. "Let's upgrade your education a bit more, shall we, hon?"

CHAPTER 15

WHEN CLARKE OPENED his eyes, he was sitting cross-legged on a basaltic rock floor, wrapped in an insulating blanket. The dark walls and ceiling were silky smooth, translucent, and with no visible joints, as if hewn from a solid piece of rock. The structure rose from the depths of a lake, where ice collected and piled against its exterior, trying feebly to topple it. The upper areas of its monolithic tower fell short of the surrounding mountain tips that pierced the clouds.

"There is no need to cover yourself," a voice said, ringing throughout the hollow structure. "I assure you. We are where we're meant to be, and you are essentially safe within these walls."

Clarke tried to laugh, but it hurt. He touched his lower lip, finding it tacky, rubbed the dark, greasy substance that collected on his fingertips, and watched as it absorbed into his skin.

"What do you find amusing?"

Clarke drew a slow, deep breath to still himself.

"No matter. Although you are recognizable, there is something characteristically different about you."

"Where am I?"

"We are all in there," the voice said matter-of-factly.

Images flashed in Clarke's mind of a shrouded figure pointing and floating closer to him—he flinched from the impending contact.

"Your mental dexterity is weak compared to the architects."

"Who are the architects?" Clarke asked, half fearing the response.

"I'll show you."

A series of hazy images flashed through Clarke's mind, leaving him dizzy and his stomach churning. However, he registered the remnant impression that this structure's creators—the architects—were once a peaceful civilization.

"What is this place?"

"More or less—it's an instructional and research tool."

"But how are we here?"

"Better to ask oneself, why are we here? That could be a more relevant question."

Clarke stood facing a projection of himself on a nearby wall. It was displaying a network of webbed tendrils running throughout the body. "What is this? Some kind of sick joke?"

"It is not. It appears your initial union was sufficient. The *how* is your *dark passenger*, as you like to call it. As for the *why*, it is baffling that it selected you. I am, however, curious as to why you chose the origination method you did. It was unconventional—"

The voice cut off as a barrage of rapid flashes and violent shakes bombarded Clarke. His arms failed to move, leaving his fresh eyes to recoil in pain behind the thin veil of his eyelids. Gradually, he heard the faint sounds of people talking, and the armor responded, providing a fuzzy view of the world. Clarke's first breath was painful, and successive ones required his complete concentration to fill his chest with a substance that ripped savagely at the soft tissue lining his airway. He thrashed wildly, trying desperately to warm near-frozen limbs and alleviate them of their stabbing pains, but he succumbed to the darkness.

CLARKE'S WORLD SHOOK again, and when he opened his eyes, a shadowy and familiar figure filled his vision. "Please stop," he requested with a croak.

"I'll be damned," a voice boomed. "You're alive. Do you know who I am or where you are?"

The owner of the voice's snowy crop of coarse hair hung loosely around his ears, obscuring the grizzled man's face. "You enjoy whittling wood," Clark said. "Mythical creatures, if I recall."

Stigg chuckled, on the verge of tears, "that was a random fact. I'm sure glad you're alive but come out of this contraption now. A bit of fresh air wouldn't hurt, and I want to get a good look at you."

Clarke found the idea of his boots touching the floor appealing. The armor parted, and the millions of tiny amoeboid-like projectiles released him. Stigg hauled him out of the machine and guided him to a nearby chair, where he collapsed into its worn supports.

"You're different," Stigg said, scrutinizing Clarke's appearance. "You sure everything's stable?"

Clarke brought his legs up to his chest and grabbed his shins. "I feel fine." He stretched, stood shakily, and wobbled to a nearby mirror to check himself out. "I could use a shave, that's for sure."

"You seem taller. And your eyes… lighter, maybe."

"Probably the lighting in here."

"There's something else."

"What?"

"Nothing," Stigg said, shaking his head. "Likely just some leftover murmurs from being around those *Mischi.*"

"Both of them are here now."

"How in the hell did you know… never mind, it's old news. Do you remember what happened to you?"

"I remember killing a big bastard with a sword," Clarke admitted, a mischievous smile spreading across his face. "That's something one doesn't do every day."

"No," Stigg agreed, beaming with pride. "That is not. You took out one of their so-called champions."

Clarke raised his eyes to meet Stigg's gaze. "I also remember you saying you were a Vanguard—that it was a story for later, and I believe now would classify as that later time."

Stigg's smile was tense as he sat down next to Clarke. "The word is mum to anyone else. Understood? I never saw myself as the tactician, nor the subtle one, and never the one with all the answers. I wasn't the one who could develop a plan that acted like a light breeze, which brought the spark and fuel together that could ignite and incite entire planets. Fires that changed the winds around them and completely masked the light breeze that instigated the whole mess. All of that was for other people, as I was a simple navigator. Eventually, I retired from the Vanguards and revived my true calling. The end."

A part of Clarke believed that if there were demons Stigg wanted to keep hidden, it was his right. Another part of him, a yet unfulfilled part, extended ethereal tentacles toward Stigg, intending to pry memories from the recesses of his mind. Right before they reached the back of Stigg's head, Clarke jerked away and toppled backward. The last thought tracing through Clarke's mind before he felt his head bounce off the stone floor was that *Stigg was gonna be pissed.*

CLARKE'S FACE BOUNCED off a smooth, damp, cold black floor. He pushed himself to his knees, relieved his nose wasn't leaking blood. He was back at the structure in the lake.

"Your augmentation will be unique as you develop," the voice said, "and the exact transformations you will undergo are unknown. Perhaps the architects' only oversight was they miscalculated the impact of one's will on the development process." A quaint laugh drifted through the area. "Do you truly think you could read someone's mind? To what end? Over time, you might tease memories and thoughts to the surface where you can judge their truth."

Clarke chuckled, disquieted with the discomfort of the place. Perhaps it was a manifestation he created so that he didn't feel crazy when he talked to the newfound voice. "Is that normal? The thought... tentacles." He jabbed his fingers at the void in front of him.

"You are rather unique. Therefore, I cannot define what is normal at this time. I am also unsure how you or your augmentation will evolve."

"You mean my dark passenger?"

"Yes. It was the most relatable classification I could find for you to understand. A silent partner, adapting to what you need."

"You said 'silent'. Mine isn't so silent."

"That could be unfortunate. It's quite remarkable you could activate it at all."

"And who exactly are you?" Clarke asked, his words echoing in the chamber. After a short while, he called out. "Hello? Are you still there?"

"Yes," came the ethereal voice. "I am here."

"And what should I call you?"

"I was once a finder of paths, of sorts. A pioneer."

"Pioneer it is," Clarke said. "Provided that's okay. But what's the purpose of this thing inside me?"

"To help. A symbiotic relationship on a primary and galactic scale. Eventually, to reveal and guide you in the architect's principles and beliefs."

"Which ones?"

"I'm not sure you're ready for that instruction, as it must be earned and your actions proved," the Pioneer responded, dropping an octave.

Clarke smiled ruefully. "Seriously? I'm not much for the fate and destiny bullshit."

The Pioneer's piercing laughter rang through the temple, reverberating and casting ripples of light through the darkened walls. "Fate and destiny. No, no, no. Think of this more as practical fail-safes to ensure it does not fully develop in unworthy subjects. It's to protect them from themselves. In another light, you simply do not meet the requirements at this juncture."

"And you're the one to judge me worthy or not?" Clarke asked.

The laughter subsided. "I would not claim that responsibility. I am simply one conduit to the vast experiences and information the architects collected and compiled."

"But saying I wasn't ready. That was a judgment, was it not?"

"It was not of your worth. The architects reveal their principles and beliefs through actions and consequences."

"To what purpose? And who are these architects?"

"There are some pieces of information in the outer banks that I cannot repossess," the Pioneer said, sounding defeated.

"Do you not remember how to, or are you just not telling me?"

"They are simply in the beyond."

"Can you tell me who Stigg Anundr is?"

"This knowledge base does not contain that type of record. I only recognize him as you do."

"Who are the Vanguards?"

"Also, not in the records. But the markings etched upon Stigg Anundr's forearms are ancient. Those who bore similar markings carried many names over the centuries. They are depictions of the path of vengeance. Their purpose is related to the energy given to the worlds—the flux—exercise caution around them."

THE COLD STONE floor steadily supported his weight and quelled the turbulence between his ears and rising from his stomach. "Sorry, Chief. I blanked out there for a minute."

Stigg turned and flashed Clarke a concerned look. "What do you mean? You want me to get the doc?"

"No, I'm fine. Just a little shaken."

As Clarke contemplated asking Stigg about architects and vengeance, a young buxom girl wielding a plate of delicious-smelling bread and hearty soup was in the room after a knock at the door. She instructed Stigg to ensure Clarke ate everything on the tray before setting it down. Hunger gripped Clarke's stomach—it had been hours since the quick rations near the alpine meadow. He tore into the bread before the woman disappeared through the doorway and closed it behind her, leaving the smell of daffodils hanging in the air.

"You heard the lady. Eat all of it."

"But what's the plan here?"

"You eat, and I'll talk," Stigg said.

As instructed, Clarke ate and listened to an account of Anzil's three objectives, which included the two *Mischi* and leaving Warbler Ridge. When he was finished, Stigg grasped his shoulder and instructed him to stay and rest because he needed to check on a few things. "Sorry," Clark said, setting the plate to the side. "Where you go, I go."

"It's not for long, lad," Stigg said, pressing on Clarke's shoulder and keeping him seated, "I'll be back to collect you in a few. I'll get you another plate. Since you gut bombed that one."

At least the food would nourish his body and give him time to regain a sure footing. Clarke shuffled over to the armor and examined it like he would a dragoon suit before attaching it to a maintenance terminal. There wasn't a scratch or dent on the cool charcoal plating, which still retained the consistency of sandpaper. He wondered how it had repaired itself and fought the sudden presence of the structure in the lake, enticing him for another session. Unable to stifle a yawn that brought tears to his eyes, Clarke climbed inside his machine, the multitude of soft-edged spines extending and contouring to his body, welcoming him back. Clarke was asleep in seconds, and incoherent dreams took over.

CHAPTER 16

STIGG DUCKED INTO the hallway, greeting his escort outside the infirmary room's door. He ignored their chorus of clearing throats and attempts to set a quicker pace toward their destination. He strolled behind them, evaluating the strides and gear the team carried—they were experienced operators. "Who exactly are you again, and where does Anzil want me to go?" Stigg asked the woman who appeared to be in charge, noting that at least two others were behind him—one who he recognized from the hallway outside Clarke's room.

"I'm Sergeant Staalke, Sir. I've been instructed to take you to *the* workshop."

"You must be new then?" Stigg asked.

"No, sir," Staalke replied over her shoulder, opening a barred gate leading to an older section of Warbler Ridge. "Chief Khilsyth assigned me here years ago."

Over the years, the rumbling of machinery and geologic episodes had marked the tunnel, exposing faint etchings along the otherwise flawlessly cut stone surfaces. Stigg dragged his fingers through the coarse grooves, noticing the hallway tapered and held a slight decline. He admired the masterful stone masonry work, but its uniformity made it challenging to commit their path to memory as the team led him through several doorways and intersecting corridors. Finally, they arrived at an unlit hallway with another nondescript and fortified door.

"This isn't the workshop," Stigg said.

"Not really, sir," Staalke replied. "Not the *regular* workshop. Another workshop, if you will? Given your rather eclectic skills and needs, we thought this one was more befitting." She deactivated the door's locking mechanism and threw her weight against its solid face to engage the counterweight—the door ratcheted inwards and out of the way.

The lights closest to the doorway flickered to life, purging the darkness from the room in a cascade of glowing blocks. Stone archways clung to side walls, extending upward to support a lavender-colored capstone for the ceiling. Metallic spherical pods filled the room, clustered in groups of seven and evenly spaced along parallel rows.

"The Khilsyths apparently discovered this room during the first expansion of Warbler Ridge," Staalke told Stigg. "A group of geologists and miners came across the stonework while drilling the south wing. They sealed the chamber shortly after that." She walked further into the room and stopped beside a canvas sheet blocking off an extensive section of the eastern wall. "Meet *Beastor,* Sir." Staalke wrenched hard on the canvas, tearing it from the wall and sending a flurry of dust swirling about the room. The grandiose gesture revealed an older-style access hatch situated between two rock columns.

"What in the hell is this place?" Stigg asked, coughing and waving his hand before his face to cut an opening through the haze.

Staalke climbed up the scaffolding attached to the side of the cavern wall. "Not sure. We were hoping you could shed some light on it. Perhaps even how to open the hatch. If you'd like, there is a better vantage point up here, sir."

Stigg trailed Staalke up the enclosed ladder to the mezzanine level, decorated with equipment reminiscent of a control room. The canvas had shrouded an object that was fifteen paces wide by nine paces deep and made of metal. "Any idea why Anzil didn't mention this earlier?"

"Not sure, sir. Maybe he didn't want to say anything in front of the specter. Or maybe he still wished to keep this place close to the vest." Staalke walked over to the most prominent board adorned with lights, knobs, sliders, and display readouts, and punched in a sequence of keys, spurring the room into activity. A series of projections leaped to life, blinked, and began scrolling lines of code.

Stigg dragged a chair across the floor, its legs chattering over the metal hexagon grating. The chair flexed and emitted faint cracks as it absorbed his weight. He drew a deep and measured breath and held it as he recognized the archaic language before him. "Is this the original text, or have you translated it somehow?"

Staalke took a seat in a comfortable chair with a cracked cushion and spun to face Stigg. "Interesting," she said, her eyes narrowing. "So you *can* read it, can't you?"

Stigg pressed several buttons on a nearby monitor until the projected text behaved for him and responded by displaying a sequence of menus. He ignored Staalke's constant requests for details about what he was reading, how he knew the language, and the warnings not to mess anything up—she seemed genuinely concerned he would break something. Eventually, something piqued Stigg's interest, and he selected the command sequences as instructed. A metallic clank echoed faintly from the box Staalke had uncovered with such zeal. "That was lucky," Stigg said, giving her a playful wink. "Shall we go see what's inside?"

Staalke was out of her chair before the pretend-mechanic finished his question. She darted to the side of the platform and slid down the parallel railings, supporting her body with both hands. Landing soundlessly on the cavern floor, she flashed Stigg a quick smile. "Come on, old-timer."

At the access hatch, Stigg pressed his hand against a control panel that had appeared. Just as he started to doubt himself, the hatch swung open, and light from the room tentatively illuminated a labyrinth of wires, tubes, and huge round drums stacked together on either side of a walkway. The machine's insides were dimly lit by indicator lights and spotless as if hermetically sealed. "Damn. I think it's a bloody marauder," Stigg said.

Staalke placed her arm gingerly around Stigg's waist and blushed weakly when he averted his gaze. "What did you call it?"

"Nothing," Stigg said, stiffening. "Just muttering to myself... do a lot of that these days."

"Those tend to be useful."

"Nah," Stigg said, moving away from the woman. "Just remembering old hacks posting theories."

"I'm listening," Staalke said sweetly.

"Just crazy rumors about mechanized units scattered throughout the systems, hidden by the Republic until needed. Guess they thought it would make mobilizing for events a little easier."

"What kind of events?"

Stigg smirked. "Events... the kind when force is a viable response. I never thought it real because, if you ask me, it's not very practical from a resource standpoint."

"Is it operational?" Staalke asked.

"Hard to tell for certain," Stigg replied. Although it was a faint scent, he could tell this machine had seen battle. "Any idea how long it's been here?"

"A while now," Staalke said, drumming her fingers on the machine. "Any thoughts on how it got here?"

"My guess..." Stigg said and tested the internal walkway's stability, finding it acceptable. "Some division of the Nova Republic deemed this a worthy planet. Their flotillas scattered these machines around Astute facilities they came across, regardless of how advanced the local cultures were. Guess they assumed they would need to visit again and wanted to be prepared if they had an unfriendly welcome. Or maybe they just needed a stopover point."

"We need some light," Staalke said and threw a device that emitted a soft glow as it skittered along the walkway. "Seeing that the Khilsyths knew about this behemoth, how long do you figure they've known about the Astute facility?"

"Why do you figure that?"

"Not long after they took over Warbler Ridge, would be my guess."

"Or they came here searching for it," Stigg said.

"It would have given them a considerable advantage to their colonization efforts, yes?"

"Yer not wrong there, lass."

"So... what was the deal the Khilsyths made with the Vanguards then? They must have offered something substantial to replace the Tersinians."

"I wouldn't know anything about that."

"Oh, come now, Stigg. The Vanguards typically piloted these machines. You really expect me to believe it was just lucky that you got this thing open?"

"Listen... how do you know about these things?"

"I'm sure an old shop Chief like you also knows. The Vanguards were part of flotillas with this type of tech, weren't they? That was back when they were part of the Nova Republic."

"I'm an old man; that much is true," Stigg said with a half-hearted chuckle. "And us old folks are chock-full of useless tidbits. Especially us backwater mechanics. As far as what happened on this planet. That type of thing is above my pay grade."

"Did you know the guard detail for this marauder has existed since Warbler Khilsyth? And you're not that old."

"What guard detail?" Stigg asked, turning to face the woman.

Staalke smirked and touched Stigg's exposed forearm. "My grandpa had similar markings. So, answer me, and please don't lie to a *wee lass*. Why are the Vanguards interested in Lindaulx?"

"Look, what I've got is just from the stories. These markings. Just a mistake I made when I was young and wanted to appear tough."

"Tsk-tsk," Staalke said, clicking her tongue against the inside of her smooth cheek and sighing deeply. "I doubt that. You really expect me to believe this is some accident that the Vanguards and the Khilsyths had the same idea for a safe place to hole up?"

"Dumb luck, perhaps."

"As was you being able to open the hatch—again, doubtful. Do you really take me for a fool?"

"No, ma'am, I do not."

"And who do you think created this place?"

"No clue," Stigg said, telling the truth. "It's not Republic, as far as I can tell. Maybe your family knew."

"Nothing they cared to share," Staalke said quietly. "But this place isn't Tersinian either."

"It is an *interesting* place."

"Quite," Staalke said, tightening her grip on Stigg's belt. "It's also *interesting* how it all works out. My guess is that there are some old soldiers here living amongst the people of Lindaulx. Vanguard's that needed a place to hide, anyway. Perhaps during the Shade Wars and the fall of House Frebel. And the Tersinians were what? Just good hosts that were taken advantage of. I understand... the Nova Republic and the Gods know who else worked together to instill world order, correct?"

"The Shade Wars were dark times, lass," Stigg said, dropping his head. "The Anacul were hell-bent on destroying entire systems." Staalke's apparent apathy for the Tersinians, or perhaps anger toward the Nova Republic, was unsettling. The thrill of finding equipment from the Strento's armada and years of complacency had dulled his instincts. The woman had a natural grace about her, and her presence faintly irritated the nausea-inducing strings of his stomach. He suspected she had *the talent*. But it wouldn't have been enough for her grandfather to have the markings—her mother would have to have been *Mischi* or *Tersa*, or worse, Anacul.

"That was back when Tersinians were made to be specters before they could become *Tersa*?" Staalke pressed. "A race for talent, if you will. But I think you were a Vanguard attached to the Strento flotilla. You were, weren't you? How the hell else could you have opened this thing?" She sighed and caressed a faint image etched into the metal. "The Strento emblem is right there."

Stigg freed himself from Staalke's embrace and walked through the marauder's wedge-shaped room, listening while Staalke pelted him with more questions. Undeniably, the markings were Strento. He climbed into the pilot's chair, which molded to the outline of his back and sent securing straps to brace him comfortably in place. He punched a few buttons on the armrests and tapped on some menu projections, and the machine's engines shuttered and started emitting a high-pitched whine as they sprung to life.

"It works after all this time!" Staalke said, stopping her verbal tirade. She peered over the back of the high-backed seat, letting her hair spill forward to rest on the exposed skin of Stigg's neck. "I can't believe it. Good job, you."

Stigg inhaled the sweet lavender scent of Staalke's hair and, from the corner of his eye, caught a warning symbol flashing on the screen. He manipulated the controls so that the machine's heads-up display showed the area of concern—it was initially disorientating because the projected images of the outside environment blurred rapidly, but the upper structure didn't rotate. Four targets were being tracked outside, and four targets inside, including him. Stigg sealed the marauder's rear hatch, undid the command chair's securing straps, and stood to be greeted with a sword pointed at his chest.

Staalke flashed a quick smile. "Easy there, big guy. This doesn't have to be difficult."

"An explanation would be appreciated."

Staalke's diminutive stature and short sword gave her freedom to move within the confined space. Her sword flashed in a vicious upward arc meant to cleave Stigg's unprotected head, and the return slash reverberated off his armored forearm, which he brought up quickly to protect his skull. Stigg ducked with unnerving speed for a man as tall and wide as he was, spun, and kicked savagely, catching Staalke in her armored midsection. The blow sent her crashing backward into another soldier and her gleaming blade scattering across the metal walkway.

A soldier stepped over his fallen comrades and stabbed wildly at Stigg, having some experience behind it. But it wasn't a match for Stigg's skill, plus some luck. He caught the man's forearm and used momentum to guide the blade safely past his midsection. He stole a large, serrated-edged combat knife from the attacker's waist and sheathed it between their eyes. The man's skull and brain matter offered little resistance to the knife. The dead soldier gyrated as bullets from Staalke's pistol slammed into their back.

Using the body as a shield, Stigg charged, hitting Staalke and sending the woman crashing backward. He grabbed a breaker bar from a nearby utility locker. Unable to swing it inside the confines of the marauder, he drove the square end of it into the nearest soldier's knee, which bent at an unnatural angle. The soldier screamed in pain as they fell; their rifle barked wildly at Stigg and plastered his armored chest and legs with smoldering metal projectiles. Stigg slammed the heel of his combat boot down on the soldier's exposed throat, turning their scream into a fit of soft chokes and gurgles.

Staalke drew knives from her forearm sheathes, crouched, and leaped at Stigg, slashing upwards at his chest. Her attacks separated pieces of his shirt from his chest and forearms as they sought the soft, fleshy parts beneath the areas where the armor was weakest.

Stigg dodged, ducked, and weaved as Staalke's relentless strikes landed safely against his armor. Until a clumsy parry and a quick shimmy led to an opening for him to deliver a stiff backhand to the side of her head; while her helmet's modern materials protected her skull from the blow, the blow's brute force knocked her off balance. Seizing the advantage, Stigg lunged, his shoulder burying into her sternum and his hands wrapping around her narrow waist. He lifted her into the air and slammed her down, leveraging his entire weight. He drew his legs up tight, cinching them against her hips and pinning her arms with the weight of his ass. The woman tried to wiggle free, kicking hard against his weight, as a wave of nausea chewed at his innards.

"Stop!" Stigg commanded.

"Get off me," Staalke screamed. "You're crushing me."

"Who are you?" Stigg growled, knowing her armor's mesh structure would respond to the downward force of his mass and distribute it safely to the sides. The woman was panicking and repeating the same plea over and over for Stigg to free her—the situation was hopeless. With the pull on his stomach increasing, he needed to resolve the situation before Staalke transitioned into the flux. In a swift motion, he unclasped her helmet, grabbed her high cheekbones with his hand, and bounced her head off the floor twice: the first time sent her helmet rolling away, and the second put her out.

Stigg stood slowly, his knees protesting and his lower back clenching, causing him to walk with a hunch. He scavenged some binding ties from the dead soldiers and bound the woman's wrists and ankles, being extra careful to secure them.

He started to make his way to the cockpit. The marauder's cabin shook violently, jostling him about, as the dull thuds of exploding ordinance seeped through the armored exterior. After a few lurches and missteps, he grasped the back of the captain's chair and the controls to steady himself. The targeting and tactical systems still tracked the four targets outside the machine and displayed solutions and response options. He cursed quietly, hoped the old armor would hold, and laughed at himself for needing instructions to operate the marauder. He consoled himself, as he was sure no one alive today had piloted this machine. He chose number five as that one felt lucky and watched the automated on-screen selections.

The marauder responded by rocking in an outcry of vengeance, liberating itself from the rusted mooring clamps and the structure encasing it.

TWO HOLLOW THUMPS originated from the machine as it deposited objects into the ceiling and sent the soldiers diving for cover.

"Must have been duds?" Artis called out, peering around a column at the machine Staalke and his other squad mates had entered.

"Stay down," Balla shouted. "Artis, keep firing that cannon, dammit!" Then muttered to himself, "simple demolition job with light resistance, my ass."

Before Artis could send another explosive projectile into the back of the machine, two green pulses reverberated through the ceiling, and the chamber's capstone vanished in a dust storm. This caused a dragoon-sized rock from a nearby stone arch to fall, grazing Balla and crushing Artis, who exploded in a wash of blood and goo. Balla shrugged and slipped behind the rock, thankful for the cover it afforded.

With the ceiling removed, dust rushed through the smoothly bored chimney, and more pieces of the surrounding stonework crashed to the floor, extinguishing the lights and plunging the room into darkness.

Balla tossed a handful of glow sticks toward the machine's noises, offering light for his night vision goggles to amplify. "How in the hell are we supposed to deal with this?" Balla asked.

Another two muted flashes came from the machine as grappling devices soared up and embedded into the chimney's sidewalls. With a rending of stone and scraping of metal, the machine began reeling in its imperceptible tethers, raising itself from its berth bit by bit.

"What the hell is it?" Koe asked.

"I think it's a marauder," Balla said, his eyes bulging.

"Impossible," Koe said, "no way there would be one here."

"Behold, exhibit A," Balla said sarcastically. He could smell that their recruit had soiled himself and was presently cowering behind a fallen support column, clutching his knees to his chest and rocking.

"We need to get outta here," Koe said.

Balla agreed, but his feet wouldn't respond even with the voice inside him and all his training screaming at him to run. As a child, he had heard stories about the Nova Republic constructing scary machines en route to or at conflict zones. This gave the storytellers ample material to spin their tales about ruthless and customizable contraptions emulating some of the fiercest natural and mythical predators. In the marauder's presence, Balla thought the abundance of armaments and its unnatural movement was enough to scare most people, even combat veterans like him.

As the marauder's legs gained traction against the cavern walls, a burst of light blinded Balla—he didn't see Koe burst backward in an expanding conical shape of burning red mist before inhaling the plasma trailing from the rail gun round, which rendered his lungs useless and set him ablaze. The impact of the round slamming into the rear portal collapsed a section of the chamber, which also crushed the recruit and their incessant rocking.

Stigg rubbed his hands together and hoped those responsible for burying the marauder deep within the mountain had the wherewithal to provide an alternate escape route. After a few false starts, he relaxed into his old familiarity with the movement of the machine and pointed it up the chimney-like tunnel leading out of the chamber. It would be good to taste some salt-laced air and have the warmth of sunlight on his face again, as all this lurking around in caves was depressing.

MOMENTUM

CHAPTER 17

DEEK WALKED TO a nearby staging area to check her unit's ready status. She worried that some of her soldiers, like the regular folks at Warbler Ridge, struggled with their alliances. Against Anzil's guidance, some folks had attempted to establish contact with loved ones and friends. Whether fear for their family's safety or succumbing to the propaganda was to blame, the Ridge's population was experiencing a slow attrition of soldiers. Deek could not completely fault those who deserted—loyalty to family and the need to protect loved ones were powerful motivators. Strategically, it meant fewer soldiers. But she consoled herself with the belief that those who remained would hesitate less when firing at people they may have called friends and comrades. For her, there was no question of loyalty. She believed Anzil was virtuous and would guide them honorably. She begrudgingly admitted that she enjoyed a slight crush on the man and went to find him.

"What about drawing off the Khilsyth dragoons and disabling them?" Lariat, a relative newcomer to her squad, was asking as Deek sat at the war room table beside Anzil.

Some lieutenants remembered the hard lesson learned in the Provings last year, although Deek fondly recalled the mock battle because of the outcome's hilarity. The Provings were annual events held by prominent Houses, such as the Khilsyths, whereby people vied to be recruited into a dragoon regiment. The contest's objective was straightforward: defeat the experienced dragoon forces or at least put up a decent effort. Event organizers provided hopeful recruits with a vast arsenal and array of dragoon armor and attachments, trying to offset some of the advantages the veterans' superior equipment provided.

As daylight broke, the battle commenced with the recruit hopefuls getting a head-start to take up positions. The sun hadn't met its apex when all potential recruits were disabled, except for Stigg and Clarke, who had somehow avoided detection by all the radars and sensors the dragoons had deposited since the battle's commencement. This feat was thought impossible in the bulky and often antiquated armor reserved for the less likely. Eventually, the dragoons started their sweep of the area and, confident in their nasty selves, strayed out of the support range of their surface-based defense systems—once in this zone, the machines suddenly dosed the pilots with onboard sedatives, trapped them all inside, and powered down. The battle concluded, and the tactical strategy became known as *sleeping giants*. Clarke had subverted the entire battlenet. Once again, he proved too valuable of a mind to be a dragoon. Within weeks, Clarke developed a defensive solution and oversaw its installation on all machines to prevent a similar attack. Around the same time, the Khilsyth's Dragoon Leader rejected Clarke from dragoon training on the premise that his body would not accept augmentations. However, they promoted Clarke's tactic to the dragoon's stratagem, which was ingrained in every Khilsyth as a method for disabling foreign enemy dragoons.

"That was an excellent suggestion, Captain Lariat," Deek said. "Perhaps we can use the *sleeping giant* tactic on any armor the invaders brought with them. The challenge: most of our computer types didn't escape the city. Clarke's condition is unknown, and we're not sure what their mobile command structure is capable of or if they have one."

"How is Willow's Ridge holding up?" Anzil asked, appearing beside Deek and taking her field glasses.

"We deployed some of our forces there as decoys," Deek reported. "Hoping to divide the invading forces or at the very least confuse them, but no such luck."

"It means that one of ours is out there and playing for the other side," Anzil said, shaking his head. "Our folks outside. Do you have a plan to get them to safety?"

"I do, sir," Deek said.

"Let's hear it," Anzil said.

Deek explained the phased plan she and her two most trusted lieutenants, Tristan and Duncan, developed for rendezvousing with the forces outside Warbler Ridge at Lake Fievre. When she concluded, the military strategists in the room offered no modifications.

"You know what you're asking of me, right?" Anzil said with a whisper to Deek. "I admire your willingness to risk your life, but…"

Deek nodded and could tell by Anzil's expression that he was trying to separate the strategic benefit of her proposal from his feelings for her. She hoped it was screaming at him to keep her safe, but in the end, to let her do her duty.

"All right, Captain Deek," Anzil conceded. "Put your plan in motion." Anzil set the binoculars down, snuck between Deek's arms, and effortlessly lifted her. "Come home safe," he whispered in her ear.

Deek burrowed her face into his neck, inhaling a light mix of musky soap and the sweet scent of exhaust fumes. "You do the same. And a specter isn't someone you can trust, darling. You grasp that concept, right? And watch Stigg. He's hiding something."

"I will be careful, love," Anzil said, unable to bring himself to tell her about the other specter. *No need to give her more to worry about,* he told himself. "It's the devils we think we know at this point." He kissed her goodbye as she reluctantly tore herself away.

DEEK'S CHEEKS FLUSHED from the rush of adrenaline as she traversed the granite tunnels leading to the staging complex of Warbler Ridge. The area was bustling with the movement of people preparing for war. She made her way to her suit, bounded up its docking station, and clambered inside. Her machine closed around her, blocking most of the outside world's noise and texture. She inhaled deeply and shivered, wiggling her shoulders to reclaim her stillness in the isolation. The commotion came rushing back in, coupled with the whine of her dragoon suit powering up, sending more chills of excitement through her spine.

Deek maneuvered into position with the rest of her dragoons in the alcove outside the main gate and took a minute to inspect her unit. The armored giants shifted and flexed, ready for battle. Her dragoons wore cadmium yellow with their nicknames over their left breast and the Khilsyth Crest on their helmet. She could hear the familiar faint rhythmic beats emanating through the protective plating of some of her comrades as each practiced their pre-battle rituals. Even though her team was a motley-clad crew with several variants of armor covered in a multitude of spikes, shields, mottos, credos, and battle scars, they were consistent in that they were all seasoned professionals. She took a deep breath, rolled her arms over to expose her forearms, and read the emblazoned words 'Titus' and 'Rend.' The two *beasts* that had relentlessly pushed them all through their training—she would make them proud.

Deek patiently scrutinized the ceiling, admiring the intricate geometric patterns carved into the rock. She traced a prominent ceiling ridge to a black panel at the front of the alcove leading outside. Behind her was the primary gate. It was constructed of a material able to withstand whatever enemies had thrown at it, including plasma cutters that had left scorch marks on the floor during a previous war. However, it was also incredibly inefficient and difficult to move. She shuddered as the gate slammed shut behind them.

IMMEDIATELY AFTER NUDA'S command went out over the battlenet to attack the deserters in Warbler Ridge, a salvo of penetrator rockets slammed into the face of the ridge, turning the canyon into a storm of flying rocks and dust. The natural curve and density of the cavern walls sent most of the blast's force skyward to dissipate in an expanding cloud of sanguine and coal. Next, they launched high-energy plasma cutter rounds that attached to the large metal entrance panels of Warbler Ridge. They burned intensely, burrowing into the metal, which flowed from the holes like melting wax. Eventually, the holy gates swung open, and with another command from Nuda, rapid thumping sounds echoed in the valley as tiny hissing canisters flew into the darkened void of the inner chamber. Noxious gas filled the Warbler Ridge entrance and billowed into the surrounding canyon.

"Why isn't the smoke flushing them out?" Harp asked impatiently.

"Perhaps they have respirators," Kifner responded.

Nuda's upper lip curled at the audacity of the two junior lieutenants. Harp was a newcomer to the House Khilsyth Guard, and Nuda didn't trust Kifner as far as he could throw him.

"What are you doing, Captain Nuda?" Valan screamed, his voice distorting in the drone's speaker. "You're at the wrong bloody Ridge!"

Nuda secretly wished he could signal someone to blot the drone from the sky but knew another would annoyingly take its place. "We've breached the gates," Nuda said, lining up to the hand-sized drone and added, "Sir." Ignoring the response from Valan and the other Command Center lackeys, Nuda ordered in his assault forces and walked from the mobile command structure to his machine. The expected resistance on their journey hadn't materialized, making the last few hours seem like they were on some slow-motion ride that was heading for disaster. It also made him briefly second-guess his gut instinct that Willow Ridge was a clever ploy, but he knew Anzil and the crew better than most. Nuda whispered a quick prayer for the good men and women he had just condemned beneath the mercury moon and another prayer that Anzil was here just for good measure. The Maw would be well-fed today.

DEEK KEYED HER mic. "This is your captain speaking. I hope you said goodbye to your families because we're not coming back anytime soon." A sad smile spread across her face. Although she hoped her forces would hold a significant advantage for this first encounter, she knew she would doom the lives of some of her comrades today and in the days to come.

"Here they come," Duncan yelled.

"Let's take some of these bastards out on our way," Deek said to her lieutenants. *And hope the Khilsyth units aren't fodder,* she thought. "Initiate Phase Alpha on my mark."

Once the invaders funneled into the Maw and approached the gate, Deek directed her first phase to commence. Her soldiers began liberally spraying incendiary rounds, flares, and smoke canisters into the canyon. Most of whatever functioning mining equipment left behind by Warbler Ridge's prior occupation began rumbling into the Maw, equipped with bulky metal shovels and protective plates. A couple of Zephyr skirmish-assault vehicles hid in the shadows behind the defensive rolling cover, launching rockets that slammed into the forward forces of the invaders.

"Our units are sitting ducks, Captain Deek!" a soldier said. "We need to help them. Now."

Deek's armored hand swung up and tapped her dragoon helmet where her temple would have been. "Hold, Private." Deek's eyes never left the projected terrain model displayed on her tactical screen.

"And so it begins," Duncan said, pointing at the wave of invaders streaming from beneath the tree lines like hundreds of ants swarming to fill the Maw.

"Light them up," Deek ordered.

As the ridge-mounted cannons began firing, their thunderous recoils sent snow and pebble avalanches skipping down the steep faces of the ridgelines. The artillery slammed into the hard rock exterior of the Maw, turning the area into a seething cauldron of flames. The antiquated armaments that did close the distance to the enemy were relatively ineffective against their armor's defensive capabilities, which shredded most of the incoming mortars. The midair explosions had little effect on slowing the forward movement of the invaders, as the area of impact of falling debris and heat was limited.

"Keep the few disabled ones pinned down," Deek cautioned.

"What we wouldn't give for some updated firepower, eh?" Lariat asked. "Lieutenant Nosup, why don't you have some of your people identify and mark House Khilsyth soldiers?"

Deek acknowledged it was agreeable to her, seeing Nosup solicit her approval. "Just remember, it's going to be confusing, as the armor might look the same." On her displays, Deek confirmed her second group was ready and motioned at Lariat to begin Phase Bravo. It started much like Phase Alpha, with a group of repurposed mining machinery rolling down the Maw, providing a modicum of protection, only this time, a wave of dragoons thundered closely behind.

NUDA WATCHED IN amazement as the second wave of dilapidated war machinery rambled out of Warbler Ridge. He tugged on his ear, struggling to understand the logic behind such a shoddy attack. Warbler Ridge could protect what was inside and had stores and various supplies that should last for months if not years. He wondered if the gas was working, and the environmental systems were out of operation. "Does anyone have any idea who might be leading this poor excuse of an exodus?"

"Not sure, Captain," Harp said. "Anzil, Deek, Lariat, Nosup... We suspect the usual suspects are still alive."

Nuda rubbed his left eye, chasing away an irritable twitch. "It's not Deek or Anzil. They're not this stupid. Can anyone make out any markings on what just exited?"

"They're showing Lariat squadron identifiers," Kifner answered.

"That tracks," Nuda said. "Lariat would be *this* stupid. Okay, folks, stay lucid and sit tight. They're making a run for it."

"We can't let them escape, sir," Kifner said.

"We wait," Nuda ordered.

"But, sir," Kifner protested.

"That's enough, Lieutenant Kifner," Nuda said, not meaning to snap so hard at the young lieutenant. He was just about to say that something didn't feel right about the current situation when it clicked—the explosions were highly suspicious. He wondered why they would sacrifice the equipment as it was uncharacteristic of Anzil's people. Nuda cursed under his breath, swung his aerial recon drone to a dragoon's eye perspective, and swept across the Maw, keeping the primary and secondary staging doors as the intended focal points. Nuda cursed, this time at his mistake. "It's cover. Hold. I repeat, hold. Do not Engage. Dammit, do not engage."

Defying Nuda's orders, the 72nd infantry, led by Lieutenant Kifner and his pride, had already spun up their machines and were heading into the Maw to make a name for themselves.

Nuda's continued orders for his forces to come back were ignored. He watched in horror as all movement inside the Maw stopped suddenly. "Sunnova bitch," he said to himself. His forces' lack of coordination, evidenced by the breakaway units, would betray his army's lack of cohesion. It would further serve to embolden the enemy at a time when his forces were off balance and needed to regroup.

"What the hell was that?" Harp screamed in panic over the broad array channel.

Nuda knew precisely what *the hell* it was—as soon as the bulk of Kifner's infantry and the other sympathetic movers were in the Maw, a powerful disruptive pulse was detonated.

The communications erupted in a flurry of chatter and typed messages, with every voice betraying its owner's mild confusion and slight panic. Nuda knew from experience that the equipment had shields to reduce, even avoid, the damage to the sensitive onboard electronics and fuel, but they needed to be active. This took precious power away from being able to move fast and have the full arsenal of weapon systems at the pilot's disposal. Nuda cursed and dropped into his seat, intently watching the moss-covered rocks for hints of what to do next.

"PICK THEM OFF," Lariat called.

Long gunners perched on ledges around the Maw began punching holes through torsos and exploding the heads of invaders as they worked their manual opening levers, clambered out onto a scorched field, and tried to bolt to safety. To avenge the assail from the ridge, the invaders who remained behind shrouded the ridgeline in flames with their short-range missiles, trying to suppress successive volleys of sniper fire.

"This adventure will be costly," Duncan said.

"But what greater thing could we fight for than our home and loved ones?" Deek asked, not really seeking an answer. The indicator light on the portal structure to the Maw flashed four successive patterns of two yellows and a green light, then went dark.

Charlie, the third phase, was underway. As the panels lifted, poisonous air rushed into the room—her dragoon suit instantly engaged the environmental scrubbing system, making it breathable again. The Zephyrs left the gate first, launching quick-fire rockets and spraying enemy forces liberally with kinetic weapon fire. They were quick when lightly loaded, and a few brave volunteers piloted the remaining machines as lead cover for the dragoons. All Zephyr pilots were taught a similar philosophy: running out of ammo was better than dying with unspent rounds. The attack dispersed with a few of the invader's batteries and dragoons before the vehicles were turned into burning piles of fodder. Captain Trull's squad commanded air support: the Death's Nemeses exited the upper aviaries and flew north to circle behind the ridgeline. When the invaders caught sight of them, they launched a barrage of surface-to-air missiles, which ate at the chaff the pilots tossed behind them.

Deek hoped the gods of war appreciated the sacrifice and that their wrath and consumption would be easy on the rest of her forces. Her display burst into hundreds of brilliant mini suns as she emerged from Warbler Ridge under the luminescent grenades and the cascade of sparks scattered between her troops and the invaders. The countermeasures should distract the enemy targeting systems long enough to give her platoon time to clear the dangerous areas of the canyon.

Deek's dragoons navigated the Maw's kill field, suffering minimal casualties, and hammered into the less fortified southern tree line. They engaged briefly with the invading forces long enough to taunt them into giving chase while sustaining some forward momentum. Once under the canopy, Deek's unit dropped scatter mines and dispersed until deep into the forest cover, where they rendezvoused and picked up a river course to the southwest. The lack of snow and icepack accumulation from the previous winter provided a navigable water flow and a passable alternative to using trails and roadways. The dragoons skirted along the rock embankments of the river on a course to the stranded House Khilsyth and Lanal forces. Every one of them was relieved to have survived the Maw.

CHAPTER 18

ANZIL STUDIED THE intricately carved wooden doors guarding the Grand Hall of the Nihkiehl Clan. He had to strain his neck upward and squint to make out the shapes carved into the upper areas and ceiling. As the doors swung open, the light from the woodsy room was captured in their metallic geodesic domes that told of the valor earned through the lifetimes of fabled warriors. The place reminded him of the charming lakeside lodges where, as a child, he would spend his summers constructing forts in the mid-branches of the dense white-clad trees. The lively conversations within faded to dull whispers, mixed with the scuffing of hard-toed soles on the stone floor as staff scurried to fulfill their various duties. The herald paused a moment, skilled in the timing of a maximum number of eyes on the guests, and, when satisfied, announced the newcomers as Corporal Anzil Stone, representing House Khilsyth and his staff.

"Stone?" a hulk of a man bellowed, striding forward with his arm outstretched to greet Anzil. "Bah, that's not his name. My bet would be on Khilsyth."

Anzil recognized the owner and shook the man's hand, Leon Nihkiehl, the current clan Chief. "The name change was supposed to be a secret, something to allow me to blend in, but that seems trivial now." He scratched the back of his head with his free hand. "Even somewhat hindering. But yes, I am a Khilsyth."

"Pretty early in the invasion for a visit," Leon said, still gripping Anzil's hand. "The Khilsyths struggling, are they? You know, it hasn't been that long since the most recent skirmish between our clans."

A lazy feud between the Khilsyths and the Nihkiehls had resulted in little blood and no loss of life until a recent incident at Carteral Dam. The Green River was the primary irrigation source for the canals that fed the southern Khilsyth farmlands. Over time, the river's flow had become a mere trickle when it made its way to the southern parts of the Khilsyth lands. This was because the Nihkiehls needed water to expand into the Arcata Range's arid areas. The Khilsyths had dispatched forces to remove one of the diversionary waterways near the dam, but their initial sweep missed a two-person dive team of mechanics inspecting the structure. Clan Nihkiehl claimed the Khilsyths staged the event and kidnapped the mechanics because no bodies were recovered—a few skirmishes ensued in the southern reaches of the Khilsyth lands, resulting in some property and equipment damage. Neither family elevated the incident further, and Anzil suspected it was the first death to have occurred in his lifetime from the family's feud.

"No, Leon," Anzil admitted. "A couple of months doesn't seem like a long time. But it also hasn't been that long since the invasion started, and I'll tell you what: it feels more like half a lifetime."

Leon laughed. "Good, you do recognize me then. Sorry about the... persuasion needed for an audience with yours truly." He chuckled as he imagined what the expression on Anzil's face must have been—upon entering Nihkiehl airspace and requesting permission to land, Anzil and crew had been given a rather stiff 'piss off' message. "Nice touch with the *Mischi* getting you in my private hanger. I didn't expect you to have that kind of help."

"To be honest," Anzil said with a breathy laugh. "Neither did I. But, about this invasion, it does seem like it's a problem for all of us."

"Right now, it seems contained and directed at the Khilsyths," Leon said, releasing Anzil. "And potentially the Lanals—poor bastards. What do you make of that, young Khilsyth?"

Anzil stemmed the anger rising inside and consoled himself that it was just his pride overreacting at the disrespect of being called young. "I don't think the invaders will stop once they've finished with us."

"That may be true."

"I think it is, given that there's also Anacul and Rift Faction in the mix. What do *you* make of that?"

Leon held up his hands and shook his head. "It's been a long while since the Anacul reared their ugly mugs," he said, leaning toward Anzil. "Go on—let's have it, then. Where do you stand?"

Anzil gave Leon a brief situational report about the invasion of Skyetook and the event at the Astute facility. After some prodding, he relinquished details about the battle on Hurricane Ridge and the situation at Warbler Ridge.

After weighing Anzil's story in a few minutes of awkward silence, Leon commanded everyone in the room to leave. The senior House members murmured in mild disapproval as they shuffled from the room, but none would dare object openly. In communal settings such as the Great Hall, the Nihkiehls considered objecting to an order as a challenge to the Chief's authority—the few people who could question Leon did so only in confidence. He chased a tickle in his throat away with a quick cough. "So, I'm just to take you at your word then? What would compel me to request action from our council?" Leon walked over, sat near one of the many roaring fireplaces, and motioned with a freshly poured beverage for Anzil to sit nearby. "I can tell you've had a busy day. But we need to have a conversation about concessions, as they will survive where we may not. And whether the rest of them do is not up to us. But a select few must live."

"Are you positive you haven't been infiltrated?" Anzil asked, taking a seat across from Leon. "Much like we were."

"We have been," Leon admitted begrudgingly. "Fortunately, many of the folks the invaders approached came forward. We used some of them as spies to root out the others. There's still a chance there are a few. We gave everyone a little demonstration of what happens to traitors in the arena about two months ago. I didn't want to do it. Wanted to believe we could set them straight. The council knew there had to be others. My niece was one of them that we made an example of. At least we hope they'll have second thoughts about pursuing any sinister objectives."

"I'm sorry to hear that, Leon."

"Are you now?"

"I truly am. Valan, my brother, and some of my friends are still in the city. We are... unsure about their allegiance."

"You're lucky you didn't find out sooner. You would have had the greater pain of watching a loved one's skin blackened and shriveled as they burned the confessions out of her."

They sat silently, staring into their diminishing pints, drowning the moment's pain with hefty draws. It was Leon who broke the building tension. "Family quarrels seem petty now. We've heard rumors that the Mar-Vhen transport has been overrun. And I don't believe Rifty and Republic star cruisers happening by our part of the galaxy are mere coincidences. My guess is that removing House Khilsyth from power is not the only mission objective. None of the people the invaders turned knew the ulterior motive or long-term plan, for that matter. We figure once they get through with you, they'll come knocking on our doors if we're still here. Also, there is something else about all this that I can't wrap my head around."

"From what we've intercepted, we have reason to believe that Valan is trying to garner a deal with the Rift Faction for extra protection," Anzil said, not hiding his disapproval. "Add the Republic and Anacul to the mix. It's interesting."

Leon nodded. "Like I said, it's getting hard to sort out who's who and what everyone's up to."

"Agreed. So. How can I sway you to help us?"

"I need something to appease the other senior members of my House. Our council is divided. They mean well but are short-sighted. Half of the reason we're fine holed up and waiting it out, the other half want to wait it out and then deal with whatever is left."

"This could just be a forward strike team."

"Most likely," Leon agreed. "Call it misguided confidence because we shot a few of their javelins out of the sky. But I call it lucky us."

"And we all know that can run out."

"Do you know how many star cruisers are up there?" Leon asked, raising his mug skyward as Anzil shook his head. "More than enough to give any reinforcements from any of our House's trouble. And that help is about ten to fifteen standard days away. It also gives me pause that the Rift Faction and the Nova Republic aren't shooting at each other."

"But that's why I'm here, Leon. I need your help. I'm planning on rallying as many people on Lindaulx as I can. I plan to visit Tallus Outpost next."

Leon arched his left eyebrow and finished his coal-colored malty beverage. "Have you contacted them?"

"We received an acknowledgment of sorts. Have you?"

Leon chuckled. "Truth is, we've never seen them. Just their robot proxies that sell their wares. They showed up one night and infested Nock's Roost." Seeing the confusion on Anzil's face, he added, "sorry, you know it as the Tallus Outpost. Nock's Roost is the old Tersinian name. Or didn't anyone tell you who lived here before the Khilsyths?"

Anzil cracked his knuckles and drew a deep breath. "Let's say the specters expanded my horizons a bit. They were a little fuzzy about what prompted the Tersinian's displacement, though."

"The Nova Republic decides," Leon said, and with a dismissive wave added, "and how those decisions get made is beyond me. Regardless. How about a joining of our families to seal a truce?" He asked with a big smile and a wave of freshly filled pint using a nearby spigot. "The old-fashioned approach hasn't been done... since your brother Valan.

Anzil shifted in his chair at this turn of events. He had expected a request for land, water, or equipment. "I take it you have someone in mind."

Leon smiled over his mug. "As a matter of fact, I do. You."

"Where did you come up with that idea?" Anzil asked, astounded. "Someone must have misinformed you. I'm... I'm not available."

Leon smiled. "I'm just hopeful you'll settle down one of these days. I sure would like to see you and my Deek make some grandkids for the missus and me."

"Wait. Deek? She's a Nihkiehl?"

Leon smiled and grasped Anzil's shoulder, forcefully shaking it twice. "Breathe, son, let it sink in. Yes, it would seem that you both have your secrets. Besides, with Trake gone—may your Pops rest in peace—there is little chance we can hold Lindaulx. All of us old-timers would be better off knowing that these lives we toiled and bled for amounted to something more than carvings on doors and stories that fade. Legacies are with the living. Trake wanted you to get your chance at the trials and tribulations of raising a family."

Anzil laughed nervously, trying to stem the sting of his heart from clouding his eyes. He turned away, biting his lip and spurning the tears welling in his eyes.

"And if you have a daughter, I just hope she doesn't have an ugly mug like yours," Leon said, then flashed a quick smile.

"Deek may not approve of children," Anzil said, shaking his head.

Leon laughed hard, a little too hard. "Son, you reckon it's going to be easy? Nah, you must earn her approval. She has a say in the matter. Failing that, maybe you'll provide me with one of your *Mischi;* I think I can offer them something they can't refuse. That would get the job done. Not pleasant. Rather, the opposite."

There was that name again, Anzil thought, which triggered an uncomfortable feeling there was an affiliation between Leon and Stigg. "Yes. I'm learning that specters can be useful, provided they maintain their end of the bargain."

"Vipers, the lot of them," Leon said with a quizzical glint in his eye. "You got them on the hook for something?"

"Not really," Anzil said and chased away an eye twitch. "Sort of. It turns out they were hired to protect two of my mechanics."

"It's mechanics they are interested in, eh?!" Leon said loud enough for any fool to hear. Then his look became distant and his voice solemn, "and whom have they come for?"

"My Chief Mechanic, Stigg. Or so they say."

"What would they want with a..." Leon said, tugging at his beard and whispering 'Stigg' a few times, changing the tonal inflections and pitch each time. "Yeah, that name sounds familiar. Big bastard. Old as dirt but could likely kick anyone's ass. Background information is pretty thin."

"Nonexistent even."

"He also tends to laugh way too loud at his own jokes."

"Wouldn't know," Anzil said, "he's a pretty serious fella." He flicked his head toward the specters and added, "he also calls them *Mischi,* just like you do."

Leon nodded, pulled at his nose, and sniffed loudly. "And the other?"

"A mid-level mechanic."

"Which one?"

"Goes by the name Clarke."

Leon sucked air in forcibly through pressed lips and mouthed a single word the *Mischi* couldn't see, 'lies.' He strolled over to the fieldstone hearth and stoked the fire more than was needed. Leon gripped the mantle to steady himself, closed his eyes, and willed his mind to cut through the distortion of Lindaulx's situation. In times like these, he longed for his life-long partner, Arbasele, even more than the daily feeling that a piece of him was missing. But she had given him instructions years ago, and he would uphold his oath. "Then it's agreed," Leon said, pounding the rings on his hand against the mantle. "My daughter, your true love, united families. I reckon there's no better reason for us to spill blood and wage war together."

"Thank you," Anzil said. "We could use your assistance."

"Don't thank me yet," Leon said, facing Anzil. "So, to the crux of the matter." He placed his empty mug on a nearby side table. "Shall we discuss how we get to dying?"

"Hopefully, that's not what happens," Anzil said, clasping Leon's outstretched muscular forearm. "First, we are going to need to rally an army."

"Great," Leon said and headed for a side room. "I'll meet you in the hangar shortly," he called over his shoulder before disappearing through an archway. "There's a couple of things I must do before leaving on this here adventure."

CHAPTER 19

THE NATIVE WILDLIFE of the Locknar Forest scattered as the machines of war raced beneath the canopies of the tall trees. The only natural movements were the clash of water over stone and the wind lashing against the feeble cling of dying leaves. Ahead of her position, Deek's battlenet screen tracked enemy armor and other equipment that bore no allegiance markings or sigils. "Captain Truul," Deek called and signaled for her platoon to slow, "any intel on the contacts to the south?"

"One sec, ma'am," Truul replied. "We'll be right back."

Deek was thankful to have an aerial reconnaissance contingent with them to provide over-cover as the invaders had disabled the satellites. She was also grateful to Mysis Rend because he had trained them to fight when blinded—the Nova Republic playbook's early engagement tactics focused on debilitating an enemy's ability to have real-time, wide-ranging data. To combat this, they developed several low-tech countering methods.

Truul and his squadron flew low along the river's course. They hugged tree-lined meadows, occasionally signaling their beasts for a few extra flaps of the leathery wings to sweep up to a vantage point, offering a line of sight to the invaders.

A few minutes later, Truul called back. "Confirmed visual on contacts. Moving southeast and quickly through the valley. They could be heading to Lake Fievre."

"They're not exactly being stealthy about it," Deek said. "I'd say we'd be a wee bit of a surprise."

"If we contact our people at the lake, the invaders will discover we're here," Duncan said.

"There's a good chance," Truul replied. "Triangulation is possible if they're skilled."

"Suggestions for conflict avoidance?" Deek asked, glancing around, only to be greeted by silence and the shaking of mechanical heads and torsos. "Come now. Nothing?" She figured her platoon was scheming for a scuffle. "Thought as much." There was a little delight creeping into her voice. It also had the unwelcome effect of raising her pitch. "They'll eventually be aware of our presence. And I didn't see a way to avoid ripping into those sons of bitches, either. Captain Truul, send a low perimeter scout around the invaders and make sure they don't have company with them." The target force was large enough that she didn't relish the thought of a tag-along support column or nearby compliment joining the fray. Taking a moment to settle herself, she relayed her plan to her strike teams. She hoped they were far enough east of the other invasion force guarding Hindish Pass that they wouldn't come to investigate or send support.

With a chorus of battle cries and encouragement from the squad, her heart swelled with pride, and a slow smile spread across her lips. She pumped her arms several times and punched her fists together twice in front of her. Her team was superb at what they did—a bunch of badasses.

"Captain Truul," Deek called, "get me an enemy unit count when you can and swift currents."

"Sure thing, ma'am," Truul responded, ignoring the Khilsyth officer's communication protocol. "We'll also drop some comm disrupters when we get the chance. No sense them calling their buddies to come play." His wyvern screeched in protest as it climbed hard to get a line of sight on the invaders. Wyverns weren't uncommon in these parts, so Truul was hopeful the invaders would overlook his contingent of riders.

"Radio battle protocols until we establish visible contact," Deek instructed.

The first volley of short-range tornado rockets followed the peaceful rush of the river. They screeched out over the cliff edge, leaving the river to crash over the ridge and break on the rocks below. The enemy units detected the attack and reacted with trained precision, dividing their forces into smaller groups and deploying countermeasures. They did not want to be caught in an unpleasant mix of armor-piercing and incendiary death.

Anticipating the invaders' response, Truul's unit sent the subsequent rockets skimming across the deck, avoiding the smoke and keeping the visual feed the missile provided relatively unhindered. At least tornadoes didn't need a direct hit to deal enough damage to incapacitate; they just needed to strike close. For all their efforts, only those invaders with the instinct to shoot down the incoming rockets were able to protect those closest to them.

Deek spurred her dragoons toward the precipice, passing a squad of Stalwart dragoons securing into something solid to counter the kick of firing their weapon. A low thump and the ratcheting of another shell into place was the signature discomforting sound of *moles* being sent downrange to bury themselves into the ground below. Worse was the unwelcome sound of the dull thud and crunch of the substrate on the receiving end for those who comprehended its implication.

As what remained of the First Dragoon platoon, loyal to Anzil Khilsyth, emerged from the tree line and over the cliff, their powerful terrain-based scanners provided a complete picture to their aerial support team—Truul's tactical screen surged into clarity.

"Where the hell did they get so much armor?" Tristan asked.

"One guess," Deek said. "Ignore their colors, boys and girls. They're not our people."

"Not anymore," Duncan said.

When Deek's forward assault squad came into rifle range, a path of smoldering shell casings and wisps of smoke began trailing behind them. They concentrated fire on the lightly armored personnel and vehicles, knowing their munition weapons would be a mere nuisance to Vindicator and Stalwart armors. The invaders answered the onslaught with a hailstorm of projectiles, marring the Khilsyth dragoon's shields like dead bugs on a hot windshield. Only a handful of invader units fled through the mole field, resulting in some being abruptly launched into the air only to land with severely crumpled and dismantled armor and a good chance of the loss of life, limb, or both.

As the two dragoon forces neared, Deek retracted her gun and drew her favored cleaver. It was her weapon of choice and had belonged to her mother. Deek waded into the battle, unhindered because on this field, she could lock swords with the strongest of soldiers—the dragoon supplying the strength and leverage needed, her augmentations elevating her reflexes to blurring heights and giving her an edge over most of her competitors. There was strictness and beauty in the efficiency of the carnage Deek and company inflicted as they executed their martial battle tactics with choreographed precision. But the invaders proved to be respectable fighters in their own right.

Deek ducked a sloppy chop slash. Her cleaver hissed to life as a carbon arc formed along its blade, and she punched it into the left hip joint of her attacker's suit. The weapon's miniature air jet cleared the cutting area in a cascade of shimmering molten metal. The effect was compounded by the internal pressure of the enemy's suit, forcing the burn-inducing material away from the pilot's skin. Deek's enemy moved as she expected. They swung their hips backward, lifting their sword arm for balance and exposing the thinner plates covering the armpit area. She exploited the mistake by sliding her cleaver into the opening, striking the pilot's heart and incinerating it. The dragoon should be dead—the experience of killing one was spooky because there was rarely notification or gratification at the moment of the kill. She chewed on the inside of her cheek to steady her doubt and sighed with relief when the dragoon armor slumped and nose-dived into the field. In her heart, she knew others wouldn't prove so easy to cut down.

As if answering the challenge, another enemy batted a comrade out of the way and pointed at Deek. The display of machismo brought a smile to her lips, which vanished as she ducked under a reckless hammer blow. She jabbed her cleaver upward, striking between the hip and torso joints of the attacker and sinking it into their armor. Deek deactivated her cleaver's cutting edge and engaged several serrated arms running the length of the blade. The dense alloy cut into the soft tissues of the invader's inner organs. Deek snatched the cleaver free from the armor with a spray of blood. The sight of her weapon dripping vermillion tears made her smile, but such evidence of prior victory would vaporize before mingling with another enemy's metal and bone.

Invaders continued to fall to Deek and her team until there were no more challengers. The gods of war had been kind as they lost a few armor sets and fewer pilots. Without having to issue orders, her unit ensured all enemy pilots were dead and salvaged what they could. Thankfully and sometimes mercifully, the base platform for dragoons was uniform, and a killing field provided ample parts to repair damaged armor.

"Captain Deek, you and your hunters are in the clear for now," Truul said, observing from aloft. "Good luck and safe travels. We'll set waypoints and pray for you all."

Deek thanked Truul and set about tending to her team. Once ready, they set off for Lake Fievre to rendezvous with the other loyalists. In transit, she relayed a secure message to Warbler Ridge using Truul's beacons. The response was grim: the invaders were gathering a sizable force outside and setting up fortified positions, meaning there was little hope of Deek getting back to Warbler Ridge by land. Anzil was hopeful Farsil would successfully capture more raptors so that a laborious process of flying her people back to Warbler Ridge would eventually be possible.

With few viable options, Deek called ahead for a defensive perimeter and tasked Truul's unit with scouting for a better location. As the evening cool air descended into the rain-dampened vegetation of the forest, a dense gloom claimed the meadow. She prayed for Anzil's success in rallying the support of the other houses. It was a selfish request, but at least she wasn't trapped behind the Maw.

CHAPTER 20

ANZIL OCCUPIED THE only dry spot in a sizable cavern where moisture collected on several stalactites, growing until it lost traction and crashed to the stone floor. The water seeping from the ceiling collected in pools that rippled and flooded into a thin chasm running the room's length. The rate of collection and dispersion created an effect like a light rain. A soft, florescent glow added to his sense of serenity and calmness, which was rudely interrupted by the now uncloaked figure in front of him. It stood almost half again as tall as him, wearing a large-brimmed hat tipped forward, touching the top of a weathered duster. It stomped toward him with measured steps that echoed throughout the cavern. At first, the steps had a metered rhythm, but the competing echoes eventually became a backdrop of chaotic applause. The figure stopped and raised its wide-brimmed hat unhurriedly, revealing a dimly glowing eye that cast a shadow of light over a metallic face.

"You are Anzil Khilsyth," a voice that sounded like a botched back-alley vocal implant said.

"Yes, I am," Anzil responded carefully. "And whom might I have the honor of greeting?"

"Why did you just hesitate."

Anzil chuckled. "If I'm being honest... you using my actual name caught me off guard."

"Yet, you laughed."

"At myself, I assure you. It's just been rather strange finding out that my name isn't the secret I thought it was. We are grateful you received us. Also, I'm sorry, but I didn't catch your name."

"You may call me Kaihaiau Vauea Laarsaa."

Anzil attempted to repeat the name and failed miserably.

"It is a challenging name to pronounce with your language skills. You may call me Laars if that is acceptable to you."

Anzil clasped his hands in front of him and nodded in appreciation. "Thank you, Laars."

"Now, as to why you are here."

"We have come to seek an alliance. We are rallying forces to take back our City. We have already gained the Nihkiehl's support."

"And you've come hoping that we can help get you off-world?"

"Quite the opposite," Anzil replied. "We are planning to repel the invaders and take back our home."

"The Tersinians?"

"Yes, them and the Anacul, or whatever they call themselves."

"Lindaulx is lost, young Khilsyth. It will also soon be time for us to leave this place."

"There's no way they can. Not with the Nova Republic and the Rift Faction here."

"That is an interesting development. But the Tersinians have been landing here for years. Recently, they've been arriving in much greater numbers, and there is justification for their reclamation of Tervessi—this planet you now call Lindaulx. Although, and admittedly, some of the relative newcomers have confusing origins to us."

"Just how many people do you track?" Anzil asked, surprise marring his words. "And do you mean to say you've identified their home worlds?"

Laars shifted his weight slightly from heel to toe and nodded affirmatively. "Perhaps. But it's not quite that simple. What fascinates us is that a handful of them can manipulate the flux."

"But these Tersinians have brought war and suffering with them, have they not?"

Laars head fell slowly, the glow from his eye dimming. "How much do you know of the Tersinian people?"

"That wasn't something that was covered in my education."

"We believe it's important for you to understand the relationship they and we have with the worlds before you make your request of us."

"Sounds reasonable," Anzil said tentatively. "Please go on."

"The Tersinians first: for most of them, religion profoundly influences their lives. Through it, they seek to expand their natural ability to touch what they perceive as divine. Many devote their lives to such lofty aspirations—almost fanatically—especially those who become their *Tersa*.

"Like specters on a crusade?" Anzil asked, wrinkling his nose and causing a drawn-out blink.

"In a way."

"And they both can use the flux?"

"In a way. But everything relates to the energy and time given to a planet. Flux is such an odd term. But you would have needed a name for the space and energy surrounding you. Yes, the ability to interact with this flux is within many objects throughout the system. Even you."

Anzil's head snapped back, his brow furrowing as he shook his head.

"That grabbed your curiosity," Laars said, the words rolling together. "These bonds, or conduits, they manifest differently in all of us. Most people only feel a faint whisper or fleeting sense of being a part of something beyond the immediate or greater than themselves. For very few, it's their sustenance. It was once said to me they need *it,* and *it, them.* Tersinian culture is driven by the need to expand these conduits to the flux—further than they were genetically prescribed. Truly, the subject is beyond me."

"And that brought them here?"

"In them lies a sense of place, of being that here is an answer to their life's greatest purpose."

"Which is?"

"Let's say that some believe there are forces beyond our comprehension that regulate how worlds evolve and take shape. And there are two camps: those that would protect what the Astutes would protect us from versus those that would undo those safeguards."

"But what do the Tersinians want on Lindaulx?"

"Ah, yes. Localized. Our theory was challenged recently when the Tersinians damaged the facility and sealed it in a manner that has threatened our home." Laars removed his wide-brimmed hat, folded it neatly in a collapsing series of metal plates, and tucked it into his duster. "And so, you must know before asking anything of us that... we may have been wrong all these years."

"We all make mistakes," Anzil said. "Nobody's perfect. I'm unsure how that would sway me."

"Because we were once clear on how life evolved, comforted by the safeguards leftover by the Astutes. Now, we are concerned that the system that would protect our worlds has been compromised."

"I don't understand," Anzil said.

"I'm afraid that we don't either," Laars said. "At least not completely. But we know that it is time for us to act. So here is what you must understand. We are uncertain what path the Astutes would have us take. By joining you, we may very well accelerate the end."

"Even so," Anzil said, mustering what he thought was confidence. "I would still seek your help. However, I have no terms or concessions prepared."

"You do realize that Lindaulx is lost."

"Then we will need each other's help to liberate it."

"Lindaulx is lost to you. That much we are certain of."

"Please hear me out. I've got the Nihkiehl's support. We've bolstered our ranks. There are still people loyal within the Capital and surrounding areas."

"I'm sorry, young Khilsyth. But Lindaulx was never yours to begin with. You must abandon this place."

Anzil cursed. "We will not lose."

"That may be true. But you must leave here."

"So, will you help us then?"

"We will."

"Really," Anzil said, standing up straighter. "I… I wouldn't have the slightest idea of what we can offer?"

Laars lumbered forward with an awkward gait and stopped an arm's length away. "How could you comprehend what we value?" he questioned in a low growl. "I assure you it won't be as drastic as producing kin."

"What?" Anzil asked with a laugh.

"We are an observant group, young Khilsyth. Intrigued by interactions, especially those close to us."

"Some would call that spying."

"Some would. But I request it for our alliance and exodus."

"What makes you think I'm leaving?"

"It's inevitable. We are not meant to remain on Tervessi any longer, nor are you."

"Would you please stop saying that?" Anzil requested.

"If you wish. But it doesn't make it less real. This planet was never truly Lindaulx. Now, our arrangement."

"I'm listening."

"We would propose a union and study your lives. It has been too long since we walked among people, and we wish to reacquaint ourselves."

"That's all?"

"It is no small request."

"No? Then perhaps some clarification is in order."

"Allow us to experience lives with you and some of your colleagues. In turn, we will provide our assistance."

"I can't speak for everyone, but I will make introductions provided no harm will come to those people."

"We require more than introductions," Laars said.

"Laars," Anzil said in a sympathetic tone. "I'm sorry. I cannot force this upon anyone. They must do this of their own free will."

"You do not command those around you?"

"Not in that way. How many of my people do you have in mind?"

"There are eight of us."

"In total? Only eight people here?" Anzil regretted his outburst as Laars withdrew several paces. "Sorry. It's been a very challenging day." If it was only eight people, he could have the specters convince them of the dire need for help.

"Introductions will be enough," Laars spoke, startling Anzil. "Your terms are acceptable."

"I will do my best to honor them, Laars."

"Noted. Now, how can we help?"

"The Nihkiehls need our support clearing a path to Skyetook," Anzil said. "Some of my forces are out of Warbler Ridge, heading to Lake Fievre, and will need to rendezvous with the Nihkiehl army."

"A siege on Skyetook seems like a lackluster plan."

Anzil shrugged his indifference.

"I understand," Laars said. "You do not reveal your ultimate plan to everyone."

"Because it's not fully baked," Anzil said with a sly smile. "I believe you need to give your team space for ingenuity and ownership when developing solutions. And you're right; it doesn't hurt to have a few secrets."

"Ah, you would like my sister. She is the warmonger amongst us. I'm curious, though. Do you have a plan to get into the city?"

Anzil wobbled his head from side to side.

"Then we shall get to it. We will need the spaceport. Getting people off world could decrease casualties of the misguided."

"When will you join us?" Anzil asked.

Laars' laugh sounded like a rock crusher, and he gestured behind Anzil. "Allow me to introduce my sister; you may call her Luna, for you will surely not grasp the complex phonetics of her chosen name."

Anzil turned to see a slim, feminine person of average height when she stepped forward with her open hand outstretched.

"The rest of our family will seek their preferred subjects," Laars said as he turned and walked toward the cave's exit. "Come now, Anzil Khilsyth," he called over his shoulder.

Anzil heard Leon step closer, betrayed by a familiar sniff. The weight of the man's hand came to rest on his shoulder and provided a fleeting sense of reassurance.

"Trake would be proud," Leon said solemnly. "Now. You take good care of my little girl, you hear. Or there'll be hell to pay. But I'm afraid it's time for me to catch another ride now."

Anzil said farewell to Leon and waited until everyone exited the cave. Then he bent down, dipping his fingers into the cool, glowing waters, and pressed his palm flat onto the smooth rock below.

Lindaulx was silent.

THE OSPREY SPED over the desert landscape toward Warbler Ridge on a course Shifty predicted would avoid potential threats. Anzil was finding it difficult to keep from staring at the two newcomers from Tallus Outpost. He imagined he appeared a little crazy, with his eyes darting back and forth between them and then down at the floor when they caught his glances. Laars was withdrawn into his oversized duster, and the visible parts of his body gave the impression he was a metal construct. His sister Luna was radiant and dressed in pants that hugged her slender frame and a fitted top with a neckline that plunged deep, revealing a precious stone hanging on a braided chain wrapped around her neck. If not for her eyes, which hinted at an age far greater than her flawless alabaster skin portrayed, Anzil would have placed Luna in her early twenties. He took a few measured breaths, trying to diminish his fears from taking hold—he felt ill-prepared for the road ahead. Still, there was comfort in convincing himself that their father had coached Valan on matters such as invasions and the Nova Republic. His last memorable thought before he succumbed to exhaustion from the day's adventure was that Luna couldn't be the warmonger of Tallus Outpost.

CHAPTER 21

ANZIL FLAILED AWAKE, grabbing his armrests, bracing his feet, and fearing severe turbulence or, worse, they were crashing. Shaking the sleep from his head, he realized Laars had doled out the rude awakening.

"We are close to Warbler Ridge," Laars said in his signature mechanical growl, releasing Anzil. "And the captain is demanding your presence."

"How long was I out?" Anzil asked.

"Not long enough," Laars responded.

Anzil stretched and made his way to the front of the Osprey, where the two specters sat together.

"Hey there, bright eyes," Tarra said with a gentle squeeze of Anzil's tense forearm and felt it soften. "We are about five minutes from Warbler Ridge."

"Any word from Leon?" Anzil asked, wondering which one commanded the ship.

Tarra turned her chair to face Anzil and snapped a crisp salute. "Colonel. They will begin their assault on the forces guarding Durges Gate in the morning."

"They have a poor chance of breaking through there," Anzil said after playing through the various scenarios and tactics. Durges Gate wasn't a gate per se but an abandoned mountain colony with a series of tunneled complexes through the Arcata Mountain Range, providing a direct route between the Khilsyth and Nihkiehl territories. On the side Leon's forces would exit, the invaders had capitalized on a defensible pinch point and moved to fortify it when they failed to take the Nihkiehl's territory. Leon's forces would be exposed when they exited the tunnel, with little space to mount an attack. It would take days to navigate the mountain passes and highland routes compared to the tunnel, and if the invaders had flying craft, they would seriously hinder Leon's jaunt through such open land.

"I wouldn't like my odds if I were Leon," Tarra admitted. "I'm not too fond of ours at Warbler Ridge either, nor of getting into Skyetook. But seriously, Leon's odds, they suck."

Luna's sweet voice filled Anzil's ears, warming his soul. "Our brother is with Leon. He will be of assistance."

"Do we have any units in the area or any way to support them?" Anzil asked.

Luna shook her head, her white silken hair shimmering. "We know very little right now. However, I can convey a message to Leon if you wish."

"Please tell Leon we'll send him whatever tactical data we can," Anzil responded. "Schematics, terrain, anything. Also, we have a team outside Warbler Ridge, likely on a southerly course to Lake Fievre. They could hook up for fire support and help provide a distraction—we'll send him a timeline. Tell him that it's Deek's unit out there. Oh, and wish him luck."

Leon's voice emanated clearly from a device on Luna's forearm. "That must have been a hard decision, son."

"Dammit, that's going to get hard to get used to," Anzil said. "Sorry about that, Leon. Yeah, it was hard. Not that I had much choice in the matter. So, how many of our friends from Tallus Outpost are with you?"

"One. I'm calling him Laand. Not even going to try his actual name. We're becoming fast friends, though. Strange company one finds themselves within conflicts?"

"What's your tactical strength at?"

"We're moving four platoons of dragoons, a Zephyr platoon with support, and an infantry division through in the morning. It was hard to convince any of the clan to stay behind. You know how that goes in these parts?" After an awkward pause, Leon continued. "Aye, sorry. Didn't mean anything by that. Will sort your kin out. Anyway, Laand here tells me you have a plan to get us into the city?"

"You comfortable with that?"

"Always wanted to see the inside of Skyetook again."

"I know a great tour guide."

"There enough lifeboats?"

"Sure, hope so," Anzil said.

"Then what?"

"Working on it. Trying to reconcile the Rifty's and the Republic's actions."

"Understood. We'll tie the invaders up long enough so they don't come searching for you right away. It may be a race to knock on the front gate, though."

"We'll be ready for you."

"See you when I see you."

"Good luck, Leon," Anzil said, intrigued by his father-in-law's fascination with death and even blatant disregard for it.

THE FORCES OUTSIDE of Warbler Ridge had swelled to about triple their size since Deek's exodus, making it impossible for a sizable force to exit without significant attrition. The recent addition of heavy artillery platforms would not bode well for any light armored or aerial units.

Inside Warbler Ridge's war room, Anzil's commanders struggled to develop a tactical strategy, let alone a decent idea for dealing with the invaders.

"Those must be some intense thoughts you carry," Laars said, gesturing for Anzil to sit across from him.

"Sorry, what was that?" Anzil asked, peering over a projection playing out simulations and reporting dismal probability numbers.

"You are weighing some considerable decisions, are you not?" Laars asked.

Anzil nodded and tapped his forehead. "Sorry, I was a little inside here. Major decisions, yes. Don't tell me you can read my mind."

"Not yet, but it can be arranged if you'd like," Laars said, erasing the smirk from Anzil's face.

"Maybe later."

"As you wish. But, your concern, it's easy enough to see."

Anzil flopped onto a nearby bench and rubbed his brow with forceful, meaningful strokes. "The paths I see have two approaches: disable the invader's artillery and rush out of the Ridge like a bunch of dumbasses. Not very inspiring or a high probability of being successful. The other approach involves a smaller task force to deal with Valan. Maybe even an Anacul leader if one's kicking around there. That also requires being able to turn people to, or back to, our side. But Stigg is apparently trapped deep within the complex in a rogue cave-in. Possibly caused by a group of rebels. And no one can account for Clarke's whereabouts."

"What would you need *them* for?"

"And to add to the fun, the specter tells me the invaders are bringing more troops and heavy equipment to the surface using our spaceport."

"Not insurmountable."

"Oh, but it gets better. The Rift Faction task force is off-loading in the wasteland under the pretense of maintenance. I suspect Valan has an arrangement with the Nova Republic he can't control. The stupid ass. And to top it all off, Deek is out there stranded, without support."

"I recommend sleep," Laars said decisively. "You are exhausted and not thinking clearly."

"No time. There are a lot of moving pieces I need to work through."

"You have time. A seven-minute doze earlier doesn't qualify as rest. Our brothers-in-arms will not engage enemy forces at Durges Gate until the morning." Laars leaned forward and touched Anzil's arm lightly—Anzil didn't finish his thoughts before the sedative quieted him.

"He won't appreciate that when he wakes," Tarra said, uncloaking in the room.

"True. But his machine failed to account for that variable. I calculate an adequately rested Anzil will improve our odds of success tomorrow. As will having the likes of you and your companion around."

"The likes of me, eh?"

"I know you, *Mischi.* I'm aware of what you hunt."

"Is that a fact?" Tarra asked Laars. "And what would that be?"

Anzil struggled against the darkness, trying to hear the conversation, but it drifted away as the light faded.

CHAPTER 22

THE PALE LIGHT cast from the few working light fixtures carved into the smooth rock flickered, barely able to dispel the darkness from the room's edges. A wisp of light hovered in the room's center, growing brighter, shifting and blurring, eventually revealing the shadowy outline of a figure. The form shifted in a swirling shade of violet and green, drawing in more light from the room and darkening its edges. "I am Harmsweld. Formally of what you call the Tallus Outpost," an ethereal voice said, startling Clarke. "Are you familiar with it? Good. It appears my kin have entered the equation. They seem to have agreed, an alliance of sorts, with some of the people of Lindaulx. I wonder: are you familiar with this new arrangement?"

"I don't think so," Clarke replied with a slight laugh. "How's it working out for them?"

"It is difficult to tell."

"Do you know what side they are on?"

"A better line of inquiry would lead to understanding what path they are on."

"Hopefully, ridding the invaders from Lindaulx."

"Irrelevant. The primary sides would claim such an objective."

"So, saving Lindaulx. Not a concern. Understood."

"Perhaps. But challenging to find a workable solution. And what version to save is the correct one? Do we save Lindaulx, Tervessi, or do we go further back? Do you know?"

"Lindaulx would be preferred," Clarke replied.

"Lindaulx is lost," Harmsweld said.

"Yeah, I was thinking the same," Clarke said half-heartedly.

"You are adapting to your new state, then?"

Clarke hesitated. "What do you mean?"

The figure's swirling hues slowed, and shades of teal darkening to a deep burnt orange appeared, weaving into patterns of violet and green. "Your ability to use Astute technology. How do you feel about its presence?"

"The dark passenger?"

"That's an interesting way to characterize it."

"It's hard to describe."

"I suppose it would be."

"Do you have a dark passenger?"

"In a way. Perhaps we all do."

"How do I remove the damn thing?"

"I'm not sure that you can."

"That sucks. Any idea why the invaders are here?"

"I have my theories," Harmsweld admitted after some hesitation. "These invaders are only the beginning. An assemblage, perhaps. Unlike my kind, they have not grown complacent."

"How so?"

"We were much like you are now. We were focused on responding to threats and reveling in the joy of life. We celebrated the multitude of events marking time's passage. And in our pursuits, we developed many wonderful and devastating technologies—"

"That's all very enlightening. But how does that help the current Lindaulx situation?"

"Truthfully, not that much. Perhaps some… maybe. But as I was trying to say. Eventually, my kind experienced repeating patterns of our existence. We encountered the same issues, but we never really solved the problems. The actual change was the creation of different technologies and approaches to achieving the same goals. The surrounding species evolved. Some died off. They were playing out lives in a similar fashion to us—but none advanced beyond our capabilities. My kind arrived at a point where they saw little value or worth in living as we were. They believed they had experienced and explored all there was to live complete lives—life was on an endless loop and could only evolve so. We believed we had arrived at what was our final state in the evolution of our species. So, some just faded away."

"That's pretty grim. Damn depressing, actually."

"I have perhaps oversimplified. There are still a few of us who remain bound by our duties. We wanted to show our kind the glory in the patterns and the subtle differences. Even the different ways that each cycle could play out—the wonderous nuances in the minutia. Some of us who stayed believed the patterns were intertwined and repeating for a reason. We started tracing the origins of the patterns through all the known living and deceased races we could. Recently, I discovered how life perdures and continues to evolve. A way to intercede with the current cycle."

"Again, how does this relate to the invaders?"

"Getting there, Clarke. I liken it to the analogy of a river system."

"Creeks and tributaries?"

"Precisely. We, everyone, are the molecules that form the water, and the flux is the stuff that binds us together. It can also destroy what's in its path. When large enough events occur, they form a confluence. This causes the magnitude of the flux to increase and the process to renew. Or perhaps feel like it starts over."

"Like déjà vu?"

"I believe your world is about to experience an unprecedented event of a significant confluence heading to a universe-altering diversion."

"Of course we are," Clarke said flatly.

"It is why the Tersinians and others have appeared. They are leading us to an event horizon—a tipping point we may not return from."

"How are they planning to do that?"

"I was hoping *you* could tell me."

"Are you serious?" Clarke asked in disbelief.

"One must explore all avenues for answers—in my lifetime, I've learned I can find them in the unlikeliest places."

"I'm guessing it's not a coincidence that we are both here then."

"I am here by my design… rather, my ambition. Although I am curious about how you are here."

"Dumb luck. Not by choice, that's for sure."

The figure of Harmsweld flickered. "Yet, you remain and seek a course to be part of current events. Have you told others about your condition?"

Clarke sighed and shook his head. "Do you understand how I can go wherever it takes me?"

"That I can answer. It is a realm between worlds. On the banks of the metaphysical world. If you will. A place *they* developed. A haven for the Astute Paragons."

"Is there a solution for Lindaulx there?"

"Probably, the course to the solution, at least. But a solution could imply an end." The haze of Harmsweld shook. "In my studies, I have identified Tervessi, which you now call Lindaulx, in this timeframe, as having a… I'll just call it… a strong focal point. The presence of the patterns and events I've been tracking verifies part of a theory I've been developing."

"Which is?"

"Sorry, Clarke. It is ill-formed and could be misleading. Though it's an assemblage—a result of answering a summons."

"Is it because you aren't sure?"

"I won't *really* understand until after it happens. But I have shared lives with ancestors of people here. What's troublesome is that you and I are from very different origins."

"Are you Astute?"

"Some would say I am sagacious."

"What does that mean?"

"Not funny? No. My kind have traced the ancestry of people here on Lindaulx that could play a significant role if a major event occurred. We didn't have the when, but understood it was abnormal to have such a concentration of… catalysts in one place."

"You still haven't answered my questions?"

"I'm doing my best."

"How did they all get here? And who are they?"

"Not necessarily the individual specifically, but their ancestors or descendants. Time is a very tricky entity. And whether they comprehend it, these people all have a strong correlation to the current events."

"But why come to me? Why are you telling me this?"

"Because Clarke. In all my years of research and life, there was never a variable like you. Or was it understood that you could even exist? Even now, I still cannot find your origin or your base purpose. It's as if you're hidden or obscured somehow."

"How did you find me here, then?"

"I am drawn here. To the signal. As I suppose you were. It quite surprised me to find you here."

"Are we the same?"

"Doubtful," Harmsweld said after a brief pause.

"Am I related to the other voice?"

"Your dark passenger—doubtful in the familial sense."

"Not that one. The other voice who spoke of the architects."

"Architects? Are you sure?"

"Positive-ish."

"Earlier, I thought you meant your inner voice, your conscience of sorts. Was that not whom you were referring to?"

Clarke shook his head and tapped his temple. "There's definitely something else trying to put thoughts into my head."

"Clarke, I may have put us both in danger by exposing myself. Find my kin."

"Why?"

"Because."

"Harmsweld, use your words."

"Because of the architects." The shadowy outline that was Harmsweld disappeared with a snap.

"What the hell does that mean?" Clarke asked the darkness, which faded as the lights flickered, humming to a steady glow. Clarke was alone.

ALTERCATION

CHAPTER 23

AURALEI COERCED HER augments to create a cocktail of stimulants, bringing her back to near-full mental acuity. She preferred to sleep, as nothing else could quite mimic the recovery process for the gray matter it provided. The diplomatic mission Anzil had subjected her to was thankfully over, although his lack of flair for politics had been comical to endure. She caught herself pulling at her eyelashes and wrung her hands together to quell her nervous habit that spoke silently of the apprehension lying just below her flawless outward projection of calmness—it was something her augments could never quite resist. She walked along a smoothly bored hallway until it opened into a massive hollowed-out cavern. This area of Warbler Ridge was her favorite so far. The construction technique gave one an appreciation for the architecture and a sense of the scale of the dwellings carved from the surrounding rock. The newer area of the Ridge, the part the Khilsyths built, was more restrictive with its functional series of hallways and doors leading to more hallways and rooms with no sense of place. Here, she could people-watch and marvel at how adaptable they were in such short order. These communities were once again filled with laughing children tumbling and spilling across playscapes with plush mossy areas. Water splashed and bubbled along little spillways and pipe courses that the wee ones would alter to see where it would spout from next. She paused, closing her eyes and raising her face upward to catch the warmth from the crystal spheres bathing the area in a sun-like natural light. In the stillness of her mind, she glimpsed a towhead girl in a brilliant sun dress running through a mossy forested area. *Was that me,* she wondered, summoning a false memory for her augments to burn away, but her internal machines were still. The hunt for Clarke proved to be more challenging than she expected, as the sightings from the guards and civilians were inconsistent. Accounts of Clarke's whereabouts were perplexing, but a common thread emerged: he would suddenly appear and spook someone. To which many boasted that he was lucky he didn't get punched, stabbed, kicked, or shot in the face. To a few, he had appeared as an apparition. *A spirit come to haunt these simpletons,* she thought, laughing aloud. Reason was often an afterthought amidst chaos and on backwater planets.

A klaxon horn began wailing its mournful warning call, tearing Auralei from her thoughts. A series of screens mounted above sprung to life, displaying a simple message—Warbler Ridge was under attack. The corridor lit up with a series of alphanumeric codes that she assumed these people could decipher based on the eruption of activity.

Auralei smiled. The gore and stench of an eminent battle tickled her base primal instincts; however, her augments dissipated her euphoria. If they were to survive, she would need to convince Clarke to flee and to kill again. She knew he would disapprove of what she would ask of him and wondered briefly if she should have at least some kind of emotional reaction regarding what he might think. Either way, it was a risk she needed to take to get off this rock and cobble the pieces of her past together.

By now, Shifty had deciphered the instructions on the walls and walkways, which provided directions for everyone: They diverted civilians further into the facility to a fortified area, which would protect them for months, and they sent military personnel to the place of most need. Auralei used the indications to guide her to a larger, smoothly bored tunnel leading to the dragoon staging areas, hoping Clarke would observe his unit's orders.

As she walked, Auralei touched the side of her neck, activating a minuscule implant that translated and encrypted the movements of her larynx and vocal folds and transmitted them to the desired recipient. "Princess, you there?" she called to Tarra. It was a tricky skill, but she was comfortable with it now.

"Loud and clear. How may I be of service?"

The sound of scattered weapon fire bled through. "It's time we got the hell outta here," Auralei said.

"I couldn't agree more. I'm with Anzil and folks from Tallus Outpost."

Auralei confirmed her two side arms were snug in their holsters, hugging her lower back, and broke into a run. "Heading your way. Any idea where Clarke is?"

"Haven't had time for your boyfriend, sorry."

Auralei swore under her breath.

"I heard that," Tarra said.

"What's the situation where you are?"

"We're pinned down with too many exits to cover. Not sure how long the barricades will hold."

"They've breached the Ridge?"

"I would say yes because we're getting shot at."

"Sweety," Auralei said scornfully. "Are they distinguishable?"

"Yeah, they'll be the ones shooting at you."

"You're pissing me off a little bit." Auralei rounded the corner and came face-to-face with three surly-looking fellows. Each soldier guided their rifle with their sight line, and all of them were trained on her. She was thankful for their trigger discipline.

"Identify yourself," a soldier barked.

Auralei scanned them for discernible House Khilsyth markings, failed, and wondered if they meant their menacing face shields to scare her. She smirked at how childish they seemed. Auralei tilted her neck to shut the larynx device off and adjusted her voice modulator to mimic Tarra's voice. "Where is the rest of your unit, soldier?"

The soldier hesitated. "Ah... ma'am, we need you to identify yourself."

"She's a specter," another soldier said, "one of ours."

Auralei peered around the group to the apparent leader, who held a fist-sized device pointed at her; it was the same as the device she had encountered earlier in the facility, which was smaller and something she didn't know existed. He sported a worn combat vest that bulged from the muscular frame it covered and ample refills for his weapons. He stood a head taller than the rest of the team, with spiked guards covering his forearms.

"Ma'am," the hulk said in a deep voice, "Kamp of the Bright Angels. What are you doing here?"

"Completing a contract," Auralei said, half lying. The Bright Angels were ROGs operatives tasked with supporting specter activity and occasionally retrieving an errant one. She didn't recognize Kamp.

"Ma'am, we have everything under control here. You should make your way home for a debriefing."

"Lieutenant Kamp—"

"It's Colonel Kamp, Ma'am," he interjected politely.

"Sorry, Colonel," Auralei said respectfully. She wondered what was so important that a full bird came here to Lindaulx. "I believe there is a renegade specter at play here."

The Colonel didn't flinch at the accusation and laughed. "You are all renegades, as far as I'm concerned. But regardless—"

The screeching of the Bright Angels' rifles drowned out the rest of Colonel Kamp's words as the men surged toward a group of soldiers who appeared through an archway about fifty paces behind Auralei. Kamp barked some commands and signaled her to accompany him to an adjacent room, which provided some respite. The soldiers followed and expertly established watchpoints.

"I'm sorry, ma'am," Kamp said, resting his hand on her shoulder. "What contract did you say you were working on?"

"I'm assisting contract LIN-2-5-6-2," Auralei said, giving them enough leeway to assume she might be the one on a directive. She hoped Shifty hadn't wholly severed her from the Nova Republic network, or it would be challenging to explain her current state.

"Ma'am, we need a brief sit-rep," a soldier asked.

"Seriously? You're asking me. You're the ones that work under directives."

Kamp stiffened and pursed his lips. "We are aware of how we operate, ma'am. Honestly, I'm a little confused. We received notice that you left this rock earlier today."

Auralei took a deep breath. "I lied and sent a decoy. I wanted to investigate the Astute facility before leaving." *Was this the group who shot Tarra down?* she wondered. "What was the last mission request received from me, Colonel?"

"Add Anzil Stone to the list," Kamp said, catching a brief glimpse of confusion across the woman's face. He pocketed the device and involuntarily rested his hand on the rifle slung before him.

"What list?" Auralei asked, regretting it instantly.

"Ma'am?"

"Sorry, Colonel. I can't interface with my ship through this damn rock. I'm not sure what information made it to you."

"Whoever built this place knew what they were doing. It's actually a great place to hole up. Even the damn relays are struggling. At least this device pegged you."

"Then let's have it, Colonel. Tell me what you're up against, and I'll see if I can help."

Kamp sighed and consulted another device, studying it intently. "I wish we knew. There's evidence of several specters operating here." He shook the device and throttled it with his palm. "These are practically useless at tracking anyone in here."

"Colonel, I think someone has infiltrated our operations."

"Bastards," Kamp said, nodding.

"Either that or they are playing both sides here. Have you received any orders or notices from ROG operations on Lindaulx lately?"

The Colonel's facial expression was calm and unwavering. He released his grip on her shoulder and scratched his beard. "Funny thing. We can't reach the Ward Inquisitor. There should be one operating nearby."

Auralei laughed. "You know how they love you all."

"Ma'am?" Kamp asked, concerned. "Just how long have you been operational?"

"Too long, Colonel, too long."

"Ma'am, are you sure you're straight?"

Auralei started pacing. "Someone has created a doozy of a confused situation. The infiltration by the Republic and maybe of the Republic, and the death of Trake Khilsyth," Auralei said over another question of concern from Kamp. She moved her hands to rest on the small of her back and stretched. "And now the Bright Angels and the bloody Anacul."

"What?" Kamp asked, clearing his throat. "Anacul. Seriously?"

"And a couple of hours ago, more than that now, a Rifty group that was passing by also landed. We believe Valan Khilsyth has formed an alliance with them."

"Are you certain?" Kamp asked. "We're aware they have resources in the area."

"They could plant someone within the Republic or perhaps change a person's loyalty," Auralei thought aloud. "No, Colonel. I'm not certain. We're both familiar with *our* relationship with the Rifty's."

"Sir, we need to keep moving," a soldier said from the hallway.

"Ma'am, just tell me—and honestly—where your loyalties lie."

"With Transom," Auralei said truthfully, matching Colonel Kamp's penetrating gaze.

"I sure hope so, ma'am," Kamp said. He leaned in close and said something only for her, "for when you need us. And I think you will." Kamp handed a tiny transponder to the specter, then stepped back. "We'll contact you when we're leaving, ma'am." He turned and issued a command to the soldier next to him, who then tapped the shoulders of two other soldiers and proceeded with his squad through the doorway. "Ma'am, you're welcome to come with us if you wish," he called.

Auralei left the room behind the Bright Angels and reestablished her communication with Tarra so she could listen. "Colonel Kamp, I could use some of your magic getting into Skyetook. I bet that's where we'll find whoever is in charge."

The Colonel agreed, and she joined his fire team, moving with trained precision along the corridors.

"Colonel Kamp, as in Bright Angel Colonel Kamp," Tarra said over her link with Auralei. "What the hell are you up to, young lady?"

"Was going to ask *you* that?" Auralei said to Tarra only.

"The Bright Angels being here..." Tarra said, and with some prompting from Auralei, she continued. "Unless you called them, but no, not you. Wow. What the hell is going on here?"

"Are you aware of the Lindaulx list?" Auralei asked Tarra.

"Yes. At least, I think I am. Names of people to extradite should things go sideways."

"Which they clearly have, wouldn't you agree?"

"Agreed."

"Interesting that the Bright Angels have this list."

"Don't make your way here, darling. It's rather congested."

"Not to worry, love. I'll think of something." It wasn't long before she was on her own again and hunting for Clarke.

CHAPTER 24

DAWN APPEARED AS a faint band of gray-blue on the horizon, growing brighter as it began its slow feast on the night. Leon parked his mechanized armor near a culvert buried under the rail line leading to the southern portal of Durges Gate. He walked along a gorge, trekking beside a watercourse a short way upstream, where he stumbled upon a waterfall with a slender ribbon-like stream plummeting from high above. He plunged his hands into the crisp glacier-fed waters. He lingered, his hands floating in the shallows, rippling the reflection of his aging face. The person gazing back at him was calm, content with their station and the family life had provided. Leon brought his hands to his face, the cold water biting his cheeks and his eyes and the warmer air burning his skin. He steadied himself for the task that lay before him. Vengeance was in its familiar place, a dark recess of himself he was all too familiar with and had hoped never to disturb again. The markings on his arms had faded throughout the years, but as the heat of his vengeance surfaced, they pulsed, and their scarlet state was gradually restored.

Leon stood as the wind picked up, carrying the sound of heavy footsteps approaching.

"It is I," Laand said in his throaty voice. "And it's time, Leon Nihkiehl."

Leon retraced his route with his new comrade back to the culvert where others had gathered in the shadow of the mountains. He watched a hovering screen displaying a brilliant white spot of the sun, which blanketed the side of the mountain with warmth against the morning frost he had just been enjoying. The scouts reported the invaders had moved two large haulers from a nearby switchyard and parked them on the northern portal's bridge, between the daylight of the tunnel and the opposite approach slab. Anything coming out of Durges Gate would have to go over or around the haulers, and then heavy steel pilings would have to be navigated immediately off the track on the far side of the bridge. It would significantly slow any force's movement out of the tunnel and leave them exposed. Leon respected the enemy for devising a good kill area.

"The Khilsyth's forces are ready to engage the enemy," Laand said. "Are you?"

"Hell yeah," Leon said, grasping the man's shoulder. "It's going to be a long bloody day." He wasn't thrilled that Deek would be out and fighting toward them.

Laand pulled a helmet from his pouch and covered the significant amount of metal hardware that comprised his face. "This should work," he said to Leon. "In theory, at least." Laand fastened his helmet, ignoring Leon's questioning glance, and attached himself to a device his robotic minions had created. He motioned for Leon to do the same. The machine had two primary arched corridors that spanned its length, and inside, narrow gauge vertical rails provided anchoring points for dragoon armor.

"You're magnetic?" Leon asked, climbing into his dragoon armor and maneuvering to the silver rail, which oscillated and snugged his armor into position beside Laand.

"We have many surprises."

With the first group of dragoons nestled into the arched corridors, the primary casing spun on end and began launching the mechanized armored units in lazy arcs up the valley. When empty, the casing retracted and was reloaded with dragoons for another volley.

As Leon broke over the ridgeline, he looked for where his heads-up display showed his infantry were supposed to be and was relieved to see them rocketing down the eastern hillside with the sun at their backs. The Nihkiehl dragoons unleashed a maelstrom of death on the invaders as they screeched through the sky, first decimating some of the burlier invader equipment. As Leon neared the enemy, the remnant piece of the rail pulsed and set him down safely before it detached. He hefted his mace and waded amongst the shellshocked enemy forces, and a battle roared to life.

WITH BLOOD AND pieces of machines and soldiers littering the terrain, Leon kneeled, his armored knee spikes sinking into the rock. He whispered a gentle word for his fallen comrades in arms.

Are you praying? When he opened his eyes, Laand's text was flashing in Leon's display.

"Just wishing them well on their journey and letting them know they died with honor," Leon responded.

"A custom of comfort," Laand said. "A luxury afforded to the living."

"True."

"And what of our enemies."

"Just misguided people who didn't need to die."

"It is true. By my account, a peculiar group of Republic soldiers, mercenaries, vagabonds, and Tersinians. It made for an odd arsenal. A discomforting battle."

"More cannons like yours would provide our living even greater comfort."

"It might be possible with some modifications. An interesting challenge."

"By the way," Leon said, inspecting Laars, "and don't take this the wrong way... but you are a little worse for wear, bud." Laand's clothes and some metallic material he wore were charred or missing, revealing a partial robotic exoskeleton. "I'm not sure how, but catching a plasma grenade with your chest and escaping relatively unharmed is a trick you need to teach me."

"Indeed. You have much to learn, Leon Nihkiehl."

"So does everyone else, it seems."

"We are more similar than you might care to admit. Perhaps it is our obsession with longevity."

"Life everlasting?"

"No, I assure you we can die."

"If only we could all be so lucky. Just how old are you, anyway?"

"In this form... ahh... let's just more than a millennium."

"How in the hell?"

"My people have a deep affinity for the elements that preserve life. For better or worse, we are tied to it closer than most. But it is a conversation for another time, yes?"

"Shall we check in? I want to find that daughter of mine."

"I will contact the others. Deek survived, and she's on her way to us now."

Leon nodded his head, his eyes softening in relief. This was not an experience he desired to have again—it was time to get the kids off Lindaulx.

CHAPTER 25

CLARKE SAT OFF to the side of a bustling cafeteria, seeking refuge from the solitude of the abandoned infirmary ward and the discoveries of his latest rendezvous with the apparition calling itself Harmsweld. A simple shirt, combat pants, and thin tuque he *borrowed* masked his appearance so that his presence went unnoticed. Fresh-faced images of him displayed on the projection screen loops around Warbler Ridge were barely recognizable to him anymore. The people nearby were primarily discussing the invading army or how the fugitive Chief Trake Khilsyth's killer was still alive. The theories about the murder and the invaders' motives were rampant and taking on a life of their own. A nearby fellow engaging in a boisterous argument proclaimed Clarke masterminded the events while his contender believed Clarke was merely a pawn. However, both agreed he must be Anacul, born of the mercurial moon and definitely someone they should eliminate.

The sudden onset of a Klaxon horn blaring to life caused the cafeteria to erupt in a mix of panic and organized chaos. The trained professionals left their food forgotten and hurried out of the room in an orderly fashion. Family members and other folks inhaled the remaining food scraps and put trays away, leaving enough time for essential personnel to clear the room before they dispersed.

Rushing people filled the hallways on their way to their destinations, which were displayed on the walls and floors. A brief pang of guilt reminded him he should have been heading to one of the advanced armories per his duty assignment and not retracing his steps to the infirmary. In moments like these, his job was to marshal other mechanics in preparing dragoon suits and triaging the myriad of problems that arose. He smirked—that would have been more normal. Undoubtedly, some pilots would fail to step through their start-up checklist and be irritable for benign and easily solved reasons. He admitted begrudgingly to himself that he missed it.

Eventually, Clarke's route became less traveled until he caught the unmistakable sound of assault rifle chatter. Clarke hugged the nearest doorway and heard someone shout orders, followed by heavy foot strikes in his direction. A group of technicians appeared from an intersecting hallway, slowed, and then simultaneously gyrated. The sprays of crimson mist belied that tiny metal objects were to blame for their frenzied movements and not spontaneous seizures.

Clarke punched the control panel on the side wall and ducked into a small office area where unwelcomed lights greeted him with a slight flicker. The handle of the doorway at the far end turned, and the door slammed open. Clarke dove between two cabinets as bullets ripped past where he had stood, and hard footsteps came rushing into the room—the type made by the sturdy protective soles of combat boots. Clarke scanned the area for anything he could use as a weapon, came up empty, and listened for the attacker's next move. In the drone of the lights, Clarke thought he could hear the steady rhythm of heartbeats, which tore away his thoughts like the grip of dry ice on moist skin. For a moment, his mind was serene. But the renewed sounds of pounding hearts and heavy breathing gnawed away at the serenity. His heartbeat was present in the mix, sounding like the disruption of thousands of tiny pebbles left behind by the receding ocean surf.

"We are not here to hurt you," someone yelled. "Sorry about shooting at you... a misunderstanding... It's safe to come out."

From another direction, someone responded. "We may have meant to shoot at *you*. Identify yourselves."

What ensued was an eventual breakdown in communication, and the limited discourse devolved to shouts of 'die bastards' and 'for Trake,' supervened by the brilliance of muzzle flashes and the crack of bullets over Clarke's head. *Get your ass moving,* he told himself. Clarke scurried on all fours between the cabinets to the cover of a nearby desk. A shadow appeared overhead, its owner omitting a scream of pain and dropping their assault rifle just out of his reach. Its dark metal taunted him with a semblance of dying with a fight. He tried to retreat deeper under the desk, but the hollow space it provided was pathetic as the bullets continued to split the air overhead. When it seemed like the opposing squads would tire of the battle over this shabby, long-abandoned office space, a shiny silver can bounced off the filing cabinet and landed in front of Clarke.

Clarke swiftly kicked it, sending it clattering across the floor. When it stopped, it erupted in a spray of sparks, and a dark, cloudy mixture poured out of it, filling the room. He took a deep breath and hoped that his exposed skin wouldn't react negatively to whatever it was. Boot strikes entered the room from his left and fanned out in coordinated movements. Clarke pressed himself against the back wall of the desk, willing his body to blend into the plain gray paint he knew covered it. In the haze, a rifle barrel appeared. Clarke exploded off the underside of the desk, catching the soldier's rifle, spun them around, and slammed his fist into their face mask. The high-density plastic of the face shield offered little protection as the soldier's nose busted with a meaty crunching sound like a cleaver into bone, and they slumped backward, their nose streaming blood. Clarke stooped and picked up an abandoned rifle. It squelched in protest as he depressed the trigger, warning of an eminent electric surge from a lack of proper clearance. Clarke's stomach clenched. He hurled the rifle at the nearest soldier and watched it bounce harmlessly off their body armor. A string of curses ran through his mind as he readied to lunge over the desk. The chaotic noise of the gunfight slowed until it was barely a whisper in the room as Clarke's tightened leg muscles released and exploded like compressed springs. The rushing sound of a strong wind blowing through dry pine trees filled his ears. Clarke watched as the soldier's finger applied a steady and increasing pressure to their rifle's trigger, which then caused the weapon's hammer to release. This set off a chain reaction of a flash, a jump of the barrel, and the abrupt replacement of another round into the chamber to be punched out again by the rifle. *Rinse and repeat*, Clarke thought. The projectiles clawed through the air on a course to his chest. The rushing noise in Clarke's ears crescendoed, then went still as he found himself standing next to his would-be killer just as the first projectile passed over the desk where he had stood.

Clarke stole a combat knife from the soldier's belt, buried it to the hilt in their neck, and twisted it for good measure; as the remaining projectiles in the assault rifle's magazine spun out, a charging soldier collided with Clarke. The momentum carried them out of the room. Mid-tumble, Clarke spun, allowing the attacker to provide their neck graciously as a cushion for landing on the hallway's brick floor. A quick search of the dead soldier and he had another combat knife. Staying low, he pressed against the wall just past the door's threshold, hiding in the gas smoke seeping from the office into the hallway. Another soldier rushed from the room and tripped over his dead comrade. Clarke's sinuses flared with a sharp pain, which he tried to alleviate by squeezing the bridge of his nose pitching his head forward. As his vision stabilized, a grenade skidded to a stop at his feet. Clarke lurched into the room using the door for leverage and hoped the walls would protect his tender flesh from the detonation.

Inside the room, a soldier let loose a torrent of projectiles from a box-shaped device on their forearm. But the hallway explosion was disorientating and affected their aim. The tiny metal shards ripped through Clarke's shirt and burned as they tore into his flank. He lunged and swung the combat knife wildly: the blade plunged into the unprotected joint in the soldier's body armor just below their ear and slid easily into their neck, obstructing the airway.

The soldier flailed, which tore the knife from Clarke's grip. Panicked, they grabbed the hilt of the blade and freed it. The blood from the wound fanned out in a mist as the soldier injected a healthy amount of air into their windpipe in an attempted scream.

Clarke fell to his knees, clutching the burning wound swelling in his abdomen. The fiery sensation spread from the wound to his fingers as a slimy and slippery substance oozed between his fingers and began clawing its way across his palms. Snapping his hand away in pain and examining it, he saw tiny flecks of shrapnel slowly pushing their way free from underneath the skin. Clarke turned his hand over, and the pieces in his palm fell to the floor, where they shattered like brittle glass. He shook his head to clear the pain, wiped the blood from his hands on his pants, and ran his hand across the tender but undamaged flesh of his abdomen. *That's not normal,* he thought and wondered if the gas was making him hallucinate.

Clarke scavenged some bladed weaponry from the dead soldiers and walked out of the room into the hallway, slipping a little on the wet mess. Another group of soldiers was there and commanded him to stop, the distinctive slap of their boots pursuing his disobedience.

A woman stepped out from a nearby doorway as Clarke rounded a corner. "Get down," she instructed.

Her authoritative tone and a mild sense of urgency led Clarke to oblige. He slid feet first across the stone floor, putting his hands out to brace himself, and stopped between the woman's legs. He was staring up at her outstretched arms, gripping large pistols that jumped four times, sending a bullet for each of the pursuers' skull cavities.

She lowered herself gracefully to rest on his pelvis. "There you are, my dear, safe and sound," she said with a wink.

Clarke wheezed. The air in his lungs was stale. There was something familiar about the devilish glint in those dark emerald eyes, but where she belonged in his memories was sketchy.

Auralei smiled. "Temporarily anyway... you need to move that ass of yours."

Clarke took a deep breath. "Who are you really?"

Her arms blurred when she holstered her death dealers to their resting spots on her lower back. "For now... an ally. So, where is that armor of yours?"

"You are the other *Mischi*," Clarke said with a cough.

Auralei's weapons blurred from their holsters, and her rear ground into him as she spun. Her guns screamed in protest as two more soldiers appeared around the corner and dropped dead without argument.

"How do you know they aren't friendlies?" Clarke asked the woman's back.

"Does it matter right now?" She replied flatly, hauling Clarke to his feet. "We need to move. I like your chances of survival better in your armor. Now. Where is it?"

CLARKE PASSED THROUGH the doorway to his infirmary room ahead of the *Mischi* and slipped inside his armor.

"That's disturbing, you know," Auralei said, breaking the silence.

"What is?" Clarke asked.

"You just sort of vanished."

"The armors cloaked?"

"Don't play games with me, smartass. Yes. It's cloaked."

"That's odd. I can see it. There have been weird things happening to me since that Astute facility. Sort of like right now, where, for no reason, I'm just babbling and trusting you. A *Mischi,* of all people."

"So, you trust me?"

"Should I?"

"I think so."

"Comforting," Clarke said sarcastically.

"As much fun as it is here, we need to get the hell outta Warbler Ridge and off Lindaulx."

"I seem to hear that a lot lately."

Auralei pressed her lips together and flashed a sympathetic grimace. "It's simple," she said, resting her arm on the pauldron of the now visible armor and seeing her reflection in its visor, "I'm here to protect you."

Visions of interlocking rings bombarded Clarke's mind's eye, and he knew the thoughts were not his own. He sensed she spoke the truth, but it brought discrete pain like slightly acidic fluid through the soft tissue of the sinuses.

Auralei's eyes softened. "Please trust me."

"I'm so bloody confused," Clarke said, pressing his gauntlet against the battle helmet.

"Don't worry. We specters are very good at what we do." She tucked a stray wisp of hair back into place behind her faintly elfish ears.

The armor snatched her forearm and lifted her off her feet. "Clarke! What the hell are you doing?"

"It wasn't me... it was this suit." Clarke's display targeted an object clinging to the woman's wrist and displayed characters he could not translate. "That bracelet. I recognize it. Where did you get it?"

They stared at one another for several moments in silence.

"Ellane?" Clarke asked, lowering and releasing the woman.

Auralei shielded her face, spurning the tears that welled in her eyes. She twisted deftly, freeing her forearm from the armor's grasp, and left the room. Clarke pursued.

AFTER HOURS OF tromping in dark caverns and smashing through rocky barricades expertly disguised to deter would-be explorers, Stigg finally emerged from a long-forgotten cave at the ocean's edge. Sitting on a rock, watching the surf patiently, there was a mechanical construct that identified itself as Enas, a resident of Tallus Outpost. After a quick exchange of pleasantries and a status update, Stigg granted its request for permission to board.

"Stigg!" Anzil's voice emanated from a device on Enas' arm. "You sunnova bitch. You're alive."

"I am," Stigg replied. "Would you expect anything less?"

"Where have you been?"

"Got sidetracked. Decided to do some spelunking after being attacked by one of yours."

"What the hell?"

"Yeah. Inside the Ridge. Some would-be assassins."

"Can you give us a little more to go on there, Stigg?"

"Sure. Saw the lad. Your folks dragged me to what I think was an old Republic armory. They wanted a tussle, only we caused a cave-in, and I decided to leave. Oh, and I think the unconscious sycophant in the back who calls herself Staalke has *the* talent."

"You think she's a specter?" Tarra asked. "Wait. There was never a mention of an old armory here. Did you know if there was a *watcher* in this sector? What does she look like?"

"Short, fit, unconscious," Stigg said.

"Stigg," Tarra said disapprovingly. "Are there any distinguishable marks on her body or her weapons?"

Stigg cursed and went to search the woman's body and possessions, leaving Enas at the helm. He removed her clothing, and she let out a faint moan in protest. He stilled her with another meaty thud of her head off the floor. "On her back leg, there's a symbol. It's red, black, and white."

Enas, having engaged the autopilot, also inspected the detainee and relayed the image of the woman's face and markings.

"Don't recognize her," Tarra said. "Doesn't mean much, though... other than she wasn't with us."

Stigg grunted. "You didn't rule out *one of* us. I figure I'll have a little chat with her once I find a quiet place."

"That tattoo on her ass," Tarra said, caressing her thigh, "it's familiar but I can't recall where I've seen it."

Stigg raised Staalke's sword and rolled it back and forth to catch the different angles of the cabin's dim light. "It's on her weapon, too. There's an engraving with mountains, and one has more snow on it and a double-stacked infinity symbol."

Tarra threw both her hands up in the air. "Gods. It could be anything. What did she say?"

"That she was one of Anzil's," Stigg said.

"Nobody I knew, Stigg," Anzil replied, rubbing his upper lip. "Can you explain more about this *watcher*?"

"Best not to delve into Republic business," Tarra warned but caught her error. She needed to build trust and continue to expand his worldly view if he was going to be helpful. "*Watcher* is slang for the Nova Republic agents assigned to oversee the sectors of the known universe. Embedded, silent, unidentifiable. Always reporting."

Stigg whistled. "Damn, that's cruel. Giving him inner club-level knowledge. You're never getting out now."

"Heads of major houses should be integrated," Tarra said calmly, "and it's conceivable that Trake informed Valan."

"But if no *watcher*, would Trake have had anything to pass along?" Anzil asked.

Tarra shook her head. "That... Ummm... There was, or is, no *watcher* per ROG. One sec." She keyed her embedded larynx device and relayed the conversation to Auralei.

"Impossible," Auralei shot back, her pale cheeks flushing.

"Tell me then, cutie," Tarra said. "Who did you notify you were here on contract?"

Auralei took a deep breath to steady herself and ran a quick diagnostic on her augments. All reported they were functioning normally. *But I'm not calm,* she thought. "I sent notice to the where ROG provided." Her insides fluttered as she said the words, and the conversation slowed to a crawl. She could envision the implication of what she said registering on Tarra's face. She wondered how she could have missed it—the part of the network she had used to research the contract in this sector had been an elaborate cover.

"When?" Tarra asked Auralei quickly. "When did you send it?"

Auralei checked the device in her side pocket and frowned. There, in a code she could decipher, was Shifty's analysis. She looked up from a device that cast an eerie glow across her stoic face. Auralei's voice was quiet and serious. "We've been played on so many levels. Princess, this may extend to our Overseers... Are you with me?"

"Always," Tarra said, meaning it. "You should know that." She wondered just how much Auralei remembered from their time together at the Nova Republic Academy. Tarra's family had understood the implications of becoming a specter and implanted augments in her, providing her with protection for withstanding the Initiate training program—*more like deprogramming.* "Be safe," Tarra said, cutting her connection to Auralei. "We've surely been played," Tarra said to Anzil.

"By whom?"

"By whom and when?" Stigg asked. "And by who, or what, and when, again and again?" He cursed the ridiculousness of the situation.

"You might not be wrong, big guy," Tarra told Stigg. "Regardless, the answer isn't here. Although I do think you have some part to play in it. We just need to get off this cursed rock." She plucked at something on her coat that was only visible to her. "Why isn't anyone listening to me? It's really starting to piss me off."

"Finding out more about what's going on here might tell us where a safe place to land is when we leave," Stigg said.

"Marvelous idea," Tarra said, rubbing her hands together vigorously. "What's in front of us, then? The girl."

"She's tied up pretty decently," Stigg admitted, checking her binds and trying to convince himself it wasn't age getting the better of his memory.

"I'd feel better if she were in a holding cell," Anzil said, glancing uneasily at Tarra.

"Stigg, I think it's time you had that chat with her," Tarra said, her voice cold and steady. "And if you are what I think you are…" She chased a shiver from between her shoulder blades that even her augments couldn't counteract quickly enough.

After a long pause, Stigg responded. "What do you want to know?"

"Can you determine her origin?" Tarra asked.

"Like where she's from?" Anzil interjected.

Tarra shook her head. "Almost, sweety. We need info on how she accesses the flux and what side she's playing for."

"It's been a long time since…" Stigg said.

"I'm sorry to have asked this of you," Tarra said quickly, hoping to distract him from going dark on her. "We really need your help."

"Not on you, lass," Stigg replied.

"Where are you now?" Anzil asked Stigg.

"Heading to Warbler Ridge. I think. You?"

"Wouldn't recommend that. They overran the Ridge."

"Is Clarke there with you?" Stigg asked.

"Yes," Tarra said, flashing Anzil a grimace conveying not to betray her half-truth. "Stigg, we're planning to pay Valan a visit."

"Never thought we'd see a day where the Ridge was overrun," Anzil said. "We're building alliances with the other households. The Nihkiehls are clearing out Durges Gate."

"Routing there is going to take me through some nasty invader-held territory," Stigg responded.

"Leon is also planning—"

"Leon, eh? You on a first-name basis with him now?"

Anzil took a deep breath and carefully let the air seep from his lungs to avoid a loud sigh—there had been an edge to Stigg's tone. "The *Nihkiehl's* are planning to send some scouts to Skyetook and surrounding areas to provide a safety net. They want eyes on all the players in the event the invader forces double-back to Skyetook. Or the damn Riftys move sooner than expected."

"Did Deek make it out of the Ridge?" Stigg asked, thinking it better not to dwell on the Khilsyth-Nihkiehl allegiances.

"Yeah. She's had a swim at Lake Fievre with the Lanals and is joining in the Durges Gate fun."

"I'm sorry, Anzil, that's a tough one," Stigg said.

"Yeah. Still working through options to keep her and the rest safe."

"Could fly her out," Tarra offered.

"She'd never let me," Anzil replied, his mic catching his sigh.

"True," Tarra said, a tiny smile forming at the corner of her mouth. "Strong lass, that one."

"Deek will at least be fortified by the Nihkiehl forces," Anzil noted. "Some of the other Houses are also collecting as a show of force to stop the Rifty's from going anywhere."

"This is going to get exciting," Stigg said with a weak laugh. "I'll try getting to Deek before much more fun starts. I think I can make the trip a tad bit prickly for the other side."

"Stigg, I want to get them inside Skyetook before the Rift Faction gets antsy in the wasteland and starts scrounging for trouble."

"Yeah, wouldn't be very comfortable being trapped out there with armies that we have limited situational awareness of."

"Do you trust him?" Stigg asked. "Leon, that is."

"Do you?" Anzil asked.

"We shall see. You take care of yourself, Anzil... you too, *Mischi.* Watch out for my little buddy."

"Will do," Anzil said and terminated the communication.

"You have a plan, Stigg?" Enas asked.

Stigg chuckled. "I think so."

"Care to share?"

"Sure. Once I figure it out, but first, let's have that chat with our new friend here."

AURALEI USED AN old floor layout posted on a wall to enter a hidden doorway within the facility that led to an abandoned switchback trail. She shortened her long stride so Clarke could keep up with her pace; the heavy stomps of the machine grated on her nerves.

"Haven't you learned to creep in that contraption yet?" she asked, more aggressively than she meant to. Her thoughts were jumbling: *Why had he called her Ellane? Why did it feel familiar? Why did he blame it on the armor? Was Clarke still managing his reigns?* Her anger was overwhelming her augments, and Clarke was catching the brunt of it. Then the heat came precariously along her memory threads as she scanned her past for hints until she gave it a memory of a little curly-haired girl swinging in a flower-filled park to chew on. As the memory faded, she hoped it wasn't one of her past's foundational and fundamental memories.

At the end of the switchback ramps, a Khilsyth soldier greeted them through a small cutout in a larger door and directed them to Anzil's location.

"Seems like you held the invaders back well enough," Auralei said as she approached.

Anzil greeted Auralei and embraced Clarke with a clank of their armored suits. "It's about time you two showed up. We were planning to pay my brother a visit." His suit did not hide the disappointment in his voice. "And as you're aware, we've got a breach. Not sure how they got in. They may have tunneled or came through the upper ridgeline doors—"

"Or were already inside," Tarra interrupted.

"Possibly," Anzil admitted begrudgingly.

"Nothing like having folks who conveniently switch allegiances mid-battle, yeah?" Tarra asked.

Anzil nodded. "Regardless, we're readying for an exit, given that we can't contain the inflow of invaders. It's a sad state to lose a place so well fortified."

"The enemy leader is obviously very skilled," Tarra breathed.

"You think it's only one person?" Anzil asked.

Auralei shook her head. "It's never one person or one thing. There's always a shadow group."

"What's the plan, then?" Clarke asked as Anzil released him from an uncomfortably long embrace.

"The fighting here is kill or be killed," Anzil said. "Our loyalists hold a few fortified locations that should be secure enough until we can get help. Honestly, we need control over the Skyetook's Operation and Command Centers and eventually the spaceport."

Auralei nodded her approval. "Second to leaving this rock, it is the best tactical decision."

"Agreed," Laars said. "We cannot win the battle here. With or without a commander."

Anzil glanced back and forth between the two specters. "Ladies, I would appreciate your help again. If you have a price, name it. If you decide to leave, I understand. I just ask that when you leave Lindaulx, you inform other members of House Khilsyth what transpired here."

Auralei began walking toward her ship. "I gave you my word, young Khilsyth. I'll see this through."

Tarra walked over to Anzil and patted his armored hindquarters. "Understand that my help comes at a price," she said, eliciting a chilling glance from Anzil.

Clarke could sense a slight warming inside the *Mischi*. The emotion was tricky to decipher as it was almost joyful, but something within her was fighting to suppress it.

"What about you, Clarke?" Anzil asked.

Clarke winced as the tendril to the *Mischi* was severed, and he recoiled from Anzil's question. Yet some part of Clarke wanted to grasp onto Anzil's concern. Explore it, understand it. Clarke shook his head, clearing the thoughts that were perhaps not his own. *Is that you, darkness?* There was a pressure, a slippery sensation between his ears. He closed his eyes tightly, and there was a comforting and welcoming place in the shadows of his memory's recesses. A spot that, when the soldiers attacked, had saved him earlier. He wondered if it was how he communed with the flux. Clarke's attention was filled with Auralei pounding on his visor and screaming—the comprehension of her words came gradually.

"What the hell was that?" Auralei asked. "Don't you ever do that. You hear me? Never-ever-never-again!"

"Would someone tell me what the hell is going on?" Anzil asked.

Tarra wrapped her arm around Anzil, slinking her way in closer. "I think our little engineer is learning new tricks."

"Like what?" Anzil asked.

"Shade stepping, perhaps," Tarra said.

"The flux?" Anzil asked the specter, who smiled and nodded. He wriggled free of her. "Impossible. Isn't it? You think it's the suit?"

"I don't think so," Tarra said contemplatively. "Maybe Clarke's figured it out on his own." Tarra paused briefly, watching Auralei continue to rip Clarke a new one. "We train for years to learn how to do it. Naked." She raised her eyebrows at Anzil, then winked with a seductive grin. "But slowly, we build our skill to where we can add equipment—"

"Did it have something to do with the Anacul Champion?" Anzil interrupted.

"Unlikely," Tarra said, shaking her head. "But no one has ever been in the flux with anything larger than a few personal effects and survived. In fact, and mum's the word mind you, princess over there is the most capable I'm aware of. Even she can only take a little more than what she carries. Or so she lets on. Our boy here, well, he was just trying to end himself. There are gizmos to help, but something in his records said he couldn't augment?"

"Nearly killed himself trying," Anzil said.

"Yeah, read that as well. Brilliant bit saving him." Tarra held up a device for Anzil to consider. "Any chance you can shed some light on this?" The screen depicted a recent scan of Clarke showing an unclassified structure of augmentations inherently different from expected normal body tissue.

"What the hell?" Anzil asked Tarra.

"Maybe he finally got the recipe correct for his own spec?"

"Possibly. It's been his hobby for years. I'd like to believe he would have told me."

Tarra shrugged her shoulders and bit at her lower lip. "This device," she waved the tablet depicting Clarke for emphasis, "is designed to sniff out spec, hon. It scans it, and with the help of Our Lady Majestic, we can reverse-engineer it to recreate it. Nothing resists the scanner—nothing except for whatever is in Clarke."

"Maybe a glitch. Or maybe it's not synthetic?"

Tarra held his gaze and smiled. "If you're right. And I'm only entertaining this theory of yours because the last couple of days have been ridiculously strange. Then our boy Clarke has figured out how to create a living augment."

"Enough, Tarra," Auralei said across their secure network.

"Now that it's out, it sounds absurd and disturbing, eh?" Tarra asked with a cackle.

"We'll need some help to find out more," Auralei continued. "For now, best not to alert him we're aware or to tell Anzil more."

"Sweetheart over there," Tarra whispered to Anzil and straightened her snug-fitting coat. "Is going to need our help keeping an eye on her engineer. Hey princess, you done reprimanding your boy?"

Auralei turned and took a deep breath, regaining her composure. "Let's get these fools some kittens and find a weapon for Clarke."

"Stealthy dragoons," Tarra said, smiling at Anzil.

WITH EIGHT DRAGOON armors attached to the Osprey, four per side, the alien armor loaded in the cargo bay, copious munitions, and some foodstuffs, Auralei ushered everyone onboard. "Skyetook, here we come," she mumbled.

Tarra jerked the controls of the Osprey, mashing the passengers against the side rail as they left. "Sorry, folks. In space, she's a ghost. On a planet like Lindaulx, she's the unwanted offspring of a rhino and a banshee."

Anzil chuckled. "That kind of comment doesn't exactly inspire confidence."

Tarra flashed Anzil a hurt look. "It should inspire great confidence." She threw her arms out wide. "Just think how it would feel to be staring it down. It's terrifying and inspiring at the same time."

Auralei smiled, "sounds like you."

Tarra slapped Auralei playfully with her outstretched hand. "Really, that's your best heckle?"

Alone, Clarke keyed the intercom to contact the bridge. "To avoid the sensors, I think we should duck around the back of Hurricane Ridge and head out over the Bay of Disappointment." It would have been a two-hour flight on a direct route from Warbler Ridge to Skyetook's Port. But if Clarke were the invaders, he would have deployed the safety net—a neat series of microscopic devices hovering overhead in the mesosphere that were virtually undetectable. They created a fine weave of sensor beams to detect refraction, heat, noise, air currents, and other characteristics that even the brightest scientists couldn't wholly circumvent. "If we approach heading southwest with the sun at our back and submerge a ways out, we should avoid most of the defense arrays."

"Aye-aye, Captain," Tarra said mockingly.

"We're going to have to divide and conquer, aren't we?" Clarke asked.

"You sure you're up for it, Clarke?" Anzil asked.

"Why not?" Clarke said flatly. "Anyone know where Stigg is?"

"He said he'd meet us at Skyetook," Auralei said, muting the cockpit. "Clarke's plan isn't so bad."

Anzil slid into the pilot seat, which was still warm from the specter. "Where you heading?" Anzil aimed his voice at the bridge's exit.

"To check on him," Auralei said and descended after Clarke.

"There's something funny going on between those two," Anzil said, smiling.

"You know this," Tarra said, pointing back and forth between them. "It is unexpected, unlikely, and unsanctioned."

"Worth it, though. I always wanted a friend who was a specter."

"We'll see," Tarra said, flashing Anzil a quick smile. "I'd make a great sister, though, don't you think."

"Good deflection."

Tarra stared at Anzil, weighing her response carefully, and then sighed. "Auralei once told me a story from her childhood. One, I was never to tell her until I thought the time was right. Whatever her purpose, she risked everything by hiding it. It would have taken some incredible willpower for even a fraction of the memory to survive."

"What do you mean?"

"Not a fun story," Tarra said. "ROG prefers a clean slate up here." Tarra tapped the side of her head gently. "They are very good at ferreting out memories they deem potentially problematic—anything that will hinder your operational efficiency."

"You went through the process?"

"Some other time, hun? Those two, their paths have crossed before when they were young."

"Bloody hell. It's Ellane, isn't it?"

Tarra turned her attention back to flying. "I don't mean to pry into such a potentially delicate memory, but if she is, is it a positive thing?"

"What? Why?"

"For the time being, it could be better for Clarke's health. Do you know if they liked each other?"

"I believe so. I mean, Clarke has been hunting for her since I've known him. I only have part of the story, but there's always been a sort of sad vibe about it. I know he definitely misses her." Seeing Tarra pursed her lips and cock her head to the side, he thought she wasn't delighted with his answer. "Hells... The way this day's going, who can be certain? I think he loves her."

"Okay then. For now, we need her focused on getting Clarke off this planet. Where she goes, we go. It's our best shot."

"You care for her, don't you?"

"Something like that, bro. Something... like... that."

CHAPTER 26

THE SKY WAS ominous and threatening more snow at the peaks of Petrified Ridge—a name given long ago to the desolate rock faces that towered high above the north entrance to Durges Gate. Stigg had arrived, transported by a strange egg-shaped device of Tallus Outpost construction. It had taken him a moment to get his feet under him after exiting the delicately featured craft. He directed the group's attention to a bank of fast-moving dark clouds shaped like anvils approaching from the west. "As soon as the leading edge of that storm bank hits the ridge here, we're going to be in for a doozy of a time, I'm afraid."

Leon turned his gaze away from the sky. The knee ache from an injury he received on another planet told him Stigg's predictions were likely accurate. "We need to speed this process up," he said, gesturing at the destruction and mass reclamation of equipment below. "The Riftys have started moving out of the Wasteland."

Deek nodded. "And Anzil will need his commotion soon enough."

Stigg motioned for the officers to come closer. "Enas and I have an idea for creating enough chaos and confusion while keeping our momentum toward Skyetook. We believe it should help this here adventure."

Enas summoned a holographic projection of Stigg's plan. Many of the details were being added on the fly as Stigg adjusted the timeline. Stigg's plans always had four phases: aggravation, momentum, altercation, and resolution. In this case, go piss off the invaders, get said pissed-off invaders to chase them, rough them up a bit, and the resolution phase was still a little vague on the details once they arrived in the general vicinity of Skyetook.

"It just might work," Leon said with a laugh. "How are we going to get into those perimeter depot yards? I presume that's where we're heading."

"Working on it," Stigg said.

"Who's going to ensure the hangar doors open for us?" Deek asked.

"Working on it," Stigg said quietly.

"Hope so, or our asses will be hanging in the wind," Leon said.

"Yup," Stigg said with a wink and a sly grin.

"This is probably the first time I've ever been glad I'm not going first," Leon said. "You taking a Zephyr or Stalwart armor?"

"Neither."

Leon wiggled his pointer finger at Enas' holographic display. "Based on the little fairy tale playing out here for us, I would say Enas is using a liberal representation of your ride. Unless you've had a marauder hidden here all these years."

"Something like that," Stigg said with a smirk.

Leon clasped Laand by his oversized metallic shoulder plate and shook him. "Another battle nears, my new friend. Everyone, it's time to make it happen. Let's wrap it up and head out."

Leon shambled after Stigg as the group dispersed, catching the man by his shoulder. His friend looked much older than he remembered. "Hey, Stigg," Leon said, "some words alone if you would, brother."

The two walked together, matching each other's strides and distancing themselves from the team, and rested on a rock outcrop where water drifted in wispy strands down from the overhead ledge and pooled. Somewhere within the rocky basin at their feet, the water seeped through a hole in perfect balance. Stigg knelt, removed his gloves, and pushed his fingers into the earth, picking up a handful of the damp pebbles. He let them cascade from his hands to clatter on the rocks and into the water. He chose an old dialect he was sure would keep their words secret for a while. "It's good to have you by my side again, Mauti."

Leon smirked and chuckled before inhaling deeply. "Been some time since someone called me that."

"We did not ask for these lives of duty, my friend," Stigg said, wiping his hands on his pants to try them. He refitted his gloves, pressing the protective covering between each of his fingers.

"That is true, my friend," Leon said, grasping forearms with Stigg and hauling him to his feet. "The same old pattern keeps playing out in our lives over and over, regardless of where we seek refuge. But we knew this day would come, eventually."

"That we did. Only it seems like someone had the wisdom and foresight to leave us some help."

"Is it true then? There was one here?"

Stigg sighed and nodded.

Leon recognized the sadness in his friend's weathered and battle-worn face. "You need to let go of that pain, brother. Frebel was not us. That oath is not yours to bear anymore. At least not alone."

"One of these days, perhaps," Stigg said. "Anyway, someone here has a clearer picture than us. I just can't figure out who."

"Agreed. It's making it hard to figure out where's safe."

"It's clear it isn't here anymore."

"That much we agree on," Leon said with a gentle laugh. "So, an old armory on a backwater planet." Leon squeezed his forearm. "Strento?"

Stigg gave Leon a knowing glance and nod—it was the only logical conclusion, given he could pilot the machine. "And with other equipment I've never seen before."

Leon let out a long sigh punctuated by restrained laughter and cursed. "Stigg. What did Constance get us into? You reckon they're here for the boy?"

Stigg nodded. "My hunch is that ROG is. I'm just not sure how they tracked him after all these years."

"Constance was never clear about the lad. The *Mischi* with the big damn sword—it's Constance's daughter, isn't it?"

"Afraid that's an accurate statement," Stigg said in a hushed tone. "You'll need to tell me how you made that leap. Took me a bit to piece it together myself."

"Seems like Constance's plans extend beyond the grave, but to what purpose?"

"Says she's here to protect Clarke," Stigg said, shaking his head. "Rend and Titus are here. They're probably still inside Skyetook."

"Bloody hell," Leon said. "The band is getting back together."

"I'm glad those juggernauts are here this time, to be honest."

"If we ever get the chance to reminisce," Leon said and chortled, "and I tell you I lost faith in your leadership skills and plan… well, that moment would be right now. It's good that my lass' are here to help keep everyone straight."

"Deek?"

"Formidable lady, that one, yes. And her older sister."

"The other *Mischi*?" Stigg asked with a smirk.

Leon nodded. "You'll have to fill me in on that leap. It was part of my debt fulfillment to Constance. Our daughters together to protect one another in a place of lone operators. That's how I made my leap."

"I'll be damned," Stigg replied. "For me, it was when I first saw your daughter. I thought she was Arbasele reincarnated. Her mannerisms and... wish I would have put it together sooner, though."

"Aye," Leon said. "Feisty like her mom too. May the gods save us all if we're on her bad side."

"Any idea why they would have been at odds?"

"Hell, if I know. But either way, Clarke's safer with them until he's not."

"True," Stigg said with a knowing nod.

"And what about your little prisoner? She nearly got the jump on you."

"I was slow on the uptake. That old feeling was... it's been some time, you know. If I'm being honest, I might have been in denial."

"We aren't young anymore," Leon said with a quiet laugh and rolled his shoulders, receiving a few ominous-sounding crunches. "This much is true. And now we're what? We're trusting her after she tried to kill you. Changed sides, did she?"

"My evolving theory?" Stigg asked, waiting for Leon's nod of approval. "Someone in Constance's little band of misfits indoctrinated Staalke's family and failed their due diligence on tracing the talent's origin."

"We can't all be as skilled as you, old friend."

Stigg shook his head dismissively. "They were inserted here as a Ward Inquisitor of sorts and have dutifully been handing down the responsibilities. Or at least whatever structure Constance put in place instead of the typical Republic bullshit. Regardless, Staalke.

That's not her real name. Her family carried some old and dangerous feelings that survived through the years."

"So, for now, she's against the same side of ROG that we're not fans of."

"I'm also certain her reason differs from ours."

"They could conflict down the road."

"True," Stigg said with a subtle grin, "but for now, we're aligned."

Leon cursed, his laughter sending him into a fit of coughing. "Constance really was the best, wasn't she?"

Stigg agreed and gave his friend a good whack on the back.

"Then why did this Staalke attack you?" Leon asked.

"She carried her family's pain," Stigg said quietly. "And their burden. She associates me with the source of it all."

"You still are. As am I if she puts it together."

"Oh, I think that ships sailed, my friend. Besides, I don't think she meant to kill me."

"Still can't believe Constance would use Tersinians," Leon whispered.

"May we join you two?" Enas asked.

"Dammit," Stigg said, clutching his chest. "Don't you know not to sneak up on old people?"

"Are you discussing your tactical approach? We could help."

"Something like that," Stigg said, using a common dialect. "Although, I'm wondering whether I should be with Clarke instead of leading this here charge. If that's what we're calling it."

"Your concern for Clarke is understandable," Enas said flatly.

Stigg looked questioningly at Enas, who shook his head back and forth—the answer as to why Enas couldn't contact the invasion team tugged on an invisible part of innards he learned to trust ages ago. Stigg knew he was lying when he told himself he wasn't worried about Clarke. "We need to get to Clarke before they get him off-planet."

"Our distraction should provide valuable time for the infiltration," Enas added.

Stigg agreed. "Truthfully, it's Constance's daughter I'm concerned about."

Enas nodded vigorously. "Yes. The specter. They would be a most interesting study."

Stigg shook his head from side to side. "They really aren't lad. By the way, I've been meaning to ask, which one of you is with Clarke?"

After an uncomfortable pause, Enas replied. "It seems that none of us are. Clarke was not available for our consideration."

"Figured he was a little too boring for you, eh?" Leon asked. "Engineers can be that way."

"Initially—" Enas started to say and vigorously rubbed his hands together. "I'm afraid my query has created some concern. Given his apparent ability to access Astute technology, Clarke would have been a logical candidate. It's as if he was concealed from us."

"How much do you know of Clarke's origins, Stigg?" Laars' mechanical growl reverberated through the forest edge as he stomped into view.

"Apparently not enough."

"Luna has spent much of her life studying genetics and the composition of life," Enas said. "Including developing an understanding for identifying those with *the talent,* as you call it."

"I'm familiar," Stigg replied.

"Oh yes," Enas replied excitedly. "Undeniably you would. As a Vanguard, you sought people with certain genetic traits and characteristics. Yes, yes."

"Not one of our better moments," Leon admitted, nodding and biting his lip, remembering some of the less-than-honorable round-up missions ROG had sent them on to bolster their ranks.

"That was some time ago," Laars said consolingly.

"Out with it already," Stigg said. "What does Luna's research have to do with Clarke?"

"Luna is having difficulty placing Clarke's origin," Laars said. "When Clarke was aboard the Osprey, Luna had a moment to study him."

"Impossible," Stigg said. "Wait. What the hell does that mean, anyway? And exactly how accurate is Luna's *whatever she used?*"

Laars' laugh was unsettling. "It's possible she may have missed something—"

"Luna's accuracy is always with the strictest confidence," Enas blurted. "Just like her discovery of those related to—"

"Truthfully," Laars interrupted. "We have little understanding of Clarke. What do you know of his past?"

"It's complicated," Stigg replied. "One day, a friend showed up with a wee babe in arms." It terrified him to admit he had grown fond of the fatherly protector he had become. He had enjoyed watching the lad grow over the years and was proud of the man Clarke was becoming.

"Stigg, we need details if we're going to help," Laars pleaded.

"As you seem to be aware," Stigg said, fiddling with his mustache. "I was once Vanguard. My friend said the child's mother was taken. I assumed it had been ROG. And, likely because the mother had the potential to be *Mischi.*"

"This friend of yours," Enas said quietly, leaning toward Stigg. "Was she *Mischi?* And the child, was Clarke, was he born of *Mischi?*"

"Yes, and I honestly don't know about Clarke's birth parents. *Mischi* aren't exactly known to be forthcoming."

"Clarke most likely had the talent to become a Vanguard then?" Laars asked. "Or perhaps even *Mischi?*"

"She believed he would become one of the greatest," Stigg said. "Although, she wasn't clear on the *greatest of what.* Those were some difficult times."

"The split of the Vanguards from the Nova Republic," Enas said. "Such an incredible event!"

Stigg flashed Enas an expression conveying that he was treading dangerously close to something sensitive. "So, I cared for the child and hid him from the world as best I knew how, as my friend asked of me. Eventually, we came here to Lindaulx. A quiet little slice of rock to squirrel away on away from the Republic's eyes."

"And why wouldn't they come here?" Laars asked.

Stigg shook his head, closed his eyes, and gently bowed his head.

"Because it seems Constance was four steps ahead of us," Leon said. "And peering around corners, we still don't see. Stigg—by the Gods man—she's had to have had all of this in the works for ages, even when we were with her. Damn. To get an armory secretly built without the Vanguards knowing. Including displacing entire colonies. And circumventing the *watchers.* And all while leaving behind something we could use on a planet that, in hindsight, we clearly didn't choose of our own volition."

"Don't forget keeping an Astute complex hidden from the rest of the world," Stigg added.

"That woman was amazing," Leon said with a beaming smile. "Scary, mind you. But bloody-well amazing."

"Somebody within ROG and the Vanguards knew," Stigg said with a growl. "She did not do this alone. My guess is that the structure was put in place before Constance's lifetime."

"It was here all along," Leon said, the implication causing his heart to race. He cursed under his breath. "All of this for Clarke? That can't be it. Can it?"

"Did you ever test Clarke?" Laars asked Stigg.

"Constance left this world before Clarke came of age," Stigg said, the sadness reflecting in his eyes. "And those rituals are outlawed. I feared ROG or others would sense it if I tested him. Especially if his talent flourished like what all the secrecy to hide him seems to insinuate. Besides, Clarke wasn't ready to have the Nova Republic hunting him, and I didn't want him caught up in their infernal dealings. He was better off." Stigg rubbed his forearms to chase away the old memories contending for his attention.

"Or was it you who was better off?" Enas asked.

"Careful, friend. I have my reasons."

"We apologize, Stigg," Laars said. "It's possible the vengeance may never have awakened within Clarke."

"Nah, Constance wouldn't have been wrong," Stigg said, trying to sound convincing. "Besides, I didn't want the child to suffer and was honor bound to protect him."

"What I'm trying to say, Stigg," Laars said. "Given Clarke's, ah, origin, a Vanguard may not exist within him. She may not have understood who, or even what, Clarke is."

"What the hell does that mean?" Stigg asked.

Laars laughed. "I honestly don't have a clue. It's quite confounding. There are many possibilities, yet none because we do not possess the truth. Let alone where to search for it."

"We could ask him," Enas said.

"Absolutely not," Stigg said. "I don't want him getting any ideas about being a Vanguard. Bad enough, he wanted to become a damn dragoon with his affliction and all."

"What affliction?" Laars asked.

"You aren't aware?" Stigg asked.

"Clearly we are not."

"The lad's body rejects all available spec," Stigg said.

"It was Clarke who invented his own spec that nearly did him in," Leon said. He sucked air between his pressed lips to make a squealing sound remembering a past conversation with his wife. Seeing Stigg grimace he quickly diverted his gaze.

"But augments bond to all documented organics in the most basic way," Enas said. "It's meant to mimic the host's genetic composition, so the body doesn't reject it as a foreign object."

"But it's based on known genetic compositions, and if you were of truly foreign—" Laars said flatly.

"It wouldn't have the proper protocols to produce the correct signatures for his body to accept it," Enas blurted. "Another data point in the puzzling origin of Clarke!"

"But how is this possible?" Laars asked.

"Better to ask how did we miss it?" Enas responded. "We have been cataloging events for far more years than Clarke is old."

"Good questions, Enas," Laars said. "And I don't have answers. Not even a plausible theory I would dare share at this juncture."

Stigg closed his eyes and inhaled deeply. "We need to get Clarke off planet and somewhere safe."

"That would be my plan," Leon said. "But taking him to ROG would not."

"That's where I figure they're going," Stigg said to Leon. "Just not sure which one they'll find when they arrive."

"They pro-Republic?" Leon asked.

"Hell, if I know," Stigg said, directing a raised eyebrow at Leon.

Leon laughed. "What? You think the ladies in my life tell me anything?"

"Fair enough," Stigg said with a heavy sigh. "Not sure I thought this one through, buddy."

"There is always faith," Leon replied.

"Never figured you to remain pious," Stigg said solemnly. He appreciated that Leon always had a way of seeing the light during the darkest of times. The man had rigorously taught them all about the old ways—the commandments delivered by the first Pathfinders.

"We must remember to trust the scriptures and our instincts again," Leon said, placing a hand on Stigg's shoulder. "They have both served us without fail through the years, have they not?"

"They were a necessity," Stigg said quietly, grasping Leon's shoulder with his other hand.

They bowed their heads as Leon recited an ancient passage in an archaic language meant to provide reassurance and call upon the wisdom and guidance of the previous Pathfinders.

"These markings are no accident, or have you—"

"Careful, Leon," Stigg interrupted, his voice sharp. "I remember the damn oaths."

"And he's back," Leon said triumphantly, raising his hands skyward. "The grumpy goat!"

"What in the hell are you two prattling on about?" Deek said as she joined the group.

"The inescapability of life's patterns," Leon said, smiling at his daughter as he seized her in an uplifting embrace. "And how to get you all to safety."

Deek strained against the force of her father's arms. "Sounds delightful. Now, if you don't mind, it's time to get gone!"

CHAPTER 27

AURALEI WATCHED AS Clarke inspected the battle armor. It felt like a lifetime since she had tracked him to the Cryl Tenser and subsequently placed a shadow-mole in Clarke's unit—a Nova Republic spy-type who was adequate for providing details on movements, social interactions, and other life events, but the reports were purely factual and lacked emotional detail. It made it difficult to determine the reasoning behind some of Clarke's actions, and now she wondered if that had been part of the ruse to hide Clarke. If she ever encountered the shadow mole, they would not enjoy their conversation with her. Auralei stepped forward to greet Clarke and stopped. Her understanding of the man's personality, temperament, and much more was limited. She was about to dive into a situation where the endgame didn't have a clear picture, and her tactical awareness was limited to mere seconds— she rarely operated *in the moment*. "What are you working on?" she asked, her voice faltering, and chided herself for asking such an obvious question.

"Any chance you have experience with this type of tech?" Clark asked.

"We are..." Auralei said and shook her head. It was difficult adjusting to the emotions she was experiencing when she thought of Clarke, let alone how they amplified when he was near. She knew the confident Auralei lurked somewhere within, threatening to rear her formidable self. "I've never seen a working version of this armor type. How did you get past the activation sequence?"

Clarke glanced over his shoulder, the woman startling him as she was within arm's reach. "How do you do it?"

"Trade secrets," she said with a wink but saw Clarke did not find her response as humorous as she did. "We receive instruction and a form of imprinting. And some of us happen to be more gifted than others."

"You mean *tainted?*"

"We prefer *talented*. But yes. And I'll deny it."

"What about your weapons and gear?"

"Some real, others a ruse created by our engineers. It doesn't hurt to have people believing we're carrying authentic Astute gear: fear and all that."

"We as in the Nova Republic?" Clarke asked, receiving Auralei's acknowledgment. "I still don't understand how you use the genuine stuff?"

"Implanting," Auralei said and held out her palms, "augments that transmit code. My understanding is that it mimics genetics. ROG's prevailing theory is that the Astutes had a caste system. Individuals, even groups, within their culture could access devices with higher echelon functions. Our engineers believe the key is a prime Astute or a group that could see behind the veil, if you will."

"What do you mean by *behind the veil?*" Clarke asked, his brow furrowing.

Auralei smirked. "The Republic exposes us to some pretty eccentric paradigms, including some of the oldest identified collections of datasets and their varying translations and interpretations. Some of them tell of a caste or group of Astutes that were all-knowing or all-accessing. Ascended. They may have been the authority, even thought of as prophets, saints, paragons, etcetera. Take my sword, for example; it performs basic cutting abilities for anyone, even you. Now, for me, it's lighter and cuts harder. There's no way of telling just what it would do for one of these ascended. Imagine the power that one would have if they could truly harness the ancient power conduits between worlds. ROG believes this group could travel without the aid of the Mar-Vhen transit network."

"Personally," Clarke said, shaking his head. "I think the Astutes were comprised a collection of races, and people like us ranked somewhere at the bottom."

Auralei smiled and nodded in agreement. "That could be why we achieve limited use."

"No one really knows, then?"

Auralei smiled and touched the dull exterior of the armor. "Precisely. Except, when the Republic, and anyone else for that matter, sees the likes of this thing, they're going to assume you know something they don't. Which complicates our situation greatly. People are already talking about a mechanized Astute guardian that appeared to repel the invaders. Those less inclined to superstition and fables will see the story for what it is. Someone resurrected a long-dormant Astute armor set or developed a believable fake. Either way, the Nova Republic will set contracts and directives to find it and you."

Clarke averted her gaze. "I was wondering what you intended to do with me once we're through with this little undertaking. Provided we survive."

"I don't know what you mean," Auralei said, stepping back.

Clarke stood and turned to face her, catching her piercing emerald eyes. "I know you're working with Stigg, and the collateral or payment seems to be yours truly," he said, scratching the back of his head.

Auralei wondered if Clarke was afraid of her or didn't trust her—not that he had any significant or compelling reasons to do so—and whether there was any harm in telling him the truth. Her augments carefully evaluated his biometrics and concluded he was straying into fright instead of flight. But his stance and penetrating focus told her he wasn't afraid of her.

Misreading the woman's hesitation, Clarke continued. "You are not taking me with you. Not to some damn lab, not to the bloody Republic, and no one is studying me. As cliché as that sounds."

"I don't see that you have much of a choice," Auralei said with a smile.

"Explain," he said flatly.

This conversation was not going the way Auralei had envisioned. "I meant there are people really pissed at you here on Lindaulx. I do not fully understand why the Republic saw fit to use you as the catalyst for this event. There must be a compelling reason to frame a person for murder, as the result can cause a significant imbalance in the flux."

Clarke sighed. "I'm aware that most people will rely on what they are told. I can handle that. But what about the invasion would necessitate framing me?" He could feel something resembling sympathy creeping from Auralei, so he closed his eyes and breathed in the mechanically scrubbed air. The invaders had invested a great deal of effort into making sure everyone believed he killed Trake Khilsyth. "I have a few theories about the ulterior motive behind the assassin being disguised as me."

Auralei guided an elevator platform used for working on the upper parts of dragoon suits over to where Clarke was and sat down. She adjusted the seat to bring her to eye level—his once plum blue eyes, dark like the ocean's depths, were now a wintery blue sheen-like light penetrating a thin layer of snow. She wondered if it was the fallibility of digitally augmented memories or the unshakable sense, he was staring directly into her thoughts that shaped the imperfect memory. "Clarke, whatever your theories are, I'm certain they are good. But I think they may have coincidently linked the two of us on this one."

"How?" Clarke held her gaze while his dark passenger provided glimpses of the fractured and fuzzy images racing through her thoughts. He shook his head to steady the images.

Auralei faltered, her voice croaking. "I know you would never mean any harm to come to House Khilsyth; I understand that. But I want to help you. I need to keep you safe."

"Why are you so interested in me?"

"Because I typically find that *we* are not in alignment with the Republic."

"*We* who?"

Auralei tugged the eyelashes over her left eye. "As the old timer refers to us, we, the *Mischi*."

"I still can't believe *Mischi* are real—it means that some of the so-called quack theories have potential to be real."

"I'd tell you that my life could be forfeit for telling you all of this, but I believe that to already be the case."

"Who would believe me?" Clarke asked, flashing a genuine smile.

Auralei laughed weakly. "Probably no one. Although my little princess is another matter."

"The other *Mischi*. What about her?"

"Perhaps another time. For now, some Nova Republic specters want to return our order to a time when we were proud to be

Mischi. And that is in material disagreement with the Republic's approach to world events—nothing we can solve here. But I plan to have some sticky conversations with people who likely aren't expecting to see me again. I... I had come down here to discuss plans for getting into Skyetook."

"You can really suck the fun out of a conversation once it gets good, can't you?" Clarke asked with a playful pump of his eyebrows. "By the way, did you see the weapon recovered from Trake Khilsyth's assassin?"

"What about it?"

"The marks on the hilt that the invaders broadcasted the image: the double-stacked mountains are House Leod's clandestine forces, and the double-stacked overlapping infinity symbols... I believe those are Tersinian."

"Not many on Lindaulx would piece that together," Auralei said.

"You don't think they would know the House Leod piece?" Clarke asked and added quickly. "But the conspiracy theorists would make the Tersinian leap."

"Are you certain about the other symbol?" Auralei asked with a sigh, remembering the markings on the woman in Stigg's care.

Clarke nodded again. "It shows up in Astute lore, and I was practically raised around House Leod. At least it's my working theory." Clarke made to touch the woman's cheek but stopped, his hand falling away. "What else rallies the people better than a threat from a stronger House?"

His hand's proximity to her face sent electric impulses coursing through her body, igniting buried emotions. She was on the verge of remembering something crucial and wading into uncomfortable territory by allowing moments such as this to form correctly, unfiltered by her augments. Devices that ROG technicians ensured provided a desired balance to eliminate fear-driven decision-making and reduce irrational responses. The side effect of the augments was a constant craving for the state of hyper-clarity they offered. *But where is my clarity now, Shifty?* She wondered. It was a scary prospect, but she needed to feel strongly about something or someone again. Her reactions were moderately foreign and challenging for her to name, and so she settled on a combination of comfort and homicide. She stepped backward, using distance as protection.

"Sorry," Clarke muttered.

"For what?" Auralei asked, watching his measured breathing and trying to read his eyes. She stepped forward, held his hand in hers and brought it up to meet her cheek. He held it there for a moment after she let go of his hand, then his fingertips slid delicately along her jawline to her ear. His hand lingered in the spot where her ear disappeared into her elegant neck without a nook.

"For a moment there," Clarke said taking a deep breath and smiling. "You reminded me of someone I once knew."

Clarke turned away, and his hand was gone, along with a fleeting sense of contentment. She fought hard against the urge to engage her neural augments to suppress these uncomfortable emotions and punch him in the face. "Ellane?" she whispered, watching Clarke's body language betray his sadness.

"Yeah," he exhaled. "I gave her a bracelet like the one you're wearing. So. Are you her?"

"I may have been. I'm not sure. Those memories are distorted. Obscured somehow. And I don't know how, but you and me, our past is shared." The memories of Auralei's childhood were fragmented. She knew Clarke was the bracelet's owner but wondered who the hell Ellane was. She leaned forward, grabbing his head as he tried to move away, and brought her mouth as close as she dared to his ear. Her stomach screamed with fire and her brain with fear. The years at the Nova Republic Academy had sought to eradicate this part of her life, severing all ties to the past to foster pure, unquestionable loyalty and dedication to the Resource Operations Group. The utterance of her birth name had resulted in hours of hard labor and lashings by the elder sisters. Even now, she feared Sister Malquis would appear and launch into one of her tirades with her favored wooden staves. Then, a filament of energy was there, guiding her memories, knitting them together, and providing a pathway to coalesce. There was an image of a young girl with her hand outstretched in greeting which morphed into one of it being slapped away by an overbearing woman. She felt her hand throb and spurned the emerging tears—suddenly, a familiar tune touched her lips just under her breath to steady her nerves, and then she repeated the mantra her mentor had instilled in her. "I am the shining light," Auralei said. "I am the shining light." She released an encompassing sigh and sunk into herself. There, in the quiet, was a grainy memory playing out of sync: a blonde girl beamed with happiness; in one hand, she clutched a gleaming metallic bracelet to her chest; and in the other, she held the hand of a little boy with bright blue eyes. "Holy hell. I am Ellane Leod."

Clarke allowed his head to fall to the side and gingerly rest against hers. "Is it really you?"

Auralei feared her augments would burn the memory away, even as her training hammered its resistance, but her machine side was still. The relief of her discovery overshadowed her ability to register the slippery residue from the dark passenger's intrusion fading from her mind. This left her unaware that something had coaxed her fractured memories to the surface and reformed them. In its wake, it left the other pieces of her life freedom to appear as flashes of images trying to reconstitute themselves.

"Everything okay?" Clarke asked with genuine concern, seeing the color fade from her face.

"Some memories aren't particularly comfortable to remember," Auralei breathed. "I have felt lost for some time now... and only recently started mending fragments of my past. I'm not sure if I'm correctly joining the pieces or even putting them on the right timeline. But that tune and that saying, somebody wanted me to remember." She chased away an imaginary hand on her neck with a shiver. In a brief respite from the onslaught of memories, there was an icy sensation in her veins and a metallic taste in her mouth. There were ethereal tendrils present within her, like dark filaments slipping between her memories, sorting, classifying, and mending them. In her mind, she fabricated a sense of wonder to mask her shift of consciousness into the flux. She wondered if it had detected her gambit and watched as her memories continued to be knit together. The wispy tendrils handled the memories delicately, careful not to distort or tie together incorrect pieces. Here in the place between worlds, she traced the source to Clarke, who was enshrouded by countless tendrils writhing in hypnotic patterns. She would need Shifty to scan Clarke and the ROG network secretly to see if someone had encountered this phenomenon before. It was worrisome and unnerving. Slowly, the dark material pulsed in sections around Clarke's form, developing expanding ellipses that moved toward her. Auralei shifted out of the flux before they touched her. "I remember going home at a young age," Auralei said quickly, hoping her discovery went unnoticed. "I completed my initial schooling. So much had changed. Duke, my father, had taken a new wife. He had become a tired soul, drained of his youthful vigor. Daphne, I think that was his new wife's name. She thought I was a Republic spy. They subjected me to multiple tests, eventually discerning the neural augments the Nova Republic had provided. Some I wasn't even aware of. She forced my father to banish me. Daphne's doctors claimed my augments were for sinister uses. There was a boy; his name escapes me. He lived in the city close to my school. We would sneak out and ride a fast two-wheeled machine he had built, but... there was an accident. I think the

Republic, maybe ROG, invested in my recovery and... saved my life."

"So. You really are Ellane?"

"I believe I was."

"I have been trying to find you."

Auralei slipped back with tears welling in her emerald eyes. She held Clarke's warm gaze. "It would have been impossible for you to find me."

"Nearly," Clarke admitted. "I talked to Duke about eight years ago now. He said they hadn't heard from you in a long time."

"That's true. I kept a safe distance from them."

"When I contacted the Republic, they said you died in an accident. Only I uncovered a transportation request you made that referenced the accident as a reason for your last visit home. It was also when I last saw you; you were alive. Also, the request happened after the accident, which might have been a clerical error, but I didn't trust the likes of the Republic. Since then, Stigg's contacts have been helping to track you down. I chased down leads when time permitted."

Auralei threw her arms around Clarke in a tight embrace. The side hug was awkward, and they weren't adequately braced for the force of the hug. The stool holding Clarke shot out from underneath him, sending them tumbling to the floor. They held each other's gaze and smiled.

"It's good to see you again," Clarke said. A series of fragmented images of her past bit at the edges of his vision, and he pressed his palm against the side of his face to steady himself against her damaged memories.

"Really? You don't look like it."

"Sorry." He adjusted himself so he was even with her. "A lot has happened since."

"And when was that?"

"You don't remember?"

Auralei shook her head. "Not specifically. Damaged goods, remember? Tell me one of our stories."

Clarke told Auralei of the last night they spent together on Nanser-Nine, where she had escaped the house from under the watchful eyes of the House Guards. They had set off after borrowing a reconnaissance-chopper without authorization. Luckily, it was a stealthy craft, as that evening, another house invaded, likely because they suspected weakness with Duke Leod's fragility.

"I remember the skyline of my home. Sometimes, in my dreams, I see a fire, and I'm not sure if it was attacked or if someone I loved was in trouble or, worse, dead. Sometimes, there's someone in the fire. I always thought it was me, but now I think it might be you, Clarke. But that girl you knew, Ellane… I'm not her anymore. So, tell me, have you had any exciting escapades with other girls lately?"

"No. Nothing quite as exciting until recently."

"Oh, really," Auralei said, flashing him a menacing glare.

"No. Nothing like that, but…"

"But what?" Auralei asked, straightening.

"Why now, Ellane? What made you come now?"

She sighed, turning away, and massaged the space between her eyes. "For the time being and only when alone, it's Auralei"

"That's a pretty name."

"With others, no names. It's an unspoken rule. Understood?" She was relieved he didn't object. "I took the contract for Lindaulx because I learned you were somewhere I didn't realize you were. I thought you might be in danger. It seemed like the only way to protect you, and Shifty thought it was time I met you to see if I could trigger lost memories. Also, if another *Mischi* knew I was interfering with the operation, I would compromise myself."

"You knew I was here?"

"I thought I knew where you were. But I didn't understand *who* you were. There was never a safe opportunity to approach you."

"Safe? You contacting me would compromise my safety?"

She ignored the obvious sarcasm. "I also wasn't sure how you fit into my past or future. Besides, the rumors of people going missing are true. If they discovered I contacted you, ROG would press you into service. Their methods are subtle, and you most likely would have done so without objecting."

"So now, what do we do?"

"My plan had involved this little conflict on Lindaulx explaining your disappearance. People would either account for you as dead or most likely kidnapped by a rival House exploiting the situation."

"Yeah, who would have figured my choice of work was dangerous, eh?"

"The other part of my plan," Auralei said, pinching his cheek. "The other part of my plan was taking you somewhere safe. But I have a feeling the invasions are not limited to Lindaulx."

"I would bet they targeted any planet with an Astute complex."

"And they know about Astute colonies that we don't. We also lost any actual contact with ROG at approximately the same time the attack began here on Lindaulx. Shortly before, we received a coded message requesting all of us to come home. It read more like a distress call than an ultimatum. Apparently, a faction calling themselves the Anacul Nation is appearing throughout the known sectors and infiltrating colonies. Based on the events here at the facility, it's clear they possess some advanced technology."

Clarke shook his head. "That's a lot to wrap one's head around, isn't it?"

"The funny part is that getting off Lindaulx is likely the straightforward bit."

"By the way, when you said *we* lost contact, you mean you and that other *Mischi*, right?"

"And others. Not just two."

"There was more than one contract then?"

"Yes," Auralei admitted. "Our initial contract was to provide a least-cost conflict resolution. The discovery of the Astute facility complicated matters because ROG prefers to manage those, and I have no explanation for how they didn't have this site documented. We figured the initial contract was the Republic rebalancing power amongst the major Houses, which is common enough. Besides, the Republic vetted and approved the contracts. But pining it on you, that is a strange one."

"Maybe the all-knowing Republic got this one wrong."

"It seems so. It's also safe to assume the Khilsyths knew about the Astute facility, right?"

Clarke shrugged. "Perhaps. Maybe even knew about the rather devastating war tech hidden within Warbler Ridge."

"And we've failed to determine much of anything about the communication source originating from Lindaulx. The signal wasn't like anything we knew about and nothing we had heard before. Our best hive minds can't figure out what it was. What would you say about the fact that my ship is reporting it went silent while we were in the facility?"

"The Anacul got what they came for?"

"Could be. But what if it was a distress call? Something so advanced and ancient that our technology can't relate."

"You think the facility had security measures?"

"Not really sure. But Shifty thinks something answered because it reversed right before the signal ended. Something came here. But right now, we need to help Anzil."

The loudspeaker buzzed its indifference and emitted Anzil's voice as if on cue. "You two better not be fooling around back there. We're getting close to our entry point."

Auralei pursed her lips, stood, and dragged Clarke to his feet. "There's never enough time when you need it." She grabbed him with both hands, forcing him close against her body, and gave him a chastised kiss on the cheek. "For luck."

CHAPTER 28

THE MARAUDER CRASHED through the forest undergrowth with thousands of oversized mechanized badgers trailing on a southerly course. When they burst through the tree line, Stigg unleashed the full might of the old Republic armory on the two closest gatherings of invaders.

As Stigg had predicted and confirmed with the help of Enas' reconnaissance devices, the invaders had organized into four distinct groups. The tracktor munitions the marauder carried were a lost technology, things of nightmares, until twenty-one ignited on Lindaulx after years of silence—the canisters streaked toward their target areas, each one separating into a star-burst pattern of approximately one thousand other smaller containers, disabling unshielded electrical equipment, interrupting combatant's equilibrium, and corrupting source fuel. This act was devastating and produced the intended result of aggravating the horde.

In charge of the marauder's multitude of cannons, Enas liberally covered the field of battle with precise and lethal shots. Successful hits sent dragoons and heavy equipment spinning and rolling across the rocky plain. Other enemies fell prey to the clan of badgers, scurrying through the invader ranks, rending flesh and armor. The invader's retaliation was uncoordinated and chaotic, resulting in some friendly fire casualties.

"Amazing!" Enas said. "After all this time, the machine is still operational. Mind you, some of the system's technology is foreign to me." He redirected a few incoming rockets that got close enough to the marauder to explode harmlessly elsewhere or back to the attacker. "Feast on that, bitches!"

"You sound like you're enjoying yourself," Stigg said.

"Very much so," Enas replied.

"That's just lovely," Stigg remarked.

"But I'm uncertain of the outcomes some of these buttons will produce. Willing to try anything once, though."

Once through the enemy's eastern flank and back to the cover of the northern edge of the Bercelium forest, Stigg coaxed the machine into a sweeping turn and reappeared along the east edge of the clearing, heading toward Skyetook. Enas guided the rest of the mechanical badgers on a tighter radius turn, impeding the invading forces from blocking their route from the north and west. Surprised and in a frenzy to prove themselves, the enemy forces became a swirling maelstrom of chaos. To Stigg's relief, his plan successfully motivated the northerly and westerly invading units to move, which prevented him from dealing with a stationary wall of enemy resistance.

"Is it time yet?" Stigg asked Enas over the marauders' screams of warning that its ability to maintain shields was fleeting –it had become the preferred target on the battlefield.

"The badgers have attached devices to approximately thirty-six percent of the enemy's functioning vehicles. Good enough?

"Yeah, it's going to have to be."

"Agreed. Another couple of direct hits and we'll be—"

"Scorched earth," Enas interjected.

"Quite. Yes."

Enas activated the devices the mechanical badgers had planted, which secreted an expanding gel-like substance, encompassing the invaders and sending tendrils into the ground, which hardened and rendered the enemy motionless.

"Stupid asses," Stigg said, watching some of the cocooned dragoons flash in a brilliant expansion until the shells grew beyond their structural limits and popped, spewing forth their molten contents. "Nasty little devices. I like them."

"Handy for our research. However, I failed to calculate the result of activating explosives within the pods."

Stigg snickered. "I'm sure they are quick studies."

"Now I presume Phase Aggravation is successful, and we're into our Momentum Phase. I am curious how you are planning to resolve this battle?"

"For now, let's focus on joining up with Leon and Deek. We're going to need the protection."

SERGEANT LESTER HALSTER, a ranger loyal to House Khilsyth, secured a vantage point on a ridgeline where she set about classifying the multitude of targets on the battlefield below. She believed that if the dragoons knew who they were shooting at, they would team up and form cohesive fighting units. Lester Halster hoped her brave actions would help stem the tide of the battle and turn it back in favor of those defending Warbler Ridge.

Under typical engagement protocols, Lester Halster knew that the classification and tracking of units protected forces from friendly fire by prompting pilots to override their fail-safes to attack targets designated as friendly. However, thanks to Clarke's pain-in-her-ass-device, the Khilsyth dragoons now always bypassed safety protocols and relied on their trigger fingers to act as the safety—an inherently flawed system, in her opinion.

Lester Halster soon recognized she needed help and tasked some of her subordinates with performing similar classification duties. Because she had reached the war outside Warbler Ridge a little too late, her ad hoc classification method was hauntingly similar to what the soldiers used as their engagement logic rules. She started by classifying the more stationary forces near the south clearing as hostiles since they were sending copious amounts of ordinance into the kill field. The rest of the soldiers in the alpine valley were more challenging to classify.

As the battle wore on, it was becoming increasingly difficult for Lester Halster to determine allegiances because the invaders had not taken the time, nor had the vanity, to distinguish their allegiance by courteously marking their uniforms and captured equipment. The battlefield had disintegrated to where soldiers were simply trying to destroy whatever was or looked like it was, shooting at them. Adding to her classification frustrations was the sheer volume of mud covering everything. The Ridge was situated within a vast weather convergence zone along the Esconairian Range, experiencing near-record rainfalls this season.

Eventually, she finished classifying her thirty-ninth friendly unit, a platoon of thirty-two dragoons who seemed to have banded together and agreed they could be pleasant to one another. Their coordinated efforts were wreaking havoc on the battlefield—on Lester Halster's command tablet; they were classified as friendly/Lester Halster's group 39/32 dragoons (F/LH39/32d). For an unknown reason, twenty-one dragoons separated from the group, and the battle tablet dubiously adjusted her classification, marking the offshoot group as F/LH39/32d-21 and the remaining dragoons as F/LH39/32d-11.

F/LH39/32d-21 immediately engaged a group marked F/NB7/12s (soldiers), which were classified by Nesson Braf, one of her less-than-careful privates. Lester Halster assumed Nesson Braf must have been sloppy classifying the group, so she overrode the classification from friendly to hostile or H/NB7+LH40/12s.

After several strafing runs, F/LH39/32d-21, having suffered no casualties, turned away and ran into F/LH39/32d-11. However, the two groups did not combine as expected. Instead, they hacked away at each other with the multitude of dragoon weaponry. Lester Halster never doubted she might be wrong about her grouping logic and sent a warning out over the battle network to *her* F/LH39 combined group, ordering them to cease attacking one another. She didn't consider that some of the House Khilsyth soldiers on Lindaulx were soldiers of fortune and easily swayed by the promise of more significant fiscal compensation if they conveniently switched allegiances. Eventually, after a multitude of warnings and persistent chat requests, the F/LH39 group complied and reformed, becoming F/LH39/24d, having suffered some losses.

Once again, the dragoon group was effective at dispatching other groups with fewer units until it split again, this time in half. One half veered behind the defensive barriers of F/LH1/20s, and she watched in horror as the dragoon's massive cannons shredded her comrades from her home squadron. Adding insult to injury, Lester Halster looked on in amazement as the four soldiers who had survived the dragoon strafing run were re-classified as hostile.

"Nesson Braf, you dumb sunnova bitch!" Lester Halster screamed and hurled her tablet at the unsuspecting private.

The tablet spun end over end and struck Nesson Braf in the head, who stumbled, tripped, and fell from the ridgeline. Nesson Braf's tablet's ultimate act was to override all unit classifications to blank, including those units classified with the strictest of confidence levels—this likely resulted from a poorly developed operating system and battle logic classification routine rather than spite.

Sergeant Lester Halster sat on a rock, drawing her knees close to her chest and rocking. She vaguely heard the screech of a tornado rocket before it slammed into her position and relieved a large section of the surrounding rock from its resting place. If Lester Halster had been alive to see the rocket's exhaust trail begin from the remains of her squadron, she might have laughed at the cruel joke life had played on her.

CHAPTER 29

MAEVE SUMMONED THE console in her private quarters, connecting to a secure network and waiting for the message service authenticator. She admired the cup of tea beside her, sending tendrils of wild flower-scented steam dancing above the rim of the stone cup. The collection of status updates and briefing reports from her agents scattered throughout the galaxy were positive. Other facilities were being secured, and her contacts poised in Lindaulx's orbit ensured they were ready to receive her at a moment's notice.

Maeve marveled at her handiwork—the plan she crafted and set in motion years ago was unfolding admirably. Even now, Maeve's agents were spreading the misinformation to the other households about the Lindaulx alliances, the support of the Rift Faction, and the involvement of the Nova Republic. These actions would incite wild rumors of a move for dominance in this sector and convince people that the Nova Republic overstepped.

Maeve's Order had rejected this plan, with two of the five senior disciples refusing to accept the merits of what she could accomplish and lobbying to punish her for daring to speak of such falsehoods—*quack theories*—and code violations. *A code of convenience,* she scoffed, knowing that if she met success, they would all come swooping in to claim the glory for the greater good of the Tersinian Order and revel in the attention and acclaim it would provide. For as much as the disciples positioned for power and postulated for the endeavor of discovering a complete spiritual awakening, at their very core, Maeve believed they were corrupt and self-serving.

Through her years of service, Maeve learned that some of the missions dreamed up by the senior disciples never worked out the way one planned. She even tolerated the incitement of an element of chaos in her work because it gave the missions a life of their own. There was a strong contingent, arguably the most influential faction of her Order, who believed their cause for oneness with the flux was just. For as long as she knew, there had always been a cause for the Order to pursue, and why not one with an undefinable ending? For how does one recognize when others have achieved true oneness? So, Maeve studied hard and fought her way up the ranks by completing missions and exploring her spiritual nature. All the while getting closer to the people she believed would serve as conduits to greater power—those with genuine influence over the Order's rank and file.

A sharp, muffled rap came from the metal door to her quarters. To answer, the door's retracting mechanism produced a slight humming noise as the heavy slabs receded into the wall. The hibiscus plant on the table in front of her swayed gently with the change in pressure as air from the room seeped through the open door. Maeve closed the console and greeted her expected guest. "Sardil, it is good to see you again," Maeve said in her native language, greeting a handsome man with a husky and severe-looking face.

Sardil panted from the exertion of carrying the wrapped package braced by his muscular arms against the shelf-like area of his belly. He greeted her with a slight nod. She had met Sardil when he was nearly a teenager at a clinic on a developing planet attempting to undergo augmentation to correct what he believed were sensory deficiencies. The social affluence of Sardil's parents provided him with high-quality tutors and trainers, and, as an infant, unbeknownst to those around him, he had learned to draw on the flux to compensate for what he saw as shortcomings. But the torments of other children had clouded Sardil's mind with aspirations that augmentations would provide an avenue to normalcy and inclusion. The beating Maeve had given Sardil had been severe for his attempt at perverting his beautiful soul by willingly wanting to introduce unnatural augmentations into his body and destroy his full potential. Maeve had contemplated leaving the child to die with the others in the clinic, but in a rare moment of compassion, she had transported him to her ship and nursed him to health. Since then, she was the dutiful protective parent responsible for shaping the formidable young man he was becoming—confident and highly-proficient in mastering the flux, rivaling even her power.

Maeve walked over to Sardil and gently touched his glistening cheek. She concentrated hard to see beneath the disguise. "Thank you, my son. You can set it over there for now. May the heavens protect us." Maeve removed the blanket covering the package Sardil deposited on the floor, revealing an attractive young woman. Satisfied, Maeve initiated a ritual, bonding her with the woman before her. If the Tersinian Order ever learned of this ritual, they would hunt her without persecution and erase her from The Official Registry.

CHAPTER 30

THE SUN WAS a sphere of gray light peering through the thin veil of a cloud-soaked sky. Auralei made some slight adjustments to the Osprey's flight, causing it to lose lift and knife downward into the wind-whipped ocean below, sending sprays of mist into the air. The vehicle slowed only a fraction as it pulled itself through the frigid waters on a course to Skyetook's spaceport on the shores of Deception Bay. Entering the port by land meant passing through two fortified and heavily armed walls, and by sea, the circumnavigation of the heavy cliff cannons to access the converted shipping pier tucked safely behind an ocean break wall.

"You know what would be convenient?" Anzil asked. "If there was a secret underwater way into the city." He turned to face the specter and Clarke as they arrived at the bridge. "Any chance we could be that lucky? A maintenance tunnel? Something big enough for us to slip through. There's always a back door, right?"

Clarke shook his head, smiling, and banged his knuckles on a nearby console frame. "We eliminated all such entrances and reworked the effluent pipes to small diameter, high-velocity piping. You're aware Stigg oversaw water-based defenses, right?"

"But didn't they skimp, ignore his designs somewhere?"

"Are you kidding?"

"Had to ask."

"So, what's your plan, Clarke?" Tarra asked.

"I have two, actually."

"Elaborate," Anzil requested, "and quickly. Between you and Stigg, the suspense of this last-minute shit is not sitting well with my nerves."

"The quiet way involves sneaking in using the mantis' to cloak our movements. That's the first one."

Anzil shook his head vigorously. "No thanks. No armor. Next one?"

"The second is the not-so-quiet way. We create distractions around the port facilities and inside the fortress, make a run for Valan, and—"

"Excuse me," Laars interrupted. "There is an incoming message from Stigg."

Anzil motioned for Laars to continue.

"How's this work?" Stigg's voice emanated from a device on Laars' forearm. "Just speak? Aye. Clarke, can you hear me?"

Clarke chuckled. "Yeah, Stigg. Loud and clear."

"Good to hear your voice," Stigg said merrily. "How's things?"

"Better than ever, you?"

"Fine. Now listen, we'll be knocking on Skyetook's gates and bringing you a lot of company in a wee bit."

"Chief, you're yelling."

"These older machines are a little noisy. And I'm a little deaf."

"What do you mean by company?" Auralei asked, tugging at her ear. "What kind of trouble are you in."

"I'd show you if I could," Stigg said. "I had this brilliant plan. It involved taking this beastor of a machine out and introducing it to the invaders."

As Stigg continued explaining his plan, Laars approached a wall-mounted panel and pressed a series of commands. The large display monitors in the Osprey flickered briefly and then filled with Stigg's smiling face. He was still rambling on about his plan, Enas' brilliance, and their teamwork.

"We can see you," Anzil said, interrupting Stigg.

"Seriously?" Stigg asked, moving his meaty finger until it filled most of the screen. "You can see through Enas here?"

"By the gods, that's a marauder, isn't it?" Clarke asked.

"Get your massive paw out of Enas' face," Anzil told Stigg.

The image spun rapidly from Stigg to mountains looming in the distance. A darkening cloud of dust appeared on the screen as a volley of rockets, chased by their smoke trails, leaped toward the invaders. A boiling inferno of plasma obscured the image as the massive rail guns hurled their projectiles downrange. Then, the image spun back to the open expanse of the plains.

"Did you see those bastards?" Stigg asked mirthfully.

"They are giving chase," Enas said proudly. "Aggravation and momentum phases were a success."

"Yeah, we saw it," Anzil said.

"We are also going to try to pick up more invaders from outside of town. Leon and Deek are also en route with a contingent."

"You saw Deek?" Anzil asked.

"Yes. She was healthy and in good spirits."

"What the hell are you going to do when you get to Skyetook?" Clarke asked. "It looks like you're nearly out of the Highlands."

"Two forces are converging on that area," Tarra said, saying what everyone was thinking. "You have a plan for that?"

"Three, actually," Stigg said.

Anzil placed his thumb on his cheekbone and ran his fingers slowly across his creased forehead. "Stigg. We still haven't confirmed what team my brother is playing for. The invaders are likely mobilizing to meet you and aware you are coming. They will set up defenses. You'll be running into a massive cluster of mines and whatever tricks they have with them."

Stigg grunted and flashed a massive smile. "It's not all doom and gloom, you know. The Riftys are coming to the party. Sounds as if they're punching through the Hindish Pass as we speak."

Tarra harrumphed in disbelief. "You've lost it, old timer."

Anzil flashed Tarra a concerned look. "Seriously, Stigg, what do you have planned for when you get near the city?"

"What were the final phases again?" Tarra asked smartly. "Oh, yeah. Altercation and resolution, correct?"

Stigg shrugged his shoulders. "Working on it. So far, we've been doing our best to give you a diversion and stay ahead of this fight. Likely warrants a little appreciation from this lot, wouldn't you agree, Enas?"

"May I expand?" Enas asked, receiving no sign to the contrary. "The invader units we have engaged are suffering more casualties than expected during this altercation phase. Some units have disengaged and changed course, and others are heading toward Willow's Ridge. One sec, patching in others."

"My guess is they're trying to lure us into a field of combat rather than the moving battle," Deek said. "And they have bad intel concerning Willow."

"Some are engaging their own units," Leon said. "Not the sanest battle I've ever been in, but not the worst either."

Clarke laughed. "Essentially, Stigg and company are a rolling shit storm."

"I would not have summed up our predicament in such a fashion," Enas replied. "There is some tactical advantage to be gained by Stigg's actions."

"Which are?" the group aboard the Osprey chorused.

"I have not fashioned a complete conclusion," Enas said truthfully. "There is merit in degrading the enemy's forces, correct?"

"Provided Stigg doesn't get his ass shot full of holes," Tarra said. "It would be nice to see him survive this."

Luna's sweet laugh drifted over the communication system. "Stigg's plan, although ill-conceived and unplanned, develops the distraction for one of our scenarios. However, there are limited solutions with moderate probabilities of the survival of Stigg's forces. We are detecting tactical warships in orbit with bombardment capabilities."

"Well, shit," Tarra said, giving Luna a healthy dose of a sinister glare. "Glad you're enjoying this."

"It will all work out until it doesn't," Stigg said. "For sure, no way to override that device of yours, Clarke?"

"Sorry, Chief. We'd have more luck overriding the pilots at this point." Clarke walked over to a bank of display screens, receiving a live feed of Stigg's convoy from one of the Osprey's observation drones. The sleek devices had a razor-thin profile and were only the length of his pinky finger, making them practically undetectable. "What if we could separate the Khilsyth forces?"

"We've been talking about that all along," Stigg said. "You have any ideas?"

"We would need to hold the Ops and Command Centers simultaneously," Clarke said.

"Ah, that might work," Anzil said. "We could broadcast over the secure battlenet to direct various forces to regroup in separate areas. And shut down any instructions from the enemy."

"What makes you so sure you need both?" Leon asked.

"Status quo," Anzil replied. "The Ops Center is responsible for units outside the walls, and Command handles units inside the walls. Like a spaceport, one tower to get them into orbit and another to find a place to park."

"You'll need to maintain control of the Ops Center for a while," Auralei said, "especially if we're planning on moving lots of folks."

"If we could separate the locals from the invaders, we may get them to see our way," Leon said.

"And that means Valan's cooperation," Deek said.

"Or his death," Tarra added.

"Let's not kill my baby brother just yet. I want to have a chat with him first."

"Clarke, break it down for us," Auralei said.

"The Ops Center is a bunker. It's the only way to send a message to the joint forces. We blocked it once but deployed multiple security system redundancies into the infrastructure to avoid any chance of being compromised from the outside. There's a chief programmer, I think Lyle's his name. He might have a workaround."

"Not likely," Tarra said quietly.

He scratched vigorously at the back of his head. "Not really a bunker," Clark said. "It's more like a hardened area within a defensible compound. It's a death trap. Once in, can we use your Nova Republic list? Do you have Khilsyth biometrics to construct most of the groups? We can broadcast a message to the right people with that."

"How do we get in?" Leon asked. "And where will Valan be?"

"It is highly improbable the Anacul commanders will be on the battlefield," Laars said. "We should also expect them in the Operations and Command Centers."

Auralei sighed. "Agreed. Although we're not certain. The invaders could be operating out of separate locations. We don't have a clear picture of what's above us." She winked at Tarra. "Except for what Princess here encountered."

"Our plan is to secure the Skyetook fortress, find Valan, and get Stigg and company inside?" Tarra asked. "What about the new invaders and the Riftys? What are the chances they protected their equipment like the Khilsyths?"

"Now you're thinking," Stigg said. "We just need them to be patched into the Skyetook battlenet, which they likely are."

"Actually, that's not completely necessary," Clarke said. "If we can find their command frequency, hack into their communications, decipher their—"

"Clarke," Stigg interrupted. "Can it be done?" Seeing his mentee's shoulders droop, he knew he stifled his friend's excitement.

"Likely. But it would require a mainframe to generate the algorithms necessary for—"

"I can help with that," Tarra interrupted, freeing a device from her hip pocket and manipulating it for a few seconds. She raised her eyes from the soft glow of its display screen, glancing at Auralei, who tossed her a die-sized cube she held against the device before putting it in her pocket. "Here's your algorithm, Clarke, courtesy of Our Lady Majestic. Be very careful with it. She's precious and very protective of her pieces."

"Clarke is on the Ops Center team," Anzil said. "I'll lead the Command team. We also need to focus on getting our people inside the walls. That way they'll have some protection."

"I have faith in you all," Stigg said.

"I'd be thinking hard about a survival plan, Stigg," Auralei said. "It's getting crowded above as more warships are appearing, and our approach is failing the keep shit simple theory."

"Who's warships, ladies?" Stigg asked with a trailing heavy sigh.

"They're of mixed origins," Auralei replied, knowing the grizzled war veteran had surmised what she had. The arrival of more warships significantly minimized the odds they were getting out of this one. "Some are Republic, likely the Bright Angels. There's also Riftys and something else."

"Tersinians or Anacul?" Stigg asked.

"Wouldn't that be something," Leon said with a grunt.

"Until they engaged one another or the surface we don't know what the teams are," Tarra said.

"That's just fantastic," Stigg said. "

"When do you need an open door?" Clarke asked.

"Our ETA depends on how much we harass the bastards following us—and the longer you take, the more we bleed."

"What about wyverns?" Tarra asked.

"We haven't heard from Captain Farsil lately," Anzil said. "I expect that—"

"What about them?" Stigg interrupted, "Captain Dipstick and Kaibab's clown parade. I tell you what, a few sonic bursts in the atmosphere, some exploding wyverns, and our aerial armada turns and burns."

"That probably wasn't Farsil's unit," Anzil said. "Maybe Kaibab's. Hopefully, Farsil wrangled some more wyverns. They could start an evac for some of your troops."

"For now, it sounds like we're stalling and stemming blood loss as much as we can," Stigg said.

"We will work fast, Stigg," Anzil said in the most reassuring voice he could muster.

"Take care, everyone," Stigg replied. "Just let us in when we knock, yeah?"

"Will do," Anzil said. "And Stigg, best of luck."

Luna walked over and rested her hand on Anzil's shoulder. "How can we help?"

Anzil took a deep breath and met Luna's gaze. "I'm going to need to send a message to all forces after I confront my brother. Clarke will need some help, too, I imagine. Can we coordinate communication using your devices between the Ops Center and wherever I am?"

Luna held his gaze. "It could be possible. One of us will need to be with each of you."

"I will be with him, you mean," Tarra said to Luna. "Just give me one of those fancy communicators you have."

Luna shied away as Tarra stepped toward her. "That would be acceptable, given the circumstances."

"Valan will most likely be at Command," Clarke added. "It's near the comfort of the family residences."

Tarra punched a series of coordinates into the Osprey's navigation panel, slapped the chair's armrests, and stood. "Shall we?" she asked the group, ushering them from the bridge to pack their gear and prepare for their insertion into Skyetook.

THE SKYETOOK FORTRESS rose from a beach buttressed by an impressive sea wall constructed from nearby rocks. The fragile shoreline was framed by two peninsulas jutting outward and protected by shallow barrier islands that absorbed the brunt of the ocean's assault. Deception Bay got its name for its welcoming appearance that hid dangerous currents and high shoals that had claimed several ships at the mercy of unskilled captains.

"Ease up there, Clarke," Auralei laughed.

"Little sphincter puckering?" Anzil teased.

Clarke flashed Anzil a raised eyebrow with pursed lips while his eyes never lost focus on the screen showing what was ahead. There was one viable water passage between the barrier islands to get to Skyetook's docks, and the Khilsyths had it substantially defended.

"This ship's not so bad in the water," Tarra said, throwing a comforting arm over Anzil's shoulders.

The Osprey passed through the outer barrier island defenses, skirting a wildlife watch vessel, its passengers hoping it didn't distinguish the machine from the four apex predators trailing them. It wasn't long before the wildlife watch vessels were relaying the positions of the carnivorous beasts back to Skyetook, activating a warning indicator in the Operations Center on a Sergeant's workstation. The Sergeant obeyed protocol and implemented the standard procedures of flipping a series of switches and sending an order to dispatch a Marine Species Invasion Task Force—MSITF— to repel the attack.

"Multiple fishes in the water," Luna said, leaning over to whisper in Anzil's ear. "It's been ages since I said that. So satisfying."

Filling the forward viewscreen was a gigantic mass of swirling fish reflecting dazzling flashes of what little light penetrated to their depth. They scattered as the Osprey sliced through the protective netting holding them. The resultant savagery as the larger predators devoured the smaller fish within the ocean farming operation evoked a more significant response from the folks of Skyetook. Invasion and warnings from the harbormaster be damned, the local anglers took to the waters in their vessels to join the MSITF in protecting their livelihood.

In the Operations Center, the on-screen distortion from the number of vessel contacts, civilian and military ordinance signatures, and the amount of aquatic life overwhelmed the Watch Sergeant. He hoped the MSITFs could settle it and decided that now was a good time for a breath of fresh air and something sweet to nibble.

AURALEI STOPPED JUST before the edge of the commercial dock area, taking in the sprawling armory, fabrication, and maintenance sheds in front of her. "Where to, Clarke?" she said in a whisper. Activity along the piers and waterfront shops was sparse, with the weather and current invasion helping dissuade folks from getting out and about. However, the cranes, machines, and androids that managed varying cargo were scurrying about inside the port, readying for a possible exodus. She also heard the occasional sounds of stray animals and people rummaging through cargo cubes while avoiding Port patrols.

"The Eighteenth Dragoons' hangar," Clarke said, pointing deep into the area before them.

"Too much activity for these?" Auralei said, dismounting her mantis and coming to rest her shoulder against Clarke's armored side. "And there's no way you're walking with that armor from here. Laars, you'll need to hole up somewhere safe. Any idea on the best route?"

The diligence of protecting assets and the area would increase close to the military sheds. Cloaking was useful, but it drew unwanted attention when someone or something collided with an invisible object. "I'm thinking," Clarke whispered. Usually, this area would solicit the occasional tremble while passing through it, but his armor provided a creature comfort that was difficult to let go of.

"We need a solution here, and we're on the clock."

"We can come back for the armor with a maintenance skiff, I suppose."

"Sounds viable. And remember, act natural as we make our way. No need to draw unwanted attention."

"Do you have any idea how hard that is, especially when you think someone is watching you?"

"I don't," Auralei said, "now let's go."

"The atmosphere's different," Clarke said after passing a few groups of people who nodded in greeting but kept to themselves—most seemed resolved to be going about their various errands.

"How so?" Auralei asked.

"Not sure. Darker maybe. Foreign."

"You're reading too much into it. Just ease up a little; we're almost—" Auralei shied away from a blast of light as two men stumbled from the door they had flung open. She quickly grasped Clarke and shoved him against the building, kissing him passionately and maintaining a watchful eye on the drunkards.

The two men noticed the couple and called to them. One was even brazened enough to give Auralei a congratulatory pat on the back before they moved on into the night. The smell of sweet, fermented grapes and spiced oils hung in the air; the soothing music and indistinguishable conversations faded as the door closed.

"That was close," Auralei said.

"Did you think they would recognize me? Or did you just want a kiss?"

Auralei's shimmering green eyes narrowed under well-manicured brows, and she seized him by his belt, dragging him along with her.

Outside of Hangar 18, she stepped into the flux, becoming a shade in the spaces between the seen and unseen. After a moment, she gave Clarke the all clear that the shed was empty, and it was safe for him. At a computer terminal inside the building, she logged into the maintenance network, navigated to the repair ticket response system, and bypassed it with a previously installed hack. "Problem," she whispered, her larynx device amplifying her voice and transmitting it to the team's earpieces. "There are no critical tickets in the area identified as the Ops Center. How do you propose we take care of that?"

"You may need a higher clearance level to see those tickets," Clarke replied, walking up to Auralei.

Auralei smirked, which the device translated as a grunt. "I'm staring at the base code. It doesn't get any clearer than this."

"Then we'll need to create a reasonable maintenance problem," Clarke said. "Something to give us an excuse to use an equipment sled. We could put something in for a backup generator. Wait. A lift failure. Could we mimic that?"

Auralei flashed Clarke a pleading look, prompting him to expand upon his strategy.

"The lifts are used to transport the guard dragoons and heavy equipment from topside to the corridor ringing the Ops Center. It's perfect-ish."

Auralei contemplated the idea. "Putting aside the riskiness of your proposed endeavor. How do you propose we disable the lift?"

"Would a core magnetic failure suffice?" Laand asked.

Clarke nodded. "Yeah. They're rare, but I bet people in the Ops Center wouldn't know that. Maybe the crew chief and security commander would put it together. Maybe."

"And if we get searched?" Auralei asked.

"That's your department, isn't it?" Clarke teased. "It wouldn't be unreasonable to have a full sled. We could say the armor and our friend Laand are technician suits or fancy new invader armor—we'll lie. Besides, the Eighteenth is the House Guard, and they get away with all sorts of stuff."

"You think they'll know the Eighteenth scattered their maintenance crews between Warbler Ridge and the front of Skyetook's main gates?" Laand asked.

"Why would it matter?" Clarke asked.

"If you'd be so kind as to direct your attention to the lovely unit command status board," Auralei said, fanning her arm to emphasize its location, "the units assigned to this place are in various states of immobilization, mobile and attacking, on guard, and nonresponsive. Nothing about us, or rather who we are trying to pass ourselves off as."

"That's still your department, isn't it?" Clarke asked, flashing her a smirk.

"Company," Auralei said unexpectedly. "You better find some cover."

Clarke dipped behind the dragoon staging area, seeking shelter amongst some discarded dragoon components and scraps of metal. Heavy vehicles lumbered to a stop outside the maintenance bay doors and idled for a moment. Overhead, a pulley system screeched in protest, straining to lift a large bay door, which gradually revealed bright lights belonging to a maintenance crew and their dragoon escort. The maintenance sled was first in the door and went to its designated parking area near the computer terminal where Auralei had been. Four crew members disembarked: the three repair technicians headed into the changing area, and the likely crew chief went to a nearby terminal. The two escort dragoons parked their machines, and as they wound down their powerful engines, the scrap metal bins Clarke hid behind provided him with some protection from the heat of their thrusters. The pilots clambered out and headed to the changing area, mercifully disregarding their post-flight checklist, which would have increased the odds of them finding Clarke.

"You finished with that yet?" one of the dragoon soldiers called to the terminal operator as he walked by.

The person tapped the terminal a few more times with dedication and turned to smile smartly at the back of the dragoons. "All done. Unit upgraded—no more shit details for us. The only critical repairs in the system are for the port. A bunch of fish got loose, and some of the MSITF lads started shooting at fishers. Likely figured they were infiltrators."

"Those bloody idiots," the dragoon pilot laughed, turning away too soon to associate the muffled thud of a silenced pistol echoing through the maintenance shed with danger. "What a joke. Oh well, not our problem tonight."

The sucking sound of air rushing into the crew chief's punctured chest cavity and of liquid spraying on the floor barely registered with the dragoon pilot before a sword punctured his heart. Auralei stepped gracefully to the side to avoid the dragoon's spurting blood and flicked her sword to clear the red smear along its glistening edge. She flashed Clarke a mischievous smile accompanied by a wink and disappeared into the changing area and emerged shortly, wiping the blood from her face and sporting a devilish grin.

"You are very efficient," Clarke said.

"Thanks. As you said, my department. Now, let's move those bodies from view and get on with it, shall we?"

"Couldn't we have waited for them to leave?" Clarke asked, fearing the answer.

"We have a schedule to keep. Besides, they were infiltrators." *Probably were,* she thought.

Clarke dragged the dead crew chief and pilot with Auralei's help and deposited them in the trash room, then disposed of the others from the shower area. He engaged the automated cleaning robots, and by the time they were back to the parking area, the notification light on the computer terminal was flashing, showing that someone had issued an urgent maintenance ticket.

"There you are, pretty girl," Auralei said, keying in a code to accept the repair ticket. "Bravo, Laars."

Laars had sent a small device to the lifts, which emitted a particular burst to reduce the magnetic properties of the lift coil, creating a failure. To add to the urgency, Laars had activated his device when the central lift registered a heavy load as discerned by its power usage. Based on the video feeds attached to the ticket by the requestor, the burst had trapped a dragoon patrol.

Clarke shimmied into the driver's seat of the maintenance sled, where Auralei wrapped her arm around the back of his neck, bringing him close. "Our lives are depending on this ruse we've created. If we mess this up, we will need to fight our way out. So, let's go get Laars and that armor of yours."

The thought of killing again carried a newfound comfort for Clarke, replacing the spots where guilt and uneasiness once thrived when it came to snuffing out a life. He tried bravely to sound convincing that he was ready and guided the vehicle skillfully out of the military complex to the harbor sheds. With Laars' help, they retrieved and secured the alien armor in the back of the sled. Clarke apologized to Laars as he tucked him in beside it and covered the cargo area with a gray tarp before setting off to the inner city.

CHAPTER 31

STIGG LED THE collective mass of forces into the heavily farmed region to the south of Skyetook's protective walls, where properly manicured and drained fields and well-constructed roadways made travel through the region more accessible. He hoped the larger waterway crossings were intact. Soon, the orderly hills providing them temporary cover from the lead Rift Faction units rolling in from the east would change to flatter countryside, exposing them to Skyetook's wall-mounted batteries—he just couldn't remember the gun's range. The occasional missile from the city and outlying batteries harassed their units, but the Zephyr's and the Marauder's defense systems quickly shredded the munitions destined for the Khilsyth and Nihkiehl forces and allowed those inadvertently aimed to fall about the trailing hostile units.

"I'm afraid the wall guards will eventually stop wasting missiles," Deek said.

"Was just wondering what the range of the heavy guns were myself," Stigg said. "Enas, can you shed some light on that?"

Leon Nihkiehl broke through. "I give us about eight klicks from the wall. The Rifty's get about twelve based on their approach direction."

"Big guns to the south," Deek said. "Makes sense. Anyone coming from the wastelands would come through or around the Petrified Forest."

"And how do you know this?" Stigg asked cheerily.

"That's what I would have done if I were in charge of the wall," Deek said. "The wastelands are a practical place to assemble a force, and the drumlins provide some cover on the way to the city."

"And we haven't always been on friendly terms," Leon Nihkiehl added. "So, we may have sat around and thought about this a time or two. But, for sure, once we're within five klicks, we're easy pickings. Who knows, hopefully, darkness and weather will be our friends. Just never imagined I'd be storming the ole Skyetook fortress with the likes of y'all."

"Excuse me," Enas said, "higher rates of ineffectiveness for this combat situation are imminent."

"Enas, talk plainly, man," Leon requested.

"Most of our equipment has severely depleted levels of ammunition," Enas replied, "and based on my calculations, the impending encounter bears a low probability of survival unless we change course."

"And the wall guards aren't responding to our hails either," Laand added.

"Have they been overrun?" Stigg asked.

"It's likely an invader or rogue force has taken it over," Leon replied.

"Can you patch me into all units in the area?" Stigg asked Enas.

"We can do our best," Enas said, working furiously at his terminal. "I can recalibrate the local battlenet repeater stations for—"

"Just an open channel when you're ready, please," Stigg said, interrupting what he expected would become a verbal tirade.

Enas nodded his head furiously. "Yes, yes, of course. Go Stigg. Maybe they'll answer you."

"This is Field Marshal Stigg Anundr. Requesting the forward wall guard to permit us entry. We are friendlies. I repeat, friendlies approaching from the east." The communication link clicked and hissed only the static from the ether. "Come on, dammit," Stigg called.

"Stigg, my old comrade," someone broke through over a secure channel.

The voice was unsettling and confident, and Stigg knew the owner. "Impossible," Stigg said through clenched teeth.

"Now, now, comrade. That's no way to treat an *old friend.*"

"Old friend, my ass," Stigg said, chasing away a tickle in his throat. Kamp had abandoned them years ago, choosing the comfort of the Republic—betraying his duty as a Vanguard. "Are you leading the Republic forces?" Stigg asked, with a sharp edge to his deep, throaty voice.

"You and your friends are not making matters any easier for us," Kamp said. "Advise you lie low. Let the grown-ups sort out matters here."

"Where is Valan?" Stigg asked.

"You need to focus on other more pressing matters right now," Kamp replied. "Your very life, and those with you, depend on it."

Stigg called after Kamp, adding several unfriendly words, but the line was filled with static.

"No way that ass is still alive," Leon breathed through the line. "That tips the scales in their favor a pinch, doesn't it?"

"You think the *Mischi* knew?" Stigg asked.

After a momentary pause, Leon said, "I'm not sure. But what the hell? We may need to reconsider this plan of ours."

"Agreed," Stigg said. "That means some of those warships above us are Kamp's. Means there's a lot of Nova Republic firepower here."

"We need to warn Anzil and crew," Leon said.

"Can't you just talk to each other?" Deek asked Enas.

Enas smiled. "It's not really talking. The communication structure permits information to be transmitted to devices that are located strategically—"

"Enas, there isn't much time for details right now," Leon said. "Wait! All of you are talking together right now?"

"Why not?" Enas replied. "A dozen people are surely more proficient in developing a solution with a higher probability of success."

"There is only a dozen of you?" Leon asked.

"Approximately," Enas replied solemnly and pointed at the ceiling of the marauder. "Aurora is the youngest. Although we have lost comms with Laars and some others."

"Who the hell is Aurora?" Stigg asked.

Enas laughed, remembering a fond memory. "Aurora is our youngest brother. He attached to the exterior of the marauder—"

"Wait, no comms on Clarke?" Stigg interrupted.

Enas stuttered. "That would be correct."

"Shit," Stigg said, drawing the word out. "Rolling solutions and cover strategies. Who's got them?"

"There's only four major directions one can go, Stigg," Leon said.

"We'll put residents at risk if any of the forces get past the walls," Deek said. "Are the farming areas evacuated?"

"Those people aren't going to heed the warning," Stigg said. "We also need to plan for what's inside the walls."

"Let's hope the Rifty's don't take it upon themselves to liberate Skyetook from the supposed military coupe without the knowledge we're trying to do the same," Leon said.

"Relay another message to conserve ammo," Stigg ordered. "We're going to cover the distance to the perimeter wall quick-like."

"Is it just me, or are our *friends* slowing?" Deek asked.

Leon laughed. "Cowards. They're shying away from the wall guns."

"Or they know something we don't," Stigg said.

There would be little the dragoons could do against the shells that would streak in from the fortress wall, which were extremely difficult to track. The only defense for a dragoon was to move erratically because the shells had minimal ability to change course once in flight. However, the correlation between the time to maneuver and contact lethality significantly worked against them the closer they got to the wall.

"There is some good news," Luna said. "The artillery isn't all focused on us. Maybe they can't decide who the bigger threat is."

"The bloody Anacul," Leon blurted. "They're not bleeding as bad as we are."

"I hope the distraction we're causing is worth it, Stigg," Deek said.

"I'm starting to wonder if we're really a distraction," Stigg said. "More like a catalyst for a decision. Will the Rifty's turn and attack us, or join us?"

"We've been in worse situations for far less warranted reasons," Leon said with a laugh. "Just let me knock on the main gate if we make it. Deal?"

"Enas, can you direct units to separate areas?" Leon asked. "We want to drag those Anacul bastards with us when we turn into the Rift Faction forces."

Enas' fingers tapped and slid rapidly over the terminal for a few moments before he confirmed he could do as Leon requested.

"We should ping the Rift Faction again," Leon said, "to see if they're listening."

Enas considered his screen. "We could use the Borealis net," he said. "It's a hyperspace telecom device capable of almost instant communications."

"What the hell are you talking about?" Stigg asked.

"It was Harmsweld's greatest achievement," Enas said, disappointed that nobody knew the infrastructure existed. "Harmsweld had been exploring methods to expedite our data collection—to enhance research efficiency. The cosmos is vast, as you know. It did several fantastic things. We would point it at civilizations, and it would funnel and synthesize all the information their media sources were providing. We could then act on potentially noteworthy findings. Its core function was to decipher false or sensationalized information. To develop leads with a higher probability of being interesting. The Borealis net also—"

"Enas," Leon interjected. "That's fascinating, but how does it help solve our current issue with the Anacul?"

"And can we establish comms without appearing hostile?" Stigg asked.

"We need to know their intentions," Leon said. "They are likely operating with different information than what we're operating with."

"Aurora is trying to overcome the disruptions now," Enas said. "The interference is, er, alien to us. He is trying to send out Borealis tendrils aimed at their transmission bursts."

"It can track the Anacul?" Leon asked.

"Crudely stated, but yes," Enas said. "Aurora could plot locations provided they transmit for a long enough time at the origin point. It's problematic if the return trajectory is… displaced. Thankfully, the Anaculs are long-winded. Aurora has compiled data on some locations of other Anacul operations. Go Stigg, ready for transmission."

"This is Stigg Anundr. I am the acting field commander of the Khilsyth forces, as appointed by Corporal Anzil Khilsyth. I am requesting all Khilsyth forces and other forces on Lindaulx to band together." Hearing no immediate rejections, he heaved a heavy sigh that wasn't picked up by his headset's microphone, thanks to Enas' quick hands. "The Anacul Nation has come into our homes with deceit in their hearts and are the true enemy. They are here to overthrow our leadership by infiltrating our command structure. Their claim for ownership of Lindaulx is a false claim. They have also attempted to infiltrate and poison the other households. They have most likely infiltrated the Nova Republic. The proximity of the Rift Faction is fortuitous. Leon Nihkiehl, the leader of House Nihkiehl, fights alongside us in recognition of the Anacul Nation's threat to his family and our piece of the galaxy—"

"Someone has jammed the transmission," Enas said, shielding everyone's ears from a loud squelch by replacing it with only static. "Very impressive."

"Get it back," Stigg commanded.

"Laand informs me he has a plan for reestablishing communications," Enas said. "It has a moderate probability of succeeding."

"You suppose the Rifty's heard it?" Leon asked.

"Deek, any visual on the Rifty's?" Stigg asked, trying to redirect the conversation.

"No. Been a while since we had eyes on them. They've kept the sky full of air nets. Some of our pilots found out the hard way where they were located. We're working on un-sticking the comms."

"We could always flash signal them," Leon shouted.

"Like morse code?" Stigg asked.

"Sure," Leon said, "I poked my head over that hill, and there are other forces coming down the far side of the valley. They'll be upon us as soon as they cross the Green River."

Stigg sighed.

"Exactly," Leon said to Stigg. "This is going to get messy."

"Let's get the hell across these bridges and charge the depots," Stigg said. "Hopefully, we catch them with the doors open."

"Are the supply tunnels still active?" Leon asked.

"They were last time I checked," Stigg responded. "Another secret Trake told you, eh?"

Leon laughed. "We had a few. As did you, ya old goat."

"Could we blow their bridge to slow them down?" Deek asked.

"Leon, can you and Deek—"

Suddenly, the ground surged, sending undulating waves of dirt and rock that eventually erupted in miniature fragments of burning debris and plant material. Within mere seconds, the bombardment had churned the fallow fields into a massive dust storm, casting an eerie brown miasma over the battlefield.

Leon came to his feet slowly, hardly recognizing his surroundings. The major bridge they had just crossed was reduced to rubble, as were its approaches. He knew there was little chance the units in the direct line of fire survived. In the distance, ordinance continued to rain down from orbit, hammering the pockets of land and sending them jumping into the air to explode. Other pillars of fire and dirt were evidence that the bridges to Fort Skyetook were being systematically leveled. Leon tried feverishly to hail Stigg through the mix of jamming devices and had lost sight of most units in the haze. Frustration looming in his voice, he commanded his units to punch a path to the nearest depot, hoping to find shelter as their retreat path was blocked. Leon slowed his machine as his unit combined with the others; he wanted to circle back and search for survivors. The once pragmatic Mauti wouldn't have hesitated when a comrade fell. He would have carried on knowing the collective and the mission were critical. But many years were separating then and now. He said a quick prayer for Stigg and banked hard, finding comfort that he was saving himself from the brave-faced disgruntlement Stigg would have if he had stayed to find his friend and welcomed death's embrace instead.

The combined Khilsyth and Nihkiehl forces were tired, bloodied, bruised, and out of viable options. The westerly turn was far from graceful and difficult to hide. Lightning forked across the sky, punctuating the failing light and sending static through his headset. As if answering his small prayer for protection from the wall guns, the sky opened and sent forth a torrent of rain to cover the battlefield. The rain would be miserable for the Zephyrs and hell for the trailing dragoon armor as their turbines would spew dirty mist, soaking everything and clogging intakes. But that volley had come from orbit, not the wall batteries.

"Captain Farsil to Captain Deek," came a call.

"Farsil!" Deek responded. "Am I glad to hear your voice?"

"Kaibab and I are coming in from the east with armor," Farsil replied. "We'll mark so you know who's friendly."

"Who's armor?" Leon asked.

"Mine, sweetheart," Base Flintlock responded. "Did you miss me?"

"Is it really you?" Leon asked cautiously.

"In the loving flesh, you so cherish, my darling." Base Flintlock responded sweetly.

Leon wondered what the hell she was doing here and in command of a Rifty armada. "It's damn good you're here," he said, not betraying that it was also fortunate for them.

"You mean lucky, sweetie," Base said in her characteristic soothing drawl. "Let's focus on keeping you alive so we can deal with the how and why I'm here later."

Leon's combined forces broke over the rim of the upper embankment and plunged downward to smash themselves upon the defensive forces that blocked the massive southern depot's entry gate. The sky above darkened as wyverns whipped in and dropped an array of mechanical armor, then bailed.

Deek's unit was the first to meet the depot's protective forward armor line. Behind them, barrages from the wall guns bit deep into the land and the leading Anacul forces.

"Thank you, Kamp," Leon said, hoping they received his transmission. He wondered if Kamp had seen fit to let *bygones be bygones* and aid his old comrades. *But for what purpose did you lend a hand?* Kamp always had a motive. It wouldn't be long before the Anacul forces devised a solution to deal with the attack from the wall. Leon would make sure their sacrifice wasn't in vain. As he backtracked with a few of his veterans, a contingent of black dragoons from the Rifty's with their signature dark purple crests joined him in setting a rear guard for Deek and her squad. The remaining Anacul forces would be upon them shortly.

"It's an honor, sir," one dragoon said. "Until the end."

Leon snapped a crisp salute. "Until the end." *Although there was no end for a Vanguard save death.*

NEARING THE SHADOW of the depot hanger entrance, Deek was hailed by a worthy adversary. The enemy dragoon managed to parry a few of her attacks, but eventually, Deek exploited a weakness and drove her battle blade into their belly. Realizing Deek's error at exposing herself because of the diminutive length of the blade, the attacker laughed and swung a dangerous and potentially deadly arc aimed at her midsection. Deek smiled. A blow to the stomach was not typically lethal, but the small explosive device inside her smaller blade was. Before the dragoon's blade could strike Deek's armor, the enemy armor bulged, satisfying her desire for kill confirmation—the device turning her prey into a self-contained exploding blowfish.

With her comrades flanking her, Deek moved through the enemy, cutting them down and too tired to feel any disappointment or remorse. The last enemy dragoon Deek felled at the depot threshold, swallowed her sword in the nook between the chin and breastplate when she drove it over their shield. Deek engaged her thrusters, supplying the force to drive her sword through her enemy's armor, and delivered the coup de grâce by circling her opponent, severing the helmet and soldier's head. The headless suit fell forward, revealing a congealed mass of tissue, bone, and metal. As she roared in under the protective cover of the heavy hangar door, the surviving members of her unit joined her.

"We need to move deeper into the facility," Laand said. "We could see some orbital-guided ordinance soon."

Deek chased the thrusters ahead of her through the staging area and past the space transport craft. "That foxy bastard," she said, laughing at the brilliance, or sheer luck, of Stigg's plan—this remote depot housed interstellar and larger planetary freighters poised to leave when called upon. Somewhere within this area, a network of military tunnels would lead them into the heart of Fort Skyetook.

"It appears we've happened upon a mobilizing point," Laand said. "We should ensure these ships are ready to fly."

Leon moved into position beside his youngest daughter. "Aye, Stigg was a clever old goat. Left the Anacul hanging in the wind."

"I have a feeling there was a lot of luck with this plan of his," Deek said.

"Aye," Leon said, shaking his head once, wondering if he would have made the same bet. "There usually is with him."

"He trusted his instincts," Base Flintlock said with a sweet laugh, taking a place beside Leon. "That, and he had a guardian *angel* watching out for you all."

"Now would be a good time for that explanation," Leon said. "As in, I would love to know how you came to be here, darling?"

"Well," Base Flintlock said, swinging out of her armor and releasing the clutch on her flowing white hair. "You sent *the* signal, and we answered as instructed."

"What signal?" Deek asked, slipping out of her armor as several Rifty soldiers did the same. She sized up the six burly warriors that formed a protective backstop for Base Flintlock. The way they moved was familiar—and the way they carried themselves—they reminded her of Leon. *What interesting company,* she thought. "The one from the Astute complex?"

Base Flintlock brought a gleaming device to her mouth and inhaled, closed her eyes for a moment as she held it, and then released a pungent cloud of smoke from her full lips. She smiled warmly at Deek. "*The* signal, my dear."

Her striking turquoise eyes told Leon that she didn't know anything more. "And by who's instruction?" He asked, the familiar knot in his stomach developing, which it was fond of doing too often as of late for his liking.

"Our old friend," Base Flintlock replied, turning to Leon with a sad, soft smile.

Leon exited his armor, landed stiffly, and wobbled over to Base with the occasional crack from his knees. He stood a head and a half taller than the woman, but it was a toss-up on who would win in a scuffle. "I need to hear you say it, love," he sighed heavily.

"Do you?" Base said, gazing deep into his gray-blue eyes. She basked in the glow of his affection, sensing a deep love that he held for her, and wished there was more time. "It was Constance, my dear. But she kept most of this hidden from me. From us."

Leon hung his head, accepting the woman's warm embrace, and was enshrouded by her scent. "It's been a long time." His voice betrayed how tired he was.

"You know each other?" Deek asked tentatively, moving closer, catching the softening of Base and her brute's eyes. "Holy shit. *You all know each other!* Dad, what's going on?"

Leon pushed back but kept Base in his embrace. "Warms my heart to hear you call me Dad, love. That's been a long time since I heard that."

Base gave Leon's arm a firm but loving embrace, and he released her. She moved close to Deek and held out her arms but let them fall away. "Leon and I have known each other for a very long time. We share a magnificent union."

Leon lifted Base and Deek into his arms, squishing them together in a tight embrace.

"You never were very subtle, dear," Base said. "Now, can you please put us down?" She touched down gracefully and fussed with her clothing. Once satisfied that the clothing was in proper order and that she was presentable, she slowly removed her face scarf. The squint of Deek's eyes and the deepening furrow of her brow betrayed the young lady recognized her and was struggling with the context. Switching off the voice modulator device implanted into her neck, Base flashed a quick smile. "Hello, daughter. It's good to see—"

Deek hoisted Base Flintlock—Arbasele Nihkiehl—into the air, squeezing her tightly as the woman's augments fortified her ribs to prevent breakage.

"Just like your father," Base wheezed. "Now, please put me down, dear." It had been more than eight years since she had been home. The ruse that she was off on *research* as part of her job with the University was challenging to maintain. In all the ways she thought Deek would discover her authentic self, she had never envisioned this scenario. "There is so much to discuss, my love. But we really don't have the time right now."

"The short version, then," Deek said. "And the truth this time, *professor.*"

"Your Dad's a Vanguard in hiding," Base said quietly. "We have spent our lives protecting our family and friends."

Deek pressed her forehead against her mom's. "Are you *Mischi?*" she breathed.

Base's lips formed a soft smile. "You feel it when you fight, don't you?" she whispered. "You hear the songs of promise, feel the warmth and the rush of the planet rising to aid you. Do you not?"

Deek nodded. She had always chalked it up to being in touch with herself and in tune with her surroundings. "Am I *Mischi?*"

"Yes, but not in the way you might think," Base said, comforting her daughter. "You have the gift. Your father sensed it in you at birth. Same as your older sister."

Leon rested a hand on each of the ladies' shoulders. His stomach twisted with the familiar churn, and his tattooed forearms writhed and glowed in the dimly lit room. "Ladies," he whispered.

"Ah yes," Base said, chasing a quiver from her body. "Sorry about that, lads." She caught her daughter's gaze. "We have a distressing effect on this lot. Yes, your sister. I believe she is masquerading as a specter, possibly using the name Tarra."

Leon bit his lip and kicked gently at a seam in the concrete. "About that. So, Deek. Love. The *Mischi* with the two swords. That's your sister." He nodded, biting his lip and tensing for the blow he thought might come.

Deek let them suffer a bit before she spoke. "I know." The shock on both of her parents' faces made her laugh. "Or at least I put it together. I'm going to have words with her. She probably figured I couldn't see through her ruse and did a good job of keeping your secrets. If she knew."

Leon shook his head. "Incredible. How?"

"She visited occasionally. Never staying long. But would catch me while I was alone in the city or out on patrol. It's been strange, but at least I got to know her over the years."

Leon was still shaking his head. "Resourceful, the lot of you. Maybe it's time for that family reunion, eh?"

CHAPTER 32

LEAVING THE HARBOR area, Clarke mixed with the usual traffic congestion of the inner city and took familiar roadways and shortcuts that now seemed like ages since he last traveled. Life in the city almost appeared to be continuing normally, but the increased armored patrols and display warnings of an approaching army belied that something was amiss. Clarke scanned through the news and social media feeds displayed on the sled's navigation system, trying to find additional details on the location of military units. Auralei's hand wrapped over his and provided corrective steering action to counter the inadvertent drift. Clarke ignored the disapproving glare and allowed her hand to continue to guide his. The news was vague, repeating the same drivel on recent events and requesting that all available units report for active duty to defend the homeland. "It does sound like they believe Stigg is a credible threat," Clarke said.

"Would you just pay attention to the road?" Auralei asked, her hand squeezing his tightly against the steering wheel.

"Now would seem like a good time for our other surprises," Laars called from behind. After receiving confirmation from Auralei, he activated the devices he had sent for various errands. Throughout the city, technicians stared perplexed at the interruptions of critical infrastructure elements, such as exhaust fans, effluent removal pump stations, and parts of the power supply grid.

"You think it's too much?" Laars asked as the spaceport went dark after the primary and backup power sources failed.

"Maybe," Auralei replied. "But it's not like they could go on any higher of an alert."

"Do you think they would think about an Ops Center incursion?" Clarke asked Auralei, who shrugged her shoulders.

Clarke navigated the maintenance sled to the west gate and stopped under a decaying stone arch flanked by walls made from the local rock and semi-precious stones. This wall enclosed the inner buildings of Skyetook, some of which could be traced to their construction date before the occupation by House Khilsyth.

"Halt!" a guard said, with a strained squeak in her voice that betrayed the stress she was under. "Identification."

Clarke rummaged through his pockets, unable to find his identification badge, and realized he forgot to take it from the crew.

"Sir, identification, now."

Clarke could hear the soft murmurings of the wind playing through the deep grooves in the stone wall and the dull scraping sound it made as it brushed against the mortar. This noise deadened the guard's shouting, and the whine of the tires from vehicles passing by on the wet roads grew louder. A steady, warm hand pressed against his chest, and Auralei's confident and warm voice brought his attention back to the gate guard.

"Sorry, Sergeant, please excuse the rookie," Auralei said. "Somewhat handy, but a horrid memory. Here's mine."

The gate guard blushed and smiled at the woman as she scanned her identification and received the tone marking the system's acceptance. "Thank you, Captain." She shook her finger at Clarke. "Now, where exactly is it you're heading, Seargent?"

Clarke avoided eye contact with the guard, not out of fear or apprehension, but mixed with his heartbeat was another rhythm he struggled to let slip through his grasp. He registered a gentle squeeze of his thigh. "Maintenance from the Eighteenth, ma'am," he said, finding the words. "We are here for the critical repair."

"Show me," the guard requested.

Clarke faltered with his data tablet, and the sergeant sighed. "Perhaps a little daft?" She joked with the *captain*. "For future reference, we're the House Guard: we have better toys than you and are expecting you."

"Sorry, ma'am," Clarke managed to say. "Still learning the ropes."

"One moment," the sergeant said, heading back to her post.

"What the hell," Auralei lashed out quietly at Clarke. "You know this one? She seems to like you."

"Quite the opposite," Clarke responded, flicking his head slightly to the left at the dragoons approaching them. "We have company."

"What the hell took you engineers so long?" a dragoon asked Clarke. "In case you haven't heard, we're under attack. And where in the hell is your escort?"

"We're short-staffed," Clarke responded. "Most were called away to fight. The rest went anyway. I guess they figured we'd be safe responding within the city."

"It's your life," the dragoon said, flexing its armored shoulders, "but I wouldn't be so rash. All sorts of weird shit happening. What with the harbor and all? If you ask me, it's a perfect cover for a snatch-and-grab for some foolish engineers. Now fall in."

The sergeant lowered the barricade under the archway and hurriedly waved them through.

"Don't let them see you sigh," Auralei said through stiff lips as they proceeded away from the view of the west gate.

Once inside the inner city, the traffic congestion increased, making Clarke less confident of their cover. He inhaled deeply through his nose, holding the air until it burned, and slowly exhaled through rounded lips. It was just *another repair job,* he thought, *easy-peasy lemon-squeezy.*

CLARKE KEYED IN the code provided on the service ticket for the maintenance lift and received an immediate response from the guard detail requesting they hold.

"Is there a problem?" Auralei asked over her secure channel with Clarke.

"Not sure, as we should be cleared."

"Don't sigh or flinch," Auralei warned again as the speaker squelched, approving their entrance.

"Look at that," Clarke said and pointed at an adjacent lift that showed it was descending.

"Look at what?" a guard asked as they approached with their oversized rifle at the ready.

"Good to know at least two of the lifts are working," Clarke answered.

"That doesn't mean you can slack," the guard said. "We need this fixed fast. Not sloppy like some remote field tech, either."

Clarke bit his lip, wanting to lash out at the accusatory remark— these city guards had the cushy gig and reputations for taking longer than practical to do much of anything. "There another team here?"

The armored head shook. "Nah, Republic folks. Now get going."

They loaded into the lift, its oversized sliding doors closing and latching behind them. Clarke leaned toward Auralei, caught the sweet scent of honeysuckle, and whispered, "now what?"

Auralei grinned. "Now is an appropriate time for armor. They're going to see through our ruse quickly. If they don't already know." She motioned toward the lift's ceiling in a universally accepted sign that someone was watching them.

As Clarke exited the skiff and opened a rear cargo hatch, he glanced upward, catching the dome-shaped device from his periphery. It was undoubtedly capturing images and other information about the lift's contents and transmitting them to a security room somewhere in the facility. He wondered how fast the guard detail below would get the information.

Laars stood; the metal of his appendages hummed as he stretched, and he smiled knowingly at Clarke. "I scrambled any signal being transmitted from the elevator."

"They may think something disrupted the feed," Auralei said. "Then again, they may think that something was us."

"Okay," Auralei said, "we don't know what's all down here or what they're capable of?"

"You mean *Dreaders*, don't you?" Clarke asked.

"Afraid the lady does," Laars said.

"Sounds like suicide," Clarke said nervously.

Auralei patted his cheek and winked. "It always was. Armor on, now. No time to think about my original plan of getting off this rock under the radar. We're committed to this one."

Clarke scrounged a couple of munitions belts from the nearby storage lockers and cinched them to his legs. "One thing for certain," he croaked, "there will be dragoons." The thought of encountering another Anacul Champion was not a particularly welcoming prospect.

Auralei spun Clarke around and held his face with both her hands. She held his gaze momentarily, brought him into her sweet breath, and kissed his cheek gently. "Another one for luck. Now be safe."

Clarke nodded awkwardly and climbed into his alien armor, the thousands of sprout-like devices attaching to his body, welcoming him back. He crammed his head into the helmet, hearing the familiar chime indicating it paired with the armor.

Auralei slapped Clarke's face plate lightly. "When the doors open, move quickly and find some cover. Laars and I will secure the area." She slipped into the flux and disappeared.

Clarke blinked rapidly, straining to focus on the hazy and ethereal image of Auralei—it was like fighting to see through smudged and scratched glasses. Her figure stabilized slightly when she crouched to the left of the lift door. His dark passenger held the adrenaline level coursing through his body in check, governing his nerves so they wouldn't affect his accuracy negatively when called upon. Cramming his neck back and forth, relief came from the crack of his bones.

The elevator made slight adjustments to arrive at the level of its destination floor while the buzzer announced it had performed its conveyance duties. The eerie wailing of the warning device sounded like the slow roll of thunder on a distant horizon in Clarke's ear—a place where powerful gusts of wind were hurling leaves from the weak grasp of frost-laden trees. A sliver of artificial light crept along the floor at his feet, gradually brightening the lift's interior as its doors retracted. He fixated on the storm brewing inside him, finding the foreign material lurking and playing amongst the darkest leading edge. *There you are, you little bastard,* he thought, latching onto it, fighting past its elusiveness so that it answered. The storm in his head intensified, lashing at the tendrils binding his thoughts and trying to break their traction. He embraced the rolling thunder and bent his own will to pass through the folds of the storm into the calmness of its eye. Aided by his dark passenger, the sound intensified as the storm ripped through ice-entombed trees, shattering limbs and trunks alike as Clarke transitioned into the flux.

As you wish, the thought drifted through Clarke's head. *At least they warned us.*

Auralei watched in horror as Clarke began to shimmer, rapidly threading the edge between this place and the flux. She cried out in warning, as did Laars, but Clarke was oblivious to their screams.

CHAPTER 33

RIGIL SPRAUGE SLOWED his machine inside the Operations Center as he approached the central lift. He released his rifle from his side-mounted holster and racked a round into the polished chamber for good measure. Considering the rarity of a failure for this type of lift design, his experience told him something didn't feel right.

Rigil Sprauge was also highly suspicious of the timing of the Nova Republic visit, which coincided with citywide events and his recent assignment to a new guard detail. As the two unfamiliar dragoon pilots neared the maintenance lift, he hung back, suspecting he wasn't as equally informed as them and that having a little distance would be wise if any shooting started. Rigil Sprauge knew some people thought of him as paranoid and delusional, but he often defended that he wasn't delusional.

Of the four Operation Centers Rigil Sprauge had occupied during his career, he appreciated the design of this one the most. All corridors to the surface opened along the exterior wall of a dome-shaped complex that provided two mezzanines traversing the circumference. The uppermost level provided clear fields of fire for several high-powered weapons placed strategically at fixed intervals that his comrades—ones he trusted and depended on. The main floor was expansive, providing maneuverability for dragoons and other military craft. At the heart was a three-story darkened geodesic dome with a spiderweb of cabling disappearing into the ceiling. There were also rumors of tunnels accessing areas within Skyetook and outside to places like Warbler and Willow Ridges. The Khilsyths had apparently sealed the passageways to the Ridges when they were no longer needed to house primary functions like the Operations Center and secure residences. But he doubted those rumors and was relieved to have options if the situation went sideways.

Silently and instantly, Rigil Sprauge watched as the area around the central lift vanished, ferociously severing in half the two lead dragoons and removing a section of the lifts and surrounding walls. Before he could shake the fuzz from his head, the material reappeared with a rending screech, tearing of metal, and cracking of rock, crushing what remained of the dragoons. The alcove went dark until the emergency lights awoke sluggishly, revealing a lone armor-clad silhouette standing amidst the wreckage and the feeble attempts of the fire suppression system. A flash from a far gun foretold a projectile was arcing toward the figure, who threw open an arm shield and deflected the projectile.

"Cease fire, you idiot," Rigil Sprauge said to the shooter. "If you've just harmed someone important, I'll have you flayed and hung up as a warning to other morons. Newcomer, identify yourself." He approached carefully, raising his rifle and directing a few other dragoons into a semi-circle. It was an advanced platform that he hadn't encountered before and most likely something dreamed up by the lesser-known side of the Nova Republic. He tried to rectify what he saw with what he remembered from past missions, but his Nova Republic soldier's memory was slipping away.

"I am here for Valan," Clarke said.

Rigil Sprauge didn't recognize the accent, but the person sounded confident enough.

"What would you have with him?" a sergeant asked.

"What he would with me," Clarke replied.

"They called for you then?"

"I am here, aren't I?"

Rigil Sprauge raised his hands and commanded the sergeant to stop further questioning. "Allegiance?" he asked the dark armor.

"Nova Republic," Clarke said, punching out each word.

"Any particular unit, division, distinguisher?" Rigil Sprauge asked. The armor cocked its head to the side and nodded.

"Keep calm," Auralei said only to Clarke. "This ruse could work. As far as your little stunt. We are going to have a wee chat about that later."

Clarke knew that wouldn't be a pleasant conversation and took a deep breath to steady his disappointment. His armor warned of multiple target locks and rapidly showed options as if taunting, even begging, for him to pick one.

"Where is your entourage?" Rigil Sprauge asked, wondering why this person was so tight-lipped. The dark armor moved its head to show they were behind it. Peering to the side, he took in the wreckage, realizing this poor chap likely lost some comrades in that mess and didn't seem phased. "Ah, yes. Fair point. And um… Sorry about that. Whole place has gone haywire. Please hold while I relay this into command."

While they waited, two nearby dragoons started chatting, indifferent to the soldiers and maintenance staff rushing to see if the damage warranted a rescue or salvage operation. They recounted stories from Hurricane Ridge about a dragoon who fought *the* Anacul Champion. Clarke hoped their intonation of 'the' meant 'the one and only' champion. One soldier tried to convince the others that the mysterious dragoon was a dreadnaught reborn under Lindaulx's mercurial moon sent to punish them for their transgressions. His proof was based on the recent rise of the long-lost marauder and rumor of its course to Skyetook, although the story lacked details of what transgressions had occurred and who they impacted.

Command finally answered on Rigil Sprauge's third attempt with an excuse about their long queue of requests. There was no shortage of unfamiliar faces these days. The gatekeepers were frantically trying to clear everyone for passage into and out of the central dome, and since some requests came from people unaccustomed to maintaining possession of their identification devices, this further increased processing time. "They say you're the Nova Republic emissary?" he asked the armor, then hushed the dragoons and dismissed all their talk of Anacul with a wave.

Clarke wasn't sure how to respond, so he nodded, unaware that a contingent from the Nova Republic had also been making their way to the Operation Center in the adjacent lift. During Clarke's shift in and out of the flux, the emissary and their staff were stuck in the elevator because of a faulty leveling sensor that wouldn't permit the doors to open. The resultant dismantling of the lift and crumbling of the support structure around it would take time for the rescue team to remove and discover the identities of the bodies.

"Lord Valan requested your presence here?" Rigil Sprauge asked.

"That is correct," Clarke said, employing his authoritative voice. "Per Lord Valan's request, I am here."

"Right," Rigil Sprauge said. "After you." He gestured for the armor to take the lead—he preferred anyone or anything from the Nova Republic to be in plain sight. "It's just that we expected more of an entourage. Caught us off guard, you did—except for that dumbass up there." He pointed to where the round had come from. "Nerves are a little thin around here. I'm sorry about you being shot at, ah… sir. Fair warning that it's getting crowded in the Ops Center. The City is going a little nuts right now, you know? Anyway, the name's Rigil Sprauge, but Rigil works just fine.

"Could you say more about that, Sergeant Sprauge," Clarke requested, slowing his pace and capitalizing on the moment to learn more from an inside person.

"Rigil if you please," he said curtly and sniffed loudly. "Now take this," he emphasized his point by jabbing an armored thumb back at the wreckage. "When have you ever seen something like that happen? The lower structure of a lift doesn't just fail and catastrophically fail at that. Never in my time, I tell you. The engineering team responding to our request for service is even late. You're lucky you were in armor, as it probably saved your life. And how shall I introduce you when we arrive?"

"I must admit that I've never seen a lift car fly off the rails and out of the conveyance tubes," Clarke said. *The sergeant was self-medicating and pushing his body beyond the normal limit*—this thought drifted dangerously close to Clarke's own. "Anything else we should be aware of?"

Rigil Sprauge rubbed his faceplate vigorously. "Yeah. We've had reports of some weird system failures all over the city. Even the aquatic farms. They tell me the wildlife is even rebelling— superstitious dunces. And there's armor in the depot hangars now. May the Gods help us. Now. Your name again, if you will?"

Clarke nodded in agreement. "I've heard about the events at the ports," he said, his pulse racing briefly as his body reclaimed calmness. "The dragoons in the depot are with me. They instructed us to have them stage there."

Rigil's eyes darted around the complex, passing over everyone before him, checking for signs of a threat. "Honestly? By whom? Thought that was the separatists."

"What the hell are you doing, Clarke?" Auralei asked tersely over their private communication line.

"We infiltrated some of them," Clarke said. "My people moved to safety and left the *separatists* outside. I would advise you to authenticate and permit them access."

"With Khilsyth and Nihkiehl armor?" Rigil asked, his eyes narrowing.

"Some in house armor. However, we received House Khilsyth ident codes so we could discreetly provide help."

Rigil Sprauge laughed. "Bloody Republic. How do you expect us to tell you apart if you're embedded on both sides?"

"That's why I'm here," Clarke said. "It also makes negotiating conflicts easier when you know what both sides are up to and what they potentially want."

"Seems like there's more than two sides," Rigil said, stopping short of the entrance door and letting a swarm of people scurry past. "Glad to know the Republic is still into spying."

"As much as I have enjoyed our chat," Clarke said, "I need to press the matter. I have time-sensitive information that I must relay to Lord Valan and my forces."

Sprauge ordered his men to form up around the Nova Republic emissary. "That armor of yours sure is different. Where did you come by such hardware, if you don't mind me asking?"

Clarke chuckled. "You wouldn't believe me if I told you, Sergeant."

With a diminutive click, the entrance door to a fortified vestibule slid open, and Rigil Sprauge led the way into the structure. Clarke scanned the area, finding the hazy outline of a noticeably irritated

Auralei trailing behind but no sign of Laars. The door closed, sealing them all inside.

"Deactivate weapon systems," someone requested through a wall-mounted speaker.

Good to know you're an invader, Clarke thought, relieved that the armor hid his smile. The Khilsyth dragoons could not shut off their weapons or relinquish control to either the Operations or Command Center—thankfully, their weapon systems would show as offline here.

"Thank you," the wall-mounted speaker responded. "Identifications."

Clarke knew that each dragoon pilot would punch their identification buttons as requested, sending a brief, unique signature transmission to verify it within the system, something his armor could not do.

"All of you *ident,* please," the request came again.

Clarke would have sweated a little under pressure, but his dark passenger ran interference and kept his emotions and internal chemical levels in check. His armor also displayed no identification markers or insignias, which a little paint could have fixed— *hindsight is always twenty-twenty,* he thought.

"I need you all to identify yourselves," the voice said.

Rigil Sprauge turned to Clarke. "Is there a problem? Do you have your emissary ID, sir?"

"It's a new unit," Clarke blurted. "Regrettably, folks... I'm not sure how to send the identification code."

Rigil Sprauge moved closer. "Your Republic ID will be sufficient. Or you can remove your helmet for a biometrics scan."

Clarke could sense the mood of the surrounding soldiers darkening, tensing in preparation. Even those at odds with the Nova Republic, especially emissaries from other nations, still benefitted from carrying their Nova Republic-issued interstellar passports.

"Wait," he requested and rattled off a House Khilsyth terminal code used by engineers when running root diagnostics on the systems.

"Enter," the speaker growled as the door leading into the Operations Center opened with a diminutive whoosh. "Why are some people so damn difficult?" the voice protested, its owner unaware they were still transmitting.

"Excellent memory," Rigil Sprauge said to Clarke, sucking air across his lips to produce a high-pitched whine he kissed off. "Let's get out of this armor, shall we?"

The dragoon exited the vestibule into an inner staging area—the bailey—which was scattered with soldiers of varying ranks, allegiances, and armor. Their arrival was a complete surprise to most inhabitants, as the entryway guards failed the handoff procedure to the inside security detail. Clarke closed the distance to Rigil, becoming uncomfortably aware that an increasing number of people were watching or moving toward them.

"And who might this be, Sergeant Sprauge?" a short and haughty fellow said, taking long strides with his hand in the air, motioning them to stop. "Does Lord Valan not believe we have the situation contained? Dammit, Sprauge, what kind of bloody armor is that person wearing?"

Rigil Sprauge stuttered. "General Trunasder, this is the Nova Republic emissary."

Trunasder stopped his strut toward Sprauge and turned to yell at his subordinates as more of them emerged from the doorways leading to the inner building.

Clarke pegged the guy as an off-worlder based on his heavy accent, which was likely intensified by having a native language that sounded like a series of growls and throat clearings. "I see my reputation precedes me," Clarke interrupted, receiving a merciful glance from Rigil Sprauge.

General Trunasder shot the *Nova Republic emissary* a narrow gaze over his broad shoulders. "Truth is, Emissary Munge, I do not know what Commander Maeve wants with your outfit," he said with a dismissive wave of his gauntleted hand. "I have limited patience for infiltration operations. I despise being ordered around. I want you to deal with your Rift Faction nuisance." He turned to face Sprauge, his words and spittle tripping over each other as they left his mouth. "I especially loathe being uninformed, and—"

"We're here to explore standing down all militaries on Lindaulx until we can sort out this mess," Clarke interrupted. "We also plan to have talks with the Khilsyth loyalists."

"The… what!?" Trunasder said in an exasperated tone, stepping closer—he had sneaked a throat clearing between the two words he fought to get over his lips and through his thick beard. "Those that are calling themselves *loyalists* are the traitors." He spat a murky substance and wiped his lips. "Hilarious, I tell you. Bloody hilarious. Surely, Emissary Munge, you don't mean to protect those who fled to Willow Ridge? Damn this infernal politicking."

"I fail to see the humor in the present situation," Clarke replied. "There are concessions the Nova Republic would see made to reduce the losses for all parties on Lindaulx and still achieve mutual benefits."

Trunasder laughed. "Mutual benefits. More people to help spread your narcissistic balance and the lie of the Greater Purpose. For as well-traveled as the Nova Republic claims to be, you still have much to learn about this world."

"Commander Maeve is in charge of Lindaulx now?" Clarke asked. "Where can I find her?"

Trunasder laughed. "No, no, no, emissary. The younger Lord Khilsyth is in command here. This was an overthrow—blood on blood. Do your job and deal with the Rift Faction; they have no reason to be here. This is a simple family spat that will be resolved soon enough."

"And your manner of involvement?" Clarke asked.

"Protecting T—," Trunasder said, wiping his mouth. "Protecting territory on Lindaulx."

"That's what this is really about then?" Clarke asked. "You expect me to believe it's only about land? Commander Maeve and Lord Valan have plans that we must understand."

"Yes, they do," Trunasder said. "But you have no business in meddling here."

"But we do have the right to be here," Clarke replied. "The Nova Republic must evaluate and judge. We must see how these plans align with our glorious Republic and the Greater Purpose. So, do you represent the Khilsyths?"

"Yes, of course," Trunasder responded, thrusting out his chest. "I am a House Khilsyth General."

"When will the Nova Republic recognize the true claim and rights of the Tersinian People to Lindaulx," someone blurted from the growing crowd.

Trunasder laughed, coughing twice and spewing spittle. "Now, that would be something sensible to talk about. Tell me, emissary, are you here to discuss reparations and ways to rid Lindaulx of the scourge that has fallen upon it?"

"That's an interesting proposition," Clarke tried diplomatically. He wondered if the Anacul had infiltrated the command structure more than Anzil knew. "Let me understand and get my bearings correct: Lindaulx belonged to the Anacul, and the Tersinians are the scourge?"

Trunasder shook his head. "You bore me with your feeble education and attempted trickery, Emissary Munge. Begone, fool."

From Clarke's peripheral view, he saw two familiar faces, Xon Titus and Mysis Rend, walking purposefully to the minor commotion he and the General were creating. Xon Titus was a hulk of a man who, rumor held, appeared on a routine supply ship one day, claiming no memory of his past. A short while later, Mysis Rend arrived similarly. The two were inseparable and had a real knack for training soldiers, so the Khilsyths invited them to stay.

"The Nova Republic's presence is growing wearisome," Xon Titus said dismissively. "Did I not make myself clear? We do not need or appreciate anyone meddling in our affairs."

Clarke was unsure if Xon Titus meant only the Republic or was also extending his sentiments to Trunasder. "Now listen here," he said, recapturing Trunasder's attention with a lack of diplomacy unbefitting the Nova Republic, "someone from this planet requested our aid. It has also not been made clear to me who killed Trade Khilsyth."

"Lord Khilsyth," Mysis Rend corrected.

"Forgive me," Clarke said, clearing his throat, "of course, Lord Khilsyth. Now, we believe the murderer to be Anacul."

"But you have not confirmed this," Trunasder said. "You don't even have a reasonable theory or evidence of how that could be. And as we have made clear, the Nova Republic has no right to interfere in a House Khilsyth internal matter. However, you are within your jurisdiction, even obligation, to deal with your Rift Faction dissidents."

"Let's go ahead and take a pause here," Xon Titus said, forming an accepted sign for holding still with his hands.

"Come to think of it," Trunasder said, stepping closer to the emissary, "we would probably question how the Rift Faction ever came to be here. Routine stop? Bah! You likely alerted them yourselves so they'd come and incite chaos. Give you a reason to intrude in our affairs."

"Trunasder," Xon Titus said forcefully, "that's enough. "Now, and calmly. What in the gods is happening here?"

"Allow me to present the Nova Republic Emissary," Trunasder said in a demeaning tone, rolling his hand. "They've come all this way to meddle in our affairs. Likely an elaborate ruse so they can implore us to believe in their pathetic Greater Purpose. But there is no need for their meddling here. So, I propose we send them on their merry way. I mean, their reputation proceeds them so infamously that this ass is still in armor."

"You know," a woman said, stepping forward, "by coming here, your pathetic Nova Republic life is forfeit. Commander Maeve will not have—"

"Silence, Bars'zul," Trunasder said, causing the woman to shrink back into the crowd.

"I implore the Khilsyths to reevaluate the situation," Clarke requested. "The Anacul are—"

"Would you stop saying Anacul?" Trunasder interrupted. "There is no indication of them here or anywhere else in ages."

"Fine," Clarke said, "I'll rephrase. The claim is that a Khilsyth engineer killed Lord Khilsyth. If true, why would the Khilsyths call upon the Nova Republic for aid? There would be no need for such intervention unless something larger was at play. Also, even if the Republic summoned the Riftys, do you think they would be that inept to fall for that trap? I tell you all, what is being shown here is not the truth—"

"Your lives could be forfeited by coming here, friend," Rigil Sprauge said. His comprehension of the present situation lagged from the influence of high levels of foreign chemicals in his bloodstream.

"Thank you," Clarke said, turning to Rigil Sprauge. "That much we've already established." Facing Xon Titus, he continued. "Someone took a contract out on Lord Khilsyth. And the sorry excuse of pinning the murder on Clarke, a field engineer, is ludicrous."

"You would know, Emissary Munge," someone from the crowd said, "or is the Republic that piss-poorly managed?"

"The responsible party clearly had the support of the Nova Republic and ROG," Clarke said.

General Trunasder raised both of his hands and pumped them back and forth. "Woah-woah there, big guy, nobody said anything about ROG."

"Potentially even tricked the Republic," Clarke added.

"The assassin appears to be one of our own," Xon Titus interjected, raising a meaty hand to silence everyone. "That is true. Therefore, it is our problem to deal with."

"I knew Clarke," a voice said quietly. "No way he did it."

"Lieutenant Andover," Xon Titus said, giving the man a reprimanding glare. "This is not the place nor the time."

"He wouldn't be capable of such an act," Andover continued. "Let alone have the skill to assassinate the Chief."

"That's enough, Andover," Xon Titus said, projecting his voice. "Just because you kept Clarke safe doesn't mean that dog is loyal."

"Oh, come on, Xon," Andover pleaded. "We're all thinking it. We're all wondering who *really* killed Trake. It would have to have been someone very skilled or close to him—someone he trusted."

"It likely just means Clarke fooled your dumb ass," Xon Titus said with a slow shake of his head.

Andover flinched; Xon Titus' words had stung, but he knew he could be right. "Fooled all of us, you mean. So, how did he do that?"

Clarke pointed at Andover. "Your Lieutenant Andover is onto something there. How could Clarke have been in two places at once? He was on a service call in the Hidden Valley area at the time of Lord Khilsyth's death. Was he not?" It was a risky play, for none of the news reports told of Clarke's movements before the murder.

By now, the group of onlookers had grown and was stressing the thin band of sanity holding the mix of allegiances in the room together.

"Exactly!" Andover said, pointing and stomping his foot. "You see? That's what I've been saying all along."

"I know you've had your doubts, Andover," Xon Titus said. "I thought I was clear that the discussion was closed. And where in the hell is operational security? Even the damn Nova Republic knows about—"

"Respectfully," Andover said, his voice shaky but gaining confidence. "We know Clarke was on a repair job with Anzil and me. We also know a repair was waiting for him at the workshop, and he accepted it on-site. And then, for some unknown reason, he took a job out of the city."

"Why in the hell are we still talking about this?" Rigil Sprauge asked.

"Because the timeline doesn't work," Andover said. "And nobody seems to give two shits."

"Who led the investigation?" Clarke asked.

"I did," Mysis Rend said flatly. "Now, Lieutenant Andover, this discussion is closed."

"I disagree," Andover said. "The gate sergeant's notes identified two people in the maintenance skiff, but the logs show only Clarke. And the escorts returned with invaders piloting their armor."

"So, Mysis," Andover said, shaking his head. "You're telling me Clarke managed all that. Bullshit. The Nova Republic Emissary needs to know—if the loyalists didn't kill Lord Khilsyth, and the Nova Republic did approve of it, then the Republic would have the cause to support Anzil's faction. But, if the Republic sanctioned all of this, then the Riftys could back Anzil's faction."

"Unless the Republic is backing the Tersinians or the Anacul Nation," Mysis Rend said.

"Backing a culture they hunted and tried to eradicate," Xon Titus said, with a shake of his colorfully inked head. "Unlikely."

"It was no member of the Anacul or Tersinian Nation who had a hand in Lord Khilsyth's assassination," Trunasder said. "So, pack ass and jet, Nova Republic spy!"

"And if there were specters involved?" Clarke asked, ignoring the belligerent General. A glance from Auralei told him he had best know what he was doing.

Trunasder broke the silence. "It would only mean that Anzil and his traitors likely had the means to hire expensive assassins. And, the Nova Republic would have—"

"You don't know ROG's place, Trunasder," Xon Titus said. "Unlikely, they would replace father with son. You know all that business about family bonds and regret. However, Emissary Munge being here means there is a good chance that ROG's meddling thumbs are on the scales."

Clarke positioned himself in front of Xon. "Right now, I'd wager the Nova Republic is most concerned about why the Tersinians tried to hide their presence."

"Wait," Andover requested. "So, specters *were* involved!"

It occurred to Clark that Xon Titus might know there were Tersinians here, perhaps even Anacul. "Then who killed Trake Khilsyth?" Clarke asked the crowd. "Our sources report Clarke Anundr was outside the walls. You're telling us he could teleport here to kill Trake Khilsyth while Anzil and Miles Andover were with him?"

"Just a second," Andover said, holding his hand up to silence any retorts. "Is our security really that frail? Our names…"

Andover's eyes squinted, his brow furrowed as he leaned forward, catching only his reflection in the dark armor's reflective visor. The intentions floating to the surface of Andover's mind were not pleasant regarding the Tersinians or the Nova Republic. Still, he couldn't determine if they carried enough conviction for him to act violently and insubordinately—he would have loved to wrap his hands around Trunasder's neck and choke the life out of him slowly.

"What about the names?" Xon Titus asked Andover.

"Regardless," Trunasder said, regaining the crowd's attention. "Plead your case to be admitted to the party, Emissary Munge. Name your price?"

Clarke kept his attention on Xon Titus. "We have reason to believe an infiltrator killed Lord Khilsyth, and there is a Tersinian-Anacul alliance behind this attempted liberation. They embedded into the houses of Lindaulx and tricked the Republic into helping. Regarding the Riftys, I don't know their true reasons for being here. However, their presence is too convenient to be a coincidence."

General Trunasder slapped his hands together slowly while Rigil Sprauge and a few others burst into laughter. "Little man—" he said, pointing at Clarke.

Clarke held up his hand and thundered. "Let me finish. Valan Khilsyth is also potentially unfit to lead, making Anzil the rightful leader here on Lindaulx."

"Then, Emissary Munge," Trunasder said quickly. "You are more misguided than I imagined. Anzil is no more born of Khilsyth blood than I am. The Khilsyths have their internal spat. We are simply here to protect the planet and ensure rightful succession."

"Actually," Mysis Rend said. "Interestingly enough... Anzil is a Khilsyth. If the house commanders judged Valan unfit to lead—by House Khilsyth code—the closest kin to Trake would reign."

"Silence!" Trunasder screamed. "I will not have this insubordination. Detain—"

The rest of General Trunasder's words turned into a gurgling stream of blood frothing from an expanding red slit that appeared across the middle of his pale neck. The man's legs gave out, and he pitched forward onto the floor, leaving a lone woman standing over his fallen body, a bloodstained blade in her hand.

"You talk too much," Auralei teased Clarke. "Trunasder was Anacul." With a wink, she disappeared back into the flux, avoiding the mad flail of a nearby soldier.

"What the…" Andover said in a nasally high-pitched shriek.

"Who's with Anzil?" Clarke asked.

Andover took a timid step toward Emissary Munge. "Clarke?" he asked.

Clarke nodded. "Gents, I swear by Stigg's beard that I'm right about this."

"Is the old goat with you?" Xon Titus asked.

"He's leading the charge outside," Clarke replied.

"That bloody fool found a marauder, didn't he?" Mysis Rend asked.

"That he did. Will you help?"

Clarke took Xon Titus and Mysis Rend's answer as a resounding yes when heated projectiles from their pistols snapped at the air past his head only to be caught by several of what Clarke suspected were invaders' foreheads and exited in sickly explosions of goo.

"Andover, highlight the targets we discussed," Xon Titus instructed, turning to continue venting the brain material of nearby attackers. "Mysis, the big guns, if you will."

Clarke hurriedly surveyed the room and noticed someone leveling a cannon toward him. Instinctively, he released the forearm shield, but his muscles were defiant and clumsy, straining against the weight of the armor. He deflected a burning, acrid ball of death to slam into someone else. It engulfed the man in a caustic wreath, melting his face like spent wax from a candle. Clarke dropped to a knee with his lungs straining to feed his body. Darkness was at the edge of his vision right before he diverted the attack. He wondered what the dark passenger was thinking trying to resist his attempt to protect them—a direct strike would have been fatal.

Clarke shook his head to clear his exhaustion. He figured lack of sleep was catching up to him, playing tricks on his mind. He stood on shaky legs. His vision was foggy, and its edge darkened again as he failed to resist. Clarke took two wobbly steps and lunged at the nearest person, who was too terrified to move. His blade stopped a hair's width from their crooked nose—the person had formed a protective barrier with ethereal tentacles that flowed between their bracelet-clad wrists and the shield it produced. Their eyes were soft, sympathetic, and even inviting to Clarke, but they were disingenuous and patronizing to another part of him. His body coursed with a purpose he could only name as survival as the armor clamped onto the tentacles, diverting the energy from the bracelets for its use. When the barrier collapsed, Clarke stabbed his knife into the person's chest, and the tip emerged from between their shoulder blades; the weapon released gentle vapor trails of burning blood once the dead body fell away.

Clarke was vaguely aware that Andover and Xon Titus had moved to form a protective flank. The brilliant spark of another device and the energy it drew from the flux caught the attention of the dark passenger. Clarke watched, captivated, as the faint hints of energy pulsed and writhed through the air, coaxed by a simple crystal to take shape. But the person's wild eyes betrayed a lack of mental fortitude and rule over the power they were trying to harness. Unhindered and ill-formed, the device released the energy as a raging gout of molten heat, setting the owner ablaze—the purifying fire sucked at the air around it as it indiscriminately burned through tables and workstations, scorching its way toward him. He shouldered Andover hard, knocking him to safety, and dragged Xon Titus out of harm's way. The brunt of the heat missed them and burned into the stone floor until it was devoid of sustenance and was called back by the device.

"Sorry about that, fellas," Clarke said before leaping over a desk and dashing toward a woman fashioning a protective barricade from several devices on the floor and one in her hand. The energy arcing between the devices shied away from his armor as he passed through it, grabbed the woman by her frail shoulders, and spun her into the path of an attack meant for him. She held her hands in front of her, and the whip of hellfire cracked against the shield and engulfed them both in flames.

"I can't sustain this much longer," the woman said, her thick, accented voice straining. "I wouldn't have harmed you." She tried to say more, but the fire ate greedily at the air, and the heat burned within her lungs.

The woman fell limp into Clarke's arms, and he wrapped his body around her, hoping his armor shielded her from the heat. Bile rose in his stomach. Displeased, his dark passenger sent several ethereal antennae to lash out and find purchase on the crystals scattered on the ground. Clarke heard faint, indecipherable whispers through the connections to the crystals and wondered about the promises of the power they carried.

The woman's eyes opened gradually. *We are here for you.* Her voice slammed into the forefront of Clarke's mind and mingled with his thoughts. *Why do you move against us? You do not know, do you? But wait... I feel something else... Something inside you... It shouldn't be here.*

Explain yourself, Clarke thrust into the ether. The power coursing through his body was exhilarating—every one of his senses magnified with an intense clarity. A thread in the back of his mind cautioned him against the lure of power and scratched at the thin veil of his consciousness. Clarke tried to understand and peer through it, but there was interference. He stilled his mind and embraced the bestial hunger inside him, believing it would offer a respite—in this state, his dark passenger became virulent. The woman's mouth snapped open in a silent scream, and a painful, shrill scream reverberated through his joints. She transmitted a few incoherent images before succumbing to the flames—the scale of the battle extended beyond Lindaulx, and she was seeking refuge.

Clarke reeled, sundering the ethereal antennae from the focusing crystals, which caused them to shatter. He wondered what the Tersinians were so afraid of.

CHAPTER 34

THE ENERGY FROM distant galaxies ripped Clarke from the waking world in a rush of streaking colors, fracturing his spatial awareness and sending him spiraling downward. His descent stopped, replaced by wild ocean surf that was trying to suck him out into deeper waters. Spitting sand and rubbing the sting of salt water from his eyes, he stood and took slow and steady steps against the pummeling of the silent walls of water until he was free of the ocean. He shielded his eyes against the harsh overhead light and discovered a temple protruding from the small island's core.

"You are learning the design quickly," the familiar voice of the Pioneer said approvingly. "I feared you would lack the moral righteousness and the proper constitution to act when needed."

"I'm not exactly sure what you mean," Clarke said, shaking the fog from his mind. "But thank you. I guess." He turned to find the source of the voice and met only the dull roar of the sea.

"Really? Are you unaware? Tell me what you think you know."

"This place, this temple, time moves slower in here than—"

"I do not believe we leave our bodies," the Pioneer interrupted. "Rather, we act within our minds."

"Wherever here is."

"This place. It is the archetype of instruction. A place to reveal design and check morality."

"And one's constitution, correct?" Clarke asked, interpreting the silence as a clue to continue. "Earlier, you said I wasn't ready. Am I ready now?" Again, silence greeted his question. "Is the armor's design to destroy the flux?"

"No. I don't believe that to be the case."

"I can feel its…" Clarke said, rubbing his chin out of habit. It was hard to wrap his mind around his sentiments at this juncture. "Let's just call it desire."

"Interesting. But it's not the machine's desire."

"Mine then?" Clarke asked with a nervous laugh to mask his concern.

"Not quite."

"My dark passenger's?"

"That would be a way to describe it," the pioneer replied. "The matter in you is that what you call it—your dark passenger. And yes, we might include the armor. They are… rather, the architects designed them for the Paragon Program—originally a venture for civil applications. Perhaps one received skills in fields such as medicine and other trades. These paragons would be the perfect embodiment, or perhaps a range, of functions. Devices could have also delivered the structure or guidance to perform the learned tasks. Anyway, it's a working hypothesis."

"Are we talking about the armor or the dark passenger?" Clarke asked, walking toward the pyramid through the soft, deep white sand.

"The devices would not have resembled armor. Too bulky. Too restrictive. And why would there have been a need for such tools?

There wouldn't have. The program would have relied on simple garments, even trinkets. There are no records of major events of violence during the adoption of the Paragon Program. Mysterious. Although they could have been hidden. Buried. Kept secret."

"Maybe the program wasn't supposed to have existed. Based on my experience, most folks wouldn't appreciate the side effects."

"Possibly. However, there are records of an Astute confederacy of sorts. It maintained alliances with several other races, fostering an age of relative peace. Perhaps the program was in its infancy when the cataclysm occurred."

"Go on, please," Clarke prompted. The temple loomed before him. It was constructed from a dark mineral substance with an internal crystalline structure that captured the light. He could make out intricate carvings along a series of short switchback ramps that provided a viable path he could ascend.

"The cataclysm. An event, some marker of significance, caused the Astute population to decline rapidly. To all but vanish. And based on your presence here, it appears a remnant of the paragon program has survived and chosen you. Which, if I may, you seem to be doing rather well at adapting."

"Do you know what the cataclysm was that wiped out the Astutes?"

"Fascinating," the pioneer said with a gentle laugh. "All of this information and your focal point is devastation. It's hard to pinpoint a single event."

"A war?"

"Perhaps. I believe it had something to do with their technology. It is related to the energy the Astutes could harness and direct it wherever they went. They built networks and structures within planets and around suns that they joined, allowing them to potentially manipulate time and space on an unprecedented scale."

"And what?" Clarke asked, tilting his head. "You think this stuff inside me gives me a front-row seat."

"No, I think it's teaching you."

"About what exactly?"

"Is it not obvious?" the voice responded.

"To fight?"

"I believe it is to be a *Reaver.*"

"Sounds ominous," Clarke teased.

"From my investigations, Paragon *Reavers,* by design, were constructed to seek disruptions—perhaps contaminations—in the energy streams. Or perhaps the way it was being used or even by whom. There's a slight possibility it also deals with time."

"And do what?" Clarke asked.

"Doesn't the armor give you some hint?"

"So, they developed a class of Paragons to protect this network?" Clarke asked. "Something to ensure they had reliable power for their civilizations?"

"I don't believe that's entirely accurate. I've uncovered translations for guardians or protectors elsewhere. There was more emphasis on something like a separation, but it was more visceral and vengeful. I believe they were nearing the end, perhaps nearing extinction, when they turned to creating these *Reavers.*"

"Or they were on the precipice of a major evolutionary shift," Clarke said nervously. He took a few tentative steps to ensure the structure supported his weight. The steps were uneven and, with his taller-than-average frame, required an awkward gait to maintain balance and a steady rate of ascension. "But why create *Reavers?*"

"I believe they wanted to ensure the survival of a race," the pioneer intoned.

"What race?" Clarke asked.

"Yours. I believe."

Clarke laughed. "You're telling me some long-vanished civilization wanted *us* to survive? They left all of this behind for *us* to find. To what end?"

"Clarke. Do you not find the composition of their environments oddly similar to yours?"

"The Astute were just like us."

"Not I, Clarke. Just you, as far as I can tell."

Clarke laughed. "You're crazy if you think I'm descended from the Astute?"

"It's plausible," the pioneer said.

"But it makes no sense," Clarke said dismissively.

"You may be one with the dark passenger, not separate."

"That doesn't make sense either. Why are you saying this now and not earlier?"

After a long pause, the pioneer spoke. "Moral righteousness."

Clarke was nearing the halfway point up the pyramid. "Whether I'm a good person or not?"

"Close enough. The architects instilled a way to guide the development of paragons within this place. How you develop your actions, skills, and responsibilities will shape your—" the voice hesitated. "Let's say metamorphosis. Or maybe evolution."

"Can't wait," Clarke said sarcastically, picking up the pace. "Why the lesson now? Why during the middle of the fight?"

"I did no such thing. You direct coming here."

Retribution, the thought burst into the forefront of Clarke's mind like slamming a finger in a door. He missed a step, stumbled, and took a few deep breaths before standing. *Are you gaining traction?* he asked his dark passenger.

"Are you okay?" the pioneer called.

"Quite," Clarke lied. "Little surreal of a message. Given tools and training, you can shape your destiny."

"Did you arrive at that just now?"

"I stole it from a recruitment poster," Clarke admitted. "But since you've taken on the moniker of my spirit guide, how do I end this fight on Lindaulx?"

"I do not know. It is time for you to leave, though."

"Because I'm almost at the top?" Clarke asked.

"No. Because people are moving unnaturally where your physical form resides, return when it's safer."

Clarke called after the pioneer, but it was silent. He increased his upward pace, bounding two steps at a time, ignoring the ache in his legs. As he neared the structure's precipice, the lightless material evaporated, and he plummeted through the darkness into the inner structure.

RESOLUTION

CHAPTER 35

THE SCENE IN the Operations Center reconstituted for Clarke in a reverse rush of images, noises, and a slight nausea-inducing wrench on his innards. Most people had moved a fraction of an inch, except Auralei, who was halfway across the room, blurring toward another group of enemies. Clarke watched as Mysis Rend's finger supplied pressure to his rifle's hair trigger, the reaction sending a few rounds toward where he figured there were enemy soldiers.

"That one's dead!" Mysis Rend called to Clarke.

Clarke released the lifeless woman's body, and it crumpled to the floor as he scanned the room, finding a lone soldier lobbing plasma-filled rounds indiscriminately at anything that moved.

"Take him out, Clarke!" Mysis Rend called.

Clarke recovered a simple sword carried by the woman, then bounded across the floor, skidding through blood-slick areas. He vaulted a workstation toward a soldier, hacked wildly, and missed as they blurred backward. With a little trial and error to test the limits of the person's travel distance, Clarke's borrowed sword flashed through the air, finding little resistance as he stumbled off balance from the force of the attack. The person's face contorted in shock and then relief, which vanished when the upper half of their body slid away from their lower half. The unnatural fire from their weapon erupted skywards, tearing through the roof of the geodesic dome. It spread out along the cavern's ceiling, burning away chunks of molten rock, which crashed onto the roof as micro-meteors.

The soldier used their necklace, releasing a wave of energy to stem the blood loss from their exposed torso. Then, dragging himself across the floor, he carefully aligned his halves, and the device released tentacles that began knitting him back together.

"Why won't you just die?" Clarke asked and thrust his blade through the man's heart. "This just isn't right." He slammed the hilt to the side, trying to drive the sharp edge out through the man's rib cage, but the weapon did not budge. He wondered what was so important in this life that the soldier had such a ferocious will to live. He wondered if he would find the same determination. Clarke grabbed the sword with both hands and jerked hard, dragging the screaming torso across the slick ground with the lower half trailing loosely. Frustrated, he sought the sticky darkness within his mind and beckoned for its aid, which it gave freely—it tore along the man's protective shielding, tracing its way back to the embedded crystal structure, which darkened at its touch, extinguishing the light and shattering it into tiny, brilliant shards. Clarke placed his heavy armored boot on the person's face to provide some traction and, with a crack of bone and a spray of innards on the side of a nearby cabinet, he freed his sword. The person was finally still.

"Sunnova bitch, Clarke!" Mysis Rend yelled. "That's awfully bloody dark, lad."

Clarke looked up from the gory mess he'd created. Several people were staring in horror with the blood draining from their faces, and a few were bent over, spilling the contents of their stomachs onto the floor.

"Ah yeah, buddy," Xon Titus said with a snort. "You're supposed to kill them, not play with them."

"They just wouldn't die," Clarke muttered.

"Enough," Mysis Rend shouted, motioning for his dragoons to round up the remaining enemy forces and escort them from the Operations Center to nearby confinement chambers.

Approaching Mysis Rend, Clarke banged knuckles with the man's extended gauntlet. "I'm glad you're on our side, Rend. I was getting nervous you wouldn't recognize me."

Mysis Rend laughed. "You bloody fool. I'm surprised these bastards didn't figure it out." He swept his arms at the mess of dead bodies in the room. "Good thing for us they didn't."

"It's good to see you alive and well," Xon Titus said to Clarke, grabbing his shoulder and giving them a shake. "You and your friend proved to be the catalysts we needed to deal with the tensions here."

"Anytime," Clarke said, removing his battle helmet.

"We've also intercepted some back-channel messages we think are from Anzil," Mysis Rend said.

"Valan's entourage said the invaders killed Anzil at Hurricane Ridge," Andover said. "The bastards even claimed to have seen evidence or had eyewitnesses. The story changed slightly depending on who told it. Anyway, we had to do what we had to do until we figured out what was going on."

"With the comms compromised, we did not know if the folks at Warbler Ridge were what they claimed," Xon Titus added. "For all we knew, it was the invaders at work. Whoever organized this little game here has impressed me. I'll have to remember this for the challenges."

"I'm assuming there's a plan with you and the mech," Xon Titus said, nodding in appreciation to Laars. "We are crawling on very thin ice here with precious little time."

Auralei appeared, startling the small posse that was forming. "Messages from Anzil?" she asked. "What of them? Are you sure they're real?"

"Gosh dang it," Xon Titus said with a jump and an arm wave to protect his center of mass. "And you're playing with *Mischi* now, too?" He gave Clarke a wink, who, now that he was inspecting him closely had changed. "Let me see you." He took Clarke's head in his blood-stained hands. "Ah yes, you've killed those with the talent." He was unsure if Stigg would be proud or start upending things. "I see the warrior you're becoming. Until the end."

"Don't you put that rubbish in his head," Auralei said. "Now, what about Anzil?"

"We received messages on an old sub-comm the Khilsyth dragoons sometimes use during training," Andover replied. "Something Anzil would—."

"We figured it was unlikely the Tersinians knew about it," Mysis Rend interrupted.

Xon Titus' deep laugh was startling. "But seriously. Who came up with the idea that you should pass yourself off as an emissary? A Republic emissary, no less. What in the world would come of us on such a day?"

"We're glad it was cut short," Mysis Rend said, giving the *Mischi* a friendly nod and wink.

"Enough chit-chat for now," Xon Titus said. "What's your plan, Clarke?"

"Valan was the plan, and he's not here," Clarke answered. "So, now we move to help Anzil."

"What were Anzil's messages?" Auralei asked again, stiffening her stance.

"Last we heard, he's pushing through some resistance on his way to Valan," Mysis Rend responded. "And that some of his forces were on their way and to find a way to let them in."

"And you did, correct?" Laars asked.

"Sort of," Andover responded. "Someone let them into the depot staging area and hangars. But we'll keep them there until we verify their identities. At least it seems like we're doing something or nothing, depending on their allegiance and how this all plays out."

"We can vouch for them," Auralei offered.

Mysis Rend laughed. "Oh, misguided *Mischi,* that means nothing."

"And for some reason, the wall guard went easy on them," Andover said.

"And that's very suspicious," Xon Titus added.

Mysis Rend clapped his armored hands in excitement. "You see. Kamp took the wall from us. And why would Kamp support the attacking forces?"

"Because Stigg was leading the charge and devised this whole schema," Auralei answered.

"Bloody hell," Xon Titus exclaimed. "You could have led with that, *Mischi.* Always dolling out the truth when convenient, you lot."

"But Kamp wouldn't have helped Stigg," Mysis Rend said. "Not the happiest relationship between those two."

Clarke shrugged. "Maybe they thought Stigg bringing an ass load of trouble to the doorstep was a pleasant distraction for them as well?"

"What's the matter, *Mischi?*" Xon Titus asked, catching the woman's curse under her breath. "Kamp's not on the same side of ROG as you, is he?" This earned him a dangerous glance from the woman. "Hon," he said quietly and scratched at his thick beard.

"Those *Mischi* glares stopped working on me a long time ago. So, what is Kamp up to? Bright Angel duty, no doubt."

Auralei laughed and shook her head. "What is it with these backwater places? I've never met a group of old farts that knew so much about ROG—"

"She's putting it together," Mysis Rend interrupted and laughed. "At least some of it. But will she share what she knows? That's the real question."

"Who the hell are you anyway," Xon Titus asked the woman. "Is Kamp here for you?"

"Be nice," Auralei said, flashing him an extended lower lip. "I'm here to help."

"You don't know then," Xon Titus said. "Shit. That's not good."

Auralei put her arm around Clarke's armored pauldron. "It sounds like we will not solve this here and now. So, how do we get to Valan?"

Mysis smirked. "Let's not be hasty. The problem is we don't have a view into Kamp's operation. However, we suspect he's still running around inside of Skyetook somewhere."

"Then the faster we get to Anzil, the better," Auralei said. "Maybe before Kamp or more Anacul get there. Do either of you boys know the way?"

"What about Stigg?" Clarke asked.

Xon Titus flashed him a look that conveyed Stigg was still on his own. "We'll open up the pathways."

"We have eyes on Commander Maeve," Mysis Rend offered. "I have a hunch she might be Tersinian. She might even be Anacul, but she doesn't feel like one. I would bet she knows who is behind this invasion. It might even be her."

"Laars, can you send notice to our forces when needed?" Clarke asked.

Laars nodded. "I believe so. I should be able to establish a link with my siblings." Laars pointed to a nearby door leading to the control room. "I will provide assistance from in there."

"Let's hope Trunasder's version of the Tersinians reclaiming Lindaulx isn't held too strongly by those folks who willingly turned on the Khilsyths," Clarke said.

Mysis Rend clapped his armored hands together. "You folks all stay here to support Laars. Xon and I are heading to check on Anzil."

"Not so fast, Rend," Auralei said. "In case you hadn't noticed, there are some who are a tad peskier to kill than others. You'll need my help to chase down Anzil. And where I go, Clarke goes."

Xon Titus' laugh reverberated throughout the area. "Lass. I know that boy; there's no way he's going any further into danger than you've already brought him."

"Like I said. Where he goes, I go," Auralei said.

"Fantastic," Xon Titus said. "My original plan it is. You both stay here. End of discussion."

Auralei vanished just as Xon Titus turned to leave, bringing the brute up short as she reappeared and placed her outstretched hand on his chest. "Are you all this stubborn?"

Xon Titus snatched the *Mischi's* arm and lifted her. "Probably," he said with a smirk.

As Auralei spun out of his grip, she unsheathed a tiny knife from her waist and snugged the honed edge against the corded lacing of Xon Titus' forearm guard. She cut the cord as she descended, and the covering fell away, revealing intricate scarlet patterns tracing along his arm. "Besides. It's not every day a *lass* finds a bunch of old Vanguards seeking refuge on an out-of-the-way planet."

"She's got another piece of it now," Mysis Rend laughed.

"I call on your oath to aid me," Auralei said with a smile.

Mysis Rend's face fell still. "It's been far too long for that. Afraid the great *Mischi* have fallen too far."

"Not so far as you," Auralei said, her eyes narrowing.

Xon Titus shook his head dismissively. "You don't know what you're asking."

Auralei tilted her head to the side, arching an eyebrow. "It holds true, though. Doesn't it?"

Mysis Rend coughed. "You don't even know why you can call on it, do you? Or what was and is sacrificed."

"Clarke is not trained for this sort of thing," Xon Titus said. "Stigg will have our hides if we put the lad in harm's way. Please don't ask this of Rend."

"A private word if you would," Laars requested, catching Clarke's armored forearm. "Their conversation is no longer meant for us, for it carries the pain of ages."

"Can you hear me, Clarke?" a melodic voice asked, echoing inside the battle helmet.

"Yes," Clarke responded. "Is that you, Luna?"

Her voice was steady and inviting. "It is Clarke. We... I cannot see how you fit into these events. I feel the need to advise caution. The others we have encountered are like bright droplets within the flux stream. But you are hidden beneath the surface." After a brief pause, she continued. "It is difficult for me to explain."

Clarke laughed and, as he recovered, could see the confusion looming on Laars' face. He cleared his throat and raised his hands. "Sorry. I'm getting a little punchy from lack of sleep. Please go on."

"We don't think this is funny, Clarke," Luna said.

"Sorry. I'm just not sure how to feel. You're saying I'm hidden, not supposed to exist or be here. Cryptic conversations, on repeat, are wearing on my nerves."

"Who else has said similar things?" Laars asked Clarke.

"A *Dreader* that... I'm not sure was going to kill me now. And your brother."

"Harmsweld?" Laars asked in a hushed tone. "Clarke, are you sure it was Harmsweld?"

"Laars, we discussed this possibility," Luna replied.

"We haven't heard from Harmsweld in many years," Luna told Clarke. "Did you see him?"

"Sort of," Clarke answered.

"When?" Laars asked hurriedly. "Where?"

"Recently at the Ridge," Clarke replied, knowing he had struck a nerve.

"Impossible," Laars said, shaking his head in disbelief. "Are you positive he was present?"

"Not exactly present, per se. More like an apparition. A projection from somewhere, but where and how, I don't know."

"Harmsweld's form is not important," Luna said. "What is important is what he said."

"He didn't say much that made sense," Clarke said.

"Please," Laars pleaded with Clarke. "Can you tell us anything?"

"Why is Harmsweld avoiding you?" Clarke asked. "His Family. And why are you all helping us, anyway?"

"He sought another way to protect our livelihood," Laars responded. "We had lost contact and feared the worst. But now, I have hope as he seems to have returned. And to you, of all people."

"And that bothers you?" Clarke asked with a nervous laugh.

"It's confusing, to say the least," Luna admitted. "Harmsweld believes that within the Astute civilization, there is a salvation of sorts for us. He also believed they still lived, potentially amongst us but disguised."

"Or somewhere yet to be discovered," Laars provided. "Just a difference of opinions within the family. Please trust us. We are here to help."

"And I just take your word for it?"

"Judge me."

"What?"

"You need to concentrate," Luna said to Clarke.

"On what, exactly?"

"I think you know," Laars responded. "Concentrate on whatever gives you access to Lindaulx's energy stream."

The dark passenger was there when Clarke closed his eyes, like the fleeting images of the world that played on the back of his eyelids when he shut them. It was waiting, eager to emerge, filling his thoughts and senses. It delved into Laars, traversing deep and knocking around the labyrinth of emotions, memories, and foreign deductive reason pathways that had formed over his lifetime. It seized onto something of interest, concealed beneath a foggy shell, and began chipping at it, opening a small fissure wide enough to squirm through—the emotions were faint, carried a heavy sense of honor and justice. Still, before they could coalesce, the link was suddenly terminated.

"Incredible," Laars said. "I think it actually worked."

Clarke took a deep breath, exhaling vigorously. "What the hell was that?"

"A hypothesis that proved true," Laars replied. "Now a working theory. How do you feel about me, specifically?"

"Level enough for now," Clarke answered, uncertain that his experience had aligned with Laars' expectation.

"Clarke," Luna said, reigning in the conversation. "Harmsweld had some rather alternative views of reality—like theories on how we're all super connected. Please. Anything he said?"

When Clarke tried to reform Harmsweld's salient points, they sounded like something that would spew forth from the lips of an unstable street prophet rather than something developed by a rational mind. "Harmsweld believes I can commune with the architects."

"To what end?" Laars asked.

"Something about an aggregation," Clarke admitted in an unconvinced tone. "It was crazy. Like an owning or a control of the flux."

"Bloody hell," Luna blurted, the usual calm leaving her voice, "you really could be."

"Luna, silence!" Laars cautioned, taking his hand off Clarke and terminating anything further being transmitted to the man—in all of their scenarios, having a *Reaver* that didn't understand their role in the universe hadn't been fathomed. The scenarios were astounding, and the consequences were potentially dire. Harmsweld had warned him about the possibility of an unraveling from within, but it was deemed so improbable that he had brushed it off. Perhaps his old friend wasn't losing his grasp on reality after all. He marveled at the sheer luck—or perhaps fate or even karma—that would have been at play for someone to discover an unformed *Reaver*. In that state, they could have been able to manipulate their actions away from their intended purpose. He wondered if the Pathfinder, the one calling himself Stigg and masquerading as a Vanguard, had tracked down Clarke.

Auralei called to Clarke. "Move it. Play times over."

"Hold on a minute," Clarke pleaded, grabbing Laars. "What the hell was that all about?"

"I am sorry if my sister caused you some alarm," Laars said. "The way you interact with Astute technology is very confusing to all of us."

"It's my dark passenger, isn't it? Something tried to possess me in that place! Do you know how to get rid of it?"

"That level of technology seems to be beyond our comprehension," Laars admitted.

"But you obviously think that only Astute's can use it?" Clarke asked.

"These are guesses at best," Laars answered. "Our sister was out of line."

"Are *Mischi* Astute then?" Clarke pressed.

"Dammit, Clarke," Mysis Rend called. "We're leaving now."

"For now, Harmsweld seems to have chosen you," Laars said.

"And it's just not clear why, yeah?" Clarke snapped and held his hands up in apology.

"Something like that," Laars said warmly to Clarke. "Just use caution. Harmsweld does not share his motives with us. It would be best to go to Luna now, as they are in the Khilsyth living quarters with Anzil. The *Mischi* will guide you. Be careful, brother."

Clarke shook Laars' shoulder in a friendly manner and wished him luck. He took off running to catch the lift Auralei was holding and avoided her disapproving glare as he slid in.

CHAPTER 36

THE STEEL DOOR that barred the Khilsyth living quarters barely muffled the competing voices from within. Mysis Rend punched the control panel, activating a magnetic rail along the base of the floor, and the door disappeared into the wall with a slight sucking sound.

Clarke felt exposed. Mysis Rend and Auralei had pleaded with him to remove his armor as it would draw unwanted attention in an area with armor restrictions. "Not as much as my face," he muttered, knowing they would find his defense wanting. Clarke pursed his lips as he slipped into the room toward a large brick-lined hearth that threatened to unleash the fire raging inside it. Valan and Anzil were nose-to-nose and screaming at one another. With a quick scan of the room, he realized that most people had bulges at their hips or couldn't quite hold their arms naturally straight at their sides. The small pistol he had tucked in the small of his back felt insignificant.

Behind both brothers were their entourages, who fidgeted, flexed, and eyed those across from them. *Quite the powder keg,* Clarke thought, berating himself for not having a solution or an escape route. A woman near the back of the room ultimately drew his attention: he gazed into her burning violet eyes, and an icy shiver ran down his spine like the drag of a dull blade. She was petite, fresh, and innocent-looking. A sharp pinch from Auralei broke the trance the woman held over him, but he felt her allure tugging at him. Eventually, he gazed into her transfixing eyes, and a gentle, knowing smile tugged at her lips.

Mysis elbowed Clarke's ribs playfully as he leaned in and whispered. "That woman you're staring at, that's Maeve. We think she's a *Tersa*. Likely a commander or something. Although we never could quite place her. She's a cute little minx, isn't she? Too bad she'd carve your heart out, sauté it, and take the first bite."

"Brotherly love at its finest," Tarra said, stepping between Clarke and Auralei and wrapping her arms around them. "Those Khilsyth brothers have some tempers. Thoughts on defusing that don't involve knocking them out?"

Valan and Anzil were arguing with fervor that matched each other's regarding the future leadership of House Khilsyth. The brothers were starting to emphasize their words with shaking fists and sideward glances to their entourages, who were now nervously wringing their hands or caressing weapons.

"Enough!" Clarke yelled, the ferocity of his voice causing most people in the room to cringe.

Anzil snapped to face Clarke, unfazed but keeping Valan in his peripheral vision. "Agreed. Lieutenant Anundr." Anzil smiled devilishly.

"Clarke!" Valan said, frothing and twitching. "You have the nerve to interrupt us." Valan's words tripped over his lips as they fought their ill-formed way out, absent the usual spirited drawl. "Guards. Arrest him."

The room filled with the soothing hum of various edged weapons being drawn. Anzil moved fast, putting himself between Clarke and the soldiers nearest Valan. "Stop! Clearly, Clarke didn't kill our father. So, let's talk, maybe even like civilized folks, about what in the gods name is happening here."

Valan drew a slender rod from his belt, and with a flick of his wrist, it extended and snapped together into a finely pointed sword. Valan was better at swordplay than Anzil, and with a quick sidestep, he had a clear alley to lunge at Clarke—the blow would have pierced his heart but was stopped short by Luna's outstretched hand. Valan's rapier hissed and snapped as the energy released into Luna's skin, browning it near the blade. It was the only flaw on her otherwise pale and glowing skin.

Valan is being manipulated, the thought ripped through Clarke's mind, leaving wispy tracers to fog his sight. Wiping the tears from his eyes, his peripheral vision caught two of Valan's soldiers slump forward and crash awkwardly on the intricately woven rug closest to Laars. Two of the women nearest Maeve were subdued just as quickly when Auralei and the other *Mischi* appeared, slamming their fists savagely into the base of the women's necks.

"I was faster," Tarra mouthed.

Auralei shook her head back and forth deliberately, keeping her eyes on Clarke.

Anzil, the larger and stronger of the two brothers, stepped forward, grabbed Valan's sword hand, and lifted it from Luna's grasp. "Stop this madness, brother," he pleaded. "The fight is not with these people."

Valan drew a small knife from a waist sheath and slashed wildly at Anzil, drawing a thin red line across his older brother's midsection. Anzil caught the man's wrist on the return, and the two men pumped their arms back and forth wildly like an ill-constructed locomotive trying to gain ground.

Clarke took a tentative step toward Maeve, bit his lip to stop it from drooping, and lunged at the woman—his lack of experience as he transitioned through the flux and the speed it provided caused him to miss the sweet-faced Maeve and slam into a red-faced person standing behind her with a sickening crunch of crushed ribs.

Clarke rubbed his ears, chasing away the sound of frozen sap rupturing through the bark. A burst of sweet hibiscus filled his senses. He grabbed at Maeve, hammering the ends of her blonde curls left behind as she ducked out of the way. His next attack came swiftly—instinctually—and caught the woman unexpectedly with a downward jab to the top of the crystal-encrusted cane she had used for balance and shattered it. His skin crawled as the room darkened and filled with an agonizing wail from deep within Valan: once the man's lungs emptied, he fell limp into Anzil's arms. The woman tumbled backward and gracefully landed on all fours. She smiled at Clarke and disappeared with her hazy image swooping across the smooth stone floor and through a nearby doorway. As he watched her, Clarke clenched and stretched his hand to chase the numbness away. "I'm going after her," he said to no one in particular.

"Careful lad," Mysis Rend called. "Not sure that's your best idea."

Clarke turned to reassure Mysis but hesitated as the man's tattooed forearms writhed and shimmered. *Another Vanguard,* Clarke thought. *There are so many secrets.* He concentrated on the familiar vileness flitting through his thoughts, trying to summon its aid, which it gave willingly. With a roar of crashing waves and splintering rock, he shifted into the flux and pursued the faint scent of hibiscus he now recognized as Maeve's.

Clarke didn't have to chase her far as she was in a nearby room pressed against a fireplace, running her hands over the cladding of bricks, probing for something. She turned to face him, a soft smile touching her lips. The patterns she drew from the flux and guided it into the necklace held by her pale hand mesmerized him. He could sense the energy that the distant celestial bodies provided to Lindaulx and the overwhelming possibilities it held. There was a shyness to it, laced with an eagerness to serve and a confident and unlimited promise of power. But Clarke could also feel his hunter lurking and waiting to reave. The woman let loose a scream from deep within her, and the device in her hand pulsed and emitted a ball of burning acid that hurtled toward him. He acted hastily out of instinct, or perhaps driven by his dark passenger, and slipped sidewards through the flux. The acid bolts tore past the space he had occupied, unable to touch him in his state, and burst into an ethereal scream of torment that dug deep into the marble walls and steel door, reducing it all to a hissing pile of white froth.

Maeve laughed. *Commendable effort.* Her voice was soothing when it touched Clarke's mind, but the experience brought intense pressure, like diving into the depths of frigid waters. *It doesn't have to be like this,* she offered.

Clarke's hands unclenched as Maeve's presence left his mind. *What doesn't?* Clarke tried to project across the wisps left from their brief interaction.

Maeve's thoughts came again, but with less pressure this time. She transmitted flawed images of sceneries and snippets of conversations and experiences that were incomprehensible to him. However, the images' traction and brilliance dulled as his tendrils crawled toward her.

What in the world is this? Maeve asked weakly and stumbled, grasping her midsection. She knew her eyes would betray her pain and confusion as she could taste the sickening retribution left by the now-severed coupling. She took a deep breath, wondering if she had betrayed her last thought. It was slow to register, but the fleeting sweet floral fragrance reminded her of the banyan trees of her homeworld. She threw a tiny thimble-shaped device on the floor. It teetered, spun rapidly, collapsed in on itself, unceremoniously hauled the two *Mischi* from the flux, and flung them gracelessly against the far wall. They screamed in frustration and pain as the stone crumbled around them. *Inferior beings,* Maeve thought: she believed their talent was weakened by the foreign components that mixed within their natural born systems. Through the doorway came echoes of heavy soles slapping the marble floors. A quick scan identified a mix of foes and needy subordinates. She retrieved a small circular device from her pockets and threw it at the ground near the doorway, where it exploded on impact, and the pressure release flung everything in the room backward against the stone-lined walls like dead leaves in a heavy windstorm. When she opened her eyes, Clarke stood unmoved. "What manner of creature are you?" Maeve asked in tempered amazement.

Clarke growled as the alien augments that had rooted him in place against the maelstrom retracted. "What kind of creature are *you?*"

Maeve recognized the confusion in the man's eyes. She had seen the same in her reflection years ago, willing it to explain her newly discovered abilities. "You don't truly know what you are, do you?" she asked. The man shook his head and growled a word she hadn't registered. "I could free you. These people are hiding and trying to manipulate you."

She transitioned into the world beyond, missing a burning pistol projectile. She wouldn't be able to linger here, but she did for a moment to take in the ragtag group. She wondered if the signal had come from these renegades and why they were working with some of ROG's finest specters. One of her contacts had told her Xon Titus and Mysis Rend were no longer part of the Nova Republic. But the betrayal was the machine people that had lived here during the time of her ancestors—they had pledged their assistance. However, given their presence here, she assumed they had broken their agreement, perhaps after her devices had impacted their precious Nook's Roost. The even greater betrayal was that they were now protecting this new creature. Something that had sought and destroyed things associated with the flux. *But what had it called itself?* Its existence was a miscalculation on her part.

She cursed. Tridal Lodestar had described a moment in Astute civilization development that represented the pinnacle of their advancement—at this precipice of their evolutionary state, they had peered over the horizon, and whatever they saw resulted in the arrival of a dissociative state and ushered in the age of *cleansing the flux.* Although in true Tridal Lodestar fashion, he couldn't settle on a definitive action to 'the flux' and had several spinoff versions such as purifying, redacting, exiting, separating, reversing, and a few more. Tridal Lodestar had classified the collective body of works as The Great Unraveling Process of Profound Indoctrination, or GUPPI. He theorized that there was the possibility of levels beyond his cultural sophistication scale—the GUPPI ether—and even greater Astute technology had resided in this space. The common thread within Lodestar's Volumes had been that the Astute had learned something so significant to their very existence that they developed a program to systematically unravel the steps they had made to evolve to that moment. The Volumes described a devolutionary process led by machines believed to remain in place to ensure a once-trodden path was not retaken. Tridal Lodestar had called these machines *Reavers* and believed that dissidents within this 'GUPPI ether' had left clues or glimpses of the puzzle as a warning.

Maeve had deduced that somewhere within the Astute civilization structure, beyond mere dissenters, there was a framework the GUPPI machines used to devolve civilizations step-by-step. Therefore, there was a way to put it in reverse—to reassemble the map. The Astutes devised their framework to work on a series of building blocks assembled based on technological advancements within a culture and to understand the interplay within the civilization landscape. As the pieces came together, they would predict the probability of how a civilization would advance. But Maeve's secret monk convent had discovered that not all blocks were created equally as there were cornerstones that represented significant breakthroughs. The monks also deduced that reconstitution of enough of these blocks would lead to unlocking the GUPPI ether—and here on Lindaulx, she had recovered a cornerstone and believed the specter she had contracted also possessed one.

Tridal Lodestar had also warned that the GUPPI machines were only dormant if their purpose was fulfilled—the revival of these machines was possible if any culture advanced along trajectories they were charged with unraveling. There was much she needed to work through: would it be possible for those machines to endure all those years since their last awakening; was it feasible that the signal originating from the Astute complex here on Lindaulx awakened or beckoned this creature; and had she, or the specter, unknowingly set the events in motions to trigger an unraveling? The machine also provoked the precognitive rumblings in her lower right ear that she trusted to foretell impending danger. She laughed at herself for such irresponsible lines of thinking. This person could be what Lodestar had warned about—she would need to find time alone with Clarke to form a better understanding.

MAEVE HAD VANISHED by the time Clarke could move again. He could still detect a faint trace of hibiscus in the air and pursued the scent through hallways and stairwells, some concealed through clever design. The hunt and desire to reave were so consuming that he missed the familiar whine of heavy armor and the wind-up of an under-mounted cannon. He dove to the floor as the windows lining the hallway exploded into a multitude of colorful shards, catching the light and flames chasing the searing projectiles. The wreckage left a haze in the hallway, providing a fleeting cover. Rising to a four-point stance and unthrottling his stranglehold on the darkness inside, he scampered down the hallway. Clarke avoided the projectiles biting lazily at the air and stones around him. He leaped to the nearest wall, scrambling upwards to run along the ceiling to the area above the doorway, obstructing his view of the soldiers. As a rifle barrel appeared through the portal, Clarke left the flux, dropping from his perch, catching the forearm of the rifle, and slamming his foot into the side of a soldier's neck with a meaty crunch. Free of its owner's grasp, Clarke stabbed the butt of the rifle through the protective visor of another soldier, crushing their nose and cheekbones. He spun the rifle around and squeezed the trigger with no response, save the warning betraying that the shock feature would bite if tried again. Not wishing to be the willing victim, he dropped the weapon.

Three soldiers were still in motion. Clarke lunged at his next victim, but his legs failed to cooperate as spasms overtook his appendages and dropped him convulsing on the cold marble floor. The dark passenger fled from his grasp, and he chased it into the recesses of his mind, only to find old memories, the pain of the outside world, and shouting. He sensed something delve into the depths and yank him back to where the blinding light of the room and soldiers burned into his view.

"Who and what the hell are you?" the soldier demanded, his rifle inches from Clarke's face.

"Only specters move like this guy, Colonel."

"I know that Bask," Kamp replied coolly.

Major Waters kicked their captive. "You can hear us, can't you?"

Clarke nodded with neck muscles that were slow to react. He hurried around in his thoughts, trying to locate his dark passenger, but it slipped through his mental grasp. Failing, he tried to open a conduit to the flux and could sense the faint embrace of the whispers of power, but another round of convulsions wracked his body.

"Yeah, I wouldn't try that either," Kamp warned. "Specters are crafty, and so are we."

Major Waters kicked again, this time adding more force to the blow. "Now, who are you?"

Clarke mumbled something imperceptible and tried to sit up, his muscles responding weakly.

Kamp sighed deeply and squatted next to his prey. "We know you're not a specter. And you've got no markings. No spec. You're not supposed to do what you did."

"The rumors are true, then?" Bask asked.

Kamp stood but kept a vigilant watch on the man whose eyelids were lazily struggling to open. "This complicates matters," he said. "Now, respectfully, what the hell are you?"

"Maeve?" Clarke asked weakly.

"What about the witch?" Major Waters asked gruffly. "She your commander?"

"Must catch her," Clarke said, digging at the tiny nodes sticking into his skin.

"Afraid not on this trip, lad," Colonel Kamp replied. "And I wouldn't touch those as they'll bite again." Kamp stretched his neck, receiving the relieving crack he sought as Waters dragged the man to his feet. "Besides, it's unlikely she'll get through the blockade without leaving a trail we can't pick up." He stared momentarily, trying to match his memory of the poor-resolution images to the man before him.

Clarke looked up at Bask and muttered something.

"Come again," Colonel Kamp demanded.

"Anacul are here," Clarke repeated.

"Never ceases to amaze me what folks will claim," Bask said with a hearty laugh.

Kamp sighed. "Lock him down."

"Why can't we just kill it?" Waters asked.

"Because of Stigg," Kamp said.

Bask cocked his head to the side and chased away an eye twitch. "So. Who cares about some backwater chief mechanic? We'll have a squad pay him a visit on the way out."

This overly confident statement almost made Kamp laugh out loud, and that wasn't easy to do these days. "That won't be necessary, Bask—no need to give the old goat more reasons to hate us. Besides, we've lost enough people today. Alright, folks, we are done here." Kamp assigned Major Water's squad to escort the prisoner to a ship they had waiting nearby, telling them he would catch them before the transit through the Mar-Vhen. *Damn you, Constance*, he thought. He had not expected his oath all those years ago would lead to him protecting the very thing they trained him to hunt. Kamp turned and went down the hallway, more soldiers joining him from the shadows. Per orders, he had a few loose ends to wrap up before leaving.

THE DEVICE ATTACHED to Clarke wracked his body with convulsions again, causing him to lose consciousness through the laughter from the Bright Angels. When his eyes opened again, he discovered he was being dragged down a hallway with plush carpet and intact windows. His body hurt. He tried to remember the sweet-faced Ellane from his childhood but could no longer catch the image in his mind. His heart tried to race and his stomach to flutter with the longing for his friend, but his elusive passenger kept him in check: the darkness of it was on the horizon, fouling the pathways to his memories, and when he tried to hold it, it slipped away.

Clarke needed its help. He concentrated on the fraction of warmth that trickled through the alien material's filter of his past, seeking one of his strongest memories. Ellane's features gradually filled his mind and gained more traction as he worked. He stretched them as wide as he could, tearing at the black filth until she flooded into the forefront of his thoughts, slamming the darkness to the periphery of his mind, coalescing and pinning it. He released the memory, lashed out, and firmly grasped the alien material in his outer recesses. It resisted. Clarke's resolve was desperate, animalistic, and fixated. The darkness writhed but eventually succumbed to his will.

"Come on, man, work with us," Major Waters said, frustrated. He pointed a small device in his hands at the captive, who tried to stand and laughed at the feeble man as they crumpled to the floor. "Wow, this guy's an ass."

"You better not kill him, Waters," Bask said, although his tone was unconcerned. "Kamp said alive."

"He's just not a fast learner," Major Waters said with a shake of his head. "Dumbass is trying again." He activated the small nodes buried in the man's skin, but the familiar spasms did not come. Waters punched the device repeatedly with his thumb to no effect, then wrapped the device against his palm and again crammed the button with no response. "Have any juice for this?" he asked. Turning, he was slow to register the progression from surprise to fear on Bask's face, as it was something he had never seen before.

Clarke's eyes snapped open. The alien material from within him seeped out through his pores, under and around the nodes, plucking them from his skin—it convulsed and expanded as it traveled over his exposed forearms and under his shirt. He scrambled backward, hitting the wall hard, clawing at the material to pull it from his skin. But it only sped its reclamation process as it emerged from under his shirt collar and crept up his neck. Clarke screamed as the material clawed over his face and silenced him.

"What in the gods have you done, Waters?"

Clarke heard the faint shouting of soldiers as he rose to his feet and the crack of automatic weapon fire. The searing gobs of metal dug into his body and produced sharp stabbing pains where they struck, but it wasn't debilitating. He circled the soldiers, who failed to keep him in their weapon sights as he phased in and out of the material plane. Clarke closed on the nearest soldier, slamming his fist into the soft, fleshy part at the top of their spine and sending them crashing to the ground. He felt nothing and shook his hand, watching his fingers slap together, the material extending from his arm and sloshing about. Clarke coaxed the material to extend further, and it morphed into a jagged, unholy blade.

The stab of pain in his abdomen warned him he was once again being shot. He stabbed the arm blade at the shooter's chest, only to have the material fan out across their armored chest plate and cushion the impact for his fist. *What the hell,* he thought and tried again. This time, the blade plunged through the protective chest plate, sheering muscle from bone as it passed out through the other side. Clarke removed his hand from the soldier's innards with ease and flicked away the blood clinging to his arm. The other soldiers fell prey to Clarke's speed and ferocity.

With a thought, the blade absorbed into his body along with the rest of the material that had coated his muscular frame. He embraced the calm serenity of the flux. He took advantage of the speed it offered, moving unhindered through the fortress, avoiding several armored patrols and checkpoints—especially the other Bright Angels—as he hunted Maeve's scent.

CHAPTER 37

"NEARING THE POINT of arrival," Captain Chetagale said, securing herself into her command chair. Her spacecraft, the *Locked Tabor*, kept a crew of seventeen souls with room for their families. It was one of the most advanced platforms for war the Nova Republic had developed, with only two currently in existence—and the only one operational. A staggering number of machines handled most functions onboard the ship. Depending on their assignment, they ranged in size, shape, and complexity, which allowed for the minimalist crew—although such a small onboard population required the crew to have a specific mental fortitude for more extended deployments.

Captain Chetagale manipulated a nearby display screen, searching again for any information on the sector the Mar-Vhen transport channel was transiting them to. Still, nothing in the Nova Republic databases nor from ROG could be considered worrisome. While Chetagale was the rightful captain of the *Locked Tabor*, this was an unsanctioned mission. She was thankful for the devotion of her crew as every one of them had risen to her request for aid, knowing that it was violating a basic principle—*don't steal really important stuff that belongs to the Nova Republic.* It hadn't been a quiet exodus either, as her crew had to pacify a few guards and technicians that would be challenging to answer for.

She plucked a small cube from her chest pocket and rolled it over in her gloved hand, letting it fall familiarly among her fingers. Its smooth metallic surface caught and redirected tiny images of her surroundings. *Damn my luck,* she thought. The device stood for a favor owed, and she knew it would cost dearly when the owner recalled the chit. It had awoken and supplied her with a location, and as instructed, she was en route with as much firepower as she could muster.

Over twenty years ago, she met the woman responsible for providing her with her current life. Chetagale had been a young, rebellious teen. There had been an invasion of her homeworld and a displacement of those in power, not unlike the many sorties she had supported since joining the Nova Republic. Chetagale still marveled at her first encounter with the specter that had liberated her as she hadn't had her typical *fuzzy feeling* that foretold of trouble when the woman offered her a better future than staying.

The journey through the years was difficult, but Chetagale had proven competent and climbed the ranks, becoming one of the Nova Republic's youngest Captains. She possessed an uncanny knack for *seeing a path through the noise,* as she liked to think of her abilities. Her comrades often credited her with knowing what they would do before they did. Even with her accomplishments, she had a hunch that her most recent commission of this new era of spacecraft had a helping hand from her mentor. She was grateful for it, as there had been many more senior and battle-tested officers ahead of her.

The *Locked Tabor* shuddered as it exited near the Mar-Vhen transit station and performed a hard banking maneuver away from fleeing ships that were ignoring transport staging area protocols. It was a common occurrence when they were inbound to hostilities. *Not their fault,* Chetagale thought, knowing the chances her ship would register on any scans would be minuscule as it disappeared.

Her ship's onboard screens sprung to life with the information provided by several friendly spacecraft in the sector and began supplementing the data with its superior scanners. The ship's hive mind surmised that the Nova Republic held the tactical advantage with the sheer dominance in firepower and noted that some of the vessels had already turned their attention to bombarding the planet.

Captain Chetagale's finger hovered over the familiar button on her console that would send her identification and start sharing her tactical information with the friendly Nova Republic warships. But she was stopped by a telltale tension between her shoulder blades and the rustling sound in her ears. "Oh, by the gods, it's the Republic we're here for," she breathed, her talent foretelling what her targets would be. "Are you all still with me?" She asked her crew.

Those nearby turned to face their captain, providing a combination of nods and subtle smiles, showing their faith in her to guide them through this, as she had several times before.

"This is going to be a bit interesting," Captain Chetagale said, taking a deep breath, flexing her fingers, and steadying herself. She concentrated on the faint rustle of the air vents around her, finding it calmed her nerves.

It is time, she thought, pairing herself with the *Locked Tabor.* There, in the ship's hive mind, she received a unanimous ready response from all stations, passengers, machines, and the *Locked Tabor.*

Within the fray of the dark skies, the Reaver of Worlds beckons, the *Locked Tabor* placed the words into Chetagale's mind. It exited the flux, appearing brilliantly on the screens of all ships in the area, knowing it was registering as a superior and unknown craft.

Captain Chetagale sent out the identification code provided by her mentor, and the *Locked Tabor* identified, registered, and communicated with several spacecraft broadcasting the same unique identifier. Her combat display showed that many of the Rift Faction ships were friendly, as her intuition had foretold. But in the allied column were also some Nova Republic ships belonging to the Bright Angels. *Let's go loud,* she commanded.

The first targets to be dismantled by the *Locked Tabor* were the non-friendly Nova Republic battle cruisers that were shelling Lindaulx. It was a near-impossible feat for a craft as small as the *Locked Tabor,* but it was in a class of its own and constructed from technology developed a long time ago.

CHAPTER 38

THE FLORAL SCENT intensified as Clarke passed through a heavy wooden doorway into a study room. Maeve waited, her feet sinking deep into a plush rug snugged against a roaring hearth. The smell of burning cedar filled the room. Her gaze held Clarke's, betraying a solemn longing he misread as defeat. Several books were hastily torn from the shelves, and the wall hangings were askew or on the ground. "Looking for something?" Clarke asked.

Maeve blinked as she regarded the metallic staff she held and slipped into the flux. Her hazy image hung brightly before emitting a brilliant flash that set part of the room ablaze in a mesmerizing swirl of flames.

The fire leaned toward Clarke like it was trying to catch a hushed conversation but failed to touch him. Curious, he brought the tips of his fingers closer to inspect the dancing flame, flinching when they blackened. He gingerly touched his thumb to his fingers, expecting to wipe the char from his skin, but it was the alien material that receded. The flaming wall pulsated and split, allowing a ball of molten fire through it. Clarke twisted hard to dodge and regained his balance. He glimpsed the woman through the shimmering gap and slammed his fist into the vacant space, stopping just short of Maeve's flowing shawl. The flames collapsed, singeing Clarke's clothing and arm hair. This close to her, he could feel the flux emanating from her, inciting a hunger that coursed through him to consume it. He could taste the sickly-sweet flavors of rage and allowed himself to feed. The alien material sent out a filament that latched onto Maeve's flux thread and closed around it like a vise. The result ripped her brutally back into the material plane, and the flames vanished, leaving tiny smoke tendrils to play amongst the stench of burning hair and furniture.

Clarke's gaze was trapped by Maeve's soft violet eyes and shy grin. Mesmerized, he spotted the ball of molten energy too late. He braced for the impact, tightening every muscle in his core. The crackling material encompassed him, and he watched with a mix of horror and amazement as his clothes incinerated and fell from his body in smoldering comets. He had misjudged the woman who was still sustaining several devices tying her to the flux.

Enraged, Clarke lashed out and clamped onto the tendrils pulsating with energy—they resisted, but he fought harder, piercing their exterior with tiny hooks to manipulate the conduit. With such a wide-open conduit, he could trace the source of the power from the distant structures created by the Astutes—galaxies and systems that were unrecognizable and had been the playgrounds of almost forgotten civilizations flashed through the forefront of his mind. They beckoned, and he felt like he could transcend through the folds of the flux.

The soft smile on Maeve's lips turned to a grimace of apprehension and amazement as the energy was unthrottled. She held her delicate hands up to protect her face from Clarke's heat as her protective shield strained to keep her safe. "Clarke, I know you."

Air rushed in to fuel the growing inferno Clarke was feeding, causing her to lose the rest of her words.

Wait, she pushed into Clarke's mind. *Please don't do this.*

She was desperate and pleading with him—raw honesty and desperation seeping from her thoughts and into him.

This cycle must be broken, but I am not the enemy. The Nova Republic seeks to suppress you. They know what you are capable of and would have you fail.

Clarke's breathing was steady. *I don't understand*, he offered. *Fail at what?*

The Anacul, the Tersinians, the Frebels, and many more before them tried to rise up to reset the balance to maintain galactic harmony. They all failed. What the Nova Republic seeks is not balance—the Greater Purpose is a lie. As history shows, the victors set the narrative.

But you invaded my home. Killed people I cared about. Why would I trust you?

I am genuinely sorry for any pain I have caused you. It was made to look like you killed Trake Khilsyth to show you the truth—the Republic will go to great lengths to protect and manage you. They have manipulated your life to their advantage. But his crystal blue eyes held only rage. She reached through the fire to touch his blackened skin. Her heart raced from the raw and boundless power of the flux. *The real threat is the Republic has learned how to circumvent the galaxy's safety protocols.* Maeve tilted her head to the side and felt her hair tickle her shoulder. She gave Clarke a glance of admiration as her moist lips slipped back into a warm smile. Then she sighed, tilted her head backward, and let her words flow to Clarke. *I understand that this is the way for now. Your desire to reave is clouding your judgment. You are not yet ready. Please find me on Transom when you are.*

Clarke tried to release her and stem the retribution, but the hellfire rushed into Maeve. At first, it had little effect, as the cells of her frail body remained together, protected by the life-invigorating energies of the flux until her body pulsed and disintegrated in a violent burst of ash.

Clarke opened his eyes cautiously, taking a deep breath. His lungs burned, and his skin ached as his chest cavity expanded. He dropped his darkened body into a sitting position, his legs splayed out in front of him. In the middle of his destruction, there was a speck of remorse in the recesses of his mind. *It's time to go*, came a thought.

He watched as the protective black matter absorbed back into his body, leaving him naked with his eerily calm mind and the stain of rage lingering between the layers of his thoughts. A hammering on the metal sliding door behind him was followed by its slow grind across the track until providing enough space to allow an armored hand. It grabbed the door, its fingers sinking into the metal frame. Clarke's stomach knotted as he was in a room with nothing for cover and nothing to defend himself. He scanned the room for another escape route and spotted a secondary panel clinging to the wall in a melted mass, exposing a slender handle. On the other side of that door, he heard shouting and the unmistakable sound of more mechanized armor.

Surrounded, Clarke scrambled to a blown-out window, which was absent its balcony. He leaned out the window and tested the walls, but they were too slick to scale, and the nearest window was too far. Below, the wall of the keep fell away abruptly, supported by a sheer cliff face above meeting the churning ocean below. He rubbed his hand on the chiseled stone walls, willing the alien material to provide traction, but he could only sense the gateway to the flux and hear its mix of playful squeals and mournful howls.

A high-pitched scream came moments before someone slammed into his back, causing him to glance off the window casing and out the window. He was silent and closed his eyes, breathed in the sweet smell of honeysuckle, and was unsure what Auralei had planned for him.

Auralei gripped Clarke tightly and steered them safely through the air into the back of her waiting ship. She rolled Clarke over and held his gaze with her smoldering emerald eyes. "You stupid ass! What was that? You just about got yourself killed. And then what?" Auralei pushed backward but still gripped the man. "And where are your clothes?"

"A little bit of bare-ass wrestling going on back here, eh?" Tarra added in a jovial tone as she appeared.

Clarke's retort was stopped short by Auralei—her lips were soft and warm, and she pressed him tightly into her sweet breath. Eventually, she released him and refocused his attention with a sharp clap on his cheeks with both of her hands. He contemplated saying something, but no words seemed appropriate.

CHAPTER 39

CLARKE WAS GLAD to be clothed again even if the outfit Auralei had scrounged up would have been at home on one of the Bright Angels—it shored up the imposter syndrome he was experiencing as he stood amongst similarly dressed people carrying themselves in a way betraying their experience. Before him was the Cathedral of Reims, barred by lavishly decorated and intricately designed golden doors that stood twice as tall as him and depicted mostly forgotten accomplishments. The Cathedral was a legacy left over from the Khilsyth's ancestors, who held different paradigms of the world from what was needed today.

Upon entry, Clarke noticed Valan sitting in a high-backed metal chair bearing the Khilsyth crest. He had positioned himself at the head of a table scattered with maps, data, terrain projections, and devices people were consulting intensely. The calm confidence in his deep hazel eyes and a healthy glow had reclaimed his skin. The late Trake Khilsyth's menacing flail was draped across Valan's lap, and Clarke wondered if he held it for posterity or sought guidance from beyond.

Valan stood and walked over to clasp Clarke's forearm in a firm and friendly greeting. "Clarke, I'm glad we could persuade you and your newfound *friends* to *assist* us." He acknowledged the two specters with a quick nod.

"Thank you, Valan," Clarke replied with a nervous laugh. "Ah, sir. Lord Khilsyth." It occurred to him that Maeve's manipulation and corruption of Valan had likely played on the man's desire to lead his family and not his greed to become Chief.

"I'm interested in your version of recent events," Valan said, resting his hands on the safe end of the mace and leaning forward, using it as a cane. "Perhaps you could shed some light on what's *really* happening around here. Or, at the very least, offer an illuminated perspective. All of which would help *us* agree on our next course of action as… there seems to be a great deal of confusion and let's call it what it is, differing opinions."

Clarke caught Valan's quick glance at Anzil. He figured Valan would have had time to develop an overall situational awareness from the assemblage of people—this likely included debriefs from Anzil and Deek, Xon Titus and Mysis Rend, the Tallus Outpost crew, and the Nihkiehl's who were milling about with a Rift Faction contingent. Clarke also wondered if Valan would be curious to know why two *Mischi* were flanking someone like him. And why, in the undertones of all these conversations, were there whispers of Stigg resurrecting an army from ancient lore buried in the depths of Lindaulx—the absence of the old goat gutted him, and he knew he would forever miss the father figure Stigg had been to him. "Has there been any word from Stigg?" he asked Valan, who shook his head. The question had struck a nerve and created an uneasiness in the collective group. Clarke felt the desire to cleave through all their thoughts and flinched, fearing that one false step and his passenger's ill-timed desires would emerge and suffocate him—the familiar rush built in his ears and was abruptly stopped as a comforting hand pressed into his lower back and a tight grip on his arm from Auralei steadied him. He took a deep breath to center himself. The need to devour and his annoyance at his lack of control agitated him.

Leon Nihkiehl stepped forward, grabbed Clarke's shoulder, and gave it a reassuring shake. "Easy lad," he whispered, leaning in close. "You're just going to need some help."

"Clarke, are you all right?" Valan asked.

Clarke nodded. "Just fine, sir. A little nervous, that's all." A tiny wisp of Leon's arm markings protruded from his shirt and was faintly glowing. All those he suspected to be Vanguards in the room had moved closer or turned toward him.

Valan flashed Clarke a concerned look. "Valan is fine. Now, if you could explain your version of events, it would help fill in some of the blanks."

"We would also appreciate some context as to how we were so fortunate to have Nova Republic operators close by when we needed them," Anzil added, eyeing the specter. "And ones that seem to run against the grain of the Republic, no less."

"With all seriousness, it's important," Valan pleaded with Clarke. "If there is anything we need to know—if you're in any kind of trouble—you know we can help."

"I doubt that," Tarra said.

This elicited from the crowd a few harrumphs, choked-back laughs of disbelief, and a mixture of mannerisms people used to distract themselves from speaking.

"Okay," Anzil said, punctuated by a sharp crack as his hands came together. "Since everyone is keeping their guard up, we'll start with the basics." He pointed at Clarke. "My *friend.* You are not who you have pretended to be all these years. You at least owe me an explanation. I know you took Stigg's name to work here on

Lindaulx, which is fine. It's great even. Although we have no view into who Stigg was or where he came from. But at the Academy, you told me your last name was Raines. I'm almost afraid to ask, but is Clarke even your real name?"

Clarke shifted and laughed nervously. "I see the confusion. I used the name—"

"He is of Clan Leod," Auralei interrupted.

An immediate hush fell over the assembled group, and Valan sunk into his chair with a dull thud. "And pray tell, which I'm afraid you will, how exactly do you know this?"

Auralei's brow furrowed as she drew her shawl over her head and snugged it tight. "It is where we met," she admitted, tucking some stray wisps of hair behind her ears. Her world had undergone a severe shake-up in the last couple of days, and here she was, confessing to a group of mostly strangers what her frail memory could only recently piece together. Apprehension rose like a wall inside her, threatening to choke her words as they formed. "I was a Leod of Nanser-Nine." As she leaped over the cobbled-together words, the free-fall drops her innards were conducting created a liberating sensation. She could sense the augments in her, panicking and attempting to assert their dominance, but a part of Shifty was there, blocking them. "I believe Clarke and I were childhood friends, and some of you know this." She pointed at the battle-worn hulk Leon Nihkiehl. "Especially you." Auralei caught the pleading glance that Tarra flashed Leon and his nod of acknowledgment.

"Wait," Valan said, raising his arms. "The Leods and the Nihkiehls are allied?"

"Aye, she speaks the truth," Xon Titus admitted, ignoring Valan's outburst. "I'm sorry it took us a while to place you, lass. You've grown. A lot. But now that we see you, you remind us so much of your mother." He smiled at the fond memory.

Auralei's heart dropped, her ears started ringing, and she felt like a spectator eavesdropping on the conversation. "My mother?" Auralei asked as some of the broken memories buried deep in the recesses of her mind began ratcheting into place and eventually slammed home. "Yes, my mother." Her heart tried hard to race against the last bastion of pesky devices that provided a modicum of defense within her—they responded with chemicals and electrons to keep her impulses and heartbeat measured and failed. "You knew my mum?"

"Aye, many of us did," Base Flintlock said, stepping forward and taking the hands of Auralei—whom she knew as Ellane—in hers. "She was one of my dearest friends. It's not a pleasant story, my dear, but this is sure to be challenging times—"

"And what's Stigg's role in all of this?" Tarra interrupted.

"The old goat," Base Flintlock said, smiling fondly at Tarra, "he was not like us. An outsider. He was a Vanguard, a Black Dragoon. One of the originals. But he forged his own path."

"Was he my father?" Auralei asked weakly.

Mysis Rend shook his head and rested his massive hand on Base Flintlock's shoulder. "No. Lucky for you, that brute was not your pops."

"The Vanguards meant..." Auralei started to say, the tears welling in her eyes and blurring her vision. "My mum was a specter, wasn't she?"

Leon walked forward and wrapped his arm around Base Flintlock's waist. "Nah. She was old school. Kept to the ways of the *Mischi*. And was a legendary one at that."

"My mother's name was Constance, I think," Auralei said. "It's hard to remember."

"Yes, Constance was your mum." Xon Titus said.

Tarra nimbly maneuvered through the crowd to stand beside Leon, her shoulder resting against his briefly before he wrapped his arm around her and brought her close. "And your relationship with Constance?" she asked Leon Nihkiehl—her father.

"Constance and I were..." Leon dug a set of grizzled knuckles into his neck and renewed his hold on Base Flintlock. "I loved her like a sister."

"And my father?" Auralei asked.

"Constance met and wed Duke on Nanser-Nine," Xon Titus replied. "Then you showed up about one year later."

"*Scandalous*," Tarra said with a devilish grin.

Xon Titus burst out laughing, recovered, and smiled at Auralei. "There was nothing sinister about your coming into this world. Constance and Duke loved one another. Very much."

"But odd pairing, no?" Tarra asked.

"Duke's family was a major player in the Republic," Base Flintlock answered. "And the Leod's didn't always see eye-to-eye with the other members of the Republic. In fact, they disagreed with some policies and the direction in which the Republic was moving. The Leods sought help from ROG, and some of the Overseers decided to help. So, Constance worked with your father, and as luck would have it, they fell in love. There was nothing scandalous about it— unless you consider ROG's fraternization policy."

"But you all aren't part of the Republic anymore," Auralei observed.

"It was a *slight* disagreement between the Vanguards and ROG that caused our rift," Leon answered.

"The Rift Faction?" Valan asked.

"Poor choice of words," Xon Titus admitted. "Let's just say that more than a few of us agreed with Duke's view, and it helped expedite the separation. He was a very persuasive individual. Practically unstoppable when paired with Constance."

"Is that when the Vanguards formed the Black Dragoons?" Valan asked.

"No, they have existed for ages," Xon Titus said. "Our generation was just a rowdier lot. Not as subtle but plenty violent. So, people assumed we were Black Dragoons, and we let them." He rested his hand on Tarra's shoulder. "But. I recognize you too, lass."

"Who me?" Tarra asked playfully, with a slight lilt. "Doubtful that you—"

"As for Stigg," Leon interjected. "He showed up out of the blue with a babe in arms."

"Me?" Tarra asked.

"Nope," Xon Titus replied and pointed at Clarke. "That kid."

"How in the hell are you involved?" Tarra said, slapping Mysis Rend on the chest as he came to stand close beside her.

"Let's just say that Maut—," Mysis Rend started to say, then cleared his throat. "Sorry. Let's say that Mr. Leon and I have a murky history together, and there were a few of us who saw fit to honor our oaths."

Tarra's eyes narrowed as she faced her father. "You're Mauti?"

Leon laughed. "Oh shit. Yes, sweety. Many, many, *many* years ago, I went by the name."

"That means you're Arbasele," Clarke said to Base Flintlock, and she responded with a playful wink.

"So, the friendly Rifty and Republic ships overhead?" Clark asked.

"Part of the Strento, yes," Base answered.

"And Clarke," Leon said, "I'm sorry Stigg kept what he knew from you. He kept a lot from us as well. But we've been with you through the years. Watching."

"Exactly why were you *watching* Clarke?" Auralei asked.

"We watched because Connie instructed us to do so," Xon Titus admitted, although he didn't know why and hoped the knowledge hadn't disappeared with Stigg. "Same with you, lass."

Auralei laughed as her eyes welled, and she bit her lip to chase away more tears. "I would have known if someone was *watching* me."

"Would you now?" Tarra asked and smiled at the confused look on her friend's face. "I was your *watcher*, princess."

"In a way, you were," Base Flintlock added with a reassuring smile. "Your Overseer was your true *watcher*. A very dear friend of mine."

"And ROG was the safest place for me when my mum passed?" Auralei asked, failing to stifle the anger from creeping into her voice.

Base Flintlock let out a deep sigh and hung her head. "Ellane, or do you prefer your ROG name?"

"ROG for now," Auralei said, more as a test.

Base Flintlock flashed a warm and knowing smile, her eyes crinkling with familiarity. "Auralei. The Republic also assigned the woman you know as Daphne, a specter, to House Leod. When she wed Duke, she maneuvered within ROG to remove us. She also banished those she suspected were not aligned with her vision of the Republic. Stigg believed she was an infiltrator, maybe Anacul, even though none of us sensed it, and he couldn't prove it." She peered into Auralei's glistening eyes. "But as you know, that old goat tended to be right about things like that. And given your mom's proclivity to the talent, we believed ROG would be a place where we could protect you. We thought that Daphne wouldn't dare move within ROG to harm you."

"But Daphne's faction of the Republic did manage to turn ROG against us," Mysis Rend added. "So, the Vanguards were forced to flee, hunted by ROG and those traitorous bastards calling themselves the Bright Angels. Stupid name if you ask me. Fortunately, Tarra and you are about the same age and could be together. Stigg and Leon took Clarke and hid here on Lindaulx while many of us hid until we received *the signal*."

"I hate to interrupt this lovely reunion," Valan said.

"But you must," Leon Nihkiehl said. "For we still have enemy troops about and a host of star cruisers, battleships, and what have you in orbit. Besides, there is only pain in those old memories."

"A question we should ask ourselves, though," Base Flintlock said, capturing the group's attention with the flair of her glimmering coat. "Was whether these recent events satisfied the responsible party's desires."

"And who they are," Mysis Rend added. "For whom are we but the objects to be commanded and manipulated for the Greater Purpose?"

"The parties we knew about are not likely satisfied," Tarra blurted, fearing Auralei would compromise their directive—her old roommate had suffered some internal failure. She feared for her safety, as ROG would wreak havoc on newfound memories once discovered. She wondered if Auralei was already too far gone and would have shuddered had her augments allowed. "We have a plan." It was a lie, perhaps a half-truth if getting the hell off Lindaulx was a plan. She was confident they could get through the Mar-Vhen transport station with Auralei's fancy ship. One of these days, she would figure out how she had come into possession of such a unique craft. But to get more of them through the blockade, Our Lady Majestic had calculated they would need more time and an unidentifiable but friendly ship currently in Lindaulx's orbit with an open communication channel.

Auralei half listened as the small contingent tried to ply Tarra for details, many of which she sensed were being fabricated on the fly. Auralei was uncomfortable with the present company knowing her past secrets—some were even part of it—but it did not please her that several Khilsyth staff members had overheard part of the conversation. True to her operational form, she filed away the pertinent information about the aide-de-camps under loose ends. She supposed they would eventually come to decide courses of action that aligned with what Shifty was currently relaying only to her–a plan for securing the surface, the immediate space above Lindaulx, and how to seek help from other families in other parts of the galaxy. All of which would require dismantling the remaining Tersinian barricade and securing the nearby Mar-Vhen transport station. The Vanguards disguised as the Rift Faction would help, but she wasn't sure it would be enough. Even her ship would be a factor, but not a significant one. So, one way or the other, the assembled group would conclude that she was in the first volley of people to leave Lindaulx. Perhaps the most challenging hurdle for this group would be the realization that they would need to come out of hiding and seek help from ROG and the Bright Angels. She wondered if they could move past old bygones and make that call for help—the continuation of their bloodlines counted on it.

Auralei stepped backward out of the huddle, towing Clarke with her. This caused the group to stagger slightly, like removing the keystone from an archway. Then, they disappeared into the flux and fled.

CHAPTER 40

WITH A GENTLE movement, Auralei tucked her head under Clarke's arm, her expression brightening as she flashed him a warm smile. "Where are we heading?"

A smirk formed on the edge of Clarke's lips. "I need a few things from home. Sound good?"

"Of course," Auralei said with a quick laugh.

Once free of the inner Khilsyth fortress, they had flown in silence. Her ship glided overhead unnoticed as it made its way across town on a direct course to Clarke's place—an old driving shed tucked behind an immaculate stone fortress of a home. The residence provided ample workshop space and modest necessities, and with the windows open, the gentle roll of the ocean's waves could be heard.

Auralei broke the silence as Clarke held the door for her. "Can we talk?"

"Always."

"So. You remember me?"

"I never forgot you. I've... been searching for you."

Auralei averted her gaze, ritualistically documenting and categorizing everything, including weapons, egresses, and some technology she couldn't register. "I know... It made my advisor quite nervous that I had someone hunting me." She laughed uneasily and pulled at her eyelashes. "You know. Based on some of these old Vanguard accounts, trying to find me was perhaps the worst thing you could have been doing. Especially if my *Mischi* mother hid you among exiled Vanguards."

Clarke caught Auralei's intense gaze as she raised her head. She had killed to protect him. "I'm sorry, Ellane."

Auralei relaxed and nestled closer. "Not to worry, right? But... I don't know if I'll ever be Ellane again. Too much has happened that separates her and me. For now, Auralei."

"We have lots of sticky conversations ahead of us," Clarke said. "And I try to avoid serious conversations with a lack of sleep."

"A bath wouldn't hurt you either," Auralei teased, bringing Clarke's face toward her with both hands. "There is a lot at play right now. Honestly, it's got me a little worried."

Clark chuckled quietly. "That doesn't exactly inspire confidence."

Auralei's eyes squinted playfully, and she slapped his stubbled cheeks friskily. "Listen, you," she said and then kissed him airily on the lips.

"What I meant was that if you're worried. I'm screwed."

"It will be fine. Now, gather what you need. We'll get back to my ship and get some sleep. Then we'll sort out how best to leave affairs on Lindaulx. I don't think we'll be coming back anytime soon."

Clarke nodded. "You know. That *Dreader*—Maeve—said she was here to help me. That the Greater Purpose was a lie, and the cycle must be broken."

Auralei rubbed Clarke's arms to comfort him and drive away his goosebumps.

"Did you know her?"

"I don't think so," she said honestly.

"Excuse me," a voice said, startling them both.

Auralei spun, placing herself between the sound and Clarke, and released tiny seeker projectiles from her armband meant to incapacitate flesh and machine alike. The sensor array she attached outside Clarke's door hadn't alerted her to anyone's presence, and there hadn't been signs of tampering with Clarke's robust home security system. "Show yourself?" she demanded.

The light spilling in the loft window shifted and blurred until the rough outline of a person appeared. "Oh my," it stated plainly, regarding the ineffective devices embedded in the wall behind it emitting soft bursts of distorted light. "Sorry to have caused you to waste such trivial toys. I apologize for startling you. Although Clarke and I are somewhat acquainted, I am known as Harmsweld. I believe you are familiar with some of my family. Those that call Tallus Outpost home." The shape transcended from the loft to the patch of light on the workshop floor. "Again, I apologize, but my time here is constrained. Clarke, what cycle needs to be broken?"

"I'm really not sure," Clarke replied.

"Fair enough," Harmsweld acknowledged.

"Do you know how it's aligned with the Greater Purpose?"

"I believe that I'm close to understanding, yes. Please let my siblings know the Tersinians seek the cornerstones."

Auralei's device alerted her to people uncloaking outside Clarke's front door. "We're not alone," she said and tossed him one of her firearms. "People approaching. Well-armed people."

Before the door to Clarke's place opened, Harmsweld vanished, permitting the light waves passing through the room to their typical trajectories.

"Clarke, we must talk," Laars called as he opened the door and waved a friendly hello. He nodded at Auralei as he walked into the room and dropped a small block taken from his satchel on the tiled floor.

The squelch in Auralei's ear and the sudden appearance of Luna betrayed the block's interference with any device that might overhear their conversation and cloaking abilities. Loud footsteps echoed up the walkway, preceding the owners, Laars and Laand.

"You won't need those," Luna said, pointing at the weapons trained on her as she moved closer.

Clarke laughed nervously as he collapsed the pistol and placed it in his pocket. "Hello everyone. Come right on in. Please make yourselves comfortable."

"No time for jests, Clarke," Laars said. "Earlier, you told me that Harmsweld had contacted you. Now is a suitable time for us to continue that conversation."

"Sure, I don't see why not," Clarke said, retrieving a drink from a small under-counter fridge. "You just missed him, by the way."

"Are you saying Harmsweld was here?" Laars asked.

"You scared him away," Auralei said. "Any idea why your brother is avoiding you?"

"I had detected something strange but assumed it was the specter," Laand replied. "Or something of Clarke's design."

"I have a name, droid," Auralei said, her eyes narrowing.

"Yes, sorry," Laand said, ignoring the crude reference. "I'm still quite curious how Harmsweld is communicating with you?"

"It must be through the ancient energy pathways," Luna said. "Somehow. But there are no residuals here."

"Wonders never cease to amaze me," Laars growled. "Regardless, what did our long-lost kin want with you?"

"Most recently?" Clark asked, unscrewing the top of his drink, which emitted a slight pop. "Or previously?"

"How about all of it," Laars responded. "And please, everything you can recall."

"And your conversation with Maeve," Luna interjected. "If you would be so kind."

Clarke recounted the conversations with Harmsweld, including the part about the Tersinians seeking the cornerstones. He skirted around discussing the temple experiences, not ready to admit he was that level of crazy just yet. When it came time to discuss Maeve, he hesitated as he had been truthful about Harmsweld, knowing there was a chance the Tallus Outpost family was sharing information. However, as far as he knew, no one present had intimate contact with Maeve and appeared to at least be moving against her. The images and words they shared had triggered a twinge of sympathy within him toward her—they were also swaying his opinion to not fully trusting his present company. "To be honest, my conversation with Maeve is a little fuzzy. It's quite strange having someone's voice inside your head. Quite painful, actually." After some prodding, Clarke continued. "My sense," he said and paused to rub his forehead to chase away the shiver triggered by the memory of sharing thoughts with the woman. "I think she was trying to tell me the Republic had betrayed or slighted her somehow."

Laand grabbed Clarke's shoulder and squeezed it reassuringly. "Perhaps we've all been swindled here. This Maeve convinced us that the cornerstone piece kept here on Tervessi was no longer safe. That she was a protector and could be entrusted with its safekeeping."

"What exactly are these cornerstones?" Auralei asked.

"You don't know?" Luna asked. "But your kind is meant to protect them. It's a component of where your talent comes from."

"Never heard of them," Auralei admitted.

"I understand," Luna said. "Information is power, which is judiciously guarded within the Republic."

"Was she *Mischi*, then?" Clarke asked. "This protector."

"We know she wasn't a specter," Laars replied.

"*Tersa?*" Clarke pressed.

"We're not sure what she was," Laars responded.

"She was very capable," Luna said and pointed at Auralei. "Perhaps even more so than you."

"Are you certain she didn't share anything else with you?" Laars asked. "Sometimes, there can be leakages. Something she might not have meant to share."

"Not that I can make sense of," Clarke replied. "I'm sorry, but it's very jumbled. As I told you, it's what I told Harmsweld, some cycle must be broken."

"Do you know what she was referring to?" Auralei asked.

"We have a theory," Laars said.

"Are you part of this cycle that needs to be broken?" Enas asked.

"I believe he is," Luna responded quickly.

"But is it the cycle devised by the Astutes," Laars pondered.

"Or have the ancient protections been circumnavigated?" Enas added. "And we're now part of a different cycle that must be stopped?"

"Any hint on where Maeve might go next?" Luna asked.

Clarke took another sip of his drink to steady his nerves. "Somewhere within the Nova Republic colonies."

"That would make sense," Auralei said. "If she's acquiring these cornerstones, then she would need to travel in Republic spaces or else risk drawing unwanted attention."

"That is a reasonable guess," Luna said.

"So," Clarke said with a smirk. "What happens if she succeeds?"

Laand released his grip on Clarke and examined the floor. "We believe the cornerstones present a pathway to the flux. Potentially at some galactic level when assembled."

"Lovely," Clarke said with a laugh. "So, you don't really know."

"We have our theories," Laars admitted.

"I'm planning on heading home to see if I can't learn more," Auralei interjected. "I know people there who may be willing to help us."

"That would be a logical course for you," Laars said, adding, "I assume by home you mean ROG."

"And which ROG home would that be?" Luna asked with a warm smile.

Auralei hesitated. She had been revealing a lot lately. "Transom," she admitted.

"Our sibling Pantest is on Transom," Luna exclaimed. "We will accompany you there."

Auralei snapped her head around to face Luna. "Overseer Pantest Pemy? The ROG operations outpost there is supposed to be discrete."

Laand clapped. "The one and the same. How wonderful! Do you know him?"

Auralei's brow furrowed. "You mean her. Right?"

Laand flicked a hand dismissively. "Bah, gender. I suppose a feminine form would be necessary to train specters on Transom."

"Interesting," Luna said deliberately. "What are the odds that you are a student of Overseer Pemy?"

"Not a student," Auralei said with a tinge of guilt for disclosing even more of the inner workings of an organization she was forbidden to discuss.

Luna smiled knowingly and rested her hand on Auralei's shoulder, only to have it immediately refused. The comforting gesture was tolerated after several more attempts and with a heavy sigh. "It is a great honor to be selected by an overseer. A rare opportunity reserved only for the best. Is it true? Are you one of Pantest's proteges?"

"There can be only one," Auralei corrected.

"Typically, that is true," Luna said gently. "But we know of another whom Pantest mentors. Leon Nihkiehl's daughter. We believe you know her as Tarra."

"Would this Pantest Pemy just happen to be the dear friend on Transom that Base Flintlock was referring to?" Clarke asked.

Laand's laugh was sudden and caused the windows to reverberate. "I'm not sure, but it would seem that Pantest knows a few things we do not. For why would a Rift Faction leader have ties to Transom?"

"So many coincidences here for us to trust in simple fate," Laars said in his characteristic rock crusher growl. "We have Vanguards and *Mischi* protecting a baby of unknown origin. A scheme that devised multiple safeguards throughout the lad's life to protect him. This includes daughters from unsanctioned bondings who, through the trials and tribulations of the Nova Republic, became specters trained in the ways of the *Mischi*. And now, we learn that another of our siblings is involved in events beyond simple observations. This is very troubling. Where do you come from, Clarke? What is your purpose that so many people have devoted their lives to ensure that you do or do not meet?"

"Do you trust me, Clarke?" Auralei asked.

Clarke smiled weakly and shrugged. "Not like I have a choice. But I have some serious concerns about going to the very place that seems to want us both dead."

Auralei giggled. "I think it's only a faction within ROG. Besides, I am quite good at what I do, you know." She grabbed Clarke's hand, and her bracelet slid out from under her shirt sleeve, glistening in the afternoon sunlight streaming through the windows. "And to think, all of this is because you gave me a bracelet." In her other hand, she held a small, inconspicuous block that chirped cheerily as it recognized her, and a small area of it retracted. She flashed Clarke a soft smile and pressed the single button on the device Colonel Kamp had given her.

INCOMING TRANSMISSION, THE *Locked Tabor* alerted Captain Chetagale.

"Little Love, are you there?" Colonel Kamp's voice came through secured.

"Yes," Chetagale said with a laugh. "I'm here. I figured you'd likely be here too, you old goat."

Kamp grunted his friendly disapproval. "No, you didn't."

"True," Chetagale replied, knowing that another request from her to share his secret would go unanswered. He was the only person she had met that she couldn't predict. But Kamp had been there since the beginning as a father figure to provide a loving and reassuring steady hand to guide her. Her mentor, the specter Constance, had entrusted him to care for her to ensure she wasn't lost in the internal politics of the Nova Republic.

"We need a lift," Kamp said politely.

"Of course. How many do you need transport for?"

"Eight. We'll have an Osprey Interceptor with us as well."

"Ditch the Osprey?"

"Can't... been instructed that one of the passengers isn't to ride on *your* ship."

"Really? Any reason we should be aware of?"

"Ma'am's orders," Kamp said solemnly.

"Fair enough. Be there shortly."

"Oh. And sweetheart, we will have specters with us."

"Fantastic," Chetagale replied sarcastically.

"And we're bound for Transom."

Of course we are, she thought, knowing this would cost her dearly. She then received confirmation that the *Locked Tabor* had predicted the same.

CHAPTER 41

SARDIL SAT CROSS-LEGGED in a dark room lavishly decorated with comfortable rugs and tapestries depicting heroic battles and sentimental representations of his home world. Lying naked on her back before him was the woman Maeve had instructed Sardil to apprehend. Her body was being preserved by a device taken from an Astute facility years ago. He relished the memory of accosting the female vessel—overpowering her and tasting her fear, muffling her screams, and slipping on bed sheets stained with the blood of her lover. The hatred her eyes held still burned into his vision, and his heart raced. Sardil fetched a small vial from his pocket, opened it, and inhaled deeply—the fresh scent of eucalyptus cleansing his thoughts and improving his focus. It was better not to have these thoughts during the ceremonial preparation lest they be unwillingly transferred. He closed the lid and returned the vial to its familiar pocket, knowing he would likely need its help again soon.

Suddenly the woman heaved, sucked in a deep, ragged breath, and opened her eyes wide. A piercing violet replaced the once warm brown eyes. The woman clutched both of her ample-sized breasts, compressed them into her chest, and exhaled. A dull thud echoed off her collarbone as she tapped it twice and sat up, cross-legged, facing Sardil.

"I am proud of you," Maeve said, admiring her new body. She had learned early that it was imperative to find a body that closely matched the one she was most familiar with to reduce the time it took to acclimate.

"As you commanded," Sardil said humbly.

She patted the man's ribs, receiving the desired grimace of pain. "Damage left from the *Reaver*." She stabbed her fingers into the soft fleshy part under Sardil's ribs, which had the desired effect of causing the man to double over in pain and grunt forcibly. "Next time, be gentler with the body. I can taste her rage. It's very unsettling."

Maeve stood and walked over to a recessed closet, where she pulled a plush robe around her and loosely tied the belt. She said a quick farewell to Sardil and gave him a brisk hug. The man deserved time to rest and tend to his affairs, as she anticipated his stay on Transom would be brief.

She touched a nearby screen, which snapped to life and displayed a cozy ocean-side village on Transom. Maeve watched the waves roll along the shoreline, dutifully pulverizing the wasted shells of past lives. The scent was familiar, and she was thankful the ocean smelled the same here as on her *home* planet. She sifted through the messages, proud of herself for setting her plan in motion— buried in the correspondence were reports of her glorious death in the line of duty for the Order.

Maeve checked the robe pocket and discovered a relatively innocuous block she had instructed Sardil to place there. It had previously resided in the underground complex on Tervessi—now Lindaulx. There had been other signatures that resembled the parameters of the devices she was hunting. Potentially, her tracker, which relied on partially reconstructed Astute technology, reported incorrect information. But her probes had captured two signatures passing near a Mar-Vhen Transport station closest to Lindaulx separate from her.

The corners of her mouth sunk into a frown. In the multitude of correspondence, there was a coded message summoning her to an emergency meeting here on Transom. She debated ghosting the meeting, as there was still work to be done to prepare for the arrival of her teams tasked with collecting items from the other ancient facilities—however, duty called.

Shortly after, she was wrapped in a warm travel cloak draped around her shoulders, concealing the traditional Tersinian Order garments beneath. At the front door, she carefully typed her code and remained still while the security device scanned her; a slight click emanated from the wall, and a concealed compartment slid open. She traced the hibiscus flower images inlaid on the mask with her index finger. She appreciated this local custom that provided some level of anonymity. The mask hummed slightly, verifying its owner to pair with the network and supplying Maeve with an augmented display of the world.

It was a short walk from her apartment to her destination through the narrow brick-lined streets, flanked by charming shops and eateries that released delicious scents tempting her to deviate from her objective. She admitted to herself that she was slightly jealous of the people who had time to browse and enjoy the company of friends: the atmosphere was light, with friendly voices and laughter drifting in the air. She wondered if a life of ignorance was a better-lived life than knowing ancient forces shaped their lives. If provided a choice, what would people choose? Like her, would they select action? She turned down an alleyway that looked like the ones she had passed, only this was where her mask directed her to go. She pushed through a heavy metal door and down a dimly lit hallway to a narrow stairway. After descending into the bowels of the building and out a portal in the foundation's sidewall, she traversed a subterranean passageway and entered a room flanked by two sentries—their tattooed forearms and masks identified them as Pathfinders. Inside, she knew other warriors were tucked away in the cloisters and standing vigilant over their charges. She made her way to her designated area, taking in the familiar group of renegades she had come to respect. Maeve turned to face the woman wearing a mask depicting honeysuckle blossoms that shimmered as they reflected the dim light of the room—the assemblage had elected this woman their leader among equals amongst the Transom Overseers.

ABOUT THE AUTHOR

RYAN ABBOTTS spends some of his weekends and vacations writing about faraway places. His debut book, Tersinian Wars, was completed with the encouragement of his wife and children. He lives in the Pacific Northwest.